People who love to eat are always the best people.
—Julia Child

A SIDE *of* MURDER

A CAPE COD FOODIE MYSTERY

AMY PERSHING

BERKLEY PRIME CRIME
New York

BERKLEY PRIME CRIME
Published by Berkley
An imprint of Penguin Random House LLC
penguinrandomhouse.com

ISBN: 9780593199145

First Edition: February 2021

Printed in the United States of America
1   3   5   7   9   10   8   6   4   2

Cover art by Julia Green
Cover design by Vi-An Nguyen
Book design by George Towne

For my mother—and all-time favorite partner in crime—Ann Warren (1928-2019)

ONE

"OKAY, SO HERE'S how it's gonna go down."

I looked sternly at my dining companions, who were eyeing me warily over the rims of their wineglasses. They were not used to me looking at them sternly.

"We order one meat, one vegetarian, one seafood, and one pasta entrée."

"Pasta doesn't count as vegetarian?"

That was Jenny, a mother of three with the body of a sixteen-year-old that she proudly claims is the result of her dedicated meat-and-potatoes-only diet. She was probably worried that I was going to make her order eggplant.

"No. Pasta doesn't count as vegetarian," I explained. "Some restaurants like to think it counts as vegetarian, but that's how vegetarians get fat. That and too much cheese. No, a real vegetarian entrée is about vegetables. Maybe with grains or legumes, but the focus is on vegetables, like a ratatouille."

"Sorry I asked," Jenny muttered to Miles, who was sitting next to her and had been quietly entertaining himself by checking out the other patrons at the Bayview Grill. "What's a legume anyway?" she asked him.

Miles looked at her like she'd just arrived from Mars. Miles is a farmer. What he doesn't know about legumes isn't worth knowing. "Beans, lentils, chickpeas—that kind of thing," he said. "How do you not know that?"

Jenny shuddered. "I don't eat 'that kind of thing.'"

I tried to continue with their instructions. "Appetizers can be anything you like—"

"Well, hallelujah," Miles said. He poked Jenny in the side with one massive elbow, almost knocking her off her chair. "I'd like that cutie-pie over there at the bar."

I ignored him.

"Anything you like," I repeated, "but it needs to make sense with your entrée."

"I'm lost," said Helene, running a ring-bejeweled hand through her mane of silver curls. Helene was Fair Harbor's new librarian. I'd known her exactly twenty-four hours and couldn't imagine anyone less like a librarian.

"I've been eating out for forty years," she said, "and I never once worried if my appetizer made sense with my entrée. I don't even know what that *means*."

I sighed. Well, no one had ever said writing restaurant reviews for the Cape Cod *Clarion* was going to be easy. Actually, I reflected, that wasn't true. *I* was the one who had said it would be easy.

I tried to clarify. "It means that if you're having the hanger steak for your entrée—"

"That's mine!" Jenny said, suddenly all in. "I call I claim the hanger steak."

I call I claim? What is she, six?

"And a half dozen Wellfleet oysters to start," she added.

Jenny always had oysters to start. And, as these were Wellfleet oysters, which are universally acknowledged to be the best on the Cape (and all Cape Cod oysters are awesome), I was surprised she wasn't starting with a dozen.

"That's fine," I said. "A classic pairing."

I turned back to Helene. "If, like Jenny, you're having

the hanger steak," I explained, "you don't want to order the barbeque sliders as a starter."

She nodded thoughtfully. At least Helene was taking this seriously. But then she ruined it by saying, "Actually, barbeque followed by steak sounds yummy."

I gave up.

"I'll order for all of you," I announced. "And once we get our food and you've had a chance to taste and consider your choices, I will *discreetly* exchange plates with each of you, one by one, and sample each dish. Then we'll *discreetly* switch back again. We'll go clockwise around the table, starting with Helene."

"I'm lost again," Helene fake whispered to Miles.

"Don't you worry, honey," he said. "Wait until she gets a glass or two of wine into her. Then we can do whatever we want."

He grinned at me, looking exactly like the overgrown five-year-old he was. If five-year-olds had big, bushy lumberjack beards.

I began to worry for real. My dining companions were definitely not taking my first foray into restaurant reviewing seriously enough. And Miles was right about the two glasses of wine. I was a notoriously cheap date. But I was also the night's designated driver, so no worries there.

"No wine for me," I said firmly more to myself than to Miles, "even if it kills me."

A poor choice of words, as it turned out.

MY NAME IS Samantha Barnes. Sam to my friends. I stand six feet one and a half inches tall in my stocking feet, six two and a half in my chef's clogs. I'm not exactly beautiful, especially when I'm sweating over a hot stove, but, as my grandfather used to say, I clean up nice. I'm blessed with my Italian American mother's clear olive skin and my Yankee father's high cheekbones, but my brown hair and eyes can be fairly described as unmemorable. When I'm not wearing the standard black-and-white-checked chef's pants and double-breasted white jacket, I have a weakness for floaty dresses and dangly earrings.

Ten years ago, I had packed my bags and headed off to New York's Culinary Institute of America (fondly referred to by its alumni as the CIA) to learn how to cook professionally and swear creatively. Before that I had lived all my life on Cape Cod, that sandy spit of land reaching out into the Atlantic from the coast of Massachusetts like a crooked arm. I grew up on the "elbow" of the Cape in a small town called Fair Harbor (pronounced Fay'h Hahbah, if you're local). Summer population, around 20,000; year-round population, 6,798.

Actually, 6,797. Now.

After graduating from the CIA, I single-mindedly climbed my way up New York City's restaurant ladder from prep cook to line cook to sous-chef and finally head chef, each time moving to a better kitchen. I was a rising star. Someday I was going to open my own place.

I was proud of being a successful woman chef in a decidedly male field. I was tough, and I didn't let the male chefs intimidate me. For the first time in my life, my height was working for me. Those macho men literally could not look down on me. Because, let me tell you, most male chefs are off-the-chart macho. They are the baddest of bad boys.

My big mistake was marrying one of those bad boys. He'd told me my love had changed him. Well, *that* wasn't true.

Things got very scary very quickly. I'd seen Stefan's temper flare at work but never at home. So I was totally unprepared the day it happened. A big screaming man with a knife in a busy professional kitchen is one thing; a big screaming man with a knife alone with you in the tiny kitchen of your New York walk-up is quite another. That we took it out into the street didn't help. Neither did the subsequent YouTube video of our difference of opinion posted by a helpful bystander.

But more about that later.

I try to be a nice person. In general, I like people and assume they are good at heart, especially if they make me laugh. I will forgive a lot for a good laugh. If my reaction to someone is not positive, I trust my radar and assume they are not nice people. Also, until recent events taught me better, I tended to take what people said and did at face value. What you saw, I thought, is what they were. This misconception has not worked out well for me (see failed marriage, above). In fact, that spring, the spring I came metaphorically limping home to the Cape, the spring when my friend Krista offered me a temp job doing restaurant reviews for the local paper, you could say it worked out very badly indeed.

But I did learn one thing: never rely on first impressions. Do not even rely on the impressions of a lifetime. Alas, I learned this lesson too late. In retrospect, I got every player in this little drama wrong. And one of them disastrously, murderously wrong.

TWO

AFTER MY 1.2 million extremely unwelcome YouTube hits, I found myself out of a job (unfortunately) and out of a marriage (hallelujah). In the great tradition of the newly unemployed (and newly single), I was spending a lot of time on the couch binge-watching Netflix. It was 2:15 in the afternoon on a dreary day in early May and I was deep into the finals of the *Great British Bake Off*, when my cell began to ring. Sighing, I hit mute on the remote and picked up my phone.

"Hello," I said crossly.

"Samantha?" a man's voice said. "Samantha Barnes?"

"Yes," I admitted cautiously. "Who's this?" One of the many lessons I had learned from my YouTube notoriety was that there are a lot of nutters out there.

"It's Roland, Roland Singleton."

I sat straight up and jabbed the TV off. Roland Singleton was Fair Harbor's most respected lawyer. More significantly, he was married to Jenny Snow Singleton, my best friend since childhood.

"What's wrong?" I demanded. "Is Jenny all right?"

"Nothing's wrong. Jenny's fine. The boys are fine. We're all fine."

I breathed again.

"I'm calling in my role as Ida Barnes's executor." His voice gave nothing away. Roland's voice never gave anything away.

My great-aunt Ida had left this vale of tears a few weeks earlier. Though we hadn't been close—nobody had been close to Aunt Ida, a taciturn Cape Codder of the old school—I'd always liked my father's aunt, ever since she'd taught me how to make real New England clam chowder with quahogs that we'd dug ourselves. (Tip: Real Cape Codders always use milk in clam chowder, not cream. Cream is an affront to Yankee frugality.)

"I see," I said to Roland, even though I didn't. I wasn't even sure what an executor was.

"The reason I'm calling," he continued briskly, "is that Ms. Barnes, having no children of her own and apparently fond of you"—*Really?* My impression had always been that Aunt Ida wasn't particularly fond of anybody—"has left you her house in her will."

I let the words sink in. This inheritance, I knew, was not exactly a windfall. Aunt Ida's house was barely habitable. But it was perched on a hill overlooking a pristine salt pond where I had spent many happy hours sailing my Sunfish as a little girl, so there was some affection by association there.

As Roland droned on about something called probate, I was surprised to find that I felt, for the first time in weeks, a faint stirring of hope. My life in New York was a shambles. This might be a short-term way out. I could go back to Fair Harbor, take some time off while I sold the house and reinflated my bank account, come back to the city when my notoriety had died down, get on with my life.

What could go wrong?

* * *

IT TOOK ME a week to actually get my tokus off the couch, but I finally managed to shove some clothes into a suitcase and hop a Peter Pan bus to the Cape. (Yes, the bus line to the Cape is really called Peter Pan. I always wanted to ask for a ticket to Neverland but didn't have the nerve.) I was going home. Only temporarily, I reminded myself. But still. It felt like failure.

Miles and Jenny had insisted on picking me up at the bus station in Hyannis. Miles Tanner, Jenny Snow Singleton and I had been a trio ever since we were drama club geeks together at Fair Harbor High School. None of us had really ever fit in. In my case this was mostly because of my height. I had almost hit the six foot mark by my fourteenth birthday. I was always the stage manager for the high school plays. It is difficult to find a part for a girl who stands at least a head taller than everyone else on the stage.

Jenny—petite, trimly built, with the square open face of her lobsterman father and the soft blond thistledown hair of her artist mother—had struggled in her own way. She was a math whiz, but because of her dyslexia, letters and words needed slow decoding. Though she would deny it, she was also a talented photographer and videographer. She took amazing candids of the actors and videoed the play itself, which the drama club then sold to the students' proud parents at exorbitant prices.

High school hadn't been easy for Miles either, who had tried, not very successfully, to hide his sexuality and regularly paid the price for it. Until, that is, he hit his growth spurt in his junior year. Suddenly this skinny little farm boy with a penchant for brightly colored socks and show tunes (he was a *fantastic* Harold Hill in the *Music Man*) turned into a great big farm boy with a penchant for brightly colored socks and show tunes. The bullies backed off.

Both of them were waiting for me in Miles's red pickup.

I knew they'd come in the truck to cheer me up. I *love* riding in Miles's truck. It makes me feel badass. Plus, I love any vehicle that is red. It is my conviction that they drive faster.

While Miles chucked my suitcase into the truck's bed, Jenny hopped out and gave me a hug.

"Now don't you worry about where you're going to stay," she announced. "You're staying with us."

By "us" she meant Roland and her three more than slightly hyperactive boys, ages nine, seven, and five, all of whose names started with *E*. Ethan, Eli, and some other name I could never remember. I just called them Thing One, Thing Two, and Thing Three.

What I don't know about kids is a lot. I am the only child of two only children. I have no cousins. My parents always treated me like a miniature adult (until I became an adult, at which point they started treating me like a child). So Jenny's kids made me nervous. And much as I tried, I found Roland, with his corporate handshake and closed face, difficult going.

"Super," I lied.

"And you can use my mom's old truck while you're here," Miles said. "I already left it at your house."

"Aunt Ida's house," I corrected him. Begin as you mean to continue.

"It goes fine. When it goes," he added.

"Super," I lied again.

We piled into Miles's truck, with Jenny riding shotgun and me in one of the two surprisingly spacious backseats. We pulled out onto Route 6, the Cape's one and only highway. Twenty minutes later, we turned off into Fair Harbor proper. I smiled, as I always did on my visits home, at the "Welcome to Fair Harbor" sign, below which was written: "Drive slowly. Densely populated." It's all relative, I guess.

The town of Fair Harbor is clustered around the shores of Crystal Bay, a dreamscape of brilliant blue waters dotted with green islands tenanted only by sandpipers and egrets. The locals divide the bay into two parts—Little Crystal, a smaller body of water surrounded on three sides by the town, and then, leading out from the little bay, Big Crystal, an enormous expanse protected from the Atlantic Ocean by a narrow, five-mile-long barrier bar of sand and dune grass known by locals as the Outer Beach.

Along the bay's inland shore, narrow saltwater rivers wind from the bay through dense cordgrass marshes into various saltwater ponds. Some of them are tiny hidden coves that are not much more than mud puddles at low water. The larger saltwater ponds are ringed by gray-shingled cottages and—more recently—gray-shingled mansions. The largest and deepest of the ponds are dominated by the town's boatyards and marinas.

Fair Harbor, when I was growing up, was very much a small town. It had grown, of course, since I'd left, but it still maintained its old-fashioned charm. It had been spared by the chain stores, which had preferred the nearby and much larger shopping hub of Hyannis, so Nelson's grocery store, Livingston's pharmacy, Karen's Penny Candy, the Shear Beauty hair salon, and Taylor's department store were all still lined up like cheerful soldiers along Main Street. The town hall, department of public works, and the post office were all to be found on our other major thoroughfare, called, unsurprisingly, Municipal Road.

As Miles, Jenny, and I drove through the intersection of Main and Locust Streets, I craned my neck to see the house I'd grown up in. There it was, halfway down Locust, a white clapboard foursquare, solid and respectable, as had befitted Robert and Veronica Barnes's solid and respectable position as the editor in chief and senior journalist, respectively, of the Cape Cod *Clarion*. It had been two years since they'd retired and moved to Florida, but I still thought of the house on Locust Street as theirs. As mine.

The house slipped out of sight as we continued down

Main. We turned right onto Memorial Road with its Civil
War monument bearing a bronze statue of a Union soldier.
As a child I'd been very impressed by his extravagant mus-
tache. We always called the statue Andy Clyde. I have no
idea why.

Soon the truck was humming by Mirror Lake, one of
the many freshwater, spring-fed kettle ponds on the Cape
formed when the glaciers retreated some fourteen thousand
years ago. Around the lake's shores, tidy shingled cottages
owned by year-rounders rubbed elbows with the far larger
but equally tidy shingled houses of the summer people. It
was a peaceful coexistence that had lasted for generations,
cemented by a mutual love of the Cape and its traditions.

Another quarter mile and Bower's Pond, with its twist-
ing saltwater river leading out to Little Crystal Bay, came
into view on our left. I craned my neck to see if I could spot
Aunt Ida's house on the opposite bank. Once upon a time,
the house on its little square of lawn had been visible
through the tall locust trees. Now a wall of briars and underbrush had grown so high that only the chimney showed.

Halfway around the pond, Miles slowed down and
turned off Monument onto an unpaved, sandy road with a
large wooden sign reading "Bayberry Point, Private Way."
On the Cape, "private way" does not mean "keep out." It
just means travel at your own risk. Because virtually every
private way on the Cape (and there are hundreds of them)
is a sandy, unpaved road booby-trapped with deep ruts and
potholes carefully preserved in order to keep cars moving
at a snail's pace. This protects the kids and dogs walking in
the middle of the road while daydreaming about dinosaurs
or squirrels. It is, in my opinion, a good system.

Miles slowed the truck. "Do you remember where the
house actually is?" he asked. "Because all I know about
Bayberry Point is that it's a maze."

I shook my head. "I haven't been there in years. But I
have the street address in my e-mail, Roland sent it to me."

I scrolled hastily through my Gmail. "Here it is: twelve Snow's Way. I'll put it into Waze." I tapped a few more keys on my phone and within seconds an annoyingly cheerful virtual woman was saying, "Let's get going!"

We bumped around Bayberry Point for a few minutes until the virtual woman got us to Snow's Way. A tangled wood of beeches, pitch pine, and locust trees lined the sandy road on either side, interrupted by the occasional crushed-shell driveway (made by throwing your empty oyster shells and clamshells onto a sand driveway and crushing them with your 4X4) leading back to well-hidden cottages. Eventually, we pulled into the sad, dilapidated excuse for a drive at number 12, which opened up on to a sad, dilapidated excuse for a lawn and Aunt Ida's sad, dilapidated excuse for a house.

This made the virtual woman very happy.

"You," she announced cheerfully, "have arrived at your destination!"

THREE

The three of us sat in the truck, unmoving, and surveyed my destination.

It was, if anything, even more bedraggled than I remembered. The original house had been built in 1795 by a certain Eliakim Higgins, who had made a comfortable living as first mate on the whaling ship *Bathsheba* out of Barnstable. It was a full Cape, which meant that it looked like a child's drawing of a house—a door with two windows on either side and a chimney in the middle of its peaked roof. The front of the house was painted clapboard, the rest sided with cedar shingles faded to silver. Over the years, the house had been added to in the typically haphazard Cape Cod way—a small formal dining room leading off the living room to a full, eat-in kitchen in the back, a downstairs bedroom and adjoining bath in addition to the three attic bedrooms above, and a large screened-in porch to defeat the mosquitoes in summer. An ell built off the kitchen wing contained the studio apartment that Aunt Ida had added on when the main house had become too much for her. It was an architectural crazy quilt that I'd always loved.

But sitting there with Miles and Jenny, my heart sank.

The structure was definitely showing its age. The once-bright yellow paint of its clapboard facade had faded to a sickly, peeling beige. Long patches of damp streaked the shingled sides where the gutters had long since ceased to do their job. Shutters hung at limp angles.

The house was separated from its neighbors by an acre or so of woods on one side and a dense yew hedge on the other. The woods were the handiwork of Mother Nature. The yew hedge was all Aunt Ida's. She'd planted it back in 1961, when a young couple from Boston had bought the property next door and commissioned Luther Crowell, a local builder descended from a long line of early Cape Cod ship captains, to build them the first of the modest "modernist" houses that later made his name. Aunt Ida had no truck with modern and no time for off-Capers. She had planted the yew hedge the minute construction had begun. When my father had gently pointed out that this wasn't particularly neighborly, she'd responded tartly, "Good fences make good neighbors, and besides, I like my privacy."

Well, she'd gotten it. As Jenny, Miles, and I climbed out of the truck, you could believe that we were alone in all the world. Scrub oak, beach plum, and pitch pines encroached on all sides. Even the once-beautiful view of Bower's Pond was now obscured by a great barricade of briars that only served to heighten the shabbiness of the house.

"What a pile of doo-doo," Jenny said. Or words to that effect.

"Not really," a bright voice responded. "It just needs some love."

The bright voice, it turned out, belonged to a sixtyish woman with electric blue eyes and a halo of curly silver hair who had materialized rather alarmingly at our side like a genie out of a bottle. On that cloudy, chilly day in May (there is no spring on the Cape, just mud season), she was dressed in several layers of hand-knitted outer garments, none of which could have reasonably been called a coat.

"Helene!" Miles said, "where on earth did you spring from?"

"I live next door, you big dope," the woman replied, smacking him on the arm with a hand that appeared to have a ring on every finger. "Bought it from the original owners when I moved to the Cape. I saw your truck through the gap in the hedge and thought I'd come over, see if I could help."

Miles remembered his manners.

"Helene, this is Samantha Barnes, the new owner of this charming property. Sam, this is Helene Greenberg, your neighbor. She moved here from New York two years ago. She's the town's new librarian."

Really? I wanted to say. *Because you look like no librarian I ever met before.*

"How do you do?" I said instead.

"I'm great," Helene said. "And I'm very happy to meet you. Miles has told me so much about you."

Oh god, really? What exactly?

"And I've got a surprise for you," Helene continued.

Oh dear.

Helene put two fingers to her mouth and let out an ear-splitting whistle. A blur of fur came flying up the steep path that led down to the salt pond. I had a confused impression of a wet nose and large pink tongue in my face and enormous muddy paws on my chest.

I'd had dogs as a kid. I knew how this was supposed to work.

"Down!" I shouted. Nothing. The creature continued to lick me to death.

"Down!" Miles shouted, also to no avail.

"Down, Diogi," Helene said calmly, holding up a dog treat that had miraculously appeared in her hand.

In a nanosecond, the beast turned his attention to Helene and stood gazing fixedly at the dog treat.

In this brief moment of calm, which I suspected was only the eye of the storm, I could see he was your typical

Cape Cod mutt, part yellow Lab, part whatever. Great water dogs, good with kids, gentle. This one was remarkable in no way except for his size. He was ginormous.

"You'll have to forgive his manners," Helene said. "He's still just a puppy,"

"You mean he's going to get *bigger*?" I yelped.

"Oh yes," Helene said. "He's still just a baby. But he's a fast learner."

She handed me a dog treat. "Tell him to sit. Diogi will do anything for a treat." She pronounced the name dee-OH-gee.

"Thank you," I said, taking the treat gingerly just in case the dog got overexcited and jumped me again. "That's an . . . unusual . . . name."

"It's a joke," Helene said, blue eyes dancing. "Dee, oh, gee. D-O-G. Get it? *Dog!*" She laughed delightedly as if hearing the joke for the first time. "It's spelled D-I-O-G-I."

I had to smile.

"Is there a cat called C-A-T?" I asked.

Helene rewarded my wit with another peal of laughter. "See, ay, tee," she crowed. "That's rich!"

I held the treat up and said, "Sit, Diogi" in my firmest voice.

Diogi ignored the command, instead leaning against my leg with all his considerable weight. I gave him the treat anyway.

"I think your dog needs some more training," I said to Helene.

"Well, we're working on that," Helene acknowledged. "But he's not *my* dog."

"Whose dog is he?" I asked.

"Why, he's yours, Sam," Helene said, as if the answer was obvious. "Diogi comes with the house."

It took me a moment to absorb the fact that in addition to leaving me her wreck of a property, Aunt Ida had left me her untrained dog. Why she'd seen fit to lumber herself with a puppy in her eighty-seventh year was a mystery to me.

"I can't take care of a dog," I protested. "I really haven't decided what I'm going to do about the house. Or how long I'll be around. I've got a few things to handle, but then I'll be heading back to the city. Can't *you* keep him?"

"Oh no," Helene said firmly. "He's yours. Ida got him for you."

Well, that solved that mystery. I was beginning to see Aunt Ida's evil plan. She'd never approved of me moving off Cape. *Sorry, Aunt Ida, but if you think you can trap me into coming back by giving me a falling-down house and a not very bright dog, you have another think coming.*

Helene bent down and waggled her head at Diogi. "You *wuv* Sam already, don't you, sweetheart?"

"He *wuvs* the treats," I corrected her.

"Whatever," Helene said, moving on. "Time to take a look at the house."

Helene trotted briskly toward the one element of the house that actually looked fairly sturdy, Aunt Ida's studio ell. I'd never been in it. I hadn't been back to the Cape since my parents had moved to Florida, and before that, on my annual visits home every August, Aunt Ida had preferred to catch up at our house on Locust Street, where I would make her China tea and her favorite raisin scones and she would try to talk me into coming home for good. (Tip: For featherlight scones, use pastry flour, not all-purpose flour.)

Helene bent down and picked up a conch shell from the patch of weeds next to the front door of the ell. She shook it briskly and a key tumbled out of the shiny pink interior. Everybody in Fair Harbor hides their spare key in a conch shell by the front door. That way the burglars know where to find it.

"When Ida knew she was dying," Helene said over her shoulder, "she asked me to keep the ell ready for you."

My heart ached a little bit. Aunt Ida had been so certain that I would love her house as much as she had. And I didn't. I really didn't love it at all. And I *really* didn't love her dog.

Helene unlocked the door, reached in to turn on the lights, and stepped back to let me enter first. Jenny and Miles peered in over my shoulder.

The studio was not what I'd expected. The uncluttered space was painted white and was open to the rafters, which made it feel larger than it was. The wall opposite the front door featured a casement window that, before the briar patch took hold, had once had a view to the pond and still offered lots of natural light. A small cherry wood table with two harp-backed chairs stood in front of the window. To the right of the window was a mahogany four-poster bed, neatly made up with linen sheets and a handmade blue and white quilt. Next to it, along the wall to our right, was a door leading to a bathroom, another to a small closet and a handsome burl-wood bureau. To the left of the front door was a sitting area with floor-to-ceiling bookshelves flanking a small Vermont Castings woodstove. A couch, its deep down cushions covered in faded chintz, faced the stove, with a small flat-topped trunk serving as coffee table. A Dutch door in the wall to our far left led from the sitting area to the rest of the house, but it looked like it hadn't been opened in ages. Taking up the rest of that wall were two built-in closets with louvered doors. Helene walked over and folded back one of the doors, revealing a small desk and an Internet router.

"Aunt Ida was online?" I asked in surprise.

"Of course she was," Helene said. "There was nothing wrong with Ida's mind. She ordered groceries, paid bills, all of that on her laptop. Not to mention playing Angry Birds and online solitaire."

She closed up the workspace and pushed back the other louver, uncovering a tiny kitchen comprised of a two-burner electric cooktop, a minifridge, a tiny sink, and just enough butcher block counter to chop an onion on. She must have seen my face fall, because she said brightly, "This will have to do until we get the old kitchen up to speed."

Until we get the old kitchen up to speed?

While I was processing this assumption, Helene touched a match to a small pile of logs and kindling in the stove, which she'd clearly prepared for just this occasion.

"Take a seat," she said, gesturing to the couch. "I'll just make us all a cup of tea."

She filled a kettle that had been waiting on one of the burners and pulled out sugar and tea from a small cupboard above the counter. Miles and Jenny pulled over the harp-backed chairs, and within minutes, the four of us were sipping Earl Grey and watching the flames dance behind the stove's glass window.

Diogi padded over to me, and put his head in my lap. The knot of tension that had lived in my chest ever since I'd starred in my very own YouTube video somehow began, ever so slightly, to loosen.

Okay, Aunt Ida. You win.

Then I shook my head. I wasn't giving up that easily.

For now, I amended. *You win for now, Aunt Ida.*

FOUR

I DECIDED TO STAY at Aunt Ida's house for the duration
of my exile. The ell was more than habitable and did
not come with a lawyer husband and three little hellions.
Perfect.

After Jenny and Miles had driven off and Helene had
disappeared through the gap in the yew hedge, I sat on the
couch engaged in a kind of staring contest with Diogi.
Clearly I was expected to do something, but I couldn't
imagine what.

I was relieved when my cell began to ring. I recognized
the number. It was Krista, Krista Baker. Krista had assumed the role of editor in chief of the Cape Cod *Clarion*
two years ago, when my father had suffered a mild heart
attack and my mother had decided within days that both of
them needed to retire and "concentrate on a healthy lifestyle." Within weeks they'd sold the house on Locust Street
and moved to Florida. *Florida?* I'd wanted to wail. *Who
are you? And what have you done with my parents?*

Krista was an old and good friend, but I felt myself hes-
itate just a moment before answering her call.

Krista is a force of nature. Not one of those nice forces

of nature, either, like sunshine or a gentle rain. More like a lightning bolt or a forest fire. In high school, Krista had been part of our little group, though she was everything Miles, Jenny, and I were not—beautiful and talented and super smart. Always the lead in the high school play. President of the debating team. Almost perfect SATs. And yet somehow she liked us, awkward Drama Club geeks that we were. Maybe it was because Miles and Jenny and I made her laugh. Krista hardly ever laughed. She was too busy being successful.

I took a deep breath. "Hi, Krista."

"I hear from Jenny you're back in town for a while. Something about your Aunt Ida's house?"

"I'm fine thanks, Krista," I said. "How are you?"

"Yeah, yeah, I get it," Krista said. "How are you? Good. Me, too. Now tell me what's going on." Pure Krista.

"She left me the house in her will."

Krista snorted. "Oh, jeez. Thanks a lot, Aunt Ida. That place is a dump. Unload it fast is my advice."

"That's exactly what I plan to do," I said. "I'm between jobs for the moment. . . ."

Krista snorted again. She'd never been one for euphemisms. Plus, she knew the whole sorry story.

"I'm *between jobs for the moment*," I repeated firmly, "so I'm staying here for a few weeks while I see what needs to be done to the place so I can sell it. The house is probably a tear down, but the property is waterfront and has a view of Bower's if you can get past the briars, so it should be worth something."

"Yeah, I know, I know, Jenny told me," Krista said, dismissing the topic (as if she hadn't been the one who'd brought it up). "Listen, I have a problem and I thought of you." *Uh-oh. Danger, Will Robinson.* "Felicia, our lifestyle reporter, is off with this new baby of hers—" Krista made it sound like Felicia was just making lame excuses not to be in the office where she belonged.

"Well, good for Felicia," I interrupted, feeling that someone should be supporting the sisterhood here.

"She'll be back in a few months," Krista continued as if I hadn't said a word. "But in the meantime I need someone to write the restaurant reviews and food features."

"Why me?"

"You're a good writer. I remember that blog you did while you were at that cooking school. You certainly know food. You know the restaurant biz. You know the Cape. You could cover for her. What do you say we give it a try?"

"Look, Krista," I said, "I may not be here long. A couple of weeks, maybe a month at the most."

"Not a problem. You do a bunch of them and I'll bank them, space them out over Felicia's leave."

Then she said the magic words. "I can pay you decent money."

Before I could even say yes, she'd assumed my agreement. "I need five hundred words on the Bayview Grill, that new restaurant that replaced the Logan Inn."

Really? I wanted to whine. *This is where you want to send me for my first assignment? Back to the Logan Inn?*

"You remember the Inn, right?" Krista asked.

"Yeah," I said as neutrally as possible. "I remember the Logan Inn."

The summer before our senior year of high school, Krista and I had worked at the Logan Inn as waitresses. I have to admit that the experience had been valuable in a *Alice Through the Looking-Glass* kind of way. The Logan Inn had taught me everything a restaurant should not be. And everything a first love should not be.

"Here's the deal," Krista continued. "Mr. Logan sold up a couple of years ago. The place was on its last legs, and I think the new owners got it for a song. Now it's called the Bayview Grill. New look, new menu, and, according to their fancy-schmancy press release, a new direction, whatever that means. Take Jenny and Miles, whoever, try it out, write me a column. What day is it today? Tuesday?"

Krista never knew what day it was. That's what happens when online news gets posted around the clock and you work seven days a week.

"It's Wednesday," I said.

"I'm always a day off," she muttered to herself. "Anyway, get a table for tonight. I need the content by Friday. We'll put it online then and again in Sunday's print edition. Okay by you?"

Sure, it was okay by me. First of all, I was broke. Second of all, I was broke.

"Absolutely," I said. "Thanks, Krista. Thanks a lot."

"Don't thank me," Krista said. "Just write me a good piece."

"I will," I said. "I absolutely will."

Then she did that Krista thing that she does that makes her such a good journalist. She made a connection that her victim never saw coming.

"So, have you seen Jason Captiva around town?"

And, just like that, all my good mood evaporated.

"Um, no," I managed to say. "I didn't even, um, know he was back."

"Oh yeah," Krista said. "He's back."

And then she hung up.

IT HADN'T TAKEN much to convince Jenny and Miles to be my guinea pigs at the Bayview Grill.

"Free eats?" Miles had exclaimed. "Oh, girl, I am totally in. Nothing tastes as good as free eats."

"A night off from wife and motherhood?" Jenny had said wryly. "Please add my name to the guest list."

I began to think this might actually be fun. It had been a long time since we'd sat down together for a meal. On a whim, I'd also asked Helene, who'd rather dazzled me at our tea party in Aunt Ida's ell with her wild silver hair, clothes that seem to be made entirely of paisley scarves, and opinions firmly expressed on every issue, whether requested or not. I was interested in what she, as someone from off Cape and clearly pretty sophisticated, would make of the Bayview Grill. I had a fairly good idea of what she would have made of its predecessor, the Logan Inn.

When I was a kid, the Logan Inn was the only "fancy" restaurant in Fair Harbor. You knew it was fancy because it had white tablecloths and offered exotic fare like French onion soup and chicken cordon bleu. My parents always took me to the Logan Inn for my birthday. By the time I was twelve I was re-creating what I'd ordered the night before using an old Julia Child cookbook I'd found at a yard sale. The Logan Inn, my twelve-year-old self discovered, was not actually a French restaurant. Their salads were mostly iceberg, their stock clearly from a can. Garlic was shunned. They didn't even offer ratatouille, probably because they would have to translate it, and "vegetable stew" wasn't going to tempt the good people of Fair Harbor.

I now suspected that the Logan Inn survived as long as it had because it was the only waterfront restaurant in town. The Inn had a great location, right next to Alden Pond boatyard, where in the summer sailboats bobbed at their moorings and neat rows of powerboats were slotted into berths along the boatyard dock. The sturdy four-square building had originally been a sailmaker's loft, turning out acres of canvas to supply the sail-powered catboats used by fishermen and lobstermen back in the eighteen hundreds. It had sat empty for years before the Logans bought it. They'd turned the first floor's dark, cramped offices into equally dark, cramped dining rooms where sad tea lights in red hurricane lamps struggled unsuccessfully to dispel the gloom. The open space on the second floor, the actual sail loft, they had turned into the "cocktail lounge," an equally dim cavern of dark bloodred carpet and matching flocked wallpaper.

In short, the decor was as bad as the food. And yet, and yet . . .

B EFORE LEAVING FOR my assignment, I fed and walked Diogi (kibble and leash provided by Helene) and watched, shaking my head, as he settled down for the evening on Aunt Ida's couch. *This is never going to work.* I'd offered to take everyone in Miles's mom's truck, as I didn't plan to drink anything, being on the job and all. The truck had coughed ominously when it first started but behaved itself the rest of the trip. The four of us had blown in through the Grill's front entrance on a particularly strong gust of chilly May wind. While Miles struggled to close the door, I took a moment to prepare myself.

Time to get to work, Sam. Step one, note ambience upon arrival.

Well, I thought as I looked around at the new Bayview Grill, things had changed.

"Niiiice," I said.

The two downstairs dining rooms had been knocked into one large, freshly whitewashed space. A small service bar with a few stools for those waiting for the rest of their party stood against one wall. I knew from reading the press release that the new owner continued to use the upstairs space as the main bar area. I hoped they'd done as good a job with that as they had with the dining room. The original pine floors, freed from their wall-to-wall carpeting, had been waxed to a deep, honey-colored sheen. The tables were well spaced and the lighting was low but not so low that you couldn't read the menu or see your food. Small vases filled with red tulips graced every table and candles offered that warm glow so flattering to the female complexion.

Ambience noted and approved. Next, note professional-

*ism of host or hostess and whether reserved table is ready
for party or if establishment tries to deflect said party to
bar for extra drink income.*

More good news. The hostess was welcoming without
being obsequious, and our table was ready for us. All good
signs. I was cautiously optimistic that the evening would go
well. I only wished my friends would take my job a little
more seriously. Their initial reaction to my instructions had
not been encouraging.

"Please," I begged them as the server came toward us to
take our food order, "this means a lot to me. Please don't
give me away, please don't draw attention to our table. I
need to be invisible, anonymous, okay?" Like I could ever
be invisible. But I could be anonymous.

The three of them looked properly abashed and promised
to behave. And to give them credit, they did. Jenny even
tried Helene's eggplant terrine and pronounced it "not disgusting" (it was excellent). She loved her hanger steak and
truffle fries (which every chef knows are an easy A). Miles
worked hard on being discreet, which had never been his
forte, and slurped his seafood chowder with gusto. I dug into
a plate of gnocchi and was transported by the lightness of
the handmade potato dumplings in their tomato and cream
sauce. The wine that the server had suggested, a cheerful
California pinot noir, managed to work well with all the
various plates. I poured myself a few delicious sips just to
check it out and reluctantly handed the bottle back to Miles.

All in all, everyone agreed that the free eats had been
terrific. This was an enormous relief to me. The last thing
I wanted to do was write a negative review. A fair review,
yes. But I didn't want any part of shooting down someone
else's dream.

For most of the meal our conversation had centered
around the food, but by the time dessert rolled around Helene could no longer contain her impatience.

"So," she said, looking straight at me and taking a sip of

her double espresso (I ask you, who has a double espresso at nine o'clock at night?), "tell me about this . . . er . . . encounter with your ex-husband."

I knew she'd been itching to ask. I knew she'd seen the video on YouTube. *Everyone* had seen the video on YouTube. Miles and Jenny settled back happily. They loved this story. Absolutely loved it.

Well, better to get it over with.

"My husband and I hadn't been getting along—"

"You can skip all that," Helene interrupted. "That part was obvious. What with the knives and all."

"Okay," I said. "Point taken. Well, Stefan and I were at home making dinner, a cassoulet, and arguing about his latest conquest, a new pastry chef at the restaurant where we both worked. I was used to his wandering eye, but this one really annoyed me. He'd break her heart and then we'd lose the best pastry chef we'd ever had."

Miles sniffed dramatically and touched his napkin to his eyes. "This is *so* moving."

"So," I continued, ignoring him, "just to get Stefan's goat I might have said, not entirely truthfully, that I was having a little fling with the sous-chef."

"Sauce for the goose, sauce for the gander," Miles put in gleefully. "To use a culinary metaphor."

I ignored him again.

"Stefan didn't take it well."

"Understatement," Jenny said.

I ignored her, too.

"He started screaming and waving his knife at me. He'd never done anything like that before, so it freaked me out. Chef's knives are razor sharp and he'd been drinking, so I turned and ran out of the apartment."

"Taking your own knife with you," Jenny put in.

"Right," I admitted. "Taking my own knife with me. I'd been chopping leeks. I didn't even know I had it in my hand until I got out on the street."

"Good thing you did have it though," Miles said. "Better notorious than dead."

Helene shushed him. "Just let her tell her story."

"Yeah," I said, glaring at Miles. "Just let me tell my story." I took a deep breath.

"The next thing I know Stefan is chasing me out onto the sidewalk and backing me into the alley where the garbage cans are kept, screaming he's going to fillet me like a fish."

"I saw that part on YouTube," Helene said with some satisfaction.

Of course she had. So had about a million other people, thanks to a passerby who'd videoed the whole encounter on his cell and immediately posted it online. Within hours it had gone viral. You know the kind of thing: *He Threatened to Fillet Her Like a Fish—You Won't Believe What She Did Next.*

What I did next was I parried Stefan's thrust wildly with my own—and neatly sliced off the top joint of his pinkie finger.

The digit then arced into the air toward the battered aluminum garbage cans and landed on one dented lid with a tidy little *ping.*

Miles calls it the ping heard round the world.

"You saw what happened," I said, looking at Helene uncertainly. I really didn't want to put it into words. Plus, I never knew what someone's reaction was going to be to this series of unfortunate events.

"I did," Helene said and reached across the table to pat me on the arm. "Well done," she said. "Very well done indeed."

This woman, I thought, *is my friend for life.*

Which was a good thing because in about ten minutes, I was going to need all the friends I could get.

FIVE

B Y THIS TIME it was almost ten o'clock, which for off-
season Fair Harbor was practically the wee small
hours. I was exhausted, but it seemed that Miles, Jenny, and
Helene were just getting started.

"The kids and Rolly are asleep by now," Jenny pointed
out. "Why should I rush home? This is the first night off
I've had in months. I'm not going to waste it."

"Here, here!" Helene said, lifting her empty wineglass
in salute, then staring at it in dismay. "It appears we are out
of wine."

"Garçon, more wine for the ladies," Miles said to me
grandly.

"I'm not your garçon," I pointed out. "And the *Clarion*'s
expense account does not run to another bottle of wine."

"Okeydoke," Miles said agreeably. "Ladies, will you be
my guests for after-dinner drinks upstairs at the bar?"

I took care of the bill (with Jenny's help determining the
tip) and followed my dining companions upstairs. The new
owner had ripped out the bloodred decor and again gone
with the airy, whitewashed look. Small groupings of comfy
chairs kept the vast space cozy and intimate. I stood chatting

with the friendly bartender as she expertly mixed Miles's old-fashioned. The summer that Krista and I had worked at the Inn, the Logans had decided to draw in a younger crowd by making the deck off the second-story cocktail lounge a beer and oyster bar. If the tide was high, the water came all the way up to the concrete breakwater down below and you could be forgiven for imagining you were on the prow of some wonderful yacht heading out to sea. But now I could see that the door to the deck had been nailed shut and asked the bartender about that.

"Yeah," she said, as she put the old-fashioned and two glasses of ice-cold dessert wine on the server's tray. "The building inspectors say it's not up to code. The plan is to put in sliding glass doors at some point, once they get the deck rebuilt. Until then, no go. It's too bad, since it's got a great view of the pond."

I agreed and followed our server back to the rest of my party, who settled happily into their cushioned wicker chairs with after-dinner drinks in hand. But I couldn't relax. Something was bothering me, something more than the natural jitters of starting a new job. Whatever it was, I was determined to ignore it.

"I'm going out for some fresh air," I said. "I need to clear my head."

I trundled back down the steps, out the front door, and walked around the building toward the boatyard and the path along the edge of the pond. I hadn't bothered to stop for my coat, and I wrapped my arms around my torso in a vain attempt to keep warm. To my right, shrink-wrapped pleasure craft lined the shore in their jack stands, waiting patiently for summer. The only illumination came from the yellow safety lights lining the dock and the moon rising over the pond itself. To my left, rickety wooden steps led up to the quiet, deserted deck that had once been loud with college kids drinking Sam Adams Summer Ale and slurping freshly shucked oysters.

Moonlight guided my steps to the sandy path along the

concrete breakwater under the deck. The tide was high, almost to the top of the four-foot wall, but beginning to recede, and the water, rippling in the fresh breeze, sparkled in the moonlight. But even with the moon, the overhanging deck created a cave of dark, enfolding shadow.

The past tried to thrust itself forward. I tried to push it back. The past won.

W HEN KRISTA HAD told me her crackpot idea about working at the Inn that summer, I was skeptical, given that we had literally no experience waiting tables. Krista did not consider this a problem. She simply pointed out to the notoriously cheap Mrs. Logan that they could call us interns and just let us work for tips.

Krista had assured me that we'd make a killing. "We're young," she'd said. "The wives will think we're charming and the husbands will think we're hot."

"You're charming and hot," I'd shot back. "I'm goofy and look like Big Bird."

But we got the job, and, I have to admit, once we'd learned the ropes, the tips weren't bad.

On our breaks, Krista and I would wander up to the deck where the college boys would chat her up and somehow fail to see the almost-six-foot-tall girl standing next to her. But truthfully, I didn't care if those frat boys with their backward baseball hats and BU T-shirts talked to me or not.

I only had eyes for the bartender; I only had eyes for Jason Captiva.

I watched him hungrily at his post behind the bar, his long black hair pulled back at the nape of his neck, the muscles of his forearms sliding smoothly under his tan skin as he deftly shucked bivalves and uncapped beer after beer. He was a good bartender, calm and friendly, but always quietly on the alert for the guy who needed to hand over his car keys or stop hassling the girl in the corner.

Though much the same age as his customers, Jason Captiva, it seemed to me, was a man among boys.

For two months I flirted with him with all the subtlety that seventeen-year-old girls are known for. Which is to say, no subtlety at all. I was eager to get better at this new area of study, but Jason was not prepared to be my teacher.

"You're a kid," he'd said, all Older Man just because he'd celebrated his twenty-first birthday three months earlier. "I don't date kids."

"Particularly not really tall ones?" I'd asked, pretending it was a joke.

"Not even really pretty ones," he'd responded, taking the sting out of his rejection.

So, with romance off the table, we developed a kind of easy banter, a gentle teasing that grew over the course of the summer into a real friendship. Everything had been great.

Don't go there, Sam.

Until that kiss under the deck.

Until Estelle.

Estelle was a piece of work. She was in her early fifties and had a passion for flat red lipstick and hair in a clashing orange shade never seen in nature. She was a little overweight but still what my grandfather would have called a fine figure of a woman. She was the kind of waitress who called her regulars "hon" and knew their drink orders by heart. She had ruled the Logan Inn cocktail lounge for years, and she made it her mission to keep Krista and me in our place. It seemed she found me, whom she insisted on calling Miss Daddy's Girl, particularly objectionable.

Don't go there, Sam.

The enfolding darkness under the deck. Jason's lips finally on mine.

Then Estelle's face, gargoyle-like in the flare of a cigarette lighter. "You're gonna pay for that, boy."

No, Sam. You exorcised that ghost years ago.

* * *

I SHIVERED AND BROUGHT myself firmly back to the present. Why, when all was warmth and light inside, was I standing outside under an abandoned deck in the cold and dark? It was a lonely spot and something about it, not just my own bad memories, made my flesh creep.

I was turning away from the shadows when I saw it.

As with all impossible sights, my brain struggled to make sense of it. My first thought was that it was the reflection of the moon, round and white, floating on the rippled surface of the water. You could almost see a face in it.

But the body knows what the brain refuses to acknowledge. If this was just the mirrored moon, why was I covered with a cold sweat? Why was my heart pounding?

I forced myself a step closer to the concrete bulkhead. The thing, whatever it was, was about six feet out from shore. I leaned forward, straining to understand what I was seeing. And then I wished I hadn't.

It was a face. Not the moon. A face.

Estelle's face.

Estelle floating on the surface of the pond, her sightless eyes staring skyward, her mouth, smeared black-red with lipstick, open in a silent scream.

SIX

∼

I STUMBLED BACKWARD, TURNED to run away, then caught myself. *What if she wasn't dead?* If not, every minute would count. I forced myself to look at the terrible sight again. Estelle was wearing a dark foul-weather jacket, its rubberized fabric cinched at the neck and waist. This had created enough of an air pocket to keep her afloat, but I could see that the body was being rapidly pulled out by a receding tide made doubly strong by the full moon. Gingerly, I crouched down, then eased myself over the bulkhead. I gasped with the shock of the waist-high, ice-cold water. I forced myself to wade out toward the body. At one point something solid brushed against me, and I visualized Estelle's ghostly hands reaching for me. My stomach lurched.

Get a grip, Sam, I told myself. *You cut a crazy man's finger off with a knife. You can do this.*

Finally I was close enough to touch the body, though it was the last thing I wanted to do. Nonetheless, I grabbed the slippery fabric of the foul-weather gear and pulled Estelle's head and shoulders up high enough to really see what I was dealing with. The tide tugged against me as if determined to claim its prize. Exhausted and freezing, I looked at Estelle's face.

That she was dead was inescapable. Her skin was gray white, streaked with mud, and her head lolled like a rag doll's. As I stared at her, I noticed a tiny snail crawling along her cheek.

And just like that, I whooped up all my free eats.

I REALLY CANNOT TELL you how I got back into the restaurant. I do remember dropping the body in horror and stumbling back to the shore. I have a vague memory of my friends' shocked faces and the restaurant's owner—a short, no-nonsense woman with short, no-nonsense salt-and-pepper hair who'd introduced herself as Carol—calling 911 after I'd blurted out what I'd seen, what I'd found. Then she wrapped me in a blanket and gave me a glass of brandy. Then, looking at my friends' strained, white faces, she poured out three more slugs. By the time she could get outside to check out the situation, as she called it, the body was no longer visible from shore.

The restaurant had emptied by that point and while we waited for the police to arrive, I, in some kind of strange aftershock, felt obliged to make small talk with Carol. It was a way not to think about what I'd just seen.

"The place looks good," I said. "A big change from when the Logans had it."

"I still see Mr. Logan," Carol said. "He comes in once a month for a drink and a chat. Always the first Tuesday of the month, always one Manhattan, no more. Very supportive of what we're doing. He's a lovely guy."

I could tell Carol was talking out of nerves, but that was okay, so was I.

"And you're so lucky to have this waterfront location," I said. A second later, the inanity of that statement hit me. *Yeah, you're so lucky to have this waterfront location so that people can conveniently drown just steps outside your front door.*

"I mean, not tonight you're so lucky," I said, backtracking madly. "Just in general."

"I know what you mean," Carol said kindly. "And, yes, we are lucky. Estelle not so much though."

"You knew her?" I asked.

"Everyone knew Estelle," Carol said, and I could tell there was no love lost there. "In fact, all my bartenders have . . . that is, had . . . strict orders not to serve her."

Then what was she doing here? I wanted to ask, but somehow that seemed rude, like I had some right to question this nice woman who was giving me brandy. And anyway, the police had finally arrived in the form of a cop who looked to be all of twelve years old.

When he understood the situation, he pulled out his cell phone, punched in a number, and asked someone called Denise to get the harbormaster out to Alden Pond.

"Tell him he's gonna need a searchlight and maybe a frogman. We got a floater out in the pond or the bay somewhere and we need to fish it out before it makes it to the ocean."

A floater. For a moment I was afraid I was going to whoops up that expensive brandy, too.

"Can I leave now?" I asked when he'd put his phone away.

"If you could just wait a couple of minutes," the young policeman said. It wasn't really a request. "The harbormaster shouldn't be long. He lives above the office at the municipal pier. He can come now in the Whaler. His team will follow with the cutter."

Helene spoke up then. "If Sam's got to wait around and go through all this again, we need to get her out of those wet clothes."

She turned to Carol.

"Have you got some spare chef's whites?"

Carol came back with the standard double-breasted white jacket and black-and-white checked pants, and Helene pointed me to the ladies' room.

"In you go," she said.

I sighed, and did as I was told. I stripped off my sopping clothes, including bra and underpants, and stepped commando into my borrowed finery. Carol's chef, it seemed, was both much wider and much shorter than I. The jacket flapped around me like a giant pillowcase, and the pants stopped attractively at mid-calf. A pair of men's black socks, donated to the cause by Miles, completed the ensemble. Not that I really cared, but I had had a difficult evening and this did seem like the final insult.

Which it wasn't.

I wandered back out to the dining room, carrying the blanket and my wet clothes. I dropped the mess onto a chair, at which point my bra made a break for freedom and tumbled to the floor. I was just picking it up when the door to the restaurant opened with a whoosh of cold air.

The man framed in the doorway was tall by most standards, though not by mine. I guessed he had an inch or two on me. He had a wild tangle of dark hair that looked like it had landed on his head rather than grown there. He was wearing khaki pants and a green windbreaker with a patch on the chest that read "Barnstable County Harbor Patrol," so I figured he was the fabled harbormaster. The hair was probably the result of his trip across the bay in an open Boston Whaler. He was staring at me, which wasn't surprising given the clown suit I was wearing and the soggy foundation garment dangling from my hand. He seemed to have forgotten that he was still holding the door open.

"Do you mind closing that?" I snapped. "That is, unless you want your witness dead, too."

That's what happens when I'm embarrassed. I get snarky.

The man shook himself a bit and pulled the door shut.

He stepped into the room, using his fingers to comb the hair back off his face.

His face.

Oh god, oh god, oh god.

"*Jason?*" I squeaked. It is not often that you will hear a tall, strong woman who sang alto in the high school chorus squeak, but I managed it.

"*Sam?*"

Oh god, oh god, oh god.

His eyes took me in from top to bottom. He seemed to have regained his composure. I wished I had.

"I like the outfit," he said. "Very fetching."

He looked pointedly at the soggy bra dangling from my hand, adding, "And so well accessorized."

"I picked it out specially for you," I said, grinning at him, although my one overwhelming thought was, *Why tonight of all nights did I have to wear my oldest bra?*

"I like the new do," I added, pointing my bra at the hot mess that was his hair. "Good job on the styled-by-a-Cuisinart look."

"Thank you," he said modestly. "It takes me hours."

And we were back.

It was as if nothing had changed, as if we'd just dropped into our natural banter, our old friendship. *This is going to be fine*, I thought.

I couldn't have been more wrong.

OUR LITTLE TALK didn't start out badly. We'd found our old footing, and when Jason began to segue from Friend to Harbormaster I wasn't particularly surprised. After all, he had a job to do. When had I first seen the body? Where exactly? How far out from shore?

I did my best to answer his questions and then waited while he barked instructions on a walkie-talkie to his waiting crew on the patrol boat.

"First, check the cut through the Outer Beach to the ocean. If the tide's already pulled the body through, we're out of luck, but I don't think there's been enough time for that. Then work your way back along the channel. Call me if you don't find anything in, say, the next thirty minutes. I'll come out."

He turned back to me. The rapid-fire questions started up again. Why hadn't I called for help? Why hadn't I brought the body in?

I stared at him. *When had this turned into an interrogation?*

"I didn't call for help because I was busy trying to see if she was still alive. I didn't bring the body in because the tide was too strong and I was almost hypothermic." *And freaked out.*

"Any chance you knew the victim? Could identify her?"

I stared at him. "Of course I can identify her, Jason. I already told Opie over there." I cocked my head toward the baby cop. "It was Estelle. Estelle Kobolt, from the Logan Inn."

Jason got very, very still.

He hadn't known. The cop hadn't told him.

Then he seemed to gather himself and pulled out a notebook from his hip pocket. "Estelle Kobolt," he repeated neutrally, writing the name carefully in his notebook.

What? Did he think he might forget it? Why was he acting like the name meant nothing to him?

"You remember our old friend Estelle, Jason," I said.

Now, it is true that I meant to get under his skin with that crack. But when he looked up at me from the notebook, I was not prepared for the coldness in his dark eyes.

"We're done here," he said very quietly.

He snapped the notebook closed, stood, and without another word walked out the front door, followed hurriedly by the patrolman, who'd been watching our little show, rapt. As had my three partners in dining.

"Woo-hoo," Miles said as the door closed behind them. "I didn't know there were going to be fireworks tonight."

"Shut up," I said miserably. "Just shut up, and take me home."

Did I just say home?

SEVEN

~~~~~~

I T'S TRUE, AUNT Ida's house was not my idea of home. But that night, the night I found Estelle and stared horrified at her cold, white face, the night I understood that Jason Captiva had not forgiven me for my betrayal so many years ago—that night, Aunt Ida's house saved me.

To take a long, hot soak in the claw-foot bathtub, then to crawl into the solid four-poster, to pull the warm blue and white quilt over my trembling body, to lay my cheek on the soft pillow—all this was to feel the safety and comfort of home and family enfold me.

When Diogi entreated me with those soft brown doggy eyes of his to let him up on the bed, I was too exhausted to resist. With his big puppy bulk warming my feet, I fell into a blessedly dreamless sleep.

Which was a good thing, because the next morning Krista had a little surprise for me. She called at literally the crack of dawn. Before I could do much more than mutter, "Yeah, what?" into the phone, she said, "I need you in the office *stat*."

I hate it when people say *stat*. Unless you are a heart

surgeon, you probably don't actually need whatever you are demanding *stat*. So I took my time, putting on a nice floaty dress and dangly earrings to make me feel like a pretty girl and not someone who had wrestled with a corpse the night before. If that wasn't *stat* enough for Krista, then, well, tough. I believe in self-care (*obviously not true*).

The night before, Helene had blessedly taken charge, calling a car to take us back to Aunt Ida's house and insisting on the nice hot bath and nice soft bed. Carol had promised to have someone deliver Miles's mother's truck back to me in the morning, and looking out the window I could see that she'd been as good as her word. So I wouldn't be totally un-stat.

I T WAS STRANGE to be sitting in my father's office at the *Clarion*. No, in Krista's office, I reminded myself. That was Krista, not my father, sitting across from me at the old wooden desk. Krista, beautiful and remote, sitting slim and upright in her navy suit and crisp white blouse. Krista with her straight, jet-black hair cut in a chic Anna Wintour bob.

"I want you to write up this drowning story."

How had this happened? I was supposed to be a chef. Then I was supposed to be a restaurant reviewer. And now I was supposed to be a reporter?

"I beg your pardon?" I said.

"You heard me," Krista said distractedly, her attention caught briefly by something that had flitted across her computer monitor. "I want you to write up this drowning story."

She looked back at me. "Harbor Patrol found the body in the rocks off Skaket Point last night. I want you to go to the police, talk to whoever's in charge of the case, probably Chief McCauley. I want to know how Estelle died. You were at the scene; you know the background. You can hit the ground running."

"I'm not a reporter," I protested.

"Don't be ridiculous," Krista said. "You practically grew up in this office. Veronica Barnes is your mother. She was the best reporter this newspaper ever had."

This was true. My mother had been a crack investigative reporter who covered the Cape's environmental beat. The tension between the Cape's old industries like fishing and boatbuilding and the new industries of tourism and development had only increased over time, so there was always plenty to investigate. And she was very, very good at it.

"Anyway," Krista continued, "there's no trick to it. Who, what, where, when, how. Five simple questions."

"But what about my Bayview Grill review?" I asked in a desperate attempt at distraction.

"Oh yeah, I need that, too," Krista said. "Great timing. We can run the drowning story online today and the review online tomorrow and both in the Sunday print edition. You should get going—you've got a busy day ahead."

Then she noticed my gauzy dress and my silver Indian earrings. "But next time try to dress a little more professionally, okay?"

"I didn't know I was playing girl reporter today," I pointed out. "And I haven't actually agreed to do this."

"News pays twice as much as lifestyle," Krista added unfairly.

"I give up."

"Good," Krista said, waving a beautifully manicured hand toward the door. "Go."

So I went. *Stat.*

Diogi was waiting in the passenger seat of the truck (or, as I was beginning to call it in my own mind, Grumpy), his nose sticking wetly out of the few inches of window I'd left cracked open. I'd tried to leave him home that morning, but he'd given me a "please don't desert me" look that no amount of "I'll be back soon" had made any headway against. When I slid into the driver's seat, he greeted me as if I'd been away for twenty days instead of twenty minutes.

"Lay off," I said, pushing him back to his seat. "We have to go to the police station."

He lunged at me again, giving me another slobbery kiss. I pushed him away again, more firmly this time. He looked at me balefully, but stayed where he was. Clearly I'd wounded his feelings. Which was fine by me. He'd taken advantage of a moment of weakness the night before and this morning. I wasn't going to fall for that again.

"You behave," I warned him, "or my nice friend the policeman will put you in the pokey."

But Police Chief George McCauley, a big, beefy fellow with a neck that merged so seamlessly into his head you couldn't tell where one ended and the other began, wasn't really interested in being my friend.

"You're a witness, lady," he said flatly. "You can't report on this case."

That got my dander up. Mostly the "lady" part. If he'd wanted to get me all fired up about reporting on this case, he couldn't have found a better approach.

"It's my job," I said. Like I'd been doing it for years instead of about half an hour. "Witness or not, I have a job to do. And you have an obligation to answer my questions unless making the information public might jeopardize your investigation."

It seemed I was, after all, my mother's daughter. And I kind of liked it.

Very reluctantly indeed Chief McCauley conceded that I was entitled to some information. The "who" was about all he was willing to give me. And even that was like pulling teeth.

The dead woman was indeed Estelle Kobolt. (Tell me something I *don't* know.) Sixty-seven years old, retired from waitressing two years ago. Childless, no next of kin as far as anyone knew.

Then he clammed up. I needed background. Time for a

switch from pushy journalist to friend and neighbor. I gave him my biggest smile and put down my reporter's notebook.

"You're the expert here, Chief," I said ingratiatingly. "I've been away a long time. Off the record, what's your take on all this? I remember Estelle from when I was a kid waitressing at the Logan Inn. She was . . . one of a kind."

I waited to see if he would take the opening.

McCauley couldn't resist. "Off the record," he said, "that old girl could really put it away. About a year ago, we had to take her license away for DUI. Not surprising she finally ended up in the drink."

He laughed at his own crude pun.

I chuckled falsely, hating myself, and slid in a question. "Where'd she live?"

"Out on Sandy Neck."

"That's on the other side of town from Alden Pond," I pointed out. "What was she doing at the boatyard, do you know?"

"Maybe she'd been boozing it up at that new restaurant."

"But there are three bars closer to Sandy Neck."

"You're forgetting the lady wasn't allowed to drive a car," McCauley said with a smirk. "But that doesn't mean she couldn't use her boat to get around. And the Inn or the Grill or whatever they're calling it now has the only bar in this town on the water."

I didn't mention Carol's ban on serving Estelle at the Grill. If McCauley wasn't going to share, I wasn't either. Mistake number one, as it turned out.

But what he'd said about Estelle using a boat to get around made sense. Pretty much everybody in Fair Harbor kept some kind of a skiff, usually with a little six-horse outboard, for getting around or doing a little fishing.

"Is that how she got to the boatyard?" I asked. "Did you find her boat?"

"Yeah," McCauley said. "An old aluminum Jon boat tied up to the end of the dock."

Jon boats are low-sided, flat-bottomed motorboats. They offer no shelter from wind or from the water that comes flying up as the boat smacks through the waves.

"That would explain the foul weather gear," I mused, all Sherlock Holmesish.

McCauley ignored me. He wasn't interested in amateur speculation. From a lady amateur, no less. "My theory is she was getting out of the boat, fell in, that's all she wrote. Probably drunk."

"But not so drunk that she couldn't navigate through the river out of Town Cove into the bay, through Alden's River, and then dock the boat," I pointed out.

McCauley looked at me balefully and declined to address that fact. I moved on.

"And besides, the tide was going out. If she fell from the dock, she wouldn't have floated in toward shore. And another thing—"

But McCauley cut me off. "Anyway, none of that is your problem. On the record, we're proceeding along the assumption that this was a tragic accident."

It seemed to me that the police chief didn't seem to find anything particularly tragic about Estelle's accident. And he was, in my opinion (and in my vast—*not*—experience of police procedure), being awfully casual, maybe even cagey, about her last hours. I was feeling pretty skeptical about Chief McCauley and his handling of the case, such as it was, and I wasn't ready to let it slide. It's entirely possible that my feelings showed on my face. My feelings usually do.

McCauley stood up to indicate the interview was over. I tried not to look at the way his khaki shirt strained against his stomach. I thanked him politely and went back to the truck, where Diogi again greeted me as if I'd been gone for months.

"Come on, Watson," I said. "We've got some sleuthing to do."

EIGHT

T HE SINGLETON *MÉNAGE* inhabits an enormous old
captain's house just off Town Square. It had been
something of a wreck when Jenny and Roland had bought
it, and Jenny had overseen its restoration with sensitivity
and respect for its heritage. Indeed, it may have been the
only rehab of the last two decades in which a wall had not
been ripped out to "open up" the kitchen to the dining room.

"Believe me," Jenny had said to her architect, "nobody
wants to see my kitchen after I'm done cooking." Which
was true. Jenny did not believe in clean as you go. She believed in making a huge mess and then leaving it for the
next morning.

She brought me into the kitchen and shooed Diogi out to
the backyard, where we could see him paying goofy court
to Jenny's cocker spaniel, Sadie. This consisted of sniffing
Sadie's butt while Sadie ignored him and then bounding
around her in exuberant circles while Sadie continued to
ignore him. *Men.*

Jenny's kitchen is wonderful. It is big and sunny and
painted yellow and has a big old farmhouse table in the
middle. Today the table was covered with kids' drawings

and littered with Legos. Jenny swept all this aside, saying, "Eli is building the Washington Monument for his history project." Eli, I was pretty sure, was Thing Two (*seven years old, second grade, blond hair, an info kid, the kind that memorizes the state capitals for fun*).

"I'm sure you'll get a good grade on it," I said dryly, well aware of Jenny's propensity to take over her kids' projects.

"I'm sure I will," Jenny said unapologetically. "I usually do. My science fair volcano won Best in Show. My projects are always the best."

She began excavating under a pile of drawings of what looked like space aliens—nobody in them had the proper number of limbs and their heads were the size of pumpkins. Crooked crayoned letters identified the subjects as MY FAMBLE. Clearly the work of what's his name, Thing Three (*five years old, kindergarten, red hair, no filter, the kid who had once looked up at me and asked, "Are you a giant?" I liked him anyway*).

Jenny knocked over a pile of Great Shelby Holmes and Diary of a Wimpy Kid library books (*Thing One, nine years old, brown hair, big reader, athletic*) and finally pulled an iPad out of the mess. "Take a look at this video I made," she said proudly.

She tapped a few icons and the next thing I knew I was watching a video of Thing Three's kindergarten play, *Our Garden*. But this was no ordinary helicopter-mom video. Jenny had combined voice-over with clever cutting and close-ups to create a perfect parody of an online review. Thing Three had apparently played Dead Lima Bean, the one that, Jenny's solemn voice-over informed the viewer, had tragically failed to germinate in its wet paper towel.

"Evan Singleton's role"—*Evan! That was Thing Three's name!*—"though not a big speaking part," the announcer continued, "was played for full dramatic effect."

Close-up on Evan—hair and face spray-painted green—

clutching his chest and crashing to the stage. His performance was greeted with thunderous applause from his
fellow kindergartners up onstage, who had not quite grasped
that applauding was traditionally the role of the audience.
Evan was so inspired by this response that he proceeded not
to germinate two more times. Three little nasturtiums were
particularly enchanted with his performance and jumped up
and down so enthusiastically that their papier-mâché flower
petals fell off. It was with some difficulty that the teacher
brought order back to the proceedings.

I was gasping with laughter when the video finished.

"That was brilliant," I said. "How did you learn to make
something like that?"

"It's all the iPad," Jenny said modestly. "The video itself
is better quality than I can get on my iPhone and the editing
tool is totally intuitive." For someone who found written
instructions more of a hindrance than a help, intuitive was
important, I knew.

"But it's your creativity and smarts and humor that
make it," I said. "Don't sell yourself short."

"I'm working on that," Jenny said with a little inward smile.

She put the iPad away and, when she saw me trying to
cover a yawn, fetched me a cup of coffee. This is why I love
Jenny. She understands that a yawn is a silent scream for
coffee.

"Sorry," I said after a few sips. "Krista woke me at the
crack of dawn this morning." I ran through the day's events,
by which point my coffee cup was empty.

Jenny smiled and topped up the mug. "I can't believe
you let her talk you into this reporting thing."

"I didn't let her talk me into it," I said. "I let her money
talk me into it. And you are the best person to help me with
the cast of characters."

Which was true. What Jenny Snow Singleton—with her
vast network of Snow siblings and aunts and uncles and

cousins and second cousins—didn't know about the good people of Fair Harbor wasn't worth knowing.

"Tell me about Estelle Kobolt," I said.

"Well, mostly she was famous for complaining about her feet or, as she so colorfully called them, her 'dogs,'" Jenny said. "She was really too old for that gig. But she was a cocktail waitress, for Pete's sake. It's not like she could retire, like she had some nice pension waiting for her. But somehow, about two years ago, she just up and quit. My cousin Pammy who works at the post office—you know how everybody stands around gossiping while they wait in line at the post office?"

I nodded impatiently and did that circle thing with my hand that means get to the point, please. Jenny's stories had a tendency to meander.

"Well, anyway, Pammy says the rumor is that Estelle found herself a rich old boyfriend a couple of years ago, probably married, since nobody ever saw them together. Anyway, she really left poor Norman Logan in the lurch."

"Whatever happened to Mr. Logan?" I asked, now distracted myself from the topic at hand. I'd always liked Mr. Logan. "I heard somewhere that he got cancer."

"Well, there's some good news there," Jenny said. "He was down to skin and bones after all his chemo, had to stop working, finally sold the restaurant after Mrs. Logan had her stroke."

"Mrs. Logan had a *stroke*?" Boy, I really was out of touch.

"Yup, two years ago. It was Fourth of July and everybody else had cleared out early to go see the fireworks at Shawme Beach so she was there alone. Mr. Logan was really sick with the cancer then. He hadn't been to the restaurant for weeks. So Mrs. Logan stayed to close up and then went out on the dock—you can sort of see the fireworks way off in the distance from there—and, wham, stroke. They didn't find her 'till the next morning. My sister

Meghan, who does the books for the hospital, she says she might have made it if they'd found her earlier."

I adored Jenny, but she dearly loved to make a dramatic or tragic story even more so. "And the good news is?" I reminded her.

"The good news is, Mr. Logan's doing a lot better lately. Meghan says it was that new immunotherapy. It's expensive, and you never know who it's going to work for, but it sure worked for him. *And* he's opening another, smaller place, lunch only, all healthy food." She wrinkled her nose in distaste. "Whatever that means. He's taken over that empty building that used to be the bait shop—you know, down by Reedie's landing?"

I nodded. Reedie's landing was a public boat launch in south Fair Harbor on the shore of Crystal Bay. It was a little out of the way in the off-season, but it was busy in the summer with day-trippers and weekend warriors sliding their trailered boats down the concrete slipway into the water.

Jenny again felt compelled to fill in all the details. "When Reedie died a few years ago, he left most of his land, almost twenty acres I think, to Cape Cod Conservation. He was dead set against development. He left his son, Levi, the quarter acre that included the bait shop, though, and Levi sold it to Mr. Logan for his restaurant."

"I love the idea of turning a bait shop into a restaurant," I said. "That's hilarious."

"Yeah," Jenny agreed, laughing. "But I hear it's going to be really nice. My second cousin Charlie, he's a carpenter, he's working on it and he says it's the exact opposite of the old Logan Inn—lots of blond wood and windows and light."

"Well, the Inn was definitely created in Mrs. Logan's image," I said. "She was not a woman with a lot of taste or imagination."

Jenny nodded. "But she had family money and she controlled the purse strings."

"Not a good recipe for any partnership," I noted idly. "When one person has all the cash and calls all the shots."

Jenny looked stricken, and I wanted to shove the words back into my stupid mouth. I'd just described Jenny and Roland's marriage.

I was suddenly very anxious to be on my way. "Well, I've gotta go."

"You're leaving already?" Jenny looked bereft.

"Some of us have work to do," I said. And once more wished I hadn't said anything. I knew perfectly well that Jenny was at loose ends since Thing Three (whose real name had already deserted me) had started school.

"I'm sorry," I added quickly. "Of course you have work to do, too." I waved vaguely to indicate all that I imagined was involved in taking care of the Three Things, a big house, and a rather old-school husband.

"Not really," Jenny acknowledged. "A lot of it's been outsourced." By which I knew she meant the twice weekly house cleaner and after-school mother's helper.

Jenny's cell buzzed. "Sorry," she said, "I have to take this." She moved out into the hall, which I thought was weird. I played with the Legos for a while until I heard her coming back. As she walked into the kitchen, I heard her saying, "Thanks so much, Brooklyn. I've gotta go now, but it sounds like just what I need. Just don't say anything to Roland, okay?"

This was not good.

There was only one person named Brooklyn in Fair Harbor (quite frankly, it's amazing that there's even one). Brooklyn Stever, a local real estate agent. I'd read *Big Little Lies*. I knew what it meant when a wife was talking to a real estate agent *and didn't want her husband to know.*

Did I ask Jenny what this was all about? I did not. I suppose I could have pushed things a little, tried to help her open up about whatever troubles she was having in her marriage. But Cape Codders, though happy to talk about others' woes, are on the whole very reluctant to discuss their own. We are stubborn, prideful people. I knew that Jenny would be as embarrassed as I was. She'd tell me what this was about in her own good time. I didn't really think Roland was beating her or anything like that. But something was definitely up.

Instead I said, "Well, I'm off to interview the harbormaster."

Jenny seized on the new topic with relish. "Oh yeah!" she said. "Jason Captiva. What was that ruckus all about last night? How do you know him?"

For some reason, I'd been reluctant to talk about my feelings for Jason with Jenny and Miles that summer, particularly after the magnificent flameout. Normally I didn't mind their good-natured teasing, but this had felt too real, and later too painful, for jokes.

"We worked together at the Inn one summer," I said as casually as I could. I didn't tell Jenny about Jason then, and I wasn't about to tell her now. "It's nice to see that he's done so well for himself." I couldn't help myself. I was curious. "How did that happen?"

"Search me," Jenny said, clearly annoyed at not being in the know for once. "He's not very forthcoming. Remember there were a lot of rumors about him and drugs when we were in high school? Everybody thought he was going to end up on the other side of the jailhouse door. But after his mom died—that was just after you left for cooking school—he got his act together, went to the police academy in Boston, then joined the Harbor Patrol up Cape in Provincetown."

"But why come back to Fair Harbor?" I asked. "It wasn't like he'd had such an easy time of it here."

"Not his choice," Jenny pointed out. "He made a name for himself in P'town and got promoted to master level last year, but the only opening for a harbormaster was Fair Harbor."

"And how did he make this name for himself?" I asked. It was ridiculous how much I wanted to keep talking about Jason Captiva.

"He busted some drug ring," Jenny said, and added, "Takes a thief to catch a thief, I guess."

Suddenly I felt sorry for Jason. Jenny was not a malicious person, far from it, but if she was any indication, he'd never outlive his youthful reputation.

Which I happened to know was undeserved.

OVER THE COURSE of that summer at the Inn, before that disastrous kiss, Jason and I had come to know each other in a way that was somehow more intimate than any physical relationship could have been. He told me things that I was certain he'd told no one else. Sitting on the heavy, scarred workbench under the deck, I listened, while Jason paced and talked. About his mother's stage four breast cancer. About the marijuana that he bought for her, the only thing that eased her pain. How he went down to Stone Harbor every week to meet his dealer, a guy from P'town who brought it in from Boston by speedboat.

"You don't smoke it yourself?" I'd asked. "Because you kind of have a reputation, you know. People, kids at school, they've seen you with that guy. . . ."

"I wish," he said with a little laugh. "But my mom needs it all. Really needs it. She totally bogarts that joint."

He smiled crookedly at me and I smiled back, even though it wasn't really funny. I knew his mom, of course. Everybody did. Mrs. Captiva, until she'd gotten so sick, had been the school nurse at Fair Harbor Elementary for years. She was as straitlaced and proper as, well, as my *nonna*, my grandmother on my mom's side and a woman who, I am quite sure, never had *anything* to report at her monthly confession at St. Anthony's. But maybe even my *nonna* would have smoked weed if she was in as much pain as Mrs. Captiva.

SITTING THERE IN Jenny's kitchen, I reflected on how much had changed in the decade or so since Jason had had to buy from drug dealers what would now be considered medical marijuana. And I wondered not for the first time if I would have been as brave as Jason if it had been my mother who had been in that situation.

I thanked Jenny for the coffee and the information and headed back to Aunt Ida's, where I banged out the article on Estelle's death on my laptop. It was short and just the facts, ma'am. Or such facts as Chief McCauley had seen fit to share with me.

FAIR HARBOR WOMAN FOUND
DROWNED IN ALDEN POND

Fair Harbor police have confirmed that the body of a woman found late last night in Alden Pond is that of Estelle Kobolt, 67, a longtime Fair Harbor resident.

The body was discovered at approximately 10:30 p.m. by a patron of the nearby Bayview Grill who attempted unsuccessfully to bring it ashore. By the time police arrived, a strong ebbing tide had pulled the body out into Crystal Bay. Search efforts by the Harbor Patrol were initiated, and Ms. Kobolt's body was discovered at 3:42 a.m.

Fair Harbor Police Chief George McCauley said that although the circumstances surrounding the death are under investigation, "We are proceeding along the assumption that this was a tragic accident."

Tragic accident. As I typed, I kept seeing Estelle's face, blurred with lipstick and mud. *The snail.* I was sure I was right. There were things about Estelle's death that really didn't add up.

At 5:50, I e-mailed the story to Krista, with a note saying, "Here's the article. If you're still in the office, I want to come over to talk this through."

Krista responded with "k. here 'till 7." *"k"? She was too busy to type "ok"?*

I figured I had time for an early dinner before heading over to the paper. I stood up and stretched, and Diogi, who had been snoozing at my feet recovering from his exhausting courtship of Sadie, immediately sprang into action. I coaxed Grumpy to life and we trundled off to Mayo's, the venerable clam shack at Shawme Beach, where I ordered a crisp, golden mound of fried clams (made with whole, fresh clams—frozen clam strips are an abomination) and a lacy nest of gossamer onion rings. When I realized that Diogi was expecting me to share, I went back and ordered him a hamburger and a small fries. Onion rings and fried clams are brain food, and I needed to think. Thinking was not Diogi's strong suit. This was a dog who honestly thought he was going to catch one of those seagulls dive-bombing us for stray fries.

Comfortably full, I drove over to the *Clarion*'s offices. I parked and, leaving Diogi in Grumpy with his window cracked open, wandered back through the empty newsroom to Krista's office, where I found her peering into a mirrored compact and applying her signature Chanel Rouge lipstick. *Oho*, I thought, *Krista has a date—on a Thursday night no less.* But I said nothing. Krista and I didn't really talk about her personal life. She knew that I thought she had an amazingly *casual* approach to love and sex. Back in the day, when she was at college and I was at the Culinary Institute, she used to call me and laugh about her exploits. But try as I might, I just couldn't hide what she called my "Yankee Puritan streak," and so her confidences had ceased. We talked about many things—her studies, my internships, our families, Miles and Jenny, what was happening back on the Cape—but by mutual unexpressed agreement, we did not talk about men.

When Krista saw me at her door, she snapped the compact shut and quickly tucked it and the lipstick back into the desk's second drawer (also known by any woman who has ever worked in an office as the makeup drawer). She looked back at me and picked up a hard copy of what I took to be my story.

"Thanks," she said, waving the paper at me. "This should cover it."

"Really?" I asked. "Because I'd like to do a little more looking into this drowning thing."

Krista shook her head no. "McCauley called me. Wants you off this story. Said you couldn't be objective."

"McCauley's the one who's not objective," I protested. "He pretty much told me Estelle was not worth wasting his time on."

"You got him to talk?" Krista said, a note of admiration in her voice. "McCauley never talks. No wonder he doesn't like you."

"It's more than that," I said. "Maybe he's just a lazy SOB, but he's determined not to look at the stuff here that doesn't make sense."

"Like what exactly?"

"Like why, if she fell off out on the dock when the tide was going out, she floated *into* shore right up to the breakwater."

"Maybe she didn't fall off the dock. Maybe she fell in off the breakwater."

"Even at high tide, there's only four feet of water there. Hard for anyone to drown in four feet of water, unless they were blind drunk, which apparently she wasn't, given her ability to navigate from Town Cove to Alden Pond."

Silence for a bit as Krista chewed on that. "Maybe," she acknowledged finally. "But I'll handle it from here."

Then she stood up, shrugged into her Burberry, hoisted her shoulder bag, and sidled past me out the door of the office, her straight black hair swinging like a silk curtain around the nape of her elegant neck.

"Gotta go," she said over her shoulder. "And remember, you're off the story."

I was more than a little surprised. It is one thing for the editor of the local newspaper not to deliberately offend the authorities. It is another thing to meekly do their bidding.

Since when are you in McCauley's pocket? I wanted to ask.

Instead I said, "Okay, boss. I'll get to work on that Bayview Grill review."

Which, of course, was exactly what I wasn't planning to do.

NINE

~~~

THE NEXT MORNING, Diogi and I set off for the municipal pier. Krista wasn't going to listen to me—that much was clear. I needed an expert opinion. Someone had to help me figure out the answers to my questions. And Jason was that someone. I just hoped things weren't going to be made difficult by our shared history. As our little encounter at the Grill had made abundantly clear, he hadn't forgotten what had happened between us so many years ago.

IT HAD BEEN a quiet Thursday night in mid-August. We'd finished our shifts and were talking under the deck in the glare of the naked light bulb that Mrs. Logan had recently installed to deter what she called "troublemakers." By which she meant teenagers making out. *As if*, I thought miserably.

The tide was high and the water slapped softly against the breakwater. Something was bothering Jason, I could tell. For one thing, he'd been drinking. Just a few beers, but even a beer or two was unusual for him. I didn't ask what was wrong. With the narcissism of youth, I'd hoped it was because he was working his way up to *finally* kissing me.

Jason tilted his head back to take another swig from his bottle of Sam Adams. I watched the muscles in his throat working as he swallowed and thought I would pass out. He looked at me. Then he bent down and picked up a smooth gray rock, which he hefted in his hand.

"I hate that light," he said, his voice thick with an emotion I couldn't name, perhaps had never encountered in my short, sheltered life.

"Don't," I pleaded, suddenly frightened. "Leave it."

He paused and leaned into me. I could smell the leather of his motorcycle jacket, could hear his rough breathing. I was, just slightly, afraid.

"Can't," he said. "Too tempting."

I was pretty sure he wasn't talking about the light bulb.

And then in one sure, swift motion, he launched the rock into the offending light. The glass shattered with a report like a bullet. We both stood very still for a minute or two, waiting, listening. Some footsteps on the gravel, probably someone walking toward the parking lot. Then nothing. It was late. We were safe. There was nobody still working in the Inn except for the kitchen cleanup crew. We breathed again. For a moment, I had lost my nerve, but that moment was past. Just like that, I didn't care.

Because Jason Captiva was kissing me. Gently but thoroughly kissing me. It was paradise.

And then, out of the darkness, a woman's voice, roughened by cigarettes and booze. "You're gonna pay for that, boy."

Jason and I sprang apart guiltily. Well, I sprang apart guiltily. Jason simply stood very, very still, then reached for my hand and held it firmly.

As we turned toward the voice, the woman lit a cigarette and her face was briefly illuminated by the flame of the cheap plastic lighter. Estelle. Standing not five feet away from us between the breakwater and the workbench that took up most of the space under the deck. She casually dropped the lighter into the crocodile handbag she'd placed next to her on the wooden table. Never had I despised anyone like I despised Estelle Kobolt at that moment.

"Don't look at me like that, Miss Daddy's Girl," she snapped.

"You *spy* on me and then don't like the way I *look* at you?" I said with cold disdain.

This, of course, only served to make things worse. "Does Daddy know what you're doing?" she snarled back. "And who you're doing it with?"

And at that, to my eternal shame and regret, I pulled my hand out of Jason's and stepped away from him.

I was frightened and appalled at the situation I found myself in. What was I doing here with this older boy, almost a man, who rode a motorcycle (because he couldn't afford a car, but still . . .), was rumored to do drugs, wore his long black hair in a ponytail? Why was I kissing a bartender, someone who hadn't even gone to college, a destroyer of private property? I was a good girl with a bad boy. If my parents ever found out, I'd be totally grounded. Probably forever.

Jason could have (and, in retrospect, probably should have) walked away from that shallow, self-absorbed girl, but he chose to stay and defend her.

"She's doing nothing," Jason said, his voice deadly cold. "We're doing nothing."

"Not what it looked like to me," Estelle countered. "Looks to me like you're screwing jailbait, boy."

Very slowly and very quietly, Jason said, "You keep your filthy mouth shut."

Estelle just laughed, the sound a crow might make if crows laughed. "That'll cost you, too. Both of you."

And then she turned and left us there in the dark night of what might have been and now was lost.

* * *

I PUSHED THE MEMORY away from me. I took a deep, calming breath. That never works, of course, but I always give it a try. I told myself that I was going to keep things professional. I would simply be talking to the harbormaster.

That made me smile. The harbormaster is a kind of Old Testament god to kids on the Cape. When I was a kid in sailing club, we lived in terror that the harbormaster would find us not wearing our life vests. At the first sight of the official twenty-foot Grady-White with "Harbor Patrol" emblazoned on its side zooming out from Town Cove, the cry "Harbormaster!" would go up from boat to boat and a mad scramble begun to zip and clip. I don't know what we thought the harbormaster would do to life vest scofflaws. Keelhaul us?

I could see now what appeared to be the same Grady-White that had so impressed me as a child tied up at the dock. I hitched Diogi's leash to the bike rack outside the front door, ignoring his look of despair. I wasn't giving in to his guilt trips.

In Fair Harbor, the offices of the Harbor Patrol are housed in an unassuming two-story building on Town Cove overlooking the town's commercial municipal pier. I pushed through the door into the office with its picture window permanently fogged on the outside by the salt spray that dashed against it with every nor'easter. A couple of tired plastic chairs flanked a Formica coffee table holding some well-thumbed back issues of *Boating World*. Official forms of every size and description were stacked haphazardly on a rickety card table. Most of them dealt with things like shell-fishing permits and applications for moorings, which are tightly controlled and hotly contested. I could have sworn that the tattered posters on the walls ("Safe Boating Is Big Fun; Life Jackets—Let the Good Times

Float") had been around since Mrs. Whitelaw had taken our third grade class here on *the best field trip ever* (the then–harbormaster had given us all Junior Harbormaster badges).

There was no one behind the counter marked "Reception" at the far wall, so I peered into a hallway leading off to the left, where a door with the word "Harbormaster" stenciled on it stood slightly ajar.

I walked over and looked in hesitantly. The room was entirely furnished in gray metal. Gray metal desk, gray metal filing cabinets, gray metal desk chair. Nautical charts papered dingy beige walls. Jason was sitting at the battered desk but had swiveled his chair around to look out through the window behind it. His back was to me and he was doing that very, very still thing of his. Somehow I knew he wasn't really seeing the beautiful view out to Town Cove and, beyond it, Little Crystal Bay.

I rapped softly on the doorframe. "Hey. Are you busy?"

He swiveled to face me. He said nothing. He looked extraordinarily tired. Shadows smudged the skin under his eyes, and his face, deeply tanned by years of sun and salt, had a leaden tinge to it. He must have been up all night overseeing the search for Estelle's body.

"I can come back," I found myself saying. "You look like crap."

So much for the thorough professional.

Something almost like a smile touched Jason's haggard face. Just a little lift at the corners of his mouth, but it transformed him, and for a moment I saw the boy I'd known so many years ago. He gestured me to the chair facing the desk.

"No," he said. "Now's fine. How can I help you, Samantha?"

So far, so good. Not exactly warm—Samantha not Sam—but he didn't seem to hate me. *Yet.*

"Krista's short-staffed at the paper, so she asked me to cover Estelle's . . . accident," I lied.

"So you're a reporter now?" Jason said, frowning. "I thought you were a chef."

"Long story," I said, grateful that he didn't seem to know it. "I'm . . . taking a break. My Aunt Ida left me her house. And her dog, actually. I'm just trying to figure out my next steps." *Stop jabbering, Sam.*

I sat down, pulled a notebook and pen out of my shoulder bag, and gave Jason my most levelheaded, reporter-like gaze.

"I'll try to make this brief, then." I checked my list of questions. We already knew who (Estelle), what (drowned), and where (in Alden Pond boatyard).

"Any idea when Estelle died?" I asked. We would save how for later.

"Well, the bodies of most drowning victims sink to the bottom almost immediately once the lungs fill with water. Depending on the water temperature, it usually takes a few days to a week before internal gases bring it up to the surface."

I winced involuntarily and hoped he hadn't noticed. Professionals don't wince.

"In this case, though," he continued, "the body was fresh. McCauley tells me that the coroner's first estimate is within an hour or so of the time you found it." *Funny*, I thought, *he didn't tell me that.* "The body was floating because of the air pocket created by the jacket." I found it interesting that Jason always said "the body." Never Estelle. "He'll know more after the autopsy."

"Any idea how it happened?"

"Well, the obvious conclusion is accident."

"Accident like how?" *Samantha Barnes, girl reporter.*

Jason sighed. "Like she'd had a little too much to drink, tripped, fell in, drowned is how."

"How much is a little too much?"

"Over the legal limit if she'd been driving, but not enough to incapacitate her."

"And tripped over what?" I asked. "After all, the dock had safety lights on. And even if that's what happened, how did she manage to float into shore when the tide was going out? And if that's not what happened, if she fell off the breakwater, how did she manage to drown in four feet of water? Was there any evidence that she'd hit her head, been knocked unconscious?"

Jason gave me a long, searching look, then seemed to come to some kind of decision.

"No," he said, "the preliminary examination showed no trauma to her skull." Then he sighed and added, "Look, Samantha, these are questions for the police, not me. I'm Harbor Patrol."

"Exactly," I said. I was ready for this. My mother had taught me well. I'd done some online research before coming out to see him. I flipped back a few pages to some notes I'd taken and read aloud: "'Harbor Patrol services include rescue, law enforcement, firefighting, lifesaving, medical response, and public assistance.'"

I looked up at him. "*Law enforcement*. You may call yourself the harbormaster, but you're a cop."

"It's a fine line, Samantha," Jason said, his voice thick with fatigue. "Law enforcement in our case tends to cover drug trafficking. Thank you, though. I'll make sure those questions are considered by the police. I'll take it from here."

He stood up from his chair. He combed his mop of black hair back from his face with one hand as if to tame it but, like Diogi, it continued to do whatever it wanted. "Now, if you'll excuse me, I really do have to get some sleep."

I was getting kind of tired of having my questions and concerns dismissed. *"I'll take it from here."*

Well, we'll see about that, chief.

"Sure," I said, shoving the notebook back into my shoulder bag. And then with all the snark I could muster (and I have never had trouble mustering snark), I added, "But here's a question for you, Mr. Harbormaster. I'm sure you've seen more than your fair share of accidental drowning victims in your work."

Jason nodded, his face shuttered.

"So tell me this. Were any of them floating faceup?"

TEN

A FTER FLOUNCING OUT of Jason's office, I took my
dog (*my* dog?) and went home. There I distracted myself from thinking about my singularly unprofessional handling of my conversation with the harbormaster by working
for a surprisingly enjoyable couple of hours writing the Bayview Grill review. It turns out, writing about food is almost
as much fun as eating food. And way more fun than sweating your tushy off dishing it up in a professional kitchen.

I sent the review over to Krista via e-mail, but decided
to go talk to her about it in person. I was feeling just a little
guilty about sneaking off to interview Jason to follow up on
a story that she, *in her role as my boss*, had told me to drop.
I had gone behind the back of a woman who, *in her role as
my friend*, had given me a job.

I walked through the open-plan newsroom where a couple of reporters, probably covering local politics or (even
more critical to regional papers) high school sports, chat-
tered on phones and squinted at headlines on their Macs. I
stood for a moment at Krista's open door. She was reading
something on her computer monitor with her typical intensity. When she finally looked up and saw me, she smiled
and held up two pages of hard copy.

"Thanks for this," she said.

"Make any changes you see fit," I said magnanimously.

She raised her eyebrows at me. "Thanks, I will. On account of 'cause I'm the editor."

She put the papers down and went back to her computer screen.

"Well," I said, feeling awkward, "I've got to get home. I'm wiped. And hungry."

It was six o'clock on a Friday night, and I'd forgotten to eat anything since breakfast, which under the best of circumstances makes me a hangry girl. And these were not the best of circumstances.

"Plus, I've got a dog to walk. Apparently." *And a suspicious death to investigate,* a troublesome little voice whispered in my ear.

Krista paid no attention. She really wasn't interested in my dog problem. Without looking up from the screen, she waved me away.

"Bye-bye," she said. "I got a couple more hours here."

It was Friday night. Did the woman never stop working? Although, it occurred to me, she had definitely looked like she'd had plans the night before. Plans on a Thursday night and not a Friday?

Anyway, not my business.

Without looking up from her monitor, Krista added, "I'll talk to you tomorrow. We need to decide what your next piece is going to be."

"No, you won't talk to me tomorrow," I said. "I'm off tomorrow. It's Saturday."

Krista looked up. "Really? I never know what day it is. What about Sunday? Are you making Sunday dinner?"

This took me aback. I was surprised that Krista remembered my Sunday dinners. Before my parents had been bitten by the Florida bug and gone stark staring mad, I'd made a tradition of cooking old-fashioned friends-and-family Sunday dinners during my annual visit home in August. I'd dish up comfort food like chicken and dumplings (Tip: Instead of covering the pot and simmering the dumplings, put the whole thing into a 350-degree oven and bake, uncovered, until the dumplings are golden brown on top) or meat loaf (Tip: Use the mixture of ground beef, pork, and chicken that virtually every supermarket carries) and mashed turnips (Tip: Cape Cod turnips are the best in the world). It made a refreshing change from the very fancy concoctions I was plating back in the city.

"I hadn't planned to make Sunday dinner," I admitted. "But I could." *Sunday dinner with friends*. Suddenly it seemed like a wonderful idea. "I definitely could!"

Maybe a leg of lamb larded with a paste of garlic and a touch of anchovy. (Tip: Don't be afraid of anchovies. Just smush one or two into any salad dressing or rub. They totally up the umami and nobody will be the wiser.) Rosemary roasted potatoes. A nice bottle—or two—of red wine. Apricot tart for dessert. That was the kind of cooking I loved. Simple, delicious, sweat-free.

"Yeah," I decided. "Yeah, I *am* cooking Sunday dinner. You wanna come?"

"Sure," Krista said, looking back down at her work, already distracted. "I'll be there at two."

"Great!" I said, and in an excess of zeal immediately texted Jenny and Miles: *"Sunday dinner at 2, Aunt Ida's house—you in?"*

Enthusiastic acceptances followed. Jenny would bring Roland and the kids. Miles would bring the wine and maybe his boyfriend, Sebastian. It occurred to me that I could even pump a few of my guests for more dope on Estelle when Krista wasn't listening. Things were looking up!

T O MY MIND, there is nothing more soothing than planning a menu. It is my default cure for insomnia. By the time I get to dessert, I am usually drifting off, visions of key lime pie or chocolate foam dancing in my head. But that night it wasn't working. It wasn't just Estelle, though that was distracting enough. It was the dinner itself. I realized I'd forgotten one critical thing. . . .

The next morning, as I opened the door of the ell to let Diogi out for his morning ablutions, I said, with no expectation of success, "Go find Helene."

Diogi bounded off through the yews. Literally five minutes later, as I stood in the door waiting for him to bound back, he reappeared through the hedge with Helene. She was wearing a man's camel hair overcoat several sizes too large for her and a pair of turquoise rubber gardening clogs. She looked like a human blue-footed booby.

"Diogi came over, so I knew you were up. I thought I'd come check on you, see how you're doing after the . . . excitement."

I led her into the ell and took her coat. Underneath, she was wearing a peacock blue silk robe embroidered with red dragons. In my gray flannel jammies, I felt like a clumsy goose next to an amazing tropical parrot.

I made us both some coffee strong enough to strip paint and presented my problem to Helene. Somehow I knew that she was one of those clear-sighted people you could present problems to.

"I want to make Sunday dinner tomorrow for you and Miles and maybe his boyfriend plus my friend Krista and Jenny and Jenny's husband and their three boys."

I was exhausted just listing them out.

"That sounds lovely," Helene said. "How is that a problem?"

"*I don't have a kitchen!*" I wailed. "And I don't have a table or space big enough for two people let alone ten," I wailed. "And I don't have plates, forks, spoons. . . ."

Helene cut me off. "Don't be ridiculous," she said briskly. "Of course you do."

She wrestled open the Dutch door that led from the ell

to the rest of the house. The door, I learned, opened directly into the kitchen where I had learned to make chowder so many years ago. I remembered it as a warm and cheerful room. But this was not a warm and cheerful room.

Cobwebs festooned the corners, and the traditional splatter-painted wooden floor was filthy. The stove top was caked with grease.

None of this seemed to have any effect on Helene's good spirits. She flipped a switch, and a dim ceiling light did its best to improve the gloom.

"You see!" she said triumphantly. "A full kitchen. Hot and cold running water. A stove, oven, and fridge." This was true. The kitchen was indeed outfitted with said appliances, all in that bilious shade of avocado that screams the 1970s.

"They all work?" I asked doubtfully.

"Of course," she said. "All electric." This didn't cheer me up much. (Just for the record, chefs hate electric stoves. Can't regulate the heat quickly enough.)

"And places for eight!" Helene exclaimed brightly, waving toward a long pine table at the other end of the room. A picture window ran the length of the wall behind the table with a long, cushioned window seat below it serving as the seating on that side. Three mismatched kitchen chairs flanked the other side and two rather beautiful oak captain's chairs held pride of place at each end. I could see how in some circumstances, such as when the window was not gray with grime, it might be a usable space.

"We can use an old card table of mine for the kids," Helene suggested.

I was still unconvinced. "I don't have plates, glasses, flatware. . . ."

Helene said nothing, just pointed to a milk-painted corner cupboard, its three shelves stacked haphazardly with blue willow china, everything I could need, literally from soup to nuts. I remembered Aunt Ida telling me the story depicted on the plates about the two lovers, forbidden to marry, turned into swallows by a sympathetic god, soul mates forever. This, I thought now, is how we get silly ideas in our heads about love.

"And behold," said Helene, "the *pièce de résistance*."

She reached down and, opening the doors at the bottom of the corner cupboard, pulled out a mahogany box the size of a briefcase. Dusting it off with the sleeve of her kimono, she placed it on the table and opened the hinged top. Inside were twelve full settings of silver, every piece engraved with Aunt Ida's initials.

I felt my heart lift. *I could do this.*

Helene then performed her second magic trick of the day. "And in here," she announced as she yanked open another door that I'd assumed was some kind of pantry, "is your utility closet."

She pulled a dusty string hanging from the bare overhead bulb to reveal a fairly new vacuum cleaner and a treasure trove of mops and buckets and beeswax polish and Mr. Clean. Even more welcome was the sight of a stacked washer/dryer combo. I hadn't been looking forward to the many trips to the laundromat that living out of a suitcase was going to require.

"Saturdays are our busiest day at the library, so I've got to go to work," Helene said as she stood and pulled on her coat. "But I've got some bubbly in the fridge that I'll drop off tomorrow afternoon before dinner." She pulled a dusty treat out of the overcoat's pocket and pointed it at Diogi like a gun.

"Sit," she commanded. *And Diogi sat.*

"What are you, some kind of good witch?" I asked.

"We've been working on a few commands when he visits," Helene admitted.

"In that case," I said, "maybe you could teach him 'Bring Samantha a cup of coffee.'"

* * *

I SET TO WORK with a vengeance on the kitchen, happily dusting, polishing, sweeping, scrubbing, vacuuming, and mopping. I also did a load of laundry. It was heaven.

While I worked, though, my mind was on other things, prime among them how Estelle had managed to drown in four feet of water. Second only to that was why everybody—McCauley, Jason, even Krista—was so determined to get me off the case. By mid-afternoon, the cobwebs were gone, the floor was spick and span, the windows sparkled, the stove and oven were grime free, the inside of the fridge spotless, the silver polished, the dishes washed, the table beeswaxed to within an inch of its life. But I was no closer to solving the riddle of Estelle's death.

I stood back to admire my handiwork, rubber-gloved hands on hips. It was a good room, this kitchen, I decided. Shabby and old-fashioned but cozy and cheerful.

"It'll do," I announced to Diogi, who looked up from where he had been napping in a patch of sunlight like a solar-powered dog. He drummed his tail against the floor.

A trip into town garnered me a leg of lamb, some good extra-virgin olive oil, a big handful of rosemary sprigs, some canned anchovies, a couple of heads of garlic, and some lovely new potatoes. This was not the old Nelson's Market, where the theme seemed to be if it was good enough for your grandparents it was good enough for you. And if it had been on the shelf since your grandparents' day, that was good enough, too. Nelson's had changed. Sure, it still had staples like flour and butter and sugar and Campbell's soup, but now it also stocked things like fresh goat cheese and ripe mangoes and baby arugula. They even had a chunky, not-too-sweet apricot preserve that would be perfect for a rustic tart. All these I threw into my cart, too.

Also, I'd forgotten that grocery stores in Massachusetts

sell wine and beer, which saved me a trip to the liquor store. Miles had offered to bring red wine, but I picked up a couple of bottles of chardonnay since I knew Jenny liked it. Then I threw in two six-packs of Sam Adams in case anyone preferred beer. I'm not much of a beer drinker but I had an unaccountable soft spot for Sam Adams.

To top it all off, Nelson's now stocked cut flowers. I loaded up with yellow tulips. A girl can't have too many yellow tulips.

"This," I said to Diogi, as I plonked the groceries on the kitchen counter, "is going to be fun."

Diogi really could not have cared less. All his concentration was on the paper-wrapped parcel that contained the lamb, as if he might be able to move it from counter to floor through sheer mind control like some kind of canine Kreskin. I put the meat in the fridge, and he looked at me resentfully.

"Tomorrow," I promised him. "There's a bone in that thing you won't believe. Just be patient." The tail drummed the floor again, and I knew I was forgiven.

I fell into bed that night exhausted but, despite the Estelle problem, happier than I had been in months. Maybe years.

ELEVEN

〰〰〰

I WOKE ON SUNDAY raring to go. By one o'clock, I was
ready. I'd put a bottle of chardonnay and some beers into
the ell's little fridge to chill in case anyone wanted a before-
dinner drink and set out a few glasses on the table. The
lamb—into which I'd poked my garlic-anchovy paste at
regular intervals and rubbed with lots of coarse sea salt and
freshly ground pepper—had been in a low oven for a couple of hours. (Tip: Low and slow gives you tender, perfectly
rosy meat from the inside out.) The potatoes and rosemary
were roasting in the hot fat in the bottom of the pan. The
salad—arugula with soft nuggets of tangy goat cheese and
tiny squares of sweet mango—would just take a moment to
toss in a honey vinaigrette. The apricot tart was cooling on
the counter and I'd already whipped the heavy cream for
dolloping on the top. (Tip: You do not have to whip cream
just moments before you serve it. I don't know why they tell
you to do that. It will hold happily in the fridge for hours.)
The table was set, and though the weather had turned chilly
again and the sky outside the picture window was gray, the
cheerful blue and white china and yellow tulips brought a
preview of summer into the room.

Back in the ell, I stepped into the tub, pulled the white shower curtain around its oval shower bar, washed my hair, and slathered on some nice smelly bath oil. A quick blow-dry, a little lipstick, a long floaty dress, my very favorite dangly earrings (silk tassels!), and I was ready. I lit a fire in the woodstove, poured myself a glass of Jenny's chardonnay and sat on the couch in the ell to await my guests.

I was happy. I had loved preparing the simple, homey food, so different from the concoctions I'd been plating in New York. I was looking forward to sharing a meal and a few laughs with my friends. Maybe it would stop me from obsessing about how I was going to solve what I was coming to think of as the Mystery of the Body in Alden Pond.

A knock on the door brought me out of my musings. Diogi bounded up and began barking as if the end of the world were at hand.

"Shut up, Diogi," I said wearily.

To my enormous surprise, Diogi shut up. *Had Helene actually taught Diogi "shut up" as a command?*

"It's open," I called out. I wasn't quite ready to give up my comfy spot on the couch.

The door swung open, and in walked Jason Captiva wearing a thick Fair Isle fisherman's sweater and faded jeans that clung like a promise to his slim hips.

"Do you have some time to talk about the body in Alden Pond?"

I DON'T KNOW WHO was more confused by what they saw. Me by Jason appearing at 1:30 on a Sunday afternoon looking like every girl's daily recommended allowance of man beauty or Jason by me dressed to kill at 1:30 on a Sunday afternoon looking like some kind of secret drinker.

Jason recovered first, but awkwardly.

"I'm sorry," he said, half backing out of the door. "You're . . . busy."

That made me laugh.

"I should always be so busy," I said, and patted the couch next to me. "Have a seat, I'll get you a glass." Two sips of wine and I'd already forgotten we weren't friends anymore.

"No, no," he said, though he did step back into the room.

Diogi was watching this ballet with great interest. Man steps in, steps out, steps in. Lady does not seem alarmed. Shut up command is still in place. This, of course, leaves only one option. Diogi pounced.

To give him credit, Jason took his doggy kisses without totally losing his dignity.

"Hey, fella," he said, after allowing a single kiss on each cheek, European style, "that's enough now. You can stop."

And Diogi stopped.

"What are you?" I asked. "Some kind of dog whisperer?"

"I like dogs," Jason said mildly. Diogi gazed up at him soulfully.

"Well, this one likes you anyway."

"This one does not impress me as being particularly discriminating."

"True," I admitted. "This one even likes me."

"Well, that's easy," Jason said, not flirtatiously, just as if he was simply stating a fact, but I felt myself going pink anyway.

"Please, have a seat," I said, to cover my confusion. "I'm waiting for some friends who are coming over for Sunday dinner. Have a glass of wine with me or beer if you'd prefer. I'm afraid I've only got Sam Adams Summer Ale."

"Well, given that it's about fifty degrees out, that's more aspirational than accurate," Jason said. "But sure, I'd love a Sam."

I felt my face flame at this unintended double entendre. I went over to the kitchenette and pulled a beer out of the half fridge. I was very conscious of his eyes on me.

"Glass?" I asked as I levered the top off.

"No, thanks."

I handed him the bottle and he took a long swig. Watching the muscles of his throat work as he swallowed, I was slammed by déjà vu. No wonder I'd always liked Sam Adams beer. It had been Jason's beverage of choice that summer. *You are totally pathetic, Sam.*

Oblivious to my scrutiny, Jason put the bottle down on the trunk that served as the coffee table and said, "Thanks. It's been a long day."

I settled back onto the couch. "There's something new?"

"Yeah," Jason admitted. "Can we talk off the record?"

"Of course," I said. "Let's make that the default. When you want to talk on the record, you just let me know." I didn't tell him that I was officially off the story. And I didn't say how surprised I was that he seemed to be taking my doubts about Estelle's death seriously. But I was gratified. Maybe I wasn't crazy. *Just pathetic.*

Jason gave me one of his rare smiles, and I felt somehow rewarded. *Yup, pathetic.* "I'll let you know," he said.

But before we could settle into our off-the-record chat, there was a tap at the door and Helene immediately let herself in. I don't even know why she knocked. She was draped in a long, tie-dyed tunic in various shades of lavender and lime green and was carrying two chilled bottles of champagne.

"Oops," she said when she saw Jason. "I didn't know the party had already started."

She handed me the champagne. Veuve Clicquot, no less.

Noticing my raised eyebrows, she murmured, "We had a very bad marriage, so I made sure I got a very good divorce."

"Well done," I said, patting her on the arm. "Very well done indeed."

Jason stood and greeted Helene familiarly. It turned out he was a library regular, mostly nonfiction, of course. Mostly history, of course. *I love a good romantic novel, said no man ever.* She told him that the best seller about America's founding fathers that he'd ordered was finally in.

"Ever since that *Hamilton* play," she pointed out, "the signers of the Declaration of Independence are totally sexy."

I could have sworn Jason blushed.

They chatted for a few more minutes, but soon Jason began making polite noises about leaving.

"Nonsense," Helene said firmly. "There's plenty of food. We'd love to have you join us."

We would? Because I for one did not want to talk about dead bodies over my apricot tart. I really wanted to be able to keep this meal down, thank you.

Jason looked at me doubtfully, as if he could sense my ambivalence, which, of course, made me feel guilty.

"Absolutely," I said, and the note of false enthusiasm in my voice was clear even to me. I tried to tone it down. "Really. This is no fancy thing. Just a bunch of friends over for Sunday dinner."

"In that case," Jason said, "I'd be happy to join you."

He paused, guessing at what had caused my reluctance. "And I promise, no shoptalk at dinner."

"Good," Helene said with great satisfaction, as if she'd just negotiated the Treaty of Versailles. "In that case, I'll just put these bottles in your little fridge and see you later." She clanked the champagne into the mini fridge, then, in a whirl of purple and green, vanished through the door. I had never seen anyone appear and disappear as fast as this woman.

Jason and I settled back onto the couch.

"So, since we have some time before the shoptalk ban begins, what exactly is on your mind?" I asked.

"That thing you said, you know, about the chances of a drowning victim being found faceup? That bothered me," he said. "I started going through our computer files on drownings on the Cape, knocking out those that happened in plain view of witnesses."

"Like people getting pulled out in riptides at the beach?"

"Exactly. In the past ten years there have been thirty-seven unwitnessed drownings, some in freshwater lakes, usually kids swimming alone or teenagers skinny-dipping at night. But most have been on the Outer Beach or in Crystal Bay and its ponds. In the two years I've been here, I've pulled out most of the bay drownings myself."

Pulled out. I shuddered, but said nothing.

"You were right. In my experience and in almost every other case," Jason continued, "the body is found floating facedown."

I nodded to show I was following.

"But you found the body floating faceup," he said. "How does a woman drown faceup?"

"My question exactly," I said. But suddenly I didn't want to go where my mind had already taken me. I hazarded an alternate scenario.

"She drowned facedown but then got turned over by a wave?"

"Not likely. There's not much wave action on a pond. And the weight of the arms and legs dangling down are usually enough to keep the body in the face down position."

I tried again. "Somebody found her and turned her over to see if she was dead?"

"And then walked away without telling anybody?"

"Maybe it was kids," I said doubtfully. "Freaked out?"

Jason snorted. "Kids don't freak out. They love nothing better than a starring role in real-life drama. Believe me, if some kids had found her, we'd have heard all about it. So who was it who turned her over to see if she was dead?"

He looked at me, willing me to say it.

"Her killer," I said, looking him squarely in the eye. "It was her killer."

TWELVE

FURTHER CONSIDERATIONS OF Estelle's untimely end were postponed by the arrival of Jenny, Roland, and the Three Things. The boys were greeted with paroxysms of joy by Diogi, who promptly herded them back outside to throw his slimy tennis ball for him about ten thousand times. Minutes later Helene apparated in the ell and began uncorking and pouring the champagne.

"Is there another time when we could talk about that-which-must-not-be-named-at-the-dinner-table?" Jason asked quietly, leaning in to me, very much aware of the eyes and ears around us.

I confess the feel of his warm breath on my cheek threw me. "Um, okay, sure," I said with my usual eloquence. "When?"

"Weather report looks good for Tuesday, for what that's worth." The Cape's weather is notoriously changeable, giving rise to the old saw that if you don't like the weather, wait twenty minutes. "I have to go out in the morning and check on some channel markers in Big Crystal that may need to be moved. You could come with me, we'll have that talk and then maybe we could take my lunch hour out there, too? Have a picnic on the boat?"

As he trailed off, I suddenly realized he was nervous.

"Of course," I hastened to reassure him. "I'll bring the lunch, if you want. Maybe some fried chicken, coleslaw, chocolate chip cookies for dessert? Easy-peasy." Jason wasn't the only one who couldn't seem to stop prattling on.

"That would be great," he said. "Can you meet me at the pier around eleven? You can bring the pup, too, if you want."

I was touched that he'd thought about Diogi. "He'd love it," I said. "We'll be there at eleven."

He smiled and nodded and walked away to talk to Jenny, leaving me staring after him.

Miles arrived soon after, bearing the wine and his boy-friend, Sebastian Wilkes. Sebastian is a pediatric oncologist at Hyannis Hospital. He is everything Miles is not—slight, with horn-rimmed glasses and a reserved temperament. He lives for his work and rarely has a free night or weekend, so a Sebastian sighting was a rare treat. I offered him a glass of Helene's champagne, and sure enough he declined, saying he was on call. Miles sighed audibly.

I introduced them both to Jason and left them happily discussing shell-fishing regulations, a source of endless de-bate on the Cape.

Arriving fashionably late was Krista, looking beautiful in skintight jeans, a white silk blouse, and red cowboy boots. The sleek black bell of her hair framed her almond-shaped eyes in a way that made them look even bigger than they were. Helene poured her some champagne and she joined the rest of the group over by the woodstove.

I stood to one side, marveling at how my friends had grown and changed since our high school days.

When Jenny was in her early twenties, she had surprised us all by marrying Roland, who was almost two decades her senior and was as buttoned-up and buttoned-down as Jenny was lively and open. I knew Jenny considered her role as their family's primary caregiver a career choice, and I respected her for it, though I wondered sometimes if she'd closed off her other options too soon. But she was hands down the best mother I'd ever known. Just look at that science fair volcano.

Miles, after getting his degree in agricultural science at the University of Iowa, had returned home, officially come out to his elderly parents and took over the family farm, one of the few left on the Cape. Now all organic, of course. This had been very difficult for Miles's dad to accept. Not the gay part, the organic part.

"I always knew he'd go gay," Mr. Tanner once said to me in his charmingly un-PC way, "but I never figured on him going organic."

And then there was Krista. After college, she had convinced my father to hire her as a part-time assistant at the paper. Within weeks she was writing feature stories. In two months, she was moved to news. She was a dynamo. She was brilliant at the work.

When my parents moved to Florida, I had assumed the chronically unprofitable *Clarion* would be shut down by the small New England media company that owned it. But Krista had convinced the big cheeses that the future of newspapers was local and online. She walked out of that meeting as the *Clarion*'s new editor in chief. Two years later, the *Clarion* was both a print and online publication with a growing reputation and even a small profit.

I was proud of them all. Of course, I did not tell them that. Heaven forfend.

I was also happy to see that Jason, though he said little, had been accepted into the group with hardly more than a raised eyebrow (shared between Jenny and Miles, of course). They assumed he was my friend, and therefore he was their friend. I, of course, was not sure he was my friend, as that seemed to be an on-and-off thing, but I didn't reveal that little insecurity. Heaven forfend.

Krista, it appeared, already knew Jason, and I watched in awe as she deftly cut him out of the bivalve discussion.

"You never got back to me on that dredging report for the inlet," she said, somehow making dredging sound very intimate. *Which is ridiculous, Sam. There is nothing intimate about a dredging report.* "Is there really a chance that it will spread red tide?" *Or about red tide.*

Nonetheless, Jason seemed captivated by the topic.

I left my guests in the ell and went out to the kitchen, ostensibly to take the lamb out of the oven and let it rest for fifteen minutes or so, but mostly because I'd just discovered something about myself that I didn't like very much and hoped wasn't obvious on my face. *I was jealous of Krista.*

This was something new. I'd *never* been jealous of Krista. I'd always admired her and rooted for her. I'd reveled in her successes. *What had changed?*

This emotion, I decided as I spooned the roasted potatoes onto a platter and popped them back in the oven to stay warm, was unworthy of me. Yes, I admitted to myself as I made a quick reduction from the pan drippings and a glug of red wine, my star was dimmed and Krista's was ascendant. And, yes, she was trying to block me from investigating Estelle's death, I thought resentfully as I drizzled the honey vinaigrette over the salad. But it was Krista, I reminded myself as I uncorked Miles's wine and set it on the table, who had given me the job in the first place. And it was Krista who had kept my parents' dream alive. The green-eyed monster crawled back into his cave, ashamed.

My guests wandered into the kitchen as I was slicing the lamb. The boys were directed to the kids table, and Diogi settled at their feet on the not unwise assumption that the little humans were more likely to share. The others found their way around the kitchen table with a lot of jostling and joking.

Miles poured the wine and offered the first glass to Helene.

"To my favorite librarian," he said with a little mock bow, "to whom I will always be indebted for agreeing to stock that terrific series of gay romances." *Okay, so I was wrong. Here was a man who loved himself a romantic novel.*

"I didn't order them because they were gay," Helene pointed out, but accepting the wine nonetheless. "I ordered them because they were remarkably well written. My criteria was literary merit."

"Well, that's what you told the library board anyway," Miles said, and Helene grinned at him conspiratorially.

As my guests passed the platters of food around the table, Krista and Miles and Jenny regaled the others with stories about our high school days, which, awful as they had seemed at the time, were actually pretty funny in retrospect.

Maybe someday, I thought to myself, *I'll be able to tell my finger-chopping story and find it as amusing as everyone else seems to.*

Jason, seated between Sebastian and Jenny, seemed relaxed and happy, and I wished that I could say the same for myself. In spite of my best efforts, as the conversation around the table moved to the ever-fascinating topic of environmental regulations (Really? You need a permit to spray poison ivy?), I found my mind wandering back to the shocking conclusion that Estelle had been murdered. My distracted state of mind was later to work against me. If I'd paid just a little more attention when my guests moved off the poison ivy debate and onto bigger issues, I could have saved myself a world of pain.

THIRTEEN
~~~~~~~~

I MIGHT HAVE BEEN listening with only half an ear, but the others were completely absorbed in their conversation.

"You're coming to the town meeting tomorrow night, right?" Jenny demanded more than asked, pointing a forkful of roasted potato at Krista.

"Um, yeah," said Krista, pointing a forkful of salad right back at her. "On account of because it's my *job* to cover the town hall meeting."

"No," Jenny said, shaking her head. "Not as a journalist but as a concerned citizen."

"What should I be concerned about?" Krista asked, suddenly interested. "I haven't actually looked at the agenda yet."

"We're voting on Trey Gorman's big plans for that 'gated community' he wants to build on the old Skaket sailing camp."

This was news to me. Of course, pretty much everything that had been happening in Fair Harbor for the past ten years was news to me.

"Someone bought Skaket Point?" I asked. "I thought the

Sloanes wanted that land to go to Conservation as preserved space?"

"They did," Krista said. "But when old Mrs. Sloane finally died last year, it turned out she'd never actually set the trust up."

That got my attention.

"And her kids decided to sell instead?" I was surprised. I didn't know the Sloanes' grown-up children very well, but this kind of disregard for a matriarch's wishes was virtually unheard of in old Cape families.

"Apparently some of them were in a real financial hole, so when Trey came to them with an offer they couldn't refuse . . ." Jenny shrugged. "Well, they couldn't refuse."

I nodded. This made me sad, but with the downturn in the fishing industry and ten years of construction drought during the Great Recession, a lot of Cape Codders were still barely making ends meet. If selling valuable waterfront land was the only choice, it was the only choice.

But I remembered the Skaket camp fondly, particularly the annual summer regattas between the campers and my own ragtag Nauset Sailing Club. The best part was the cookout that followed on the beach, essentially hot dogs charred over a driftwood fire and a kind of Kool-Aid concoction that for some reason we called bug juice.

The camp sat on a beautiful stretch of waterfront culminating in Skaket Point, a spit of land sticking out into the bay that marked the separation of Little Crystal Bay from Big Crystal. Except for the clearing that housed the cabins and dining hall, it was almost completely wild. In my day, quail and the occasional deer still wandered freely through the beach plum, pin oak, and pines, and once I'd even found a rare piping plover's nest in the high dune sloping down to the beach.

"So what's being voted on?" I asked. "This 'gated community' idea?"

"It's certainly distasteful," Helene put in. "I mean, whom exactly are they putting up a gate against? Me?"

"If they're smart, they are," Miles said dryly.

Helene looked at him and discreetly rubbed the middle finger of her right hand against her nose. There were children in the room, after all.

"I don't suppose it's actually illegal," Sebastian said, turning to Roland for confirmation.

Roland shook his head. "No, it's not illegal."

His voice was studiously neutral. Roland's voice was always studiously neutral. But in my heart of hearts, I suspected he liked the idea of gated communities. That made me feel disloyal to Jenny. I reminded myself that at their wedding, Roland had been so choked up he'd barely made it through the "to have and to hold" part.

The discussion had continued around me, and Jason was pointing out that the proposed project might face some obstacles.

"But the development itself might well be illegal," he said. "At least as it's currently planned."

There is something about the person at the table who sits quietly listening, and then, once everyone else has finished blathering, actually says something substantive. It kind of gets your attention. Even the Three Things looked up from surreptitiously feeding Diogi choice morsels of my very expensive lamb.

"The shoreline along the property is an important shellfish habitat," Jason explained, "which, because shellfish are filter feeders, is critical to keeping the bay waters clean. Gorman plans to build four docks along that stretch, with heavy pilings for large pleasure boats. That could be contested on environmental grounds."

Jenny's oldest boy, Thing One (*Eli?*), stared at Jason. "Is he a teacher or something?" he asked no one in particular.

"No, Ethan (*Ethan!*)," his mother replied. "He's the harbormaster."

Ethan/Thing One was awestruck.

"Really?" he asked Jason. "You're the harbormaster?"

Jason smiled at him, completely blowing his advantage. "Not on Sundays," he said.

Ethan/Thing One sat back, half-reassured, half-disappointed.

"Actually, it was your mom who first pointed out that the plans might be in violation there," Jason added.

Roland looked at his wife in astonishment, his fork stalled halfway to his mouth. "How did you know that?"

"I *can* read, you know, Roland," Jenny said. "Just slowly." *Uh-oh.*

Jason, in that clueless manner particular to so many men who *don't understand the signs*, didn't help matters by saying, "It's going to be an important argument for the Friends of Crystal Bay when she presents their case."

Roland put his fork down and looked at Jenny as if he'd never seen her before. "*Presents their case?* You're a member of the Friends of Crystal Bay?"

"You say that like it's the Communist Party," Jenny shot back. "It's just a group of concerned citizens who want to be sure that any development that touches the bay is sustainable and environmentally sound."

"Bunch of hippies," Roland muttered into his lamb.

Whoa. I could see where this was going. And so I did what any good hostess would do.

"Who'd like some more wine?" I asked brightly.

W ELL, THAT WAS awkward."

Helene and I were tidying up after the other guests had left. To be sure, the apricot tart and another bottle of wine had put my little dinner party back on its feet and Jenny and Roland had departed literally holding hands, but, still, I was worried.

Helene didn't have to ask what I meant.

"It's just growing pains," she said matter-of-factly as she dried a plate and set it on the counter next to her.

I looked at her quizzically.

"Marriages grow and change just like people," she said. "What works at one stage might not work for the next. It's growth, and it's painful. But if the marriage is strong and based on love, trust, communication, and a certain amount of practicality, the couple finds their way through. If it's not," she added, shrugging, "they don't."

This wasn't particularly comforting, but I was beginning to see that Helene wasn't particularly interested in being comforting. She was interested in telling the truth as she saw it.

"I just wish it wasn't happening now," I said. "I've got too much change going on already. I can't deal with Jenny's, too." *That's right, Sam, make this all about you.*

"You don't get to choose when change happens or how much hits you at once," Helene said mildly.

"You got that right," I said ruefully. "It's like I won the change booby prize." I took a scrubber to the roasting pan with a vigor that it did not deserve.

Helene merely said, "Do you want to tell me about it?"

Apparently I did.

FOURTEEN

<u>~~~~~</u>

"THE COMMON WISDOM," I said to Helene, "is that Cape Cod is paradise. Rolling ocean breakers on long stretches of golden sand. Tidal pools and spectacular sunsets. Lobster rolls, ice cream stands, silver-shingled B and Bs . . . all paradise."

"Which is true," Helene pointed out.

"Unless you grow up here," I countered.

What I explained to her, Helene being a newbie and all, was that if you are born and raised here, the truth is somewhat different. What Cape Codders know is that the Cape has only two seasons—tourist season and mud season. And autumn, of course, which is lovely, but even that only lasts for a month or two. But from November until well into June is mud season. Cold and gray and wet and unending.

And then, overnight it seems, it's tourist season. Hot and sunny. Roads choked with summer people and weekly renters and day-trippers. Beaches wall to wall with screaming kids. About mid-June, the mosquitoes arrive. About mid-July, the big biting flies known as greenheads join the party. Both leave with the tourists on Labor Day weekend.

Then September sashays in—crisp and cool, all greens

and blues and golds. September on the Cape is paradise, that I will admit.

When I'd left the Cape to pursue my wonderful life (*read irony there*), I'd been mystified that my friends had not done the same. They didn't want to go anywhere. They actually thought the Cape *was* paradise. They loved it, even during tourist season. They loved it even during mud season. In fact, they seemed to love it *more* during mud season.

Jenny, for instance, adores walking the long empty curve of Shawme Beach with Sadie, particularly when a blow is coming and the ocean is gray and angry. When nor'easters throw rain against the windows of her house and the wind moans and whips the tops of the locust trees, Jenny happily retreats inside, where she sets bread dough to rise, drinks tea, and plays Monopoly (at which she cheats, I might add) with the Three Things. On the rare sunny day, she takes them on the nature walk around Trout's Point to look for ospreys diving for fish or for a seal playing with a banner of kelp. They love the Cape.

As a kid, I'd loved the Cape, too. I'd been sailing the waters of Crystal Bay in my Sunfish, the *Two Bits*, since I was ten. Jenny and I spent a lot of our childhood gunkholing in our kayaks, looking for hidey-holes back in the marshes, breathing in deep, funky drafts of mud and clams and salt water. "Eau de low tide," we called it. Then we'd ride our bikes over to the spring-fed waters of Mirror Lake, where we'd wash off the mud and salt and practice our synchronized swimming. We called ourselves the Aqua Maids.

"I *loved* synchronized swimming," I said to Helene.

"I'm sure you did," she murmured, as if she implicitly understood how in the water, I was graceful in a way I'd never known on land.

"But more than anything, I loved food and cooking," I continued. This was true. My tattered copy of *Mastering the Art of French Cooking* was my closest companion. I read it the way my friends were reading *Harry Potter*, over and over again. But back then, Fair Harbor was no place for a budding foodie. Outside of the dubious French food to be had at the Logan Inn, the offerings in Fair Harbor were definitely, almost defiantly, unsophisticated.

Which is not to say that there wasn't some great food to be had. There were the fried clams and onion rings at Mayo's, for example. And Nellie's Kitchen, great for tall stacks of buttermilk pancakes and crusty rounds of hash browns. But Cap'n Tom's was a total loss with its soggy fish and chips and overcooked hamburgers, and a slice of pizza from DeLorenzo's drooped in your hands like the neck of a dying swan.

Then there was Ling's Kitchen, a Chinese takeout that—except for really good spareribs and dumplings—basically gave you Americanized glop. That is unless you, like my twelve-year-old self, expressed some real interest, in which case you walked out with plastic containers of whatever Mr. Ling was cooking for *his* family for dinner.

For me, these delicious, mysterious meals of sautéed bok choy with sliced fresh ginger or chicken stir-fried with chili paste opened a window to other tastes, other ways of cooking that I knew I'd never find on the Cape. And so, to my parents' grave disappointment, instead of going to college I took myself off to the Culinary Institute of America.

"I had loved the Cape," I told Helene. "And then, almost overnight it seemed, I didn't."

"Because it didn't have fine cuisine?" Helene asked, the doubt clear in her voice.

Somehow I couldn't find it in myself to tell her about what had happened with Jason. How he'd made sure we were never alone together those last few weeks of the summer. How his coldness had hurt, but I'd thought I understood. He'd been right all along. I was a child, a selfish child, more concerned about my parents' disapproval than standing up for a friend. I'd spent my senior year of high school in a fog of heartbreak.

And so I left paradise for the big wide world. And, as is the way when you are young, things got better.

"I had dreams," I told Helene. "I was going to be a famous chef with my own famous restaurant in famous New York City. I was planning to call it Sam's Place. I was planning to live in a glamorous glass box in the sky with views of the Empire State Building. And then for some reason, I married Stefan."

"You might want to consider those reasons at some point," Helene said meaningfully, "but go on for now."

"Suddenly I was a notorious YouTube star. Suffice it to say, the publicity cost me my job. Stefan and I agreed not to press charges against each other, but the subsequent divorce proceedings cost me my savings. None of this was part of the plan."

"Life," Helene said dryly, "is what happens when you're busy making plans."

I gave her what I'm sure was a twisted, bitter smile. "So *what happened* was I ended up writing restaurant reviews for a local paper no one outside the Cape has ever heard of, living in a ramshackle old house with a view of a briar patch, and finding a dead body that nobody but me seems to care about."

"Well, we do need to go into that dead body bit more thoroughly," Helene said, "but for now let's just think about what all this has taught you. Because, my dear, no problem goes away until you have learned all it means to teach you."

I snorted. "All it's taught me," I said, "is that I've wasted the last ten years of my life."

"Don't be ridiculous," Helene said briskly as she dried her hands on a kitchen towel. She gave me a level look. "You did not waste the last ten years of your life. You honed your craft and built a career. You learned about life and you learned about love. You are a better, wiser, more compassionate person for the challenges you've faced. You are exactly *where* you should be, *when* you should be."

* * *

THAT EVENING, AS I walked Diogi around the quiet, sandy roads of Bayberry Point and the sun dipped below the tops of the locust trees, my cell rang. The number was unfamiliar, but it was a New York City area code, so I answered it.

"Hello," I said.

Diogi, of course, chose this moment to warn off a clearly suspicious squirrel with a volley of barking.

"Shut up," I hissed at him. Diogi shut up.

"Excuse me?" said an unfamiliar voice.

"Oh, sorry!" I said. "I was talking to my dog. 'Shut up' is the only command he understands. And sometimes 'sit.'"

"Well, that's a start, I guess," the voice replied. "Is this Samantha Barnes, by the way?"

"Yes," I replied cautiously. I hadn't gotten a call from one of my crazy YouTube fans in a while, but you never knew.

"This is Caitlin Summerhill," the voice said as if I should know who Caitlin Summerhill was. Which I should and did.

Caitlin Summerhill was the chef-owner of Plum and Pear, one of the most revered restaurants in New York City, and justly so. Caitlin Summerhill had bet her life savings that New Yorkers were ready for a fusion of Asian simplicity with American tastes. Who knew that a dab of slow-roasted pulled pork on a perfect, almost translucent round of radish would become the appetizer of choice for the city's elites? Caitlin Summerhill knew, apparently.

"Are you there?" Caitlin asked, with more than just a touch of impatience.

"Um, yeah," I said. "I mean, um, of course. How are you, Caitlin?" We'd met once at a James Beard Awards dinner, so I felt I could be that familiar at least.

"I'm great," she said briskly. "But I'm losing a sous-chef de cuisine soon, and I thought you might be available."

Sous-chef de cuisine to Caitlin Summerhill's executive chef. Second-in-command at Pear and Plum. *Jump at this, you idiot.*

But I didn't jump at it.

"Yes, I'm available," I admitted slowly. "And you probably know why." Because if she didn't, now was the time to get it on the table. So to speak.

"Sure," she said. "I know why. That guy was an asshole. Him and his jerk friends are why I'm not a big fan of men in my kitchen."

Ah, I thought, *a kitchen without angry men with knives in it. Hmmm.*

"Well, I like the sound of that," I said.

"Good. When can you start?"

Whoa. This was going a little fast for me. I wasn't worried about pay or hours. I knew the pay would be good, I knew the hours would be terrible. I could live with both. So why was I reluctant to make the commitment?

"Actually, can I have some time to think about it?" *Did I just say that?*

"Seriously?" Caitlin Summerhill was not going to pretend that any chef worth her Maldon sea salt wouldn't die to get into Pear and Plum.

"I'm actually not in the city at the moment," I said. "I've got some, um, stuff to take care of, some, um, family stuff." *Not to mention a murder to solve.* "It's, um, difficult for me to make a decision right now. . . ." I trailed off miserably.

"Well, I need to know in a week," Caitlin said. "Call me by next Sunday. After that, the deal's off."

"Thanks, Caitlin," I said. "I really appreciate the offer. And the time to consider it." Finally I was talking like a professional. Unfortunately, Caitlin Summerhill had already hung up.

I started walking again, scuffing my feet in the sand, hardly seeing where I was going, just letting Diogi lead me. A few cars crawled by us, and I did not even notice them or give the obligatory little neighborly wave. My head was else-where. *Why hadn't I jumped at Caitlin's job offer?* There was no decision to make. I was being offered the chance of a lifetime.

I should have been excited. I didn't have to retreat to the Cape. I could go back to New York with my head held high. Back to the high-stakes, high-excitement, high-reward life I'd left behind.

But all I could hear was Helene's calm, certain voice. *"You are exactly where you should be, when you should be."*

If that was true, the next question surely was, *Why? Why was I here?* Not to find myself. I'd always known who I was. Not to find love. If my experience had taught me any-thing, it was that you don't find love, love finds you.

And then the answer came to me.

To find Estelle's killer.

I was exactly where I should be, when I should be so that I could find Estelle's killer.

FIFTEEN

~~~~~~

G IRL! YOU AWAKE in there?"
        I sat straight up in my Aunt Ida's bed, unsure for a moment where I was until Diogi's hysterical response to the voice outside brought me back to reality.

"Shut up!" I shouted at Diogi. Diogi shut up.

"I'll take that as a yes," the voice said.

Krista. What was Krista doing at my house at the ungodly hour of—I squinted at the clock by the bed—eleven in the morning. *Eleven in the morning?*

My existential crisis, or whatever you wanted to call it (*self-pity, maybe, Sam?*) had kept me up until the wee small hours, at which point I'd finally fallen into a feverish sleep. Now my brain felt like Jell-O.

I slid out of bed and padded over to open the door. Diogi went into paroxysms of joy at the sight of our visitor. Krista was having none of it.

"Call off the hound," she said, fending him off with one hand.

"I wish I could," I muttered as I pulled Diogi away. "Go do your business," I said, and pointed him toward a forsythia bush that I'd noticed he loved to water.

He bounded away happily, and I stood back to let Krista in. It was only then that I noticed the cardboard boxes at her feet.

"What're those?"

"Your parents' notebooks. They left them in the office archives when they went to Florida, and I need the space."

"I don't have any space," I said.

Krista waved vaguely toward the door that led to the rest of Aunt Ida's house. "You got nothin' but space, girl." *Why did everyone assume I was keeping Aunt Ida's house?*

But I knew from experience that there was no arguing with Krista, so I stooped and picked up one of the boxes. It was heavy, but I managed to get it over to my little table. Krista followed me with the other. I left the door open for Diogi's return. The morning was almost balmy, and it was nice to feel the soft spring breeze coming up from the salt pond.

I turned back to the boxes and lifted the cardboard top of the one I had brought in. Neatly stacked inside were dozens of reporters' notebooks, those steno pads beloved by journalists everywhere for their stiff cardboard covers joined at the top by a wire spiral. This made them easy to hold with one hand while taking notes with the other. For most of my life, these notebooks had been like extensions of my parents' hands. Each would be carefully labeled on the front cover with a start and finish date, each would be crammed, I knew, with notes from meetings, interviews, and research.

"They're in chronological order, the most current on top," Krista said. "They go back about fifteen years."

I opened the top notebook in the box I'd brought in and flipped through pages filled with my father's neat handwriting until I got to his last day at work, about a month after his heart attack:

8:35 am/phone call from Rowena Myers, complaint re editorial re town dump expansion

9 am/front pg meeting/top story, park service to close
Outer Beach during plover season/front pg photo, birds
2:30/editorial due, supporting park service
4:00/"surprise" retirement party god save me

Now you know where I get my snark.

This was kind of fun. I opened the other box and picked up the last notebook my mother had used before she gave it all up to ensure that my dad would live forever. Unlike his notebooks, this one was neither neat nor methodical, the pages covered with a kind of shorthand that only my mother could fully decipher. My mom had a history of leaving her stuff all over the place, so on the front of every notebook she'd write in black Sharpie: CONFIDENTIAL PROPERTY OF VERONICA BARNES. PLEASE RETURN. Once a notebook was filled, she'd use that same Sharpie to record the first and last dates of the notes it contained. This notebook, I saw from the cover, was from two years ago, running from mid-March to mid-May, ending abruptly on the day of my father's heart attack. I flipped the cover back and opened to a page at random.

pnd colish agnst cdr pd culvt
clms wil blk tdl flw
twn sys frsh wtr stm bttr re nitrgn

Well, I wasn't going to get much out of that. I flipped the cover closed again and set the steno pad back on the table.

"You don't need to hold on to these?" I asked Krista.

"I went through most of them," she said, "and flagged anything that looked like it might be relevant to later inquiries or possible lawsuits, had those pages digitized by the intern."

Then she did something that Krista almost never does. She admitted just a teeny bit of uncertainty. "But I'm new to this biz, really, and I'm not sure what else might be relevant." She paused and swallowed hard. "So I thought you could keep them for me, just in case? We really don't have the room at the office."

"Of course," I said. "Not a problem. Good idea."

Her face cleared, and Krista sat down on one of the chairs at the table. "So, what are your thoughts on your next piece? I'm thinking a feature this time, rather than a review. Any ideas?"

Truthfully, I'd completely forgotten about my temporary job writing about food for the *Clarion*. At the moment, I was still reeling from Caitlin Summerhill's offer. Also, I was completely obsessed with Estelle's death and how I could find out more about her without tipping off McCauley, Jason, or Krista. So I definitely didn't want to talk to Krista about that.

So what I said to Krista was, "Um."

"Um? That's your idea?"

I needed to come up with something else fast. Nobody can say I can't think on my feet. Suddenly I knew how I could kill two birds with one stone.

"No, I do have an idea," I said. "Jenny mentioned Mr. Logan is opening a new place, very different from the Inn by all accounts. It might be interesting to do an interview with him, you know, 'how things have changed in the Cape's restaurant scene' kind of thing." *And,* I didn't say, *pump him, as Estelle's employer for at least two decades, for information about Estelle and any enemies she might have had.*

"Good idea," Krista said, nodding. "Mr. Logan likes you. Always has." She grinned and added mischievously, "I think he kind of saw himself as playing Cupid between you and Jason Captiva."

I was mortified. "Really? I was that obvious?"

She rolled her eyes at me. "Hard to miss the way you looked at him that summer. The way you searched him out every chance you got. Girl, you were so gone on that dude."

I tried to play it down.

"Yeah, well, my first crush, you know. Live and learn. It never went anywhere. Estelle saw us one night, kissing.

Well, not kissing really. Just one kiss. She was nasty about it though. Made it sound like we were, you know, doing it. She said we'd pay for it. Jason avoided me like the plague after that."

"Aha!" Krista exclaimed. "*That* explains it." She began to dig through my father's box until she found the notebook she was looking for. The dates on the cover included the summer we'd worked together at the Inn.

"I wondered about this," she said, busily flipping through the pages. "Yeah, here it is. *'August eighth, ten thirty-five in the morning, phone call from EK, said had proof S 'doing it' with JC.'*"

Krista looked up at me. "I assume EK is Estelle, JC is Jason Captiva, and S would be you?"

I nodded, a little stunned by what I was hearing. *Estelle had called my father?*

Krista continued reading. "*'Said would consider keeping quiet re 'skank' for a 'retainer.'*"

"*Skank*?" I yelped. "She called me a *skank*? Let me see that!"

I grabbed for the notebook, but Krista was too fast for me. She yanked it out of my reach.

"Not done yet," she said calmly and continued to read aloud. "*'EK hung up when pointed out blackmail a crime.'*"

Good for you, Dad, I thought.

And then it hit me. *Estelle was a blackmailer.* And if she'd had the nerve to try to extort my father, who else had she tried this little trick on? And for how much? Enough so that someone finally got fed up? Fed up enough to kill her?

I tried to keep my face neutral. I really didn't want to alert Krista to my suspicions. That was something I would follow up on my own, starting with Mr. Logan.

So when she said, "And that's not all," I was actually relieved that she was changing the subject.

Silly me. I'd forgotten about that Krista thing that she does, the way she saves the worst for last.

SIXTEEN

"THERE'S MORE?" I asked.

Krista flipped a few more pages. "Oh yeah, here we are. *'Three p.m. meeting with JC. Pointed out S underage. JC said had been drinking after bad news about mother's illness, only kissed S, but regretted it. Agreed would not see her again.'*"

I was gutted. *Bad news about mother's illness.* I'd *known* something was wrong with Jason that night. Why hadn't I asked him what was bothering him? *Because all you wanted was for him to kiss you. Some friend you were.*

Krista shut the notebook. "Looks like your dad scared off Jason Captiva."

I suppose I could have been angry at my father in retrospect. Angry at him for not talking to me at the time, not trusting me. And, yes, I could have been angry at him for warning off Jason like some Victorian father dismissing a chauffeur who'd gotten above his station with the daughter of the house.

But I couldn't be angry with my father for dismissing Jason. Because I'd done the same thing when I'd ignored his real need that night so long ago. I'd done the same thing when I'd pulled my hand out of his, when I'd stepped away from him and chosen my reputation as a good girl from a fine upstanding family over my friendship with a troubled young man with a difficult home life who'd allowed himself to open up to me. I was ashamed of myself then, and I was still ashamed of myself.

"No," I said, more to myself than to Krista. "My father didn't scare off Jason. He only finished what I started."

We were mercifully interrupted by a knock on the still open door to the ell.

"Hello," a man's voice said hesitantly. "Ms. Baker?"

We turned, and standing there, framed in the doorway, was Apollo. Or at least a guy who literally looked like Apollo—golden hair, golden skin, golden brown eyes. The face was saved from classical perfection by a slightly crooked nose and a too-wide mouth.

At this vision, Diogi erupted into his usual crescendo of barking.

"Diogi," I shouted over him. "Shut up!" Diogi shut up.

In the sudden silence, Krista said to our visitor, "Yes. I'm Krista Baker." She added coolly, "And you are?"

"Tyler Gorman," the Apollo said. "The third, that is. Not my dad, he's Tyler Gorman, Junior." As if the distinction was important somehow. "Everybody calls me Trey, you know, because I'm the third generation with the same name."

I stared at the man in the doorway. *This was Tyler Gorman III?*

I vaguely remembered Trey Gorman. His grandmother had lived next door to us, and Trey and I had played together when his family had come on their annual pilgrimage to Grandma's house for two weeks in August. He'd been a plump boy about my age, with a fluttering mother who thought he could do no wrong and a coldly distant father who thought he could do no right. Despite the mother's protests, Trey's father had bundled him off to boarding school as soon as he possibly could.

But really? This long, lean hunk of yummy was the beta version of the pudgy, awkward boy who used to mope around in his grandma's backyard? I had felt sorry for Trey. But it seemed he had grown up into quite the hottie.

I was suddenly very aware of my gray flannel pajamas and the fact that I hadn't yet brushed my teeth.

"I'm sorry to interrupt," Trey said to Krista. I probably shouldn't have worried about my jammies. I was invisible next to Krista. "Your assistant said I could find you here. In advance of tonight's town meeting, I wanted to leave you some of the specs for Skaket Acres."

He opened a neat brown accordion file and pulled out a carefully folded blueprint and a surprisingly tasteful brochure, all tan and green and very, well, organic looking.

Suddenly aware of my duties as a hostess, and, let's face it, tired of being invisible, I said, "Trey! Hi! It's me, Sam. Samantha Barnes. I used to live next door to your grandmother."

The wide mouth broke into a smile.

"Sam! Of course! How great to see you. I thought you lived in New York. What are you doing back in Fair Harbor?"

"It's a long story," I said. *And hopefully you will never hear it.* "But come in, please. I'll make some coffee for us all, while you and Krista go over your papers."

Which will also give me a chance to get dressed and brush my teeth, I didn't add.

Trey moved into the room, shutting the door behind him.

"I hope I'm not interrupting anything," he said, gesturing toward the cardboard boxes.

I flipped my mom's notebook shut and dropped it on the table.

"No, no," I said. "We were just looking at some of my mother's old notes. Krista thought I'd like to have them."

Trey reached over and picked up the notebook idly. "Anything interesting?"

"There might be," I said with a laugh, "if it was possible to read her shorthand."

"I liked your mom," Trey said, replacing the steno pad on the table. "She was nice." *Said nobody ever about my mom.* He turned back to Krista.

"This is the blueprint that we'll be sharing tonight at the town meeting," he said. "I thought it would be helpful for you to have an advance look."

"Thanks, that's useful," Krista said. I pushed my parents' stuff aside to make more room on the table.

Krista and Trey bent over the materials, while I bustled away to make the coffee (*and* slip into the bathroom to brush my teeth *and* wash my face *and* pull on a pair of jeans and a clean T-shirt).

When the coffee had been brewed and drunk and Trey had answered Krista's many questions to her satisfaction, he finally got up to leave, gathering his materials and carefully stowing them in the accordion file.

"If you want another look anytime, just let me know. These are my only copies, so I'll just keep these in my car. It's kind of my office when I'm out on the Cape. Most of my real work is done in my dad's Boston office."

He tucked the file under one arm. "It was really great to see you again, Sam," he said, giving me his hand (*his warm, strong hand*) and another one of those smiles. "I'd love to catch up sometime, if you're free."

"Um, sure, well, sure," I spluttered.

Krista took pity on me and walked Trey out to his car while I regained my composure.

When she came back in, she looked at me with utter contempt.

"That's the best you could come up with? 'Um, sure, well, sure'?"

"He threw me," I said in weak defense. "I have to say, he's totally not what I expected. I mean for a real estate developer and all. He seems so . . . nice."

Krista looked at me thoughtfully.

"Girl," she said after a pause, "you are still a fool for love."

I punched her lightly on the shoulder.

"Nope," I said, grinning. "I'm like you. I reject love as a fanciful invention of lady novelists."

Then we smiled at each other.

"Badass," I said.

"Or just emotionally unavailable," Krista said.

"Same thing," I said, "but badass sounds cooler."

In our little moment of female bonding, neither of us noticed that my mother's notebook was no longer on the table.

SEVENTEEN

SOMEHOW JENNY MANAGED to talk me into going to that night's town meeting with her for "moral support."

It wasn't that I didn't want to be a good friend. But a town meeting is not my idea of how to spend a Monday night. Or any night, for that matter. Do not listen to people who tell you that the New England town meeting is the world's purest, most direct form of democracy. What they neglect to mention is that it is also the dullest. Plus, I was hoping to spend the evening working out how I could subtly prompt Mr. Logan into telling me who Estelle might have been blackmailing.

"Why can't Roland give you moral support?" I whined.

"Rolly is taking the night shift," Jenny pointed out. "Dinner, dishes, homework, baths, bedtime. Unless *you* want to stay with my kids . . ."

"No, no," I said hastily. "Not my strength. I'll go to the meeting."

And so we made our way with two hundred other concerned citizens into the already stifling auditorium of the Fair Harbor Middle School and settled into our unbelievably uncomfortable folding chairs.

Three rows in front of us, I could see the back of Krista's perfectly coiffed head. Next to it I saw, with an odd sinking sensation, Jason's hot mess. The man desperately needed a haircut. They seemed to be getting on well, so I distracted myself by actually trying to pay attention to the meeting.

This was not easy. After several riveting (*read irony here*) yea or nay votes ranging from a proposed $450,000 annual tax levy to pay down the town's unfunded pension liabilities (yea) to the advisability of a $75,000 survey of Beach Road for potential construction of a sidewalk (nay), I hissed to Jenny, "I am going to want these past two hours back on my deathbed."

"Just wait," she whispered back, pointing to Article 37: Medical and Recreational Marijuana Dispensaries. "The laughing grass fight comes next."

We both enjoyed the ensuing brief but entertaining skirmish over whether to allow the newly legalized weed stores within the Fair Harbor town limits. There was some concern about the "town character" (whatever that might be). But when it was pointed out that such emporiums would bring in some pretty nice tax revenue, the resolution was passed unanimously.

"At least we know we want the money," Tom Wylie, the selectman moderating the meeting, had noted dryly.

But by the time Mr. Wylie got to Article 46—the proposed development of a fifteen-unit gated housing development on Skaket Point by Gorman Properties—I'd completely tuned out and was busy creating next Sunday's dinner in my head. Aunt Ida's New England clam chowder to start, I thought, followed by a traditional New England corned beef and cabbage boiled dinner (Tip: To make sure you do not boil it to death, use a slow cooker.) with a really hot fresh horseradish sauce. Then maybe homemade vanilla ice cream with butterscotch sauce for dessert.

I was worrying about how to keep this from being an all-white meal—maybe lots of parsley garnish, which I knew was a cheat—when Jenny poked me unceremoniously in the side.

Trey Gorman, in neatly pressed chinos and a crisp white shirt open at the neck, was making his way up to the dais while an assistant began placing large placards showing the planned development on easels. At first, Trey looked both confident and happy to be there, but I thought I saw his smile falter a bit as he looked out over the audience.

I craned my neck to see who it was who had thrown him off his stride. And then I understood. Tyler Gorman, Jr., Trey's rather forbidding father, was sitting in the front row, his face just as I remembered it from our childhood—stern, dismissive, cold. Once again sitting in judgment of a son who was, it appeared, coming up short before the session had even started.

Nonetheless, Trey managed to pull it together for the presentation, going over the plans for the development thoroughly and clearly in a businesslike manner. His case was further buttressed by the promise that all construction would be done by local contractors and the houses would be certified green. He resolutely avoided looking at his father. Not that I blamed him. The man perpetually looked like he smelled something bad.

When Trey had finished his piece, Selectman Wylie opened the floor to discussion.

"We're up!" Jenny whispered.

"*We?*" I whispered back. "*I* don't have a dog in this fight."

"It's about the environment," Jenny said indignantly, turning to me and forgetting to keep her voice down. "We *all* have a dog in this fight."

A few other people in our row turned to look at her disapprovingly. You aren't supposed to voice an opinion aloud at a town meeting unless called on by the moderator. And even then, you addressed the moderator, not another person attending the meeting. It was a good rule, and one that kept the personal attacks to a minimum. Jenny looked suitably abashed and mouthed a quick "sorry" to her neighbor.

But when called upon to present the findings and concerns of the Friends of Crystal Bay, she was cool and collected and ready to apologize to no one. She went through each possible impact step-by-step, speaking without the benefit of notes, of course. I was very proud of her.

"Development is inevitable on the Cape and, when done well and sustainably, can contribute to preserving what we love best about this precious spit of land on which we live. The Friends of Crystal Bay have no doubt that Mr. Gorman is sincere in his stated wish to develop Skaket Point with those goals in mind," she went on, the very voice of reason. "And so it is *both* of our responsibilities to ensure that all possible environmental impacts have been considered and, if determined to be harmful, mitigated. I'm sure Mr. Gorman agrees with that assessment."

Mr. Wylie nodded to Trey, who stood and smiled first at Jenny, then at the rest of the town council ranged around the folding table on the dais, and finally at the sea of faces in front of him. It seemed to me that he came alive in this kind of direct question and answer format, where his charm could come through.

"Ms. Singleton and the Friends of Crystal Bay are absolutely right, of course," he said, pushing a golden curl off his golden forehead (which, I must admit, distracted me for a moment). "Skaket Point is one of the last undeveloped parcels on the bay and its unspoiled dune formation, marsh, and beachfront not only add to the beauty and environmental stability of the bay but also, I must admit"—and here he grinned boyishly—"to the value of the land on which we are proposing to build these homes." He grinned again. "I am, after all, a businessman, ladies and gentlemen. I do not wish to kill the goose that lays the golden egg."

His candor was rewarded with some quiet chuckles from the audience.

"Please refer your comments to me, Mr. Gorman," Tom Wylie reminded him, but it was too late. I could see that Trey had the crowd eating out of his hand.

"But more importantly," he continued, not even bothering to pretend he was talking to the selectman, "though I grew up outside of Boston, I spent every summer of my childhood here in Fair Harbor, sailing on that bay."

Well, *that* was stretching it a bit. Trey had visited his grandmother for precisely two weeks every August, not all summer. But he *had* learned to sail at the very snooty Fair Harbor Yacht Club and if it had made him a fan of Crystal Bay, then great. Good on you, Yacht Club.

Trey proceeded to consider each objection raised by Jenny and the Friends of Crystal Bay, agreeing with some and offering suggestions for mitigating impacts or asking for time to consider the implications of others (particularly the deepwater docks) and how they could be addressed. By the time the discussion was over and Trey had agreed to resubmit his plans at next month's meeting for further review, both sides seemed satisfied with the outcome.

I stood a bit apart from Jenny outside the auditorium as she accepted the congratulations of her fellow Friends of Crystal Bay, somehow growing taller and more self-assured as her friends and neighbors crowded around her. At one point, the throng parted deferentially for a man in an impeccable blue suit who was moving forward to shake Jenny's hand. He sported improbably white teeth, a chin like the prow of a ship, and the patently insincere smile of the career politician. His thinning brown hair had been carefully combed and gelled over the top of his head. He looked vaguely familiar, but I couldn't quite place him. He gripped Jenny's hand in both of his own and leaned, in my considered opinion, way too far into her personal space. I couldn't hear what he was saying, but Jenny looked distinctly uncomfortable, and I noticed that she did not return his smile.

I was distracted by a tap on my shoulder. I turned to find Trey standing behind me.

"I thought I saw you in the auditorium," Trey said hesitantly. "I just wanted to say hi, see how you thought the meeting went." He seemed unsure of himself, and I wondered if he'd been getting some quality feedback from that father of his.

"I thought it went well," I said truthfully. "I thought you and the Friends found common ground."

The smile grew wider. "Did you really? That's great. That's exactly what I was hoping for. I really can't afford any more delays."

"Absolutely," I assured him, adding, "You may have to make some concessions though."

"Of course," he said. "But there was nothing on the table that was a deal breaker, do you think?"

I was wary of reassuring him any further. "Well, regulations are regulations. It's up to you whether you think the plan is still economically viable, depending on the concessions you may have to make."

His face grew clouded, almost sulky, as he said, "Yeah. But the docks are a big selling point. Without that access for pleasure craft . . ." He trailed off and then smiled that smile of his. "Anyway, I was wondering if you meant it when you said we could get together sometime?"

I gaped at him, once again aware of all his goldenness. "Get together?" I repeated idiotically.

"Yeah, like for a coffee?"

"Um, sure," I said. "I'd, um, like that."

Trey noticed Jenny coming toward us, and said quickly, "How about Nellie's Kitchen, say, tomorrow morning?"

"I can't," I said, remembering my picnic with Jason. "I have . . . other plans . . . tomorrow." *I'd had no social life for months and suddenly my dance card was full. How great was that!* "And then on Wednesday I've got to work on an assignment for Krista. . . ."

"You write for the *Clarion*?" Trey's eyes lit up. I could almost see the visions of good publicity dancing in his head. Not that I blamed him. And not that I'd ever let his goldenness get in the way of my purely objective reporting. *Yeah, we'll see about that, Sam.*

"Thursday, then?" he asked eagerly.

"Thursday would be fine."

"Ten o'clock good for you?"

"Sure," I said. "I'll see you then."

I turned and walked back to Jenny who had finally escaped from her adoring fans.

"Who was your friend with the superhero teeth?" I asked her as we pushed through the double glass doors out to the school parking lot.

"No friend of mine," Jenny said shortly as she beeped the car's doors open. "That was Curtis Henson."

"Aha," I said. Curtis Henson was the Cape's district attorney. Curtis Henson also had a very high profile off Cape in Massachusetts political circles. Which was why he was now running for state DA. No wonder he'd seemed familiar. I'd seen the guy's campaign ads on local TV when he'd run for county DA a few years ago. Everybody on the Cape had.

"Was he asking for your support as he climbs the political ladder?"

"Yeah, although maybe not in those exact words," Jenny said. "But he can ask 'till he's blue in the face. The man's a disaster on environmental issues."

As she climbed up into the driver's seat she added, grinning, "And how about you? Was that Trey Gorman you were talking to? Colluding with the enemy now, are we?"

I laughed. "If having a coffee is colluding, then I guess so," I admitted. "Do you mind?"

"Of course not," Jenny said. "Trey Gorman's not a bad

guy. He grew up off Cape"—which is Cape Codder speak for not to be entirely trusted—"but I've known his grandmother since forever. She's a good lady. I'm sure he'll do the right thing."

"I'm sure he will," I said.

But then I thought about the look on Trey's face when he'd seen his father at the town hall. The same look I'd seen on his face as a boy. That insecurity, that desperation to please. And suddenly I wasn't as confident as Jenny that Trey would do the right thing at all. That father of his was one scary dude.

EIGHTEEN

~~~~~~~~~~

YOU KNOW HOW Oprah is always asking people what their one true thing is? Well, this is my one true thing: Crystal Bay is the most gloriously beautiful body of water in the world. On a crisp May morning, dazzled by the sunlight sparkling on its deep blue waters, entranced by the new green mantling its small, uninhabited islands, taking great breaths of the fresh salt breeze, one could be forgiven for thinking that this was what the dawn of the world had looked like.

I'd had a busy morning. Jason and I were going to have a picnic! *No*, Downer Self admonished me, *you and Jason are going to talk about Estelle's death.* I decided to ignore Downer Self.

By eight o'clock I was flouring the chicken pieces that had been marinating in buttermilk overnight. I'd found a cast-iron pan deep in one of Aunt Ida's cupboards, which would be perfect for frying. (Tip: Cast-iron pans are the absolute best for fried chicken. They hold the heat like nobody's business.) While the chicken was popping and sputtering in the hot oil, I sliced some red and white cabbage (much prettier to use both) as thin as I could; added some equally thinly sliced sweet onion and a little grated carrot; and mixed it all with a simple dressing of mayonnaise, caraway seeds, and white wine vinegar. (I'm not a big fan of sweet coleslaw, but you could add a little sugar if that's your thing.)

I put the fried chicken on a couple of cookie racks to keep it crisp. (Tip: Never let fried chicken cool in its own grease. That makes it—surprise!—greasy.) The cookies came next. I like my chocolate chip cookies flat and chewy with crispy edges. (Tip: Use *a lot* of high-fat butter, preferably Irish or French, brought to room temperature until it is so soft you can stick your finger through it. Unless, of course, you like your cookies puffy.) I felt obliged to sample three or four, just as a test. They were awesome if I do say so myself (*and you shouldn't*, Aunt Ida would have added).

I also made lemonade using deep cold well water from the tap, the juice of a couple of fresh lemons, and some simple syrup. (Tip: Simple syrup is just equal parts sugar and water cooked for a few minutes over low heat until the sugar dissolves. It's simple to make. Hence the name. And unlike granulated sugar, simple syrup stays suspended in whatever you mix it into.)

I showered, dressed in jeans, a white T-shirt, red hoodie, and red Vans. No makeup except for lip gloss, but I did do that thing where you brush your hair upside down and then do a dramatic slo-mo hair flip. For all the good it did. I wished, not for the first time, that I had Krista's sleek black bob or Jenny's blond curls.

I took Diogi for a short walk along Snow's Way, then drove the two of us to the Harbor Patrol offices at the municipal pier. Jason, dressed in his official khakis, was already down at the dock, throwing gear into the patrol's twenty-two-foot Zodiac rigid inflatable. Zodiacs are essentially big rafts—shallow-draft, aluminum hulls surrounded by an air-filled neoprene collar. Because they are relatively lightweight and don't have a very deep hull, they are great for shallow waters. But because they are so open, with low sides and bow, they are not so great for hair. I was surprised we were using the inflatable, and not just because it would ruin my hair.

"Are we going gunk-holing?" I asked.

"In a manner of speaking," Jason said. He took one look at my darling red, white, and blue outfit and threw me a grungy yellow foul weather jacket.

I snagged the jacket and looked at it in dismay. It was your usual rubberized model, complete with attractive brimmed hood and tastefully decorated with engine grease and dried eelgrass. I felt it did not complement my outfit.

"It's gross," I said. *What was I, ten?*

"It's waterproof," Jason pointed out with infuriating male practicality. "And it's going to be choppy out there," he said. "You'll get soaked."

I wrinkled my nose in response. *Yes, exactly. Ten years old.*

I shrugged into the foul weather gear and picked up the blue Coleman cooler holding our picnic. I'd rescued it from Aunt Ida's unfinished basement and had scrubbed it clean, in the process evicting at least seven daddy longlegs spiders (*eeuuw*) from what they obviously considered their home.

I hoisted the cooler to him over the side of the boat. Diogi, who had been eagerly sniffing seagull poops on the dock, looked up in alarm. He knew exactly what was in that cooler. I clambered into the Zodiac. Diogi took one panicked look and dove into the boat after me.

Jason laughed. "Do you think he was more worried about his human abandoning him or his lunch disappearing with her?"

"Definitely the lunch," I said. "I've made it very clear to him that I'm not his human."

"I don't know," he said. "I think you might be sending him mixed signals."

For a moment his face was serious, and I stared at him

in something like alarm. But then he grinned and the moment was gone.

"Has he been out on a boat before?"

"I wouldn't know," I said. "He's not my dog." *Yeah, keep telling yourself that, Sam.*

"Well, we'll take it slow at first," Jason said. "But these yellow dogs are bred for the water. It shouldn't be a problem."

It was definitely not a problem for Diogi. Just in case, I crouched next to him in the bow of the boat and put one arm around him, but the moment Jason pulled away from the dock and began heading out into the bay, Diogi was the happiest dog in the world. I could have sworn that he was smiling.

We scudded across the water, the Zodiac slapping the waves like a happy whale. Jason had been right about the chop. Spray flew up into my face, and my hair windmilled around my head until I reluctantly pulled up the hood of the jacket and cinched it tight around my face. *Very attractive.*

Jason sat behind the wheel amidships, squinting out at the bay and steering with one hand. As the wind blew his hair back from his face, I was struck by the intelligence and maturity revealed there. It was the same intelligence and maturity that had so drawn me to him when I was just a girl, though a decade of life and experience had added a quiet calm that I now found even more attractive. I felt my heart twist and, in self-defense, turned away.

I concentrated on the beauty of our surroundings. We were skimming through Little Crystal, the smaller, more contained part of the bay. It was still early in the season and only a few powerboats were out, most of them solid gray workhorses piloted by lobstermen or commercial fishermen. The pleasure boaters would come with the warmer weather. A few local sailors had already put their catboats in, though, and I was visited by a deep envy at the sight of their gaff-rigged sails billowing white in the fresh breeze. The spring-green marshes that edged the shoreline gleamed against the deeper green of the wooded hills rising behind them, the occasional shingled cottage or rambling old summer places known as "big houses" peeking through the pines and pin oaks.

As we headed south through the channel markers at Skaket Point—red nun to our left, green can to the right—the view opened up into Big Crystal, a vast waterway dotted with small, green, uninhabited islands. Everything else was a bowl of blue—the water a deep navy in the channel shading to cobalt over the shallows, the sky a clear robin's egg blue with puffy white clouds mimicking the sailboats below.

Entering the big bay you could almost believe you were back on the old Cape, before development, before tourism. Most of the curve of the Fair Harbor shoreline to the west was Conservation-protected land. Houses were few and far between and most were old family big houses grandfathered in when Cape Cod Conservation bought up the land back in the sixties.

To the east was the Outer Beach, a miles-long arm of low dunes and beach grass protecting the bay from the crashing breakers of the Atlantic Ocean on the beach's far side. On its bay side, the promontory was edged with the salt marshes and meandering tidal creeks that Jenny and I had so loved as children. The only thing interrupting our view toward the marshes was Nickerson Island, sitting close to the marshes but kept separate from them by a winding river between the two.

Though Jason had said that we were going to have lunch behind Nickerson, I wasn't surprised when he turned the Zodiac to the west, along the curve of the Fair Harbor shoreline. The best way to get to Nickerson was to follow the loop of the deep water channel around the Fair Harbor shoreline and then back around to the island itself. This way we would avoid the long stretches of shallow water over the sandbars that, at mid- and low tide, prevented a straight shot across the bay. At high tide, Crystal Bay holds almost eight thousand acres of water. Then it is a boater's dream. But as the tide lowers, only the foolish stray out of the marked channel between those treacherous, ever-shifting bars covered by mere inches of water.

Unless you were sailing a Sunfish, as I had as a child. Sunfish are small, flat sailboats, hardly more than surf-boards, with an eight-inch-deep footwell about the size of a farmhouse sink and one triangular sail. They were great, even at low tide. Especially at low tide. If you had the wind behind you and your daggerboard up, you could skim right over the long flats of sand bars, leaving the "stinkpots," as we disdainfully labeled motorboats, confined to the long way around in the channel.

Jason opened up the Zodiac's Yamaha 150, and Diogi's ears flew back as he leaned forward into the wind, deliri-ously happy. He looked like a doggy version of a Rolls-Royce hood ornament. Even at full speed, it took us about ten minutes to take the channel around to where it eventu-ally began to loop back toward Nickerson Island. There Jason cut the motor to barely more than an idle and began taking soundings at the buoys that marked the channel.

"That bar has shifted," he said, almost to himself, as he marked the depths carefully on a paper chart. "The chan-nel's narrower here than it used to be."

I said nothing. It was a pleasure to watch him, com-pletely concentrated on his job. He moved around the craft with the confidence and ease of someone who could tie a bowline before he could say a complete sentence. He was at home.

It was warm in the lee of the island. I ditched the hated foul weather jacket and Jason abandoned his windbreaker. He rolled up the sleeves of his khaki shirt, and I could see the long muscles of his forearms sliding under bronze skin as he pulled the markers aboard. His was not the overmus-cled, gym-built body of the men I'd known back in New

York. This man was lean and strong from real work, work that he loved, work that made a difference. Work that I knew he'd chosen despite the personal consequences of that choice.

D URING OUR TALKS under the Logan Inn's deck, I'd asked Jason about his father, whom I'd never met. All I knew was that he was from one of those enormous fishing families descended from the Portuguese sailors and fishermen who had settled in Provincetown generations ago.

"What about your dad?"

"Not in the picture," Jason had said, but without rancor. "Left a long time ago for Maine, where there's still some fish to be caught."

In the past few decades, the cod and haddock had all but disappeared from the waters around the Cape, whether because of overfishing or simply a bad cycle, no one was really sure. A lot of fishermen had moved north for their livelihood.

"I'm sorry," I said, meaning it.

"Not a problem," he said. "I figure this way I can't be a disappointment to him."

I looked at him quizzically but said nothing.

"Unlike my father, I happen to believe the overfishing theory," he said. "I'm kind of a fanatic about it. And about all the other ways we're not being the stewards of the land and the water that we ought to be."

He talked about how sad it made him when people built trophy houses on vulnerable waterfront, dumping nitrogen-rich fertilizer on their lawns that then ran off into the nearby lakes and ponds, creating toxic algae blooms that smothered the fish below. But mostly he'd talked to me about how much he loved the beaches, the bays, the harbors of the Cape. "I'm really only happy," he'd said, "when I have a boat under me." I'd thought that was both lovely and sad.

* * *

LOOKING AT THE man Jason Captiva had become, the work he had chosen, and what it had cost him, I respected him all the more. I stayed out of his way, deliberately not distracting him with conversation. This was his job, and he took it seriously. Also, I was kind of hypnotized by those arms. Diogi was clearly bored, though, and yawned conspicuously several times before giving up and taking a snooze.

Finally, Jason rolled up the chart and tucked it into a waterproof compartment in the stern of the boat. "I'm hungry," he announced. "If you're ready to eat, we can head to the river now. I have a surprise for you."

I was absurdly pleased that Jason had a surprise for me and nodded my agreement.

"The river's completely silted up on its north end, and there's a new bar silting up our entrance at the south," he said, as he moved the throttle up a bit, "but in the Zodiac and with the tide high enough now and still coming in, we shouldn't have any trouble getting over it and back again."

Now I understood why we'd taken the inflatable, which could be maneuvered through water as shallow as a foot without hitting bottom, as opposed to the Grady-White, which drew more than twice that.

Jason veered off the deepwater channel into the river that ran behind the island and separated it from the dense stands of marsh grass on its other side. I'd always loved this little river. On the marsh side the cordgrass grew as tall as a man. When the tide was high and covered the marsh's peaty soil, the dense green spears appeared to be growing out of the water itself.

Jason slowed the Zodiac to a crawl and nosed it over so close to the marsh that I could have reached out, as I had as a child, to run my hand along the cordgrass. I noticed, though, that as he steered he kept glancing over to the other side of the river toward the island, as if he was looking for something.

"Here we are," he said finally.

And with that, he wheeled the boat directly into the marsh grass.

I gasped and grabbed for Diogi, preparing for the lurching crunch as the boat ran aground on the peat bed below.

Some surprise. He couldn't have given me flowers?

NINETEEN

~~~~~~

THERE WAS NO crunch. Just tall grass surrounding us, grass sliding under and along the boat with a barely audible whoosh. And then, like a magician's trick, we came out into another, much narrower waterway, maybe ten feet wide, that snaked through the marsh parallel to the river but completely hidden from it.

I laughed with delight. "It's a secret creek!"

Jason smiled, clearly pleased with my response. "Isn't it great? All you have to do is find the spot where the creek is closest to the river and, if the tide's high enough, you can slide over that narrow hummock between them right into it."

"I wish I'd known about this when I was a kid in sailing club," I said. "We used to play hide-and-seek with the Sunfishes. The idea was to find a hidden spot back in a marsh, let down your sail, unstep the mast, and fight off the greenheads until somebody found you. It was so much fun."

"You didn't get out and walk on the marsh itself, though, right?" *Jason Captiva, ever the harbormaster.* But he was right. At low tide, or sometimes even half tide, the marshes can become vast swathes of thigh-deep mud. We'd been properly terrified as kids by stories about holes covered with scum that look like solid ground but where a man could sink out of sight in an instant.

"Of course," I said. "But mostly because we knew our mothers would kill us if we came home covered in stinky marsh mud."

I looked around at the wall of grass on either side of the creek. It rose at least five feet over our heads. I felt like Moses in the bulrushes. "This creek would have been a perfect hiding place though," I said ruefully.

"If you could find it," Jason pointed out, steering the inflatable carefully along the narrow passage.

"Yeah," I admitted. "How *do* you find the right spot?"

"It's directly across from that high sand dune on Nickerson Island—you know, the one everyone used to run down when we were kids?"

Of course I knew that dune. Every kid on the bay knew that dune. We used to pull our boats up to the beach below it, clamber up the thirty feet or so of sand, and then tear ass down, screaming with delight, in great leaps that almost felt like flying.

"Yeah," I said. "I must have face-planted a hundred times on the beach coming down from that dune."

"That was the tricky part," he said, laughing. It felt good when Jason laughed.

"Maybe we could do it on our way back? Run down the dune for old time's sake?" I suggested.

"No can do," Jason said. "The piping plovers use it for nesting now. Nickerson dune is off-limits these days from May to August."

I was disappointed, but pleased that the endangered birds had found a protected nesting ground.

"That's good," I said. "And probably not too difficult to enforce, since no one lives there or uses it."

But then all conversation ceased as Jason steered the boat around a curve in the creek. Before us was a lovely tidal pond, deep and blue and sparkling in the spring sunshine.

The water was so clear you could see the sandy bottom at least eight feet below. Though the pond was encircled by acres of marsh, across from us was a small, tempting sickle of sandy beach. Beyond that, more marsh and then, in the distance, low dunes topped with wiry grass and wild roses. On the other side of those dunes, a tough slog through deep, soft sand, you'd find the cold Atlantic breaking furiously in great, white-topped waves against the Outer Beach.

But here, in this hidden pond, all was peaceful. Jason and I were completely alone, not another boat or person in sight. Our only companions (other than Diogi, who was snoozing up on the bow again doing his solar-powered dog imitation) were a couple of ospreys building a rickety nest of sticks on one of the wooden platforms that had been built by conservationists to encourage just such domestic activity.

"Oh, it's lovely," I breathed.

Jason said nothing but looked pleased. He cut the motor. "We'll anchor here and have lunch, okay?" he said. "Then maybe pull up at the little beach on the other side and let Diogi take a run."

"Perfect," I said, and began pulling the chicken and coleslaw out of the cooler as Jason tossed the anchor over. Aunt Ida's kitchen hadn't run to plastic forks or paper plates for the slaw (I wasn't worried about the chicken. Everybody knows fried chicken should be eaten with your fingers), so I'd put in two blue willow salad plates and two monogrammed silver forks.

Jason raised his eyebrows a bit. "Pretty fancy."

"Here," I said, grinning at him and pulling out a roll of paper towels. "I had hoped for monogrammed napkins, too, but this was the best I could come up with."

"A shame," he said. "Really lowers the tone."

We shooed a grumpy Diogi off the varnished wooden seat in the bow of the boat and took his place, putting the food and a thermos of lemonade between us. At the sight of the cooler being opened, Diogi had sat up at rigid attention.

I was touched that before Jason tucked in, he stripped the meat from a couple of chicken thighs and gave it to his new BFF.

We ate in companionable silence, wiping our greasy fingers on the paper towels and taking deep gulps of the lemonade. As we bobbed quietly under the dome of the sky, the crystal water and shining dunes in the distance glowing in that clear light that you only get on the Cape, it seemed to me that we could have been the only two people on earth. I wanted to hold the moment, savor it. Maybe, like, forever.

It is a scientific fact that men are immune to atmosphere. While I was going all poetic over nature's beauty, Jason was pushing his plate away and reaching for the cookies.

"Oh, man," he said, munching happily. "I haven't had a homemade chocolate chip cookie in I don't know when."

It occurred to me to wonder if Jason had a girlfriend. I'd assumed he wasn't married, partly because he wasn't wearing a ring but mostly because Jenny definitely would have included that factoid in her biography. But maybe a girlfriend? My heart sank a little, but I comforted myself with the knowledge that he hadn't had a chocolate chip cookie in he didn't know when. It has been my experience that, at least in the initial phases of courtship, homemade chocolate chip cookies play a large role.

After polishing off a good half dozen, Jason metaphorically pushed himself away from the table, his face going all serious on me.

"We need to talk," he said.

I panicked a bit. This sounded serious. Were we at last going to confront what had happened between us all those years ago?

"About the case," he added. *Of course.* Lunch break was over. Jason was back on the clock.

"So, I've talked to McCauley and he's proceeding along the assumption that Estelle had been drinking, which the coroner confirms, though not so much that she couldn't operate her boat. But McCauley's theory is still that she was stepping onto the dock, missed her footing, fell into the space between the dock and the boat, and drowned."

"And then floated *against* the tide toward shore," I added sarcastically. "You know what I think about that theory."

"Yeah," Jason said. "And I agree it makes no sense." *Well, duh. But thank you.* "But we still need some idea of where she did go in."

I remembered something. *The snail.*

"Jason, when I found her she had mud on her face and"—I gave a small involuntary shudder—"a snail crawling on her cheek. One of those little periwinkles that live in the mud along the pond edges. How could she get a snail on her face, if she drowned in deep water?"

Jason absorbed this in silence. Okay, so maybe it was just a small thing, but it was significant. At least *I* thought it was significant.

"But," he pointed out, "even if she drowned—or was drowned—where she was found, by the breakwater, the water there was at least four feet deep. If somebody drowned her, why push her face four feet down into the muddy bottom?"

"I don't know," I said slowly.

"Well," Jason said, "it certainly bears looking into."

He glanced at his watch. "The tide's going to start going out soon. We've got time to give Diogi a quick run and then I've got to get back to the office."

We motored over to the other side of the pond and landed the inflatable on the little beach. Diogi leaped off the boat and began running up and down the sand, sniffing the dried eelgrass that marked the high tide mark. Jason and I followed at a more sedate pace.

At one point, Diogi brought me back an empty horseshoe crab shell, laying the treasure proudly at my feet. I have never been a huge fan of horseshoe crabs, which can grow as large as dinner plates and always look to me like prehistoric tanks, creeping along the bottom of the bay dragging their long barbed tails behind them. I took the shell gingerly by the tip of its tail and winged it out into the water. Diogi plunged in after it, swam back with it in his mouth, and dropped it again at my feet.

"Oh no," I groaned. "The dog wants to play fetch."

"Now you're in trouble," Jason said, laughing. He took pity on me and tossed the by now rather raggedy shell back out in the water. Diogi got to play this incredibly fun game for about ten minutes, at which point Jason ruined everything by insisting that he get back in the boat.

"Time to go home, boy," he said.

Diogi retaliated by doing one of those doggy fur shakes, spraying both Jason and me with a lovely mixture of salt water and sand.

By the time the inflatable slipped back out of the secret creek into the Nickerson River, I could tell Jason was a little worried about getting the boat over the shallow delta where the river opened back up into the channel. He tipped the outboard up a bit and Diogi and I scooted up to the bow, using our weight to keep the stern of the boat and the engine's propeller as high in the water as possible. I leaned over, peering down through the water at the sand below, shouting my best estimates as to depth back to Jason at the wheel.

"Two feet, maybe three. Now two again. Getting shallower. Maybe a foot. Okay, deeper again. Two feet. Three. Yay, we're in the channel!"

It was fun. A little nerve-racking but fun. That's the thing about being out on the water. It takes you completely out of yourself. You are perpetually monitoring the wind, the currents, the tide, other boats—you are completely in the moment, as my yoga-mad friends would say.

We jounced our way back to the municipal pier. I was happy with the way the day had gone. I felt like Jason and I were on our way toward our old friendly footing. I did wish I'd had the nerve to bring up our history. But that was okay. We'd have other opportunities to talk now that we were working together to find Estelle's killer.

Back on dry land, Jason followed me over to Grumpy and watched while I coaxed the old truck back to life. He leaned into my open window.

"So," I said brightly, "what's our next move on the case?"

Jason pulled back a bit.

"Thank you for your information," he said, his face suddenly as closed as a summer house in January. "It's very helpful. I'll take it from here."

Whoa. Samantha Barnes, Girl Reporter, gets shut down.

I just nodded coldly and began to raise the window. *Okay. If that's the way you want it.* And as the glass slid up, Jason Captiva turned and walked away.

I SPENT THE REST of the afternoon hacking at Aunt Ida's briar patch with some old loppers I found in the toolshed. This was hugely therapeutic. By dinnertime, I was too beat to do anything but scarf down some cold fried chicken and soggy coleslaw and run my grievances with Jason in a loop over and over again in my head.

Was that all the day had been? A chance for Jason to get the information he needed?

To cheer myself up, I reached for the Tupperware container that should have held at least a half dozen chocolate chip cookies only to discover that Jason had somehow eaten all of them when I wasn't looking. This made me mad at him all over again.

Which may have been part of the reason why I did what I did with Trey Gorman.

TWENTY

No, *NOT THAT*. Just flirt a little. Get my groove back. Of course, I had a whole day to wait until my coffee date with Trey, but I was perfectly capable of holding my grudge against Jason for a day or two.

But first I had to make a living. I'd promised Krista an interview with Mr. Logan on the changes in the Cape's dining scene. It had not escaped me on my annual summer visit to the 'rents that while I was away making myself all sophisticated, the Cape was doing the same thing. Somehow over the years it had managed to transform itself into a foodie destination. Farmers markets, country inns, bistros, and coffee bars had popped up like mushrooms after a long rain, offering everything from heirloom tomatoes to burgers made with grass-fed beef to truffle pâté to Hawaiian poke bowls (maybe the *best* food fad ever).

I didn't think that Mr. Logan was going to go as cool as poke bowls, but I was interested in this healthy food idea of his. And his ideas about Estelle, just incidentally.

So, time to get to it. On Wednesday morning, I marched out to Grumpy, who apparently did not share my work ethic. The truck refused to do much more than cough a few times before not even doing that. I called Jenny, who, with the boys off to school, was happy to come pick me up and take me to my next assignment.

The ramshackle building that had once housed Reedie's Bait and Tackle was reached by way of Levi's Way, a long narrow road off of Route 6 that led to nowhere except Reedie's landing on Big Crystal. At that time of year, the location was eerily quiet and isolated. This was the stretch of shoreline that Jason and I had zoomed by the day before, mostly protected and with almost no houses in sight except a few big houses tucked back into the woods. And even these were mostly still shuttered.

The boat launch, too, was deserted now, though by late June it would be crowded with people sliding fishing skiffs and small sailboats down the ramp into the water. There were a handful of moorings about twenty feet out from the landing, but only two with boats on them, one a Chris-Craft cabin cruiser with two fishing poles standing at the ready in their rod holders, the other a sleek gray-black number with a tall wheelhouse completely sheathed in dark, tinted glass. The name on the transom, *Mad Max*, was as macho as the boat.

Really? I thought. *Who wants a boat that looks like Darth Vader designed it? So off-Cape.* It occurred to me that I was in danger of turning into my Aunt Ida.

Jenny turned the Range Rover into the sandy patch that passed for a parking lot behind the old gray-shingled bait shack. Tacked to the back wall was a banner reading, "Coming Soon! Bits and Bites—for the Best Lunch and Best View on the Cape!" Well, as a name, *Bits and Bites* was a bit twee for me, but I liked Mr. Logan and I wasn't going to let it put me off.

Jenny and I got out of her car and followed a newly laid brick walkway that curved around to the front of the building. I noted the freshly painted white trim, the sparkling clean plate glass window facing out to the bay. The view alone, which stretched all the way across to Nickerson Island and the Outer Beach, would probably ensure Bits and Bites' success. From where we were now standing, I could see a small beach in front of the building that had been hidden to us from the parking lot. Pulled up above the tide line was a tidy little Sunfish, its sail neatly furled, ready for action. I felt a twist of envy for the carefree soul who was clearly already using that baby to escape for a few hours on the bay.

I turned back to what I couldn't help but think of as Reedie's and knocked on the front door. I could hear hammering coming from inside, and called out a hello. Within seconds the noise stopped and Mr. Logan, hammer in hand, appeared like some kind of cheerful elf in front of me.

"Well, my goodness, if it isn't Samantha Barnes!" he exclaimed, smiling broadly. "I can't believe my eyes!"

I could hardly believe mine. Was this bustling little man really the same Mr. Logan I had known a decade ago? He looked much the same—slight but wiry, thick gray hair, clear blue eyes—but where was the defeated slope of the shoulders, the hesitant smile that always seemed to be apologizing for something?

"Mr. Logan," I said, "I'm surprised you remember me."

"Come in, come in!" he said, opening the door wide. "Of course I remember you, Samantha! You were one of the best waitresses we ever had."

Which was an out-and-out lie, but well-meant and I took it in the spirit in which it was intended.

"And you were one of the best bosses I ever had," I said, laughing. There was a lot of truth to that. He'd been a lovely boss.

"Oh, this is my friend Jenny Singleton, Mr. Logan," I said. An idea hit me. "Actually, Jenny, maybe you could take a few photos of the place? The camera on your phone is much better than mine." Which was true. If you've ever wondered who it is who stands in line for the new iPhone the minute it comes out, that would be Jenny.

"Of course," she said happily. "How about a photo, Mr. Logan?" And without waiting for actual permission, she started snapping away. "And maybe I'll just take a little three-sixty video of the space while I'm at it."

Mr. Logan looked confused but didn't protest.

Jenny and I stepped into the small but cheerful dining room, with its new-construction smell of sawn wood and fresh paint. A bandsaw sat on a workbench in one corner, and I could see that Mr. Logan had been hammering freshly cut lengths of framing into place around the picture window. The window filled the space with light. The walls were painted sky blue, setting off the simple pale birch tables and chairs.

"This is charming," I said. "You've done wonders."

Mr. Logan's face glowed with pleasure and even his thick gray hair seemed springier at the compliment.

"Please," he said, gesturing with the hammer toward one of the tables, "have a seat. I was just going to make some coffee. Can I offer you a cup?"

Jenny declined, but I live on the stuff and accepted eagerly.

I was curious to see where the magic was going to be made (as we chefs like to say sarcastically), so I followed Mr. Logan into the kitchen. It was still a half-finished mess. Canvas drop cloths were bundled in one corner, painter's tape and stirring sticks had been tossed in the other. Stacks of paint-encrusted roller trays were piled precariously under a long stainless steel prep counter itself cluttered with paint cans, somebody's cell phone, some car keys, various spackling knives, empty Diet Coke cans, sandpaper, and all other detritus left behind by workmen. On the plus side, a new six-burner stove and commercial dishwasher, all shiny and virginal, were waiting for opening day.

I prepared myself for another twist of envy. This was

what I'd always wanted—my own restaurant, my own kitchen, designed to my own specs. But nothing happened. I was happy for Mr. Logan, but I wasn't envious. *What was that about? I wanted a Sunfish more than I wanted a restaurant?*

Mr. Logan turned and saw that I'd followed him into the half-finished kitchen and shooed me back out.

"No, no, no," he said. "This isn't ready for prime time yet. The workmen are off buying more supplies. You go back and sit down. I'll just be a minute."

I went obediently back to the dining room, where I inspected a series of framed black-and-white photos of sailboats that Mr. Logan had hung along one wall.

"I can hardly believe that this was once Reedie's bait shop," I shouted back into the kitchen.

Mr. Logan came out with two mugs and a French press full of some really wonderful smelling coffee. He set it on the table, then reached down to pick up a battered plasterboard sign that had been leaning against the wall. It read "1 Pint Worms $2." I laughed out loud.

"I'm tempted to remind people by putting this up," he said, "just as my little joke."

Jenny laughed at this but advised him against it. "Might put the customers off their food."

Mr. Logan and I sat down at the table. As Mr. Logan poured coffee into our mugs, he said, "Now tell me everything you've been up to, Samantha Barnes. I hear you're a top chef in the Big Apple."

I was surprised that Mr. Logan hadn't seen The Video, but then reminded myself that the man was at least sixty and probably wasn't spending a lot of time on social media.

"Actually I'm taking a little break from the chef thing," I said. "I'm doing some writing for the *Clarion,* and Krista thought we might give you a little advance publicity for Bits and Bites, maybe run an interview with you about the changes you've seen in the Cape food scene over the years."

"I'd love that," Mr. Logan said, holding up one of the mugs. "Cream, sugar?"

"No sugar, milk if you have it."

"Well, that right there is one of the changes," he said, chuckling. *When did Mr. Logan start chuckling?* "Nobody takes sugar in their coffee, nobody takes cream. Always milk now. And a good thing, too. People need to take care of their health, their bodies. That's why Bits and Bites is going to offer vegan, gluten-free, and vegetarian offerings."

This was good stuff. We talked for an hour about everything from the changing demographics of restaurant goers to the move from "exotic" foods in favor of eating locally.

"In fact, that's why all of our greens and most of our vegetables are going to be from Tanner Farm," Mr. Logan said.

"You're going to work with Miles as a supplier?" I was delighted with the news. The more steady restaurant clients Miles had the better.

"Absolutely," Mr. Logan said. "I'm taking the contract over to him today. He's local and he's organic. And an awfully good fellow to boot. Plus, we're going to credit Tanner Farm on the menu. I think it's important that people know where their food is coming from. Too many kids these days think food grows already wrapped in plastic." He smiled at his own little joke.

"It's true," I said. "There was a study in Britain a few years ago, where they found that almost a third of primary school children thought cheese was made from plants and a quarter thought fish fingers came from chicken or pigs!"

Mr. Logan laughed and Jenny, still with the phone aimed around the space, moved closer to us.

"Of course," I added, "the Brits used to be even more clueless about food. There was that great fake documentary the BBC posted on April Fool's Day back in the fifties, the one about the spaghetti harvest in Italy, with the spaghetti farmers happily plucking pasta off the spaghetti trees."

"I'm actually old enough to remember that," Mr. Logan said, his eyes sparkling. "It was on the Johnny Carson show, too. Turns out, a lot of people fell for it. Wanted to know where they could get their own spaghetti trees."

I laughed again, saying, "I've really enjoyed our time together, Mr. Logan." This was true, but all I could think of was how I was going to move this conversation to Estelle.

Jenny looked at her watch. "Sam, I hate to hurry you, but I've got an appointment to see—" She cut herself off and I wondered if it was an appointment with the real estate agent, Brooklyn Stever.

"You go ahead, Jen," I said. "I can walk back through the Point. It won't take long." This was true. Bits and Bites was only about three miles away by the sandy private ways that roughly followed the shoreline of the bay. It was a nice walk and would take me under an hour.

Jenny held her cell phone out to Mr. Logan. "I like this photo of you by the window. What do you think? Are we okay to run it in the paper? You can scroll to see the others."

Mr. Logan shook his head and backed away from the proffered phone. "I'm sure if you like it, it's fine." Then he admitted helplessly, "I don't actually know what you mean by scroll. These mobile cellular telephones are a mystery to me."

Jenny smiled tolerantly and hurried off while I leaned forward in my chair. Might as well jump right in.

"Did you hear about the . . . incident . . . at the old Inn the other night?" I asked delicately.

"About Estelle?" Mr. Logan said, his kindly face troubled. "I did indeed. What a terrible thing."

"I was there actually," I said. "I found the body."

Mr. Logan rocked back slightly in his chair. "How awful. Did you remember her from before?"

"Estelle would be hard to forget," I said.

He nodded. "You're right there." His face clouded, making him look momentarily like the old Mr. Logan. "It's a shame about her accident. She was a fine waitress once. Not everyone's cup of tea, but her regulars loved her."

Not everyone's cup of tea. I had the opening I needed.

"Well," I said with false reluctance, "she didn't make my life very easy, but maybe that was just me?"

As I'd expected, Mr. Logan rushed to reassure me. "Oh no, my dear," he said. "She was not very pleasant to a lot of people, especially the other waitresses. Suzanne complained about her constantly." Then his mouth snapped shut, and I knew he wished he hadn't said anything. He was of the school that believed in speaking no ill of the dead.

Oh, well, at least I had a lead. Suzanne. Suzanne Herrick. I hadn't thought about Suzanne in years. She was one of the few waitresses at the Inn with more seniority than Estelle. She'd taken Krista and me under her wing, taught us the ropes, even occasionally stood up for us when Estelle got particularly nasty.

"Do you ever hear from Suzanne?" I asked. "She was awfully good to me."

Mr. Logan looked unhappy. "She's not so great. Some kind of early onset dementia, they say."

"I'm so sorry to hear that," I said, meaning it. Suzanne had been a truly nice person. "Is she at Shawme Manor?"

Shawme Manor is the closest nursing home to Fair Harbor, just a few miles up Route 6. I knew it had a special wing for dementia patients, because my *nonna* had spent the last sad years of her life there, slipping further and further into the absence of Alzheimer's.

"Yes," Mr. Logan said. "I visit her when I can. She's all mixed up, of course, doesn't make a bit of sense."

"Maybe I should pay her a visit while I'm here." Now, *that* made me feel a little guilty. To be sure, I did want to be nice to someone who'd been good to me during a tough time. But I also thought I might be able to learn something from Suzanne about Estelle. I knew from my grandmother's experience that in the early stages of dementia, patients often had a much better grasp of the past than the present. It couldn't hurt to sound Suzanne out. I tried to ease the guilt by telling myself that if Suzanne were in good mental health she would certainly want to help me. Nobody thinks a killer should go free just because their victim wasn't a very nice person.

"Well, I don't know," Mr. Logan said doubtfully, as if he wished he'd never brought Suzanne up. "It might just upset her. She still knows me, you see."

I decided it was time to change the subject, as it was clearly distressing him. "And you, Mr. Logan, how are you doing? You're looking really well," I said.

"Yup," he said, cheerful again. "I was real sick for a while with Hodgkin's lymphoma. Looked like curtains, and then about two years ago my doctors at Cape General got me started on that new immunotherapy. Six months later I was in remission. It was like I was given my life back."

"That's wonderful," I said.

"It was more than wonderful," he responded, suddenly very serious. "It was a sign. A message. Nothing is more important than your life. You have to fight for it. Illness will try to take it from you. Acts of God will try to take it from you. Other *people* will try to take it from you. You can't let them. It's yours, yours to live. You can't let anything or anyone get in the way of that."

His intensity was a little unexpected and I wasn't sure how to respond.

And I certainly never dreamed at the time how important those words would be to my own survival.

TWENTY-ONE

I SPENT WHAT WAS left of the afternoon working on "The Cape Cod Food Scene: A Decade of 'Change for the Better'" featuring "veteran restaurateur Norman Logan." I was pretty sure no one had ever called Mr. Logan a veteran restaurateur before.

I e-mailed it to Krista and immediately got a reply asking me to come by in person, saying she had something she wanted to run by me.

Uh-oh.

Krista was not a consensus seeker. Krista just told everybody else what to do. So, if she was going to try to get my buy-in on some cray idea, I was pretty sure it was a super-cray idea. Like when I let her talk me into waitressing at the Inn. But I said that if I could get Grumpy to agree, I'd come in. I am congenitally curious.

Grumpy was eventually convinced to actually do his job, and I rolled into Krista's office a mere half hour later. I'd barely had time to sit down before Krista turned her PC's monitor toward me.

"Take a look at this," she said.

She clicked her mouse, and a face filled the screen. My face. My face talking.

"There was a study done in Britain a few years ago," I was saying, "where they found that almost a third of primary school children thought cheese was made from plants. . . ."

"Jenny *taped* me?" I asked. Well, screeched really.

"Shut up and watch," Krista said.

The camera pulled away from my face, and there was Mr. Logan and me, coffee mugs in hand, laughing and talking about food. It was a video, and I never wanted to see myself on a video again in my life. But it wasn't so bad. At least at the end I didn't cut anyone's finger off.

"So what do you think?" Krista asked. *Like you care what I think.* "Jenny brought it by earlier, after she'd edited it a little."

What I thought was I didn't like where this was going. I didn't like it *at all*. My face may have reflected my thoughts. It usually does. Krista was looking just a teeny, tiny bit uncertain.

"Jenny thought maybe I might want to run it as a sidebar video to the story in the online edition," Krista said. *That's right, pin it on Jenny.*

"*Absolutely not*," I said. Or maybe screeched. "I will never, ever, ever again be a part of an online video in any *way, shape, or form*." *Tell us how you* really *feel, Sam.*

"I get it," Krista said. "Once burned, twice shy. But this isn't YouTube. It's not going out into the big, bad interwebs. It's nothing controversial. In fact, it's really good. Short, funny, informative. You've got to admit, Jenny's good, right?"

Still playing the Jenny card. But it was working. I nodded reluctantly.

"I called Mr. Logan," Krista said. "He liked the idea, gave me permission to run it. Said we'd be doing him a great favor."

Oh, jeez, now play the Mr. Logan card why don't you?

"And you look terrific," Krista lied. "Those cheekbones, those sparkly eyes. And those great earrings. They could be your trademark." *Cheekbones? Sparkly eyes? Trademark?* "Anybody who sees this is going to see the real you—charming, knowledgeable, an expert in her field. Also strikingly attractive, what with being so tall and all, like a model."

My mother once told me that if you want someone on your side, compliment them. Extravagantly. "In my experience," she had said, "you cannot flatter people too much."

I *knew* this, and yet I fell for it. "An expert in her field." *Not a woman without a job.* "Tall like a model." *Not oversized like a giraffe.*

"And think what it would do for Jenny's self-confidence . . ."

Again. Unfair. What was I supposed to say to that?

I nodded slowly.

This was all the okay Krista needed. "Great," she said. "We'll run the story and the video clip as the first in the series."

I should have known there would be more.

"What series?" I asked dully.

"'The Cape Cod Foodie' series," Krista explained patiently, like I should have known. "A twice-monthly feature article and accompanying video on food, where it comes from, new trends—that kind of thing. Starring you."

"Oh, *that* series," I said with a heavy sarcasm that Krista chose not to hear.

"You can maybe do Miles's farm next. He's great talking about all that organic crap."

Krista existed on a diet of microwave popcorn and black-and-white cookies from the Sunoco Ready Mart. She couldn't care less about organic. But she knew a good story when she saw one.

And I have to admit, I was hooked. There is nothing in the world I like more than talking about food. Where it's grown. How it's grown. How it's used and how it's misused. What's real food and what isn't. How it's cooked, and how it *should* be cooked. Food encompasses all the really important things—family, community, creativity, health, politics, the environment, even sex. (Yes, sex. Case in point, the famous scene in the movie *Tom Jones*, where Tom and Mrs. Waters go through five courses of what can only be called foreplay. Never has eating a pear been so hot.)

"Okay," I said. "We'll give it a try."

Somehow, I'd completely forgotten about my job offer from Plum and Pear.

TWENTY-TWO

T HURSDAY MORNING DAWNED clear and brisk.
Even Grumpy was happy and started up at the first try.
I was still a little pissed off at Jason. I was looking forward
to meeting Trey for breakfast at Nellie's Kitchen. I thought
it would be nice if someone started treating me like the
charming, terrific-looking, tall-like-a-model eye candy I
apparently was.

Toward that end, I was wearing a floaty dress—a very
short floaty dress—platform espadrilles and eye makeup. I
hadn't applied eye makeup since my marriage went down
the toilet. That my mascara hadn't dried up in the tube I
took as a sign. A sign that I should flirt with Trey Gorman.

With admirable foresight, I remembered to remove my
ratty fleece jacket before I pushed open the door to Nellie's
Kitchen. I could have sworn Trey gulped when he saw me
come into the diner dressed more for cocktails than pancakes. He had been sitting at the Formica counter drinking
a cup of black coffee and looking at some official-looking
papers but stood up abruptly at my entrance, shoving the
materials into his brown accordion file.

"Wow, you look great!"

I looked down at my outfit as if to say *"What this old thing?"* "Thanks," I said breezily, batting my mascara at him. "You look great, too."

Which was true. He was wearing a pair of pretty darn tight jeans and a crisp white cotton shirt casually rolled up at the cuffs. My eyes somehow got snagged on the golden hair on his forearms, and I had to pull them away like reluctant toddlers in front of an ice cream store.

"I'm starving," I announced, plopping myself down on the red pleather seat of the stool next to his.

"I'm starving, too," Trey said meaningfully. It was a good line. The problem was I'd never much gone for guys with good lines. *Uh-oh. What had I gotten myself into?*

I ordered a nice big stack of banana and walnut pancakes with bacon on the side. Trey ordered an egg white omelet.

"That's what you eat when you're starving?" I asked, dabbing at the melted butter and maple syrup dripping down my chin with a paper napkin manifestly inadequate for the job.

"I don't know if you remember," he said, smiling that charming smile of his, "but I was a fat little boy."

"No," I protested. "Not fat. Plump, maybe."

"Whatever," he said. "When I started boarding school, I was teased like crazy. So I decided I'd never be called Porky again. Without my mother force-feeding me, it was pretty easy. Skip the carbs, stick to lean protein and vegetables. And I started working out. By the end of sophomore year, I'd lost twenty pounds and had a six-pack."

Do not think about his six-pack, Sam. "And that's still your routine? Just lean protein and veggies?"

He nodded. "No red meat, no dairy, no carbs, no sugar."

I wasn't sure how to respond to someone for whom food was the enemy. Food was my friend. What do you turn to when you can't turn to a grilled cheese sandwich?

"Well, good," I said finally. "That leaves more for me."

He laughed, and I was struck again by how white his

teeth were against the golden tan of his face. To distract myself, I turned back to the bacon that had been playing second fiddle to the pancakes. When I'd finished tucking into every food group that Trey couldn't or wouldn't eat and when he'd finished his teeny tiny bites of what I didn't even consider sustenance, we looked at each other solemnly.

"Jack Sprat and his wife," he said, shaking his head in mock sadness. "Surely we can think of something we *both* like." *Another line.* I tugged down the hem of my very short skirt, which Trey was looking at suggestively. I had changed my mind about the whole flirting thing.

"We both like sailing," I reminded him. Sailing was a nice, neutral topic.

"True," he said. "The best hours of my childhood were spent on the *Milagro*, my grandmother's Wianno Senior." For once there was no doubting his sincerity. And I totally got it. There is no boat more lovely than a Wianno, with its graceful lines and old-school, gaff-rigged sail. For goodness, sake, John F. Kennedy had sailed a Wianno Senior.

"Does she still have it?"

"Well, in a way," he said. "She wanted to give it up a few years ago, but I bought it from her, had it completely reno'd—all new paint, new sails, the brightwork stripped and revarnished, the works." Okay, so he hadn't done the work himself, which was a strike against him. But he loved the boat, which made up for a lot.

And I was frankly jealous. My parents had sold their modest eighteen-foot Baybird (named the *Nellie Bly* in honor of the first woman investigative journalist) when they'd defected to the Sunshine State, so I was landlocked. And Trey had a twenty-five-foot classic wooden boat that he could use whenever he wanted.

"Is she in the water now?" I asked, not even bothering to hide the longing in my voice.

"She is," he said, his eyes dancing. "You want to take her out for a spin?"

"What, now?"

"Why not?"

"Well, for one thing, I'm not dressed for it."

"So, how long will it take you to dress for it?"

I stopped to think about this. Not how long it would take me to dress for a sail (about five minutes to scrub my face clean and put on an old pair of jeans and a flannel shirt), but whether this was actually a good idea. I really hadn't enjoyed flirting with Trey. He was a little too self-absorbed and finicky for my taste. I knew enough of his history not to blame him for it. We all carry family baggage. I'd been lucky that mine was lighter than most. But maybe we could be friends. And besides, I hadn't been sailing in years. I yearned for the feel of a boat leaning into the wind, the sight of a taut, white sail against a blue sky.

"About five minutes," I finally said.

"Great," Trey said, "I'll meet you at the yacht club in fifteen."

THERE IS NOT a lot of time for flirtatiousness when sailing a rather large boat on a rather windy day on some rather tricky waters. I was glad about that. Which isn't to say that the sail wasn't fun. It was delirious fun. The *Milagro* was perfection—she seemed as happy to be slicing through the water, sails flying, as we were. Trey took the tiller, and I was kept busy trimming the unfamiliar mainsail and jib. The brisk breeze meant a lot of hiking out, that is, leaning back over the water on the side of the boat that the wind was coming over to hold the boat on a fairly even keel.

So we didn't talk a lot, but there were moments, skimming along like a bird, the wind in our faces, when we just looked at each other and laughed in common delight.

"That was great, Trey," I said as we made the *Milagro* shipshape again back at her mooring. "I can't remember when I've had so much fun." *Actually, you had fun on Tuesday*, a little voice in my head said. *With Jason.* I ignored it and continued coiling the mainsheet neatly. "I really owe you."

I swear I didn't mean it like that. I didn't mean I actually *owed* him anything. I believe absolutely that when a man asks a woman out on a date (or for a sail), she owes him nothing more than the pleasure of her company. And if the man assumes otherwise, she owes him not even that.

But Trey assumed otherwise.

"That's easy to repay," he said, leaning toward me.

This was not what I wanted.

"Hey, whoa, fella," I said, trying to keep things light while at the same time backing up a few inches. But there is not a whole lot of backing-up room on a sailboat. I'm not sure what would have transpired next, if the wake from a motorboat speeding by hadn't violently rocked the *Milagro*. Trey and I tumbled onto the floor of the cockpit in an awkward tangle of arms and legs.

As I scrambled to my feet, I muttered, "This is a no-wake zone, moron," and looked to see who the moron was. And as the Harbor Patrol Grady-White roared by, Jason Captiva looked back, and he and I locked gazes. It was just for a moment, though it felt like an eternity. And then he turned away and was gone.

Trey hoisted himself up and gave me a rueful smile. "Sorry about that," he said. "You just looked so fine."

You just looked so fine. Is there a woman in the world who doesn't like to hear that? But I could still see the Grady-White over Trey's shoulder. Time to change the subject again.

"Can I help with that?" I asked and without waiting grabbed the sail bag holding the jib that Trey had decided was a little threadbare and needed to be replaced. "You have enough to carry."

This was true. Trey had also lumbered himself with the

boat's cabin cushions, which he said smelled moldy and needed to be aired. They'd smelled fine to me. I was beginning to wonder if he spent his entire life with his father's voice in his head telling him that nothing he did or had was good enough.

We tossed the cushions and the sail bag into the pram and rowed back to the yacht club's dock. In front of us loomed the clubhouse—if you can call a ten-thousand-square-foot mansion built by the first governor of Massachusetts a clubhouse. A silver-haired gentleman was standing on the bluestone terrace waving at Trey to come over. Trey looked torn.

I nodded at the cushions and sail bag and said, "I'll take this stuff to your car. You go see what he wants."

"Thanks. I really should go say hello. He's an old friend of my father's." He lifted his shoulders helplessly. "And a prospective investor in Skaket Acres."

"Go," I said. "I can throw these in your car before I leave. Just give me your keys and I'll drop them at the club desk when I'm done."

For a moment, Trey looked conflicted. What did he think, I was going to untidy his precious car? But his future investor was beginning to look just a little impatient and finally Trey seemed to come to a decision. He shrugged and tossed the car keys to me. Which I missed, of course. *Why do men do that?*

"Thanks," he said as I bent to pick up the keys off the dock. "It's the black Lexus SUV. Just toss it all in the back."

I wouldn't know a Lexus if it bit me. As far as I am concerned, cars are just boxes on wheels. Except for red ones, of course. But I found the SUV easily enough. In a sea of shiny cars, Trey's was the shiniest. I knew enough about Trey now not to "just toss" anything of his into anything of his. I beeped open the back hatch and carefully wedged the cushions and sail bag in next to a clear plastic box containing neat stacks of brochures and blueprints for Skaket Acres.

Which was kind of surprising. If Trey had all these promotional materials, why had he taken away the brochures he'd shared with Krista, saying he didn't have extras?

I shook my head. *None of your business, Sam.* But as I was beginning to close the hatchback, I spotted something else. On top of the plastic box was the brown accordion file folder that Trey had brought with him to Aunt Ida's and that he had been looking through at Nellie's Kitchen. It was the old-fashioned kind that you close by winding a string around a cardboard button on the front. I might not have noticed it except that it had a few papers and notebooks spilling out haphazardly, which wasn't like Trey. Apparently he had been too startled by my appearance at the lunch counter to close it properly. I leaned back in to tidy up the papers and notebooks and close the file properly.

No, not notebooks. *A* notebook. I picked it up. And not just any notebook. My mother's reporter's notebook.

TWENTY-THREE

ET ME GET this straight," Krista said, speaking slowly and carefully, as if to a child, and pointing to the steno pad lying open on the desk between us. "You stole this from Trey Gorman's car."

"No," I said slowly and carefully, as if to a child. "I did not steal it from Trey Gorman's car. Trey Gorman stole it from *my house*."

We were sitting in Krista's office. I'd taken the notebook, given Trey's keys to the club receptionist and then driven Grumpy straight to the *Clarion*. I wasn't ready to talk to Trey about what I'd found. I needed some time to think, someone to help me figure out what was going on. My mind was awhirl.

"Or," Krista said, "he accidentally picked it up when he was gathering up his materials."

"But he had it with him when I met him at Nellie's Kitchen. Why didn't he tell me then, give it back then?"

"Maybe because you were coming on to him and he was a little distracted?"

I gave her a little "okay maybe" sideways nod. I wished I hadn't told her that part.

"But why did he even take those materials back from you?" I countered. "He has literally dozens of brochures and plans in his car. I saw them. He took the blueprint and the brochure to hide the fact that he was taking the notebook, too."

"But why?" Krista asked wearily. "Why take the notebook?"

"He could see the dates on the front. He wanted to know what was in it."

Krista didn't say anything, just gave me a long, considering look.

I didn't blame her for not understanding why I was so worked up. So Trey had had my mother's notebook? So what? So he had forgotten to tell me about it, was that so surprising? Not really.

But here's the thing. I knew for certain that I had shut the notebook before setting it down on the table when Trey had arrived at my door. What *was* surprising was that when I found it in Trey's car, the pages had been flipped back open to a page of notes my mother had scribbled down a few weeks before my father's heart attack.

I handed Krista the notebook.

"When I found it in Trey's car, it was opened to this entry," I said, pointing to the page in front of her. "Read that."

The entry read:

ek cl re sa
sd III stpng on pps
bn drnkng & no prf or rsn y

"'Eck cluh ree sah,'" Krista said obligingly, and looked up at me blankly. "Means nothing to me."

"Keep going," I said.

"'Sid three—'" cl she began, but I interrupted her before she could go any further.

"Three!" I said triumphantly. "You read *I, I, I* as the Roman numeral three!"

"Indeed, I did," Krista acknowledged. "So what?"

"What else can the Roman numeral three be read as?"

Enlightenment dawned. "The third," Krista said slowly.

"Exactly," I said. "As in?"

"As in Tyler Gorman the third," Krista said, scribbling it down on a pad of paper in front of her: Tyler Gorman III. "Trey. So you think your mother was referring to Trey Gorman?"

"I do," I said.

"And why do you think she was referring to Trey Gorman? I mean, aside from the coincidence that he had her notebook in his possession, probably by accident."

"Because I've had more experience reading my mother's notes than you have," I explained. "I haven't figured it all out. But some of it is suggestive."

I pointed to the first line: *ek cl re sa.* "I read this as 'EK call about'—*re* means about—'SA.'"

Krista looked serious and nodded. "Go on."

I pointed to the second line: *sd III stpng on pps.*

"'Said Trey stepping on pee pees.'" I looked up at Krista. "I admit I don't know what pee pees are."

"Doesn't matter," Krista said briskly. "Keep going."

I stared hard at the next line: *bn drnkng & no prf or rsn y.*

"'Been drinking and no proof or reason why'?" I guessed.

Krista shook her head slowly. "Even in your translation it doesn't make any sense. Trey was stepping on pee pees? What does that even mean? And who's EK? And who's SA? And who's been drinking?"

"Estelle Kobolt," I said triumphantly. "EK is Estelle Kobolt, of course. And SA isn't a who, it's a what. Skaket Acres. And if history is any guide, it was Estelle who'd been drinking. And whatever she was accusing Trey of, she had no proof that he'd done it or, if he did, any reason why."

What I didn't say was that this might be further evidence that Estelle was in the habit of digging up dirt about people.

I wanted Krista to think my interest was in Trey and Skaket Acres, not Estelle. Maybe that way she wouldn't shut me down.

"Oookaaay," Krista acknowledged slowly. "That sounds like Estelle."

I reached across Krista's desk and pressed the speaker button on her phone, then started punching in numbers.

"Hey! What are you doing?"

"What *we* are doing is going straight to the horse's mouth," I announced. "We are calling my mom."

Krista sighed. "Why didn't you just do that in the first place?"

The phone on the other end started ringing.

"You'll see," I said.

TWENTY-FOUR

~~~~~~~~~~

IT TOOK A bit of time to actually go straight to the horse's mouth. After ten rings, there was radio silence for three seconds, then a kind of scrabbling noise and then my mother's voice.

"Hello, hello, hello?" she yelled into the phone.

"Mom, it's me, Sam."

"Is anybody there?" she responded. This was par for the course. I waited patiently while she swore quietly to herself, realized that she had the sound off on her end, punched it on again. We went through the whole "hello, hello, hello" and "Mom, it's me, Sam" routine again, this time more successfully.

"Is everything okay?" she asked, her voice anxious. This is always the first question. *Always*.

"Everything is fine, Mom," I said. Before I could get any further, she interrupted.

"Hold on, hold on, hold on, sweetheart. Let me get your dad. He'd never forgive me if he missed you."

Krista and I waited while my mother searched the house for my father (who was, of course, in the garage) and while

the two of them figured out (for about the hundredth time) how to put my mom's phone on speaker.

"Sam? Is that you, honey?" my father shouted.

"Hi, Dad. Yeah, it's me. No need to shout, I can hear you fine."

"Is everything okay?" he shouted.

I sighed. "Everything is fine. I've got Krista here, too."

"Krista!" both the 'rents shouted simultaneously. "How are you! Is everything okay?"

"I'm fine, Mr. and Mrs. Barnes," Krista said, rolling her eyes at me. "Everything's great. We, Sam and I, we just wanted to ask you, Mrs. Barnes that is, about something . . . something work related."

And suddenly my helpless, technology addled mom turned back into a professional journalist. It was a relief quite frankly.

"Absolutely," she said firmly. "How can I help?"

"Mom, do you remember what story you were working on in the days just before Dad's heart attack?"

She said nothing for a moment, but I could almost hear the wheels whirring in that steel-trap brain of hers. Veronica Barnes never forgot anything about her work.

"Yes," she said definitively. "That was almost exactly two years ago. I was looking into the specs for the septic system at that proposed development on the old Skaket camp."

Krista raised her eyebrows at me.

"Any new developments and resorts planned for waterfront are subject to strict regulations because their septic's gravel disposal fields are so close to the water," my mother continued. "The big danger, of course, is nitrogen seepage and algae blooms."

"Right," Krista said, pulling a notebook over and beginning to take notes.

"I was checking with the Conservation Law Foundation to make sure the developers, Gorman Properties, had presented an accurate discharge estimate, based on similar projects."

"And had they?" I asked. I was beginning to get excited. I'd completely forgotten about pee pees and Estelle. Sewage treatment! This was the stuff of cover-ups!

"Absolutely accurate," my mother said. "If anything, they had overestimated the septic needs in an excess of caution."

Talk about a letdown.

"So, it was all kosher," Krista said, pushing her notebook away.

"All kosher."

Which, in hindsight, made sense. My mother wouldn't have given up on the story if things hadn't been kosher. No matter how many heart attacks my dad had.

"Mom," I said. "The reason we're asking about this is because we . . . found . . . were looking at . . ." I just couldn't face trying to explain Trey and the saga of the traveling notepad.

I started again. "We're just doing some follow-through on the latest plans for the development, and I was looking through your old notes and saw something about an EK? Did someone named Estelle Kobolt call you?"

"You mean the woman who drowned last week in Alden Pond?"

I should have expected her to know all about that. Old journalists don't die, they just read it all online.

"Yeah," I said, swallowing hard. I knew I should tell her and Dad that I'd found the body, but something held me back. "Her. Did you talk to her back then? Something to do with Trey Gorman?"

"Oh yeah," my mother said with a little laugh. "Well, sort of. She'd been drinking or was high on something and she called me with some wild story about Trey killing piping plovers."

PPs. Piping plovers. "Killing them how?"

"She said she was out on her boat and saw him up on that dune at the old camp, the high one over the beach, stomping on the chicks, she said."

"But that's awful," I exclaimed. *Who stomps on baby birds?* I didn't want to believe it of Trey. I mean, the guy had his issues, but surely he wasn't a bird killer.

Then I reminded myself that I was, at least temporarily, a journalist. If piping plovers were nesting on the Skaket dune, no one living at the proposed Skaket Acres would be able to use the beach through most of the summer. And that, I suspected, was a deal breaker. But still, *Trey killing baby birds*?

"Estelle had to be at least a hundred yards away," I pointed out. "She might have been able to see him, but those chicks are tiny and the nests are just shallow holes in the sand. Could she really see what he was stepping on?"

"Exactly what I asked her. She said she could see it by zooming her cell phone's camera," my mother said. "But I just couldn't take her seriously, you know? She was rambling—she really seemed to have it in for Trey, kept calling him 'that snotty preppie.' Finally, I just told her that unless she had some proof, one, that piping plovers actually nested in that area, which to my recollection they don't"—a hazy memory tugged at me, something from last Sunday's dinner, then drifted away as my mother continued—"and, two, unless she could send me a photo of Trey actually destroying nests or birds or whatever, I couldn't help her. She said she didn't have the 'first frigging idea' how to send anything from her cell phone, but if I came to the Inn she'd show the photo to me. Then I said if she really had something to show me, she could bring the phone to my office. Then she called me an asswipe and hung up."

"Niiice," I said.

"I've been called worse," my mother said dryly. "And actually, I'm glad I didn't follow up on it because she called me a few days later, sober as a judge, and took it all back. Said Trey had stiffed her on a tip at the Inn and she wanted to get back at him."

"That sounds like Estelle all right," I said.

"She said she saw him on that dune and came up with that piping plover story. The new conservation restrictions had just come into play, so everyone was talking about it." In my mind's eye, I again saw my father's note about the editorial favoring protecting the nesting grounds. "She told him she was going to call me, make trouble for him. I'm guessing he, in turn, reminded her about libel laws. Once she sobered up, she called me back, retracted the whole thing."

Krista looked at me and made a cutting gesture across her throat.

"Thanks, Mom," I said. "I'm sorry to interrupt your day. We've gotta go. We just wanted to check on that."

"Well, it's important to keep in mind that even though most whistleblowers are trying to do the right thing, there are always a few who just like making trouble," my mother said, ever the objective journalist. "That doesn't mean they aren't telling the truth. But in this case, it was pretty clear to me that there wasn't any 'there' there."

The rest of the conversation was basically me trying to get off the phone while my parents tried not very subtly to find out what my plans were for the rest of my life. I danced around that for a while until Krista finally stepped in with a "Great to talk to you, Mr. and Mrs. Barnes!" and punched the off button on the phone.

"So that was much ado about nothing," she said to me.

"I guess," I admitted reluctantly. Maybe I should try again with Krista, now that we had what looked like a pattern of Estelle of at least threatening blackmail. "But I have a bad feeling about this. There's a couple of things that bother me—"

"Don't start," Krista said, raising a hand like a crossing

guard. "Unless you have something substantive to base your bad feeling on, I don't have time for it."

She didn't have time for it? We were getting close to proof that Estelle was a blackmailer, and she didn't have time for it? What was she afraid of?

"What I do have time for is another restaurant review," Krista said firmly. "How about that new Thai restaurant in Chatham?"

If you want to distract me from any subject at hand, there's no better way than to say the words "Thai food." I absolutely *love, love, love* Thai food. Give me a plate of good pad Thai—*very* spicy hot and *not* sweet—and I am your slave for life.

But I wasn't fooled or happy about Krista once again fobbing me off the Estelle inquiry. It wasn't like Krista not to follow up on a dodgy story. But I figured I had time to think that one out.

I figured wrong.

TWENTY-FIVE

~~~~~~~~

THE EVENING WAS drawing down as I drove back to Aunt Ida's. In spite of my best efforts, I couldn't stop replaying the coldness in Jason's eyes when he'd roared past the *Milagro*. As I crunched into the driveway, I was actually looking forward to seeing Diogi. I really needed a little unconditional positive regard.

Diogi greeted me at the door and performed his role to perfection. He didn't care that I'd been caught almost kissing a man who, as it turned out, I really didn't like all that much by a man who, let's face it, I liked a lot and who now didn't seem to like me at all. Diogi, however, was like Colin Firth in *Bridget Jones's Diary*—he liked me just as I was.

When we were done exchanging greetings, I said to him, "I would love a glass of wine right about now. Why don't you go find Helene?" I didn't really expect him to go find Helene, of course. I was just doing that thing where you talk to your dog because it's nice to have someone to talk to. But Diogi cocked his head at the sound of Helene's name and then took off through the hedge like a man on a mission.

Sure enough, in about two minutes he was back with the

lady in question. My neighbor was wearing what can only be described as harem pants and a T-shirt emblazoned with the words "Fortune favors the brave." Best of all, she had a glass of wine in her hand.

"Hey!" she shouted as she came through the bushes, "Diogi seemed to think I was needed."

I laughed and said, "He's smarter than he looks, that dog."

Helene lifted her glass to me. "You want to come over for a drink on the deck?"

She didn't have to ask twice. I grabbed a leftover bottle of wine from Sunday's dinner and followed her back through the hedge.

I'd seen the house next door once or twice as a child, before the yew bushes got too thick. But back then I'd been well primed by my great-aunt to view its boxlike shape and spare lines as somehow an affront to traditional Cape architecture. I came through the sandy path between the bushes and stopped short.

Looking at the house now, I could see that, in fact, with its simplicity and focus on function, it both echoed those traditions and made them work in new ways. First of all, it was not a large house. It was modest, really, in the old Cape fashion. The roof was flat, though, not peaked, and slanted up from the front of the house to the back, giving it a decidedly mid-century modern feel (which was not surprising, since it had been built in the sixties). And, yes, the side of the house that faced the pond was essentially a wall of glass. But the rest of the house was sheathed in traditional cedar shingles, with crisp white trim outlining the windows and doors. There had been no attempt to create a grass lawn, but I could see that in the summer the grounds would be a lovely tangle of native plants like wild roses and beach plums. The front door was painted a brilliant and, needless to say, untraditional neon yellow, but I was very pleased to note a conch shell next to the front step. I was willing to bet it held a spare key.

Helene led me into what was essentially one large living space whose ceiling soared to almost double height at the wall of windows overlooking her deck and Bower's Pond beyond. The kitchen area was to the left, dining area to the right and, ahead of us, a low-slung couch and two equally low-slung chairs faced the expansive view of water and sky.

"I love this," I breathed.

"I love it, too," Helene said. "I knew as soon as I saw it that we were meant to be together." She laughed. "Of course, I said that about my ex-husband, too. But this has been a much better marriage."

Diogi, Helene, and I sat companionably on her deck, watching the sun setting in great red and gold streaks over the pond. We chatted about books for a while, and she promised to hold the new Lisa Scottoline for me when it came into the library.

"And in return," I said, "I'd like to invite you to be my guest at the new Thai restaurant in Chatham next week."

"Will you be providing another dead body?"

Helene's sense of humor, it struck me, was sometimes in questionable taste.

"Oh dear God, I hope not," I said, taking a big gulp of my wine. "The one I already found is being *such* a pain."

Helene must have heard the unhappiness that I was trying to keep out of my voice.

"Really," she said thoughtfully. "In what way?"

So I told her the whole story, beginning with that fateful kiss twelve years ago with Jason up to today's almost smooch with Trey.

"Is your life always going to be marked by ill-considered snogging?" Helene asked, only half kidding. "First you tell me about this Trey's dysfunctional family and how you don't really trust him because he's still under his unpleasant father's thumb, and then you make out with him in public?"

"Almost make out," I corrected her. "And, believe me, it

gets worse. Wait until you hear the other rumors about this guy."

I told her the tale of the traveling notebook and gave her the gist of the phone call with my mother, adding, "So we already knew that Estelle threatened to blackmail my father and now we know that she tried the same trick with Trey."

"And got nowhere," Helene pointed out.

"But that doesn't mean she wasn't bleeding somebody else dry. And maybe they got tired of it."

Helene nodded thoughtfully.

"So, am I crazy?" I asked. "Because both Jason and Krista are really keeping me at arm's length on this. McCauley, too, but I don't expect anything from him."

As we'd been talking, the sky had faded to a pale lilac, then cloaked itself in deep purple. The stars began to come out.

"So let me see if I've got this straight," Helene said as she lit a couple of candles in their hurricane lamps. "One, you think Estelle might have been murdered, but the police don't agree. Two, you think Trey stole your mother's notebook, but he might have taken it by mistake. Three, you think, or thought, that Estelle might have had something on Trey, but your mother says not. And four, you think Estelle was, in fact, blackmailing somebody who might have killed her for it, but you don't know who."

I nodded miserably. Put that way, I sounded like a real nutcase.

"And, five, you're angry at Jason for eating all your cookies," she added.

"No," I snapped. "I'm angry at Jason for keeping our relationship strictly professional."

Helene raised an eyebrow. "And what would you like your relationship to be?"

"I want to be friends," I said quietly, all my anger gone. "I just want us to be friends again."

"And that's why you flirted with this Trey Gorman? Because Jason wouldn't be your friend?"

I nodded glumly. *Again, nutcase.*

"Do you really want to know what I think?" Helene asked.

"Maybe not," I said.

As it turned out, her question was rhetorical. I was learning that Helene always told you what she thought, whether you wanted to hear it or not.

"Well, I think you're right that Estelle was murdered," she said. "I think your questions about her death are good ones, and I trust your instincts. Also, Jason clearly agrees with you, and I trust his professional judgment. I also think you're right that she was a blackmailer. Even if she made up this piping plover story, it's pretty clear that she tried to pressure Trey Gorman with it. I think he knew Estelle had talked to your mother, and he deliberately took that notebook to find out what Estelle had said to her even if it was a pack of lies. Or at least keep anyone else from finding out about it. And, finally, I think Estelle Kobolt was murdered because she was successfully blackmailing someone and they'd had enough. The problem is going to be finding out exactly who that someone is."

I stared at Helene. I'm pretty sure my mouth dropped open. Always an attractive look. "So you don't think I'm a nutcase?"

Helene shook her head. "No, I don't think you're a nutcase. But I do think you need to be very, very careful."

TWENTY-SIX

I THANKED HELENE FOR the wine and the validation and took myself and Diogi home for dinner. I had some eggs I'd picked up at a roadside stand with a hand-lettered sign reading "Fresh Eggs from Happy Chickens." There is nothing better in the world than a fresh egg from a chicken that spends its day running around eating bugs. These are the absolutely best eggs for spaghetti carbonara, which I suddenly had a huge hankering for. (Tip: For a truly rich carbonara, but only if you have really good eggs, just use the yolks, not the whole eggs, one yolk for every two servings.) I had some salt pork that I'd planned to use in a batch of clam chowder one of these days, but, diced and rendered into crisp little bacon nuggets it would easily substitute for Italian pancetta.

I gave Diogi his usual dinner of dried doggy nuggets while I feasted on the pasta. He ignored his bowl and looked at me pathetically. I will give him credit though. He did not beg. Diogi has too much dignity to beg. So I took the couple of tablespoons of fat left over from rendering the salt pork and poured it over his nuggets and both of us were happy.

But lying in bed that night, I couldn't hold on to the mood. I hadn't actually asked Helene what she meant by "very, very careful." Careful about making assumptions? Careful about missing clues? Or careful about annoying someone who had already killed somebody who had annoyed them?

I had the awful feeling it was the last one.

Maybe Krista and Jason were right. Maybe I needed to step down on this. I knew I should just tell Jason what I'd learned and then let him convince Chief McCauley. I had no other leads anyway.

But wait. I *did* have another lead. I'd forgotten about the other waitress at the Inn, Suzanne, Suzanne Herrick. It was a long shot, I knew. Mr. Logan had said she had some kind of dementia, but depending on her recall of the past, she might know something about Estelle's little blackmailing game, about who else might have had it in for her. It was worth a try. It might give me some further leads.

And it would be an excuse to put off seeing Jason again. The memory of our eyes locking that morning still made my face burn. Yup, definitely I needed some time before facing Jason.

I CALLED THE NURSING home the next morning to check on visiting hours and spoke with the manager, a nice woman who introduced herself as Jillian Munsell, to make sure it was okay to spend some time with Suzanne, maybe talk a bit about old times at the restaurant we'd both worked at.

"Of course it's all right," Ms. Munsell assured me. "Suzanne loves having visitors."

"Norman Logan told me she has some kind of dementia?"

"Oh yes, Mr. Logan was just here yesterday. We hadn't seen him for a while. But, yes, he's right, it's the early stages of Lewy body dementia, I'm afraid," she said. "LBD isn't the same as Alzheimer's. People hear 'dementia' and they think LBD sufferers can't remember anything. But for them it's more short-term than long-term memory loss. The bigger problem is real-time confusion and hallucinations."

"That sounds awful," I said.

"It can be very difficult," she conceded, "but in the early stages, like Suzanne's case, the delusions are fairly benign—often seeing children or small animals, that kind of thing. And if you talk about the past, it would be a real tonic for her."

We agreed on early afternoon for my visit, and hanging up the phone, I felt better. By just doing something, taking a step forward, my natural optimism had kicked in. I would see if Suzanne had anything substantive to add. Then I would call Jason—not go in person—and tell him what I'd learned. *And then he'll tell you that he'll take it from there.*

Fine. I would get on with my life. I had a yummy restaurant to visit as part of my new job. I had another, incredible job offer in the wings. *An incredible job offer that is only going to be open for two more days*, I reminded myself. But still. I had options. I was young and healthy and I had a really nice dog.

Whoa. When had Diogi become *my* dog?

I WASN'T SURE WHAT the proper attire was for visiting a nursing home these days. When we'd gone to visit my *nonna* at Shawme Manor, Sunday best was the dress code, partly because we usually visited on a Sunday after church, but also, I thought, as a sign of respect for *Nonna* herself. When I'd packed my bag for the Cape this time, I'd included a vintage navy shirtwaist dress with white collar and cuffs that I'd always liked for its retro *Mad Men* sixties vibe and thought might be suitable for meetings with lawyers and real estate agents. That would do for today's visit.

Shawme Manor was your typical one-story redbrick oblong that had been the design rule for nursing homes when it was built in the seventies. But it was well-kept, with lovely grounds made wheelchair and walker accessible by concrete pathways and raised garden beds for those who might want to pull a weed or plant a pansy.

As I turned Grumpy into the closest parking space to the building, a black SUV pulled in behind me and parked at the far end of the lot. One of those people, I thought, who takes every opportunity to add to their ten thousand daily steps. I am never going to be one of those people. I am one of those people who *always* parks in the closest spot. It is a matter of principle. The person with the closest spot wins. Everybody knows that.

Inside, it was bright and cheerful, with sunny yellow walls hung with framed botanical prints and fresh flowers gracing the reception desk. Ms. Munsell, a tall, graceful woman with close-cropped hair, deep mahogany skin, and a smile as warm as her voice, greeted me, asked me to call her Jillian, and led me to Suzanne's room.

"Suzanne," Jillian said, "you have a visitor, a Samantha Barnes. She says you worked together once at the Logan Inn."

I peered into the room. It was hard to believe that the frail creature sitting in the armchair by the window was the same woman who had once balanced heavy trays of restaurant crockery on one hand.

Suddenly, I was assailed by doubts. Why was I bothering this poor old lady with my problem? Because it's not *your* problem, I reminded myself. A woman may have been murdered. To quote Jenny, that made it *everybody's* problem.

Suzanne smiled sweetly. "I remember a Samantha Barnes," she said brightly. "She worked one summer at the Logan Inn. I felt sorry for her. She was too tall for a girl."

"Hello, Suzanne," I said, stepping forward. "That's me. Samantha Barnes."

"I remember a Samantha Barnes," Suzanne said again

with that same sweet smile. "She worked one summer at the Inn. She was too tall for a girl. What did you say your name was, dear?"

Jillian gave me a look and said, "Well, I'll leave you to it."

I started to sit down on the other armchair in the room, but Suzanne stopped me, raising one birdlike hand gently. "Oh, do be careful, dear. You'll sit on the kitty."

Startled, I looked at the empty chair, then remembered what Jillian had told me about hallucinations. Well, a cat curled up on a chair struck me as a fairly benign delusion, so I didn't argue. I just parked my butt on the end of Suzanne's neatly made bed.

"I saw Mr. Logan the other day, Suzanne," I began. "He mentioned you. . . ."

"Oh, Norman Logan's a fine man," Suzanne said. "I like to talk to him about old times at the Inn. He helps me when I get confused. He was my boss, you know."

"He was Estelle's boss, too," I prompted her.

"Oh, Estelle," Suzanne said, her voice suddenly much stronger. "She was such a nosy parker. Always sniffing around other people's business."

I blinked, but said nothing. If I'd learned anything from my journalist mother it was *don't interrupt the flow.*

"One day she told me that Linette Flugal's new baby was actually Donny Klimshuk's, if you can believe that." Suzanne looked at me expectantly.

"I can't," I said helplessly. "Not Linette." Whoever Linette was.

"Exactly," Suzanne said triumphantly. "Everybody knew it was Guy Murphy's baby. All Linette Flugal's babies were Guy Murphy's. Even Frank Flugal knew that."

And there I'd been trying to protect Linette's reputation.

"Linette told me that Estelle said if she, Linette, gave Estelle one hundred dollars Estelle wouldn't tell Guy that the baby was Donny's. Because Guy is a crazy jealous type. And do you know what Linette did?"

I didn't dare speculate. Linette was a mystery to me.

"She pulled a one dollar bill out of her wallet, gave it to Estelle, and told her to stick it where the sun don't shine." Suzanne chortled. "And then she said that if Estelle did that and Linette could watch, Linette would be happy to give her ninety-nine more under the same conditions."

"My goodness," I said, actually quite shocked. "What did Estelle do?"

"What she always did when somebody stood up to her. She spread the dirt around, true or not. Mean as a snake that woman was."

"I guess she made herself a lot of enemies. . . ."

"Well, nobody liked her, that's for sure," Suzanne agreed.

"Do you think she ever, maybe, got it right?" I suggested. "Got some real proof, maybe enough to get someone to pay up?"

"Well," Suzanne said uncertainly, "once she told me that he had been there with her that night, that she had proof, but he says I got that confused."

This sounded like an illicit romance, and I wanted to ask who the he and she were in this case, but Suzanne was off and running and I couldn't get a word in.

"And she had poor Howard Sykes paying through the nose for years after she caught him red-handed out on the bay pulling lobsters out of traps that weren't his. That time she showed me the picture she took on the telephone thingy of hers."

Pulling someone else's lobsters was a pretty serious charge, though I couldn't imagine that a lobsterman had been paying Estelle's rent the last couple of years. But it was worth checking into.

"Where's Howard now?" I asked.

"Oh, he's gone to his reward," Suzanne said.

So not Howard. But at least I had some confirmation that Estelle was, in fact, a blackmailer. Nothing that would hold up in court, of course, but something that indicated I was on the right track.

Suzanne peered closely at me.

"What's your name again, dear?"

"Samantha," I said, "Samantha Barnes."

"I remember a Samantha Barnes," Suzanne said. "She worked one summer at the Inn. I remember she had a terrible crush on a boy who worked there, used to follow him around like a lovesick calf. I felt sorry for her. I could have told her it was no use. She was too tall for a girl."

Okaaaay. Clearly I hadn't been as discreet in my attentions to Jason as I'd thought at the time. Maybe that's why Estelle had followed us down under the deck.

I made a couple of weak attempts to move the conversation back to Estelle, but I could see that Suzanne was tired and I suddenly felt very guilty for pushing her. As I stood up to leave, I promised her I'd come to visit again. I told myself I would keep that promise.

"Watch out for the kitty when you leave," Suzanne warned. "She'll try to follow you out if you're not careful."

At the door, I made shooing sounds in the general direction of where I thought the kitty might be, and this seemed to satisfy Suzanne, who waved goodbye cheerfully.

"You come visit anytime, dear," she said. "What did you say your name was again?"

"Sam," I said, "Samantha Barnes."

"I remember a Samantha Barnes . . ."

I half closed the door behind me and began to walk down the hall.

"She was too tall for a girl. . . ."

TWENTY-SEVEN

~~~~~~~~~~

I PULLED OUT FROM Shawme Manor, the black SUV behind me. I hoped their visit hadn't been as confusing as mine. In the ten minutes it took me to drive back to Aunt Ida's house, I tried to sort out what, if anything, I'd learned from Suzanne.

One, Estelle did, in fact, have a history of small-time blackmail and, when that didn't work, of spreading false rumors out of spite. Just as she'd threatened to do to Trey.

Two, Estelle had taken incriminating photos with her cell phone.

I wondered what had happened to Estelle's cell. I knew from Jason that no purse had been found by the police, which presumably meant no cell phone either. If Estelle had been killed for her phone, I could only assume that by now it was lying at the bottom of the bay and her killer knew that he—or she—was safe.

That was a perfectly reasonable assumption, I thought. But only an assumption. I wasn't going back to Jason with assumptions. I mean, how much further would it get his inquiries to know about Estelle's unpleasant penchant for squeezing people she didn't like?

Until I had something solid, something really solid, to give Jason, I didn't have to go back and talk to him. He'd just tell me to leave everything to him anyway.

As I turned off the blacktop onto Bayberry Point, I noticed that the black SUV—or maybe it was another one, I couldn't be sure—was still behind me. Okay, Fair Harbor was a small town. It was perfectly reasonable that someone out on the Point also had a family member or friend at Shawme Manor. Nonetheless, I was somehow relieved when, as I slowed to make the turn into Aunt Ida's driveway, I saw Miles's truck parked by the house. As I turned in, I did a quick check of the rearview mirror. The black car slowed, then drove by. I was glad to see it go.

Miles himself was precariously balanced on a creaky wooden ladder that had been propped against the house since I had moved in and probably for years before that. Diogi, who Miles must have let out with the spare key in the conch shell, was gazing up at my friend's considerable bulk, perplexed by what could possibly be of interest to the Big Hairy Man peering intently into the copper gutter running along the eave. I was a bit perplexed myself.

I gathered up my shoulder bag and got out of the truck. Diogi interrupted his supervisory duties to lope across the yard to welcome me, and then led me over to the day's excitement.

"Miles! What are you doing up there? You're going to break your neck or, worse, Aunt Ida's ladder."

Miles turned from his inspection, and the ladder protested loudly.

"I'm checking out this clogged gutter. I don't think it needs to be replaced. That's the good news."

"And what's the bad news?"

"I'm going to have to snake the drainpipe, and from the smell of it, there's something dead in there, maybe a squirrel or a bird."

"Oh, gag," I said. "Just what I need. Another corpse."

Miles made his way gingerly down the ladder. Once the Big Hairy Man was on solid ground, Diogi relaxed his vigilance and wandered off in search of rabbits.

"What prompted this visit?" I asked.

"I finished thinning the lettuces a little early—"

That reminded me. "Congratulations by the way," I interrupted. "I hear you have a deal to supply Mr. Logan's new restaurant."

"Well, I'm not counting those chickens 'till he actually shows up with the contract," Miles said, but I could tell he was pleased that he'd landed the business.

"I don't think you have to worry about that," I reassured him. "He told me on Wednesday he was bringing it over. He probably just got sidetracked with contractors and stuff."

"I'm not worried," Miles said. "He's a man of his word." He put a beefy arm around my shoulders. "Really, I just wanted to come by and see how you're doing. I mean, after finding a dead lady floating in Alden Pond and all."

I was touched by his concern but didn't know how to explain the whole sorry mess to him without getting into the Jason thing, which I totally didn't want to do.

"I'm as well as can be expected," I hedged.

Miles looked at me doubtfully but didn't push it. He threw the grimy work gloves he'd been using into the back of his truck. "I've got a snake back at the farm. I'll go pick it up and then we'll see what you and I can do about that drainpipe. Shouldn't take me long."

I didn't actually know what a snake was, but I didn't like the sound of it. Nor did I really look forward to cleaning out a clogged drainpipe filled with rodent remains. But Miles, bless his heart, wanted to help me and I thought it would be churlish to refuse to participate in the drainpipe deconstipating process.

"Okay," I said. "I'll be here. I'll hold the ladder for you."

"You might want to change out of the Mother Superior drag."

I looked down at my prim navy shirtwaist. "Right. I'll do that."

I stood by the door to the ell as Miles drove off. I was alone. Helene, I knew, was at the library and two acres of dense pitch pine and scrub oak lay between me and my other neighbor. The house across the lane was a summer cottage and still closed up as tight as a drum. I was surrounded by silence except for a crow cawing harshly overhead and the rustle of a rabbit in the underbrush. Normally, I would have found the quiet and the isolation soothing, but today it was unsettling.

Diogi seemed to sense my unease and leaned against my leg, whining slightly. The clear weather of the past few days was changing, and a cloud slid over the sun, bringing a chilling wind that worried the tops of the locust trees. I wrapped my arms around myself against the cold, but I didn't go inside. Instead, I waited.

I wasn't surprised when the black SUV slid into the drive. Nor was I surprised to see Trey Gorman step out of it.

Had I recognized the car subliminally when Trey had followed me to Shawme Manor and then back to Aunt Ida's house? Because I was certain that it had been Trey following me. And that he had waited until Miles left and he knew I was alone to make this little visit.

I stiffened, and Diogi's whine turned into a low growl.

"Sam!" Trey called, raising his hand in greeting. "I'm so glad I found you home!"

He started across the grass to the ell, wearing that smile that I'd known since childhood.

Maybe I'd been wrong. One black SUV looks much like another. Maybe that hadn't been his car at Shawme Manor. Maybe he hadn't followed me. Or even if he had, maybe his interest was just, well, romantic. *Not that there is anything romantic about being stalked.* Nonetheless, he certainly didn't look like he had anything nefarious on his mind.

But, still, he had a lot of explaining to do. His cute little crooked grin wasn't going to get him out of this. *One may smile, and smile, and be a villain*, as the Bard says.

"Trey," I said as neutrally as possible.

He stopped in his tracks. His golden eyes grew downcast. "Uh-oh, you're mad at me."

I said nothing, and he walked toward me, smiling again. A lock of golden hair fell fetchingly onto his brow, and he brushed it back almost unconsciously. Almost but not quite. I realized it was the same gesture he'd used at the town meeting, when he'd so effortlessly mesmerized his audience. That lock-of-hair-falling-in-my-eyes routine was just one of the many weapons in Trey's charm offensive.

"Look, I'm sorry," he said. "I'm sorry we didn't get to say goodbye yesterday. That guy kept asking questions, and by the time I got out to the parking lot, you had gone."

He stepped closer, his hands outstretched in appeal, and Diogi's growl got louder. I put my hand on his collar, saying, "It's okay, boy." He turned the growl down a decibel or two.

Trey looked nervously at Diogi and stopped again a few feet from us.

"Look, Sam," he said. "Is this about the notebook? If so, I'm really sorry. I picked it up by mistake and meant to return it to you, but"—here he paused and the smile went all sexy—"then I had other things on my mind."

He gave me a significant look, reminding me that we had shared . . . what? A moment?

It was very skillful, but I wasn't going to fall for it.

"I find it hard to believe," I said evenly, "that you were so overwhelmed by my mere presence that over the course of four hours you forgot to mention that you not only had my journalist mother's *confidential* notebook but that you had, in fact, *read* it."

Trey's smile disappeared as if it had never existed. His mouth went from crooked to twisted. He looked like a different person. A different, *weird* person.

"Believe whatever you want," he said. "But you need to get over yourself. I didn't read your mother's precious notebook. Why would I? It has nothing to do with me."

Now I was angry. He was lying, and I knew it.

"Well, you were certainly interested in what she wrote about you and Estelle Kobolt."

Trey's eyes narrowed and two ugly red splotches bloomed on his cheekbones.

"I have no idea what you are talking about," he said. "Anyway, nobody could read that garbage if they tried. It's in some kind of crazy code or something."

"So you did try to read it."

Trey's hands clenched, and a muscle by his left eye began to twitch. Suddenly I was frightened. Dr. Jekyll had turned into Mr. Hyde.

He took another step closer, close enough that I could smell his sour breath. I felt the fur rise on Diogi's neck as I held his collar. The low growl got louder.

"Where is that notebook anyway?" Trey asked. "In your purse?"

In fact, I'd never taken the notebook out of my shoulder bag after my meeting with Krista. I knew that if Trey got his hands on it, I'd never see it again. But I also knew I didn't stand a chance against him. This was a guy who had been lifting weights since he was a teenager. All I had ever lifted was fork to mouth.

Nonetheless, when Trey grabbed for the shoulder bag, I clutched it with the hand that wasn't holding Diogi's collar. If Trey wanted it, he was going to have to fight me for it.

Trey pulled roughly at the leather strap, which dug into my shoulder. I cried out, more with surprise than pain, and Diogi's growl turned into a volley of shrill barks. I let go of his collar to hang on to the bag with both hands and Diogi, suddenly free from restraint, leaped on Trey, his paws against the man's chest, barking wildly into his face. Had Diogi been older and more experienced, Trey might have been in some danger, but as it was, Diogi was literally more bark than bite. Indeed, he didn't even seem to consider biting, which in retrospect I found disappointing. But his clumsy attack was enough to knock Trey off balance, and he let go of the bag to fend the dog off.

I used the moment to throw the purse back through the open door of the ell and pull the door shut. I turned back to face Trey. It was probably just the adrenaline pumping, but I was no longer afraid. And I certainly wasn't going to leave Diogi out there alone with that man.

Diogi, for his part, had backed off once the Bad Man was no longer actually fighting with his human. But he kept himself between me and my attacker, still growling, the hair on his back standing up in a ridge. My hand closed on his collar again.

"You need to leave, Trey," I said as evenly as I could, trying to turn the temperature down.

But Trey was way past that.

"Happy to," he hissed, leaning forward until his face was only inches from mine. "But just so you know, this is not finished."

And that's when he kicked my dog.

That shithead kicked my dog.

Diogi yelped with confusion and pain. I knelt down and held him close, trying to soothe him, but my eyes never left Trey's face. I was filled with a cold, hard anger. I stood up slowly.

"Do yourself a favor, Trey," I said very, very quietly. "Go home and google Samantha Barnes on YouTube. Watch what I can do with a knife to any man who threatens me."

Trey's face drained of all color.

"And then," I added, "stop and consider if you really want to come back and finish this."

TWENTY-EIGHT

I WAS SITTING ON the ground next to Diogi, running my hands along his ribs to reassure myself that no permanent damage had been done when Miles wheeled back into the driveway.

Jumping out of the truck, he took one look at my face and asked, "What's wrong? Is it Diogi? Is he okay?"

Diogi answered that himself by running over and giving Miles a big sloppy kiss and then dashing over to water the forsythia bush.

"Looks that way," I said, standing up and brushing sand and dirt off my dress.

"Are *you* okay?" Miles asked, his face concerned.

And suddenly the girl who had very effectively faced off against a very nasty guy—the kind of creep *who would kick a dog*—suddenly that girl burst into tears.

Miles gathered me into his arms and patted my back until the storm was over. Then he reached into his pocket and pulled out a clean red bandana.

"Blow your nose," he said. "You'll feel better."

Which reminded me so much of my father that I fell apart all over again. But when I finally did pull myself together and did blow my nose (noisily), I definitely did feel better.

"You want to tell me what this hullabaloo is all about?" Miles asked, deliberately trying to keep the tone light lest I dissolve again into a puddle of tears and snot. "I mean aside from me being all insulting about your Mother Superior outfit?"

"It's not a Mother Superior outfit," I said, still sniffling a little but also kind of smiling. Miles does that to you. "It's a visiting-the-nursing-home outfit."

"Of course it is," Miles said. "That was my next guess. Now, how about we go inside and you tell me what it was about that nasty nursing home that made you all boo-hooey."

Miles tried to open the door to the ell, which, of course, had locked itself when I'd thrown my bag in and pulled it shut. This made me feel even more sorry for myself.

"It's locked," I wailed. "And my bag is in there and my keys are in my bag."

Miles raised his eyebrows in mild surprise. "You're crying because you locked yourself out?"

"Not exactly," I said.

Miles shook the spare key out of the conch shell. "I'm glad to hear it. Because that's why God invented spare keys."

But before we got inside, Helene's unmistakable *yoo-hoo* sounded and we turned to see her apparating through the yew hedge. She was a vision, even by Helene standards. Her hair was wrapped in a turban of African wax cloth in a brown and orange print of a vibrancy eclipsed only by her bright yellow jumpsuit and red high-top Converse.

Miles considered her critically as she approached. "The turban is fantastic," he said finally. "Also the kicks. The jumpsuit not so much."

"Who are you, Tim Gunn?" Helene said dismissively.

She turned back to me. "I stopped at Snyder's Fish Market on the way home from work and picked up a couple of their steamed lobsters and corn on the cob." Only Helene would consider Snyder's justly famed steamed lobster and corn a quick takeout meal. "I thought you might want to join me for an early dinner."

Then she took a closer look at my face, which was, I was sure, all puffy and blotchy.

"And," she said, "we can catch up on . . . events."

She turned to Miles. "You, too, if you can stand the fashion statement."

But Miles, who was clearly relieved that someone was willing to take the crying female off his hands, demurred.

"I'd love to," he lied, "but there's only about an hour of daylight left and I've got a nasty drainpipe to snake."

"I don't even know what that means," Helene said, "but have at it."

I reached into the ell and grabbed my shoulder bag with the notebook in it off the floor. This wasn't leaving my sight.

Helene headed back through the yews with me following gratefully. For one thing, I was really looking forward to a lobby dinner. And for another, I knew that Helene, whose good sense I now trusted absolutely, would sift through my story and calmly help me decide what to do next.

Helene insisted that I settle my obviously unsettled nerves with a nice glass of chardonnay on the deck, and I gratefully complied, letting the wine and the view over Bower's Pond do their magic. While I was following the doctor's orders, she brought out two platters, each bearing a bright-red lobster, an ear of corn, and a bowl of melted butter, and set them on the table in front of us. We clinked glasses, and as I dunked the sweet meat into the drawn butter, I told her about Trey's little visit.

Helene's first reaction was to go all librarian and scold me. "I thought I told you to be careful."

"Actually, you told me to be very, very careful," I admitted.

"And were you? Very, very careful?"

"Well, I was until that maniac *kicked my dog*."

"No," Helene said, "I don't think you were."

As I excavated a claw with my lobster pick, I waited for her to list my sins.

"First of all," she said, "you let him know that you have the notebook. Before that, he couldn't be sure that he hadn't just lost it."

I nodded. She was right.

"Second, you acknowledged that you knew there was something in the notebook, some circumstantial evidence, connecting him and Estelle Kobolt."

I felt obliged to break in here.

"Circumstantial evidence of what though?" I asked. "That he was wiping out plover nests? Estelle told my mother that she'd made that up."

"True," Helene said thoughtfully, waiting for me to take the next step.

I knew what she was thinking. I was thinking it myself. But I didn't like it. This wasn't going to be easy.

"But what if *that* was the lie?" I said. "Maybe there *are* piping plovers on that dune." *Why did I think that?* And then the memory surfaced that had been tugging at me ever since that Sunday dinner when everyone was talking about environmental roadblocks to Trey's development: Those cookouts at Skaket Camp when I was a kid. *I'd found a piping plover's nest in the dune sloping down to the beach.* In my mind's eye, I could still see that fuzzball chick looking up at me, peeping like mad.

I put down my half-eaten ear of corn. "Wait. There *were* piping plovers nesting there twenty years ago. Maybe there still are. What if Estelle *did* see Trey killing chicks on that dune two years ago, took a photo, and tried to blackmail him with it?"

"But she told your mother she didn't know how to send pictures from her phone," Helene pointed out.

"Yeah," I said. "That didn't actually surprise me when my mom said that. You're about Estelle's age," I said (with not a whole lot of sensitivity). "Do you know how to do that?"

Helene took no offense. She just snorted and said, "I can use the camera on my phone for taking photos for myself, but that sharing business is beyond me."

"Exactly," I said. "So Estelle had Trey come to the cocktail lounge where she showed him the photo and in the process made it obvious that it was only on her cell and nowhere else."

"Nowhere else like where?"

I sighed. "Like on a personal computer or laptop or something."

"Oh," Helene said thoughtfully. "Yeah, that makes sense."

"And then when he didn't immediately agree to pay up, she called my mother. And then told him she'd talked to my mom, just to let him know that she meant business," I continued. "And that if he came through with the money, she would tell my mom that she'd made everything up in a fit of temper. So he paid up and she called off the dogs, so to speak. Jenny said Estelle retired shortly after that and that she lived pretty well. Maybe it was Trey's payoffs bankrolling her."

Helene just sat silent for a moment, then asked, "So what are you saying?"

"I'm saying Trey Gorman may have killed Estelle Kobolt to get that cell phone," I whispered.

TWENTY-NINE

HELENE REACHED OVER and placed a hand on my arm. "Sam, I'm not saying you're right about this. That's neither of our roles. But I do think that you need to go to the authorities with what you know, let them investigate where Trey was that night, see if he has an alibi."

I shook my head. "McCauley's a meathead. He'll just blow me off."

"I wasn't talking about Chief McCauley," Helene said. "I was talking about Jason Captiva, who, *for some reason*, you don't seem to want to put into the picture."

"I've been busy," I muttered.

But she knew and I knew that I was well and truly trapped.

"Okay." I sulked. "I'll talk to Jason. First thing tomorrow, I promise."

I have to admit though, just saying the words considerably lightened my mood. Murderer or not, Trey's behavior that day had frightened me. I could tell Jason what I'd discovered and I would be safe. I should have listened to Jason in the first place. I should have let him handle it.

On the other hand, a little voice in my head said, *if you'd been a good girl and let him handle it, you wouldn't know what you know now about Trey Gorman. And neither would Jason.* I felt better. Sometimes I really like that little voice in my head.

On the other side of the hedge, Miles sounded his horn, and I jumped up. "He'll have fixed that drainpipe. I should go thank him. Just let me clear the table."

But Helene wasn't done.

"Just a second there, Nancy Drew," she said. "I'll take care of the cleanup. But am I right that, as far as Trey Gorman knows, you are the only person who's aware of what's in that notebook?"

I felt a chill go through me. "I guess so," I said. "I didn't tell him that I'd shared it with Krista."

Helene grimaced. "Okay. You go. I need to make a quick phone call."

I didn't like the sound of that. Not at all. But the horn honked again, more insistently this time.

"Thanks for the meal and the talk, Helene," I said. "You're a lifesaver."

I turned to my faithful companion, who was sulking under the table because nobody had shared her lobster with him. As if. "Come on, Diogi," I said. "Time to go home."

It wasn't until I was walking back to Aunt Ida's through the gathering dusk that I began to feel a little uncomfortable at the thought of being alone in the house that night. *Of course,* I reminded myself, *I had Diogi to bark any intruder into submission.*

Miles was sitting in his truck with the driver's side window down. I waved and started over to him.

"How did it go?"

"Very satisfying," Miles said. "Big old dead squirrel in there. I threw the carcass in the briar patch so Diogi wouldn't roll in it. That gutter should work fine now. You're lucky, you know. Your house is actually pretty solid."

"Aunt Ida's house," I corrected him automatically, but he

was still talking, using words like *pointing* and *flashing* and other incomprehensible terminology. But I let him go on, nodding encouragingly here and there because that's what you do with friends. Especially friends who snake your drainpipes.

When he'd exhausted the topic of renovating Aunt Ida's house, I waved him off. "Thanks for being a buddy," I said.

He gave me a thumbs-up and I stood there like an abandoned child as my friend left me to deal with . . . well . . . whatever it was I was dealing with.

I N LIEU OF a walk, I threw Diogi's disgusting tennis ball for him about a bazillion times until it grew too dark for him to find it. I was just turning to go into the ell when I again heard the crunch of tires on shells. Miles coming back to get something he'd forgotten? Or Trey to "finish this"?

Neither, as it turned out. It was a white Ford Explorer with familiar lettering along the side. It was the Harbor Patrol vehicle.

The Explorer pulled up next to Grumpy at the end of the driveway. I walked over to the driver's side and peered in the window. Jason was sitting there doing that very, very still thing of his, just looking back at me. The circles under his eyes betrayed his exhaustion, and I felt my heart ache a little. This was a man who needed to be taken care of. He worked too hard.

Oh no, girl. Do not go there.

I hardened my heart and rapped on the glass. Jason lowered the window. He still said nothing. It was unnerving.

"What are you doing in my driveway?"

"No idea," he said tiredly. "Ask Helene. She called, told me to come out here. She said she was worried about you. Why would she be worried about you?"

I sighed. "It's a long story. You better come in."

Once Diogi got over the miraculous appearance of the

Man with the Boat at his house, Jason and I settled down to business. I lit a fire in the woodstove and made some coffee. This was going to take a while.

Jason settled into one end of the couch with a soft grunt. "So much better than the front seat of the Explorer." He stretched his long legs out toward the fire, leaned his head back, and ran a hand through his tangled hair, which did exactly nothing to tame it.

I handed him a coffee cup. "Helene told you to come here?"

"Yup," he said, sipping his coffee gratefully. "This is really good coffee."

"You have to get the grind just right for a French press," I said, sitting as far away from him as I could get and still actually be on the couch. "Too coarse and you don't get enough flavor, too fine and you get way too much sediment."

"Well, you got it just right then." That half smile of his again. But the eyes still looked tired. "Tell me why Helene is worried about you."

"It's Trey," I said and stopped. *Well, this is awkward.*

"You and Gorman looked pretty friendly to me." Was Jason just a *teeny* bit jealous?

"You were the one who literally threw us together," I reminded him. "Going full throttle in a no-wake zone. And you the harbormaster."

He looked momentarily uncomfortable. "I had bad guys to catch," he said. He didn't even try to make it sound believable.

"Good," I said, "because Trey may, in fact, be a bad guy."

Jason sat up, all his earlier ease gone. "Tell me."

So I told him. I told him about finding my mother's notebook in Trey's car, and what it had revealed. I told him about what I'd learned from my visit to Suzanne. Jason listened with the still intensity that I was beginning to expect from him.

When I got to the part about Trey following me home,

trying to snatch my bag from me, I thought I saw Jason's eyes narrow slightly, but otherwise he remained impassive. Even when I mentioned my threat to fillet Trey like a fish, no response. Even when I told him about *that moron kicking my dog,* he barely reacted except to reach out and give Diogi a soft pat on the head. *Which was more than I got,* I thought. That's how bad things had gotten. I was jealous of a dog.

I told him about talking with Helene and our theory that Trey might have drowned Estelle to silence her once and for all.

Jason nodded. "It makes sense."

"I agree," I said. "But something bothers me. . . ." I hesitated.

"Tell me," Jason said, putting his coffee cup down and leaning toward me, his forearms on his legs. "I'm beginning to understand that when something bothers you, there's a good reason for it."

I figured that was about as close to an apology as I was ever going to get for his earlier dismissal of my concerns. Which was fine. I would take it.

"Why wait two years to kill her?" I couldn't believe I was talking like this, thinking like this.

"Didn't Trey tell you the delays on the Skaket Point development were getting expensive? Estelle was just one more drain on his pocketbook, and with the town meeting coming up, she was not exactly someone he could count on to keep her mouth shut. Not only could he no longer afford Estelle, he could no longer risk having her alive at all."

"So why was Trey so concerned about my mother's notes?" I asked. "Presumably, if he drowned Estelle, he has her cell phone and therefore the incriminating photo, so he has nothing to worry about. A scribbled page of unfounded claims isn't proof of anything."

Jason nodded thoughtfully. "But he *was* worried. So maybe he *doesn't* have Estelle's cell?"

"Seems likely," I said. "But how could that be? How do you murder someone for her cell phone and then not take it?" I could hear the irritation in my voice. Not at Trey, but at myself. Every time I had a "feeling" about something or someone, I got blocked by an inconsistency.

"Take it step-by-step," Jason said calmly. "You get to the answer by taking it step-by-step. You know the scene, you know the characters. Visualize it step-by-step."

Hoo boy, this was not going to be fun.

THIRTY

B UT I TRIED. I visualized it.

"Under the old deck would be a good, quiet spot to meet." I stopped, suddenly overcome with embarrassment. Jason knew only too well what a good, quiet spot it was. But he was too intent on getting to the bottom of the current mystery to be distracted by old history. *Unlike some of us.*

"Agree," he said, then waited for me to go on.

"Estelle could get there by boat, and under the deck it would be private because if the light was off, it would be dark." *Really, Jason? None of this brings anything back?*

Jason just said, "It would be good to know if the light was always off or if that was unusual. If, for instance, the bulb had been deliberately unscrewed." *Instead of smashed with a rock.*

But Jason was busy working it all out. "So maybe the usual drill was whoever got there first unscrewed the light bulb, put it somewhere where it wouldn't get broken, then put it back in when they left."

"Okay," I said, following that train of thought. "So Estelle gets there first, takes out the light bulb. She's a chain-smoker, so she's smoking while she waits for Trey. She's probably near the concrete breakwater, so she can flip the butts into the water." *Just like when she spied on you and me.*

"And where's her purse?" Jason asked. "Estelle was old-school. She never went anywhere without her purse." *So he did remember that much.* Estelle's proudest possession was her crocodile handbag. I'd never liked it any more than I had liked her. It had a varnished bamboo handle and, Estelle bragged, was made of real crocodile skin. I'd pointed out that crocodiles were endangered, and she'd laughed in my face and said they could have her handbag when they pried it out of her cold dead hands. Which, it occurred to me now, was kind of what had happened.

"Right," I said. "She would have had a handbag with her if only to carry her lipstick and Kools. And these days her cell phone."

"So, a handbag or a shoulder bag, you think?"

"Well, back in my day"—*our day*—"it was a handbag. That crocodile thing. Maybe she still carried it. Those bags were made to last forever."

"So let's assume she still has the same bag when she's meeting Gorman. She'd probably want a smoke while she waited, so she'd have put the bag down on something while she got her cigarettes and lighter out. Where, then? Maybe on the ground?"

"Believe me," I said. "I know from my dad that nobody of a certain age puts anything on the ground if they can help it. Creaky bones protest."

I tried to think back to the night Estelle had spied on Jason and me. Where was her handbag when she'd been taunting us? I was pretty sure there'd been no bag on her arm when she'd been illuminated by her lighter. So, she'd put it on a table or something like that. I caught my breath. *Something like a workbench.* That heavy, scarred workbench where I used to sit while Jason talked and paced.

"There was a workbench!" I cried. "Don't you remember?" I was so excited I forgot that we weren't supposed to be talking about the past.

"Yes, I remember," Jason said quietly. "But that was then. What matters now is if it's still there." For an insane moment I thought he was speaking metaphorically about our relationship.

As if. Pulling out his cell phone, Jason began scrolling. "I have some photos I took that night of the area near where she was found." Click, click, click. "Yup, here it is. Under the deck. The workbench. Probably too heavy to make moving it worthwhile. And, look, there's the light bulb." He handed me the phone. The camera's flash showed it all. The empty light socket, the bulb tossed onto a pile of old burlap sacks, the concrete breakwater with the water lapping against it, the workbench just a foot or so away.

I nodded and handed the phone back to him and continued with my re-creation.

"So, she's been standing next to the breakwater, smoking, her handbag beside her on the workbench. It's after dark, so the boatyard would be closed, but it's during the dinner rush, so it would be unlikely that anybody working at the Grill would be out there and any patrons arriving are parking and coming in on the other side of the building."

"And if anyone saw Trey when he arrived, they'd just assume he was there to eat," Jason added.

I nodded. "They'd been meeting there for months, and never had a problem. Estelle would be completely at ease, even a little looped, waiting for Trey to arrive."

I gulped and stopped. This was where our little exercise was going to get tough.

"It might have been an accident," I hedged.

But Jason wasn't having it. "Maybe when she first went in," he acknowledged, "maybe she stumbled and fell. But the water was about four feet deep at the breakwater. How likely is it that a woman who had been living on the bay her whole life couldn't hold herself up in four feet of water with the wall of the breakwater right there to support her? And why didn't she call for help if she needed it?"

I nodded miserably. Putting the horror into words was making things way too real. But it had to be done.

"So Trey gets there and somehow Estelle falls off the breakwater, either accidentally or intentionally," I continued. "And I guess we have to think intentionally, given Trey's desperation. Trey jumps in after her and . . ." I swallowed hard, then forced myself to continue. "He holds her head under. I can't imagine she was any match for him."

"So, the logical thing to do next," Jason interrupted, "would be for Gorman to climb back over the breakwater, grab her handbag, and get the hell out of there."

"Except he didn't," I said.

"He didn't what?"

"*He didn't take the handbag*. Don't you remember the whole problem here? If he has the handbag, he has the cell phone. And if he has the cell phone, he has the photo Estelle was holding over him. Ergo, why would he care about my mother's notes? Ergo, he doesn't have the handbag, cell phone, or photo."

Jason nodded. "So who has it?"

"I don't know," I admitted. "But what if it happened like this? He's in the water with the body and suddenly he hears footsteps on the gravel, someone coming under the deck. It's dark. Whoever it is probably can't see him. But just in case, he sinks down and pushes the body farther under."

"It would have been hard to keep that body under water," Jason pointed out. "There was the air pocket created by her foul weather gear. It would have been like trying to keep a balloon underwater."

Suddenly I remembered. *The snail. The mud on Estelle's face.*

"You remember we wondered how she got that mud on her face, the snail on her cheek?" I didn't want to go on. It was horrible. I didn't want to think about it. In fact, I didn't want to think about any of this. But what I wanted really didn't matter anymore. What mattered was getting to the bottom of how Estelle had died.

"He did more than hold her under the water. He held her down with his foot, facedown in the mud."

Jason nodded. "If he was wearing sneakers, I doubt there'd even be noticeable bruising. But I'll ask for that to be checked. Go on."

"Trey stays still, only his head above water. He waits until he hears the footsteps recede. He lets the body come back up to the surface, turns it over to check that his victim is well and truly dead, then climbs back up on the breakwater to grab the handbag. But it's not there."

Jason nodded. "It's with whoever came by while Trey was hiding in the water. You're right—it's the only thing that makes sense."

"But if somebody found a handbag under the deck, wouldn't they have brought it up to the restaurant, reported it?" I asked.

Jason looked at me with enormous pity. "You really are almost ridiculously naive sometimes."

"You think they stole the purse."

"Of course they stole the purse," he said. "It's the only explanation that fits the facts."

"And now Trey has a murder on his hands but not the cell phone he did it for," I said flatly. "Which means that the only piece of evidence that links him to the victim is my mother's notebook."

"Which brings us," Jason said, "to the reason Helene called me."

I just looked at him inquiringly.

"Gorman could come back," Jason said. "Police protection would appear in order since your sole defenses are a dog who thinks that barking is the limit of his job responsibilities and your trusty chef's knife."

Oh god, oh god, oh god. Jason had seen the YouTube video.

While I was trying to absorb this latest humiliation, Jason went out to the Explorer, then came back into the ell carrying a canvas duffel bag.

"What's that?" I asked rhetorically.

"A duffel bag."

"I can see that. What's in it?"

"Stuff. Toothbrush, clean clothes for tomorrow."

I shook my head. Maybe I hadn't heard him right. "Tomorrow? You think you're spending the night?"

For the first time, Jason cracked a smile. "I have my orders," he said.

Oh god, oh god, oh god.

"You can't stay here," I gabbled. "Aunt Ida's house is a wreck. There are *daddy longlegs* everywhere."

Jason laughed outright. "Here," he said, patting the couch. "I'll sleep here."

No way you're sleeping on that couch, buddy, I wanted to say. *That couch is exactly six feet away from my bed.* The thought, I have to admit, was vaguely thrilling.

And then he said it. *Again.* "And tomorrow I'll take it from here."

And just like that, the thrill was gone.

IT WASN'T MUCH of a sleepover. No lights-out confidences, no binge watching *Doctor Who*, no giving each other manicures. I was exhausted and Jason, who, he explained, was on call for the weekend, already looked drained. I didn't really think that Trey had plans to come back and murder me in my bed but the truth was, I was glad to have Jason there. Even if I was *once again* pissed off at him.

But tired as I was, sleep wouldn't come. Over and over again, I replayed the day's events in my mind. Over and over again, I went through our reconstruction of what might have happened between Trey and Estelle. It made sense, but now something else was bothering me. An image in my head. A cell phone where there shouldn't have been one. On a cluttered countertop. *The kitchen counter at Bits and Bites.* Why did Mr. Logan—who by his own admission didn't even know how to use cell phones—have one in his kitchen? It clearly wasn't his, so whose was it? It was unlikely to be Estelle's. Unless . . .

Carol had said Mr. Logan was a regular at the Bayview Grill, coming in once a month like clockwork. Had he been at the Grill that night? Had it been *Mr. Logan* who'd found Estelle's purse?

I tried to work it all out, but I was very, very tired. It's not every day that a girl gets in a brawl with a vicious dog kicker, then solves (sort of) a murder with a member of the local marine constabulary who then takes *her* ideas and kicks her to the sleuthing curb (so to speak). Who wouldn't be tired? I'd check out that cell phone first thing in the morning, though.

The last thing I thought as I slipped into sleep was, "*I'll* take it from here."

THIRTY-ONE

~~~~~~

IOGI WOKE ME early, whining to go out. I could hear
the crows and seagulls competing to greet the sunrise,
and a gray light filtered in through the cotton curtains at the
windows. At first I was disoriented, wondering what it was
about the ell that felt different. *Oh yeah, maybe it's that guy
sleeping on my sofa.*

Gradually the events of the night before came back to
me. I remembered our reconstruction of the crime. I remembered Jason patronizing me *after I figured it all out
and gave him all the clues.* I remembered what I needed to
do. I checked the time. Not yet six. Too early to talk to Mr.
Logan, but I could go peek in the window of the kitchen at
Bits and Bites, see if the phone was still there. If I was
quick about it, Jason wouldn't even know I'd left the house.

I threw on jeans, a T-shirt, my Vans, and the red hoodie.
I let Diogi out for his wee, grabbed a granola bar that I'd
bought at Nelson's Market during a moment of madness
when I'd thought maybe I should start eating healthy, took
a bite, spit it out and threw the rest in the trash where it
belonged. When I got back I'd make pancakes.

I peeked over the back of the couch. Jason was sleeping

like he didn't have a murderer to catch. He looked so young. I hardened my heart against him. *"I'll take it from here."* He'd had no right to make that decision. I told myself I didn't need to feel guilty. All I was going to do was take a quick look in the window of Bits and Bites. If the phone was still there on the counter, I'd tell Jason. There was no reason to assume that the phone was Estelle's, but it would be worth checking out. I would look in the window, and if the phone was still there, call Jason. That was the plan.

I scribbled a quick "running some errands" on a piece of paper and left it on the table.

"Back soon," I whispered to Diogi. *Famous last words.*

Grumpy took some coaxing to wake up. The first time I turned the key, it made that whee-whee sound designed to drive you mad, but it eventually gave in and we lurched off.

As I turned into the gravel parking area behind Bits and Bites, my heart sank. Mr. Logan's green Buick was parked by the kitchen door, which had been propped open with a brick. I was pondering my next step when a high-pitched shriek started up from inside, making the hair stand up on the back of my neck.

Then I recognized it as the shrill whine of a bandsaw and cursed the man's newfound lust for life. At his age and at this hour, he should have been curled up under an eider-down, not cutting framing for windows. Not getting in the way of amateur sleuths like *moi.*

Well, no matter. If he was happily working in the dining room, I could actually go into the kitchen, see if the phone was on the counter. Maybe check it out. And if he came in and saw me, I'd just say I was passing and wanted to see if he'd liked the *Clarion* story, then casually ask him about the phone.

I did, in fact, hope the *Clarion* story would drum up some advance business for him. Because looking around, I wasn't so sure people would be flocking to this isolated place. For as far as the eye could see, there was no one out on the bay or walking the shore. Of course, it was early in the morning and the season, and the weather, which was cold and damp and windy, wasn't encouraging for either boaters or bird-watchers. That would change in a few weeks.

I peeked in the half-open door leading to the kitchen.

It was there. The cell phone. Lying faceup on the kitchen counter.

I pulled my own phone out of my pocket. Time to call Jason, tell him to meet me at Bits and Bites. I looked at the home screen and swore softly. No bars, no cell service *at all*. And obviously no Wi-Fi. Which meant no way to text or call. *Why does anyone live in this godforsaken place?*

I couldn't help myself, I swear. The lure of that phone on the counter was too much. I tiptoed in (as if anyone could have heard me against the sound of that saw) and picked up the phone, raising my eyebrows a bit at the hot-pink case wrapped around the back of it. So not a workman's. *Estelle's*? It was an iPhone like my own, not new, maybe a few years old. I tapped the home button hoping that if this was in fact Estelle's cell, she hadn't bothered to password protect it. The good news was the home screen came to life. The bad news was that the battery icon was seriously low.

I tapped the e-mail icon. Even with no cell service the app should open, and hopefully any saved correspondence would tell me who the owner was. Oddly, the app was blank, no e-mails at all. Or actually not so oddly if the phone belonged to Estelle. I couldn't imagine she had a vast network of online buddies. She had used her phone simply as a phone. And as a camera. I flipped back to the home screen, which was now frantically yelling that I had *less than 10 percent power*.

I tapped the camera icon and hoped for the best. *Yesss!* Photos. Not many, maybe a few dozen, and most were of an old and rather raggedy cat. Did Estelle have a cat? I couldn't remember. I filtered them by date and scrolled back two years. The cat again, not quite as old or raggedy. And then a first attempt at a selfie. *Yessss.* There was Estelle in all her blowsy glory. I was definitely holding Estelle's phone in my hand.

I scrolled forward, knowing the juice was running very low, very fast.

Cat, cat, cat, and . . . *jackpot*—a couple through a window, locked in a passionate embrace. Though the window appeared to be tinted, an overhead light illuminated the pair in clear detail. The woman's back was to the camera so all that you could see was a cap of short, straight black hair. Half of the man's face was visible and he seemed vaguely familiar, but I couldn't place him. On the man's left hand a wedding ring glinted. The woman's left hand, cupping the side of her lover's face, was bare. *Interesting.* Was this the he and she that Suzanne had mentioned to me?

I scrolled on.

Cat, cat, cat, and then a distant shot of an old bald guy sitting on a dock at night, lights twinkling in the distance. An old man rich enough to own waterfront property. Estelle's sugar daddy?

Cat, cat, cat, and then a snap of a very respectable-looking middle-aged woman sliding a lipstick still in its packaging into her purse. *Ooh, a shoplifter, too.*

I scrolled to the next shot, but only got a brief glimpse of what might have been a beach before the screen slid into darkness, the battery drained. I groaned out loud. Had that been the photo Estelle claimed she'd taken of Trey stamping on baby birds? Oh, well. All I needed to do was charge the phone up and I could be sure. In the meantime, I had enough to go on. I had photos that suggested that Estelle had probably blackmailed several people, any one of whom might have been her killer.

"Samantha?"

I whirled around, dropping the cell on the counter guilt-ily. Mr. Logan was standing in the doorway.

"You found Estelle's mobile cellular telephone!" Mr. Logan said, beaming. He walked over and picked the phone up gingerly. "Maybe you could help me with it. I don't know how to make it work. Estelle used to show me pictures of her cat on it. I thought maybe I could use it to take some photographs of my dog, Archibald. He's a very hand-some dog."

I was touched that Mr. Logan had a dog named Ar-chibald, but jumped in before he could continue to wax rhapsodic about the pooch. "You knew this was Estelle's phone?"

"Well, of course I did," he said. "I got it from her, didn't I?"

"Estelle *gave* it to you?"

"Oh no, no," he said. "Not exactly. You see, the other night I went to have my usual drink at the Grill—I go there once a month you know, as a show of support for Carol—and anyway, I was heading back to my car, when I noticed that the light under the deck was out. It's just an automatic thing with me. It used to drive my wife half mad when that light was out. Sometimes kids would break it. Vandals, you know?"

Suddenly I felt very guilty.

"I hoped that wasn't the case this time, so I went to the car to get a flashlight and then I stepped under the deck to check and do you know what I saw?"

I shook my head no. There was no point in trying to get a word in anyway. Mr. Logan was on a roll and I was busy enough just trying to make sense of what I was hearing, which wasn't easy since the fellow had a habit of asides and discursions that needed real concentration to follow.

"Estelle's handbag—you know that crocodile one she was so proud of?—well, it was sitting on that old work-bench. But no Estelle. I thought she must have come down for a smoke and left it there by accident. That had happened before when she worked for me, especially if she'd had a few cocktails after her shift, you know?"

He stopped and looked at me expectantly. What was I going to say? *Well, no, what actually happened, Mr. Logan, was Estelle was being drowned no more than a few feet away from you?*

"So what did you do then?" I said instead.

"I took the bag with me, figuring I could drive over to her place the next morning and give it to her." Mr. Logan's face clouded. "But the next day I heard about her accident. I knew she didn't have any family, so there wasn't anyone to give the handbag to." Of course. It hadn't occurred to Mr. Logan to give the bag to the police because he didn't know there was any reason to. As far as he (and everyone else who had read my story in the *Clarion*) was concerned, Estelle had died in a "tragic accident."

"And then I looked inside," he continued, "and saw her mobile cellular telephone and I'm a little embarrassed to admit this, but that's when I thought maybe I could keep it and learn how to use it to take pictures of Archibald so I can show them to people." He stopped for breath, then added, "Maybe you could teach me?"

"I'd be happy to teach you how to use it," I said. Which was true. When all this was over, I would introduce Mr. Logan to the wonders of cell phones. Just not this particular cell phone. "But the thing is, it needs to be charged up. It's all out of power. It needs a charger."

"Where do I get a charger?" Mr. Logan asked.

"I have one at home," I said. "I tell you what, I'll just take the phone, charge it up, and bring it back for our first lesson."

Mr. Logan looked at me oddly, and I wondered if I sounded as fake as I felt. "Can't you just bring the charger here?" he said.

Okay, second best option. I mean, it wasn't like I could rip the phone out of his hand. And it wasn't going anywhere.

"Sure," I said. "I'll be back soon."

Again. Famous last words.

THIRTY-TWO

〰〰〰

I WAS PULLING OUT from Levi's Way onto Route 6 when my cell rang. I knew it was Krista because who else would think nothing of calling me at seven o'clock on a Saturday morning. Well, she'd just have to wait. I grinned as I pictured her, probably in her office, impatiently tapping her foot, waiting for me to answer, shaking her head in irritation, her sleek black bob swinging like a bell around her face.

Her sleek, black bob.

The photos in Estelle's phone. Something had bothered me—there had been something, someone familiar. The man and the woman kissing. The man's face had been only half visible and only the back of the woman's head could be seen. The back of her sleek, black bob. Krista had a sleek, black bob. I'd noticed it particularly yesterday, as she was leaving the office, her hair like a silk curtain around the nape of her neck. *The woman in that photo was Krista.* Was Krista having an affair with a married man?

I thought about Krista dolling herself up on a Thursday night but with no plans for the weekend. In my limited understanding of married men who have affairs, they tended to spend weekends with their wives and children, weeknights with their girlfriends.

And, yes, Krista could certainly be having an affair with a married man. I didn't find this particularly shocking. Not because I didn't think it was wrong—I thought it was very wrong—but because it was Krista. Krista had always played by her own rules. Krista always went after what she wanted.

Did Krista know that Estelle had that photo? Had Estelle tried to blackmail Krista's lover with the threat that she'd reveal their affair to his wife? Was that why Krista had tried to get me off the story?

And now all I could think about was *who was Krista's married lover?* It occurred to me that even if Krista no longer confided her love life to me, she probably still did to Miles. Miles was a big "no judgments" kind of guy. I needed to talk to Miles. He'd be up, even at this ungodly hour. He was a farmer.

So I decided on a little detour before going home for the phone charger. I took the second Fair Harbor exit off Route 6 and steered Grumpy around the traffic circle onto Tanner Road, which led me back to the farm that had been in Miles's family for generations. I rolled past neat rows of bushes that in summer would be heavy with blueberries and raspberries, then past the long plastic greenhouses that sheltered early lettuces and other microgreens and finally past the brown, furrowed fields that would produce those wonderful Cape Cod turnips.

I turned Grumpy into the driveway and pulled up in front of the weathered barn that housed the farming equipment, including an ancient tractor that Miles spent hours tinkering with just to "keep it going one more season." To my certain knowledge, "one more season" was now almost ten.

As I parked the car, Miles came out of the barn, wiping black machine oil off his hands with a grimy red bandana. Trotting alongside him was Fay Wray, an exceptionally intelligent, beautifully trained Australian shepherd with fluffy, silky black fur that set off the smooth white bib of her chest and the brown and white patchwork of her face. Miles claimed that Fay Wray knew at least fifty commands, including "Go get Daddy a beer from the cooler." Diogi, in contrast, sort of knew three commands: "Shut up." Sometimes "Sit." And, apparently, "Go get Helene."

Fay Wray greeted me with all the restraint one would expect of such an accomplished dog. No jumping and slobbering for her, just a friendly wag of her butt (Aussies usually have bobbed tails) and a little nose snuffle in my outstretched hand. Miles greeted me with an exuberant bear hug. It is a sad thing when a man is less dignified than his dog.

"So what brings you to the lower forty?" he asked as he led me into the farmhouse and back into a kitchen that hadn't changed since Mrs. Tanner had had it "done" in 1962. Same white-enameled metal cabinets, same black-and-white enameled table surrounded by four chrome kitchen chairs with red vinyl seats.

"I need some information," I said as I settled myself at the table and took the mug of coffee that Miles had poured out for me without asking. We'd sat at this table with mugs of coffee more times than I could count.

Miles nodded. "Information about what?"

And suddenly I was uncertain. "Not what," I said. "Who."

"Okay, about who?"

"Krista," I said miserably.

Miles looked at me apprehensively. I think he was afraid I was going to start crying on him again. "And what information do you need about Krista?" he asked carefully. "I mean that you can't ask her for yourself?"

"I need information about her love life," I said, even more miserably.

"Ah," Miles said slowly. "Her love life. I see. Yes, I can understand why you wouldn't want to ask her yourself, seeing as every time she talks about one of her little flings you go all pink in the face and flustery."

"There's no such word as *flustery*," I said.

"There is now," Miles said.

"But you're right," I admitted. "She stopped confiding in me a long time ago because I used to get . . . perturbed."

"Flustery," Miles corrected me.

"Okay, flustery. But I need to know who she's been seeing, Miles. Don't ask me why, but it's important, really important."

Miles gave me a long look. "Okay. I don't think you'd be asking if it wasn't important. And knowing what I know, I can see how it might be."

"What do you know?" I asked. "Please, I promise it won't go any farther, but I have to know."

"Well, she hasn't mentioned him in a while, but I know she was seeing Curtis Henson."

I almost fell off my chair.

"*Curtis Henson*? Curtis Henson the district attorney?"

Miles nodded. "None other."

So not just Krista who had looked vaguely familiar. Curtis Henson, too.

"But he's *old*," I said. "He's got to be at least twenty years older than Krista."

"Really?" Miles said. "That's your objection, that he's old?"

I smiled ruefully. "No, of course not. I don't know where that came from. But I do object to the fact that he's married." I put my face in my hands.

"Oh dear," I whispered, almost to myself. "This is not a good thing. This is not a good thing at all."

"No, it isn't," Miles agreed. "Even *I* do not think this is a good thing. I never thought so. And I told her so. But you know Krista, she always knows better. It's a no-strings-attached kind of thing, she told me. Nobody was going to get hurt. They were very discreet."

"They'd better be," I said. "He's a politician and she's a pretty prominent journalist."

"Exactly," Miles said. "But Krista says they're super careful. He lives in Barnstable for his work now, but his family still has one of those big houses by Reedie's landing. He keeps his boat moored there year-round, and that's where they meet. Krista says nobody's ever suspected anything."

So Krista didn't know about Estelle's photo. Had Henson not told her?

"Nobody's ever suspected except for you," Miles added meaningfully. Then he just looked at me.

I knew what he wanted. He'd dished, and now it was my turn to dish. But I didn't know what to say to him, what to tell him. This had gone way beyond gossip shared between friends. This was essential information as part of a murder investigation. I needed to talk to Jason. *He could take it from here.* And for the first time, my feelings about that were not resentment, but relief. We'd get the phone from Mr. Logan, and I'd be out of it.

There was just one thing I needed to do first.

THIRTY-THREE

ONCE I'D ESCAPED from Miles (who was all *flustery* because I wouldn't tell him anything) and Grumpy had finally agreed to start, I headed back toward town. I pulled into the Sunoco station for gas (the Sunoco was the only gas station in town that still offered full service, which meant that I didn't have to pump my own, which was something—I'm ashamed to admit—I'd never learned how to do). While the nice gentleman filled Grumpy up, I took the opportunity to text Krista. I didn't want to explain anything over the phone.

Where you?

Work

It was 7:30 on a Saturday morning. Of course she was at work.

Don't move coming by

The *Clarion*'s offices were deserted and very quiet except for the sound of Krista clicking away at her computer. I stuck my head in her door and said "Hey, you" to her back.

She jumped about a mile and turned to me, frowning furiously. "Jeez, don't do that!"

Great, Sam. Get her all pissed off before you even begin.

"Sorry," I said. "I, um, I need to, um, talk to you about something. . . ."

Krista just sighed dramatically. "Just spit it out, girl. Some of us have work to do."

I took a deep breath. The words came out in a rush. "I know about you and Curtis Henson and so did Estelle. She took a picture of the two of you . . . together . . . probably on that boat . . . with her cell phone."

Krista was no fool. She didn't even try to pretend she didn't know what I was talking about. "And you've seen it? You have Estelle's cell?"

I nodded. Well, I *almost* had her cell.

Krista went silent. But I'd known her for so long that I could read her like a book, and I watched as something like the five phases of grief flitted across her face—denial (*This can't be happening*), then anger (*Who told?*), then bargaining (*How do I get out of this?*), to depression (*I can't get out of this*), to acceptance (*This is happening, there is nothing I can do about it*). She bowed her head and put her face in her hands.

It wounded me to see my admittedly annoying friend brought so low. I wished mightily that I hadn't been the one to bring her this news, that I'd never gotten involved in investigating Estelle's death. I'd never meant to hurt anybody, particularly not Krista.

Then Krista raised her face to mine.

"That *scumbag*."

Oops, we're back to anger. Now, that's more like it.

"Curtis?" I asked hesitantly.

"Of course Curtis. Curtis Slimebucket Henson. He dumped me, you know." Of course I didn't know, but now was not the time to interrupt. Krista was just getting started.

"About six months ago. Ghosted me, the gutless rat bastard." Krista has an amazing vocabulary when she's mad. "Just stopped answering my texts, sent my calls to voice mail. I couldn't figure out what had happened. The funny thing was, I was planning to call the whole thing off myself. In the beginning he'd had that sexy power thing going on, you know? And a killer smile. But once you got to really know him, he was kind of a weird, kinky guy." I could feel myself getting flustery, but fortunately Krista moved on.

"And then last week he called me, said he wanted to explain, asked if we could meet. Like an idiot, I agreed. He told me his wife had gotten suspicious, that was why the sudden silence. It made sense to me. The sleazeball is scared to death of her. She runs this big hedge fund and he needs her money in his run for state's attorney. He said he was sorry about the way he'd left things, that his wife wasn't suspicious anymore so he wanted to get back together. What a degenerate, horny, money-grubbing piece of crud." It was a fantastic aria, and I was kind of enjoying it, but even Krista had to stop to take a breath.

I took advantage of the opening. "He never mentioned Estelle? Or the photo?"

"Nope. But I bet that's what it was really all about. His clueless wife probably never suspected anything. What probably happened was Estelle showed him that photo and he freaked out and dumped me. And probably used his wife's moola to pay her off. And then when Estelle died, he figured he and I could get it on again." She stopped for a second as another thought struck her. "I wonder why Estelle didn't try to hit me up, too."

"Your back is to the camera in the photo," I said. "I recognized you by your hair. But I've been looking at the back of your head since ninth grade. I don't think most people would know it was you, least of all Estelle."

"Well, thank heaven for small favors," Krista muttered.

I paused, wishing I didn't have to ask Krista my next question. I took a deep breath and punched it out. "Do you think Curtis could have killed Estelle?"

Krista gave a short bark of laughter. "Do I think he could have? Yeah, sure. The guy is totally eaten up with ambition. But did he? No. That was the night after you got back, right? That night he was with me."

"I thought you just met to talk," I said. "So maybe he did it before or after your meeting?"

Krista had the good grace to look a little ashamed. "We were . . . busy . . . for a couple of hours."

I looked at her, aghast.

"I dumped him after," she said proudly. "But I wanted the dirtbag to know what he was missing."

And then I realized that this was good news. "He's in the clear, then," I said with relief. "If he was with you, nobody has to see that photo."

Krista, to give her credit, was horrified by what she thought she was hearing. "Don't you *dare* delete that photo," she said. "That's tampering with evidence and *it is against the law.*"

"But, Krista," I said, "if they bring Henson in for questioning—which they will because they'll recognize him—he's going to use you as his alibi. Your name is going to get out. Not all publicity is good publicity you know, not for a journalist anyway. But I don't see why the authorities even need to know about it. We know Curtis didn't kill Estelle. Let them concentrate on the other possible suspects, real suspects."

"Absolutely not," Krista said, and her tone brooked no argument. "You touch that photo and I'll have your guts for garters."

I couldn't help myself. I burst into laughter. "*You'll have my guts for garters?* What are you, a pirate?"

And suddenly we were both doubled up, hiccuping with laughter. It felt good. It felt like old times.

When I managed to get hold of myself, I stood up. "Look, I've got to go talk to Jason."

"Go," Krista said, pointing imperiously to the door. "Do your duty as a citizen." I could have sworn she was enjoying all this.

As I turned to leave, I saw her from the corner of my eye picking up her desk phone.

I turned back to her. "And you tell *no one* about this. Particularly that dirtbag ex-boyfriend of yours."

I didn't wait for her to respond. Krista would do what she wanted to do. But at least she knew how I felt about it.

BEFORE I LEFT the *Clarion*'s parking lot, I tried Jason again on my cell. The call went to voice mail, and I decided not to leave a message. He was probably still asleep back at Aunt Ida's. I headed home.

But Jason wasn't asleep at Aunt Ida's. He was gone. I knew he'd seen my note because he'd scribbled a peremptory "call me" below it. *Yes, sir, I thought. Right away, sir. Except you're not answering your phone, sir, so whose fault is that?*

Nonetheless, I tried the Harbor Patrol offices. The woman on the other end of the line informed me that the harbormaster had been called out to bring in a kayaker who'd lost his paddle.

"He's probably in a spot with no cell service," she said, "but he should be back soon. Do you want me to radio him with a message?"

"No message, thanks," I said. "I'll catch him later." She told me to have a nice day. I wasn't sure that was on the cards.

Diogi in the meantime was clearly jonesing for an outing, so I decided to take him with me to Bits and Bites. He'd enjoy romping on the beach while I charged Estelle's phone. I tucked the charger in my bag, and we settled into our respective seats in Grumpy. But Grumpy wasn't going anywhere. Grumpy didn't even wheeze at me. Grumpy had finally given up the ghost.

In response, I had one of those temper tantrums where you rock back and forth and bang on the steering wheel with both hands and generally behave like a spoiled five-year-old.

Tip: When the universe sends you a message, don't fight it. *Listen to the universe.*

Which, of course, I didn't. Instead I explored other options. I'd seen a bicycle in Aunt Ida's toolshed when I'd gone in to dig out the loppers for the briars in front of the house. I could ride the bike to Bits and Bites. I wasn't crazy about the idea of riding along Route 6 (I had visions of being sucked into some truck's slipstream). But if I went on the private roads through Bayberry Point, it would only be a couple of miles farther and the sandy lanes, though narrow, would be mostly deserted at this hour.

It was not an ideal day for a bike ride, chilly and gray and very windy. Through the gap I'd created in the briars, I could see whitecaps on Bower's Pond and noted with the sailor's automatic reflex that the wind would be even stronger out on the bay. Well, I wasn't planning on a sail. I was just going to take a little spin on Aunt Ida's bike.

So, full of the usual misplaced optimism that taking action, any action, tends to give me, I prepared for my bike ride. I tucked my phone and wallet into the front pockets of my jeans and the charger into the hand-warmer pocket of my hoodie. At the shed door, I zipped up my sweatshirt and cinched the hood around my face attractively. The shed was essentially a spider condo. I didn't want any of those suckers in my hair.

I stepped in and tugged the chain hanging from the bare bulb overhead. The rusted, red Schwinn was leaning against one wall. The bad news was that it looked like it weighed a ton and it had only three speeds. The good news was I'd never gotten the hang of shifting gears on a ten-speed anyway. The tires were not exactly flat but they were definitely soft. That, though, would be an advantage on the sand roads.

I pushed the contraption out onto the lawn, and Diogi erupted into a volley of barking at the monster wrestling with his human. I told him to shut up, which he did, then propped the bike against the shed (the kickstand having long since gone wherever it is that kickstands always go) and led him back into the ell.

As I pedaled away, I could see Diogi looking woefully out the window as the monster carried me off to who knew what terrible fate.

THIRTY-FOUR

~~~~~~~~~~

T HE RIDE ONLY took me about twenty minutes but it was a little hairy. The scrub oaks and pines shielded me from the worst of the wind, but the occasional gust sometimes rocked me and once actually knocked me over. But I got back on that horse and continued on my wobbly way. When I finally skidded into the parking area behind Bits and Bites, I could hear the by now familiar whine of the bandsaw in the dining room. Also good. I just needed a minute to take a quick look at the rest of Estelle's pictures without Mr. Logan peering over my shoulder. I really did not want to explain to him what I was looking for. It would only upset him.

I slipped into the kitchen. The phone was still on the cluttered counter where I'd left it. I plugged the charger into the closest outlet and then into the phone itself. Presto. We were back in business. I quickly scrolled back through Estelle's photos until I came to the beach scene that I'd briefly glimpsed before the phone had died.

It was one of two photos, actually. And not of beach scenes. As I'd suspected, they were of the Skaket Point dune. Taken from the water.

I think I stopped breathing for a moment.

In the first picture, a distant figure was walking along the top of the dune. It was impossible to identify who they were or what they were doing. But not in the next photo, which had been taken with the zoom function. Which meant Estelle meant business. Which meant she had really wanted to capture who was walking on that dune and what they were doing. Which she did.

It was Trey Gorman. It was Trey Gorman about to step on a baby bird huddling in the sand while its frantic parents dive-bombed the attacker.

I breathed out. So, yes, Estelle indeed had evidence of Trey Gorman destroying plover nests.

I should have been thrilled. My theory had been right. But all I felt was a deep sadness, for the birds, for Trey, for Estelle, for the greed and insecurity that had led to such a terrible end. For the whole sorry story.

But maybe I was rushing too quickly to judgment. There were other people Estelle had been blackmailing, other photos, probably some I hadn't even seen yet. I'd go back a few years and then scroll forward, starting with the few I'd looked at the first time. After all, I hadn't recognized Curtis Henson the first time I'd whizzed through the gallery. Maybe looking through the photos again, someone would strike me as familiar or something would give me a clue as to their identity.

But it was hopeless. I didn't know the lady with the lipstick, although I thought maybe it was taken in Livingston's drugstore. I tried again with the rich old man on his dock and though he reminded me of someone, I had a feeling it might be Mr. Burns in *The Simpsons*.

"You got it to work. You've found her pictures."

I whirled around. In my concentration, I hadn't registered that the wailing of the bandsaw had stopped. Nor that Mr. Logan had come in and was standing behind me, looking over my shoulder at the phone.

"I did," I said, putting the phone down as casually as I could on the counter. "But most of them are just of her cat."

"Oh dear," Mr. Logan said, distracted by the mention of the cat. "That reminds me, I've been meaning to check in with that neighbor of Estelle's who's taking care of it, see how it's doing."

"That's nice," I said. "You should probably do that." I tried to sound calm, but all I could think about was how I was going to explain to him that I needed to keep Estelle's phone. Mr. Logan didn't even know Estelle's death was being investigated as suspicious. I doubted very much that Jason or McCauley would appreciate me giving the game away.

But before I could say anything, we both heard the sound of tires crunching on gravel and turned to peer through the back door to see who was coming into the parking lot.

I literally felt my blood run cold as Trey Gorman's black SUV slid into view.

I grabbed Mr. Logan's arm.

"What's Trey Gorman doing here?" Even I could hear the panic in my voice.

"Probably come to talk to me about making the right-of-way he's been using for that development of his permanent," he said. "I figure it will be good for business, once I open the restaurant. Plus, he seems like a nice young man. He's given me a key to that fancy boat of his out there so I can take it out when the blues are biting. He hardly ever uses it. He's more of a sailor type, keeps a nice Wianno at the yacht club, I understand."

I liked Mr. Logan, but sometimes he just talked too much.

Actually, maybe that was a good thing. . . .

"Look, Mr. Logan, I really don't want to see him. Trey, I mean. We had a kind of . . . falling out . . . yesterday, and I just need a little time to sneak out the front, okay? Could you stall him for me, talk to him for a while?"

Mr. Logan smiled and chuckled. "Of course, Sam. I understand. The course of true love never runs smooth."

I wanted to laugh at how wrong he'd got it, but if it kept him on my side and Trey occupied while I got away, then great. He could think whatever he wanted.

Mr. Logan toddled out the back door, and I heard him hailing Trey cheerfully. I pulled out my own phone. Maybe I could call or text Jenny to come pick me up. But still, no cell service. The place, like most of the bay it bordered, was too remote.

I slipped my cell back into my jeans. Then I quickly unplugged the charger and Estelle's phone and dropped them into the pocket of my hoodie. I ran through the dining room and out the front door, then peeked around the side of the building to make sure the coast was clear. Unfortunately, I hadn't given Mr. Logan specific enough instructions. Instead of bringing Trey into the kitchen while I snuck out the front, he was chatting to him by the SUV, which was parked about five feet away from my bike. Even on foot, I couldn't get past them without being seen.

I crept back to the front of the building. The only thing Trey couldn't see from where he and Mr. Logan were chatting was the small strip of beach the restaurant looked out on. *The beach with the Sunfish pulled up on it.*

A Sunfish in a wind like this would actually be very fast. In it, I could probably be around Skaket Point and completely out of Trey's sight in about ten minutes. If, in this wind, I didn't capsize. I tried hard not to think how cold the water was, about how quickly a body can turn hypothermic. But I'd been sailing Sunfishes since I was ten. I wasn't going to capsize.

I cinched the hood of my sweatshirt over my head and dashed over to where the little sailboat had been pulled up above the tide line. I was relieved to see that both the rudder and the daggerboard were tidily stowed in the boat's footwell. I couldn't steer without a rudder, and I needed the daggerboard to keep us from simply sliding sideways instead of moving forward when the wind was coming across the side of the boat.

I pinwheeled the boat around in the sand so that the bow was facing the water. Across the stern some proud owner, probably a kid, had stenciled the name *Swallow*. I couldn't help smiling to myself. Then, grunting with the effort, I began to push the boat out to the water.

The tide was getting low, and the minute or so it took me to push the boat fifteen feet down to where the water lapped the beach seemed like hours. I looked behind me quickly. No sign of Trey. *God bless you, Mr. Logan*.

I pulled off my Vans, threw them into the footwell, and pulled my jeans up to my knees. I pushed the *Swallow* out until there was a good foot of water under it. The water was bitterly cold on my legs. No matter.

Still standing behind the boat, I slid the rudder into the gudgeons on the boat's stern and straightened out its attached tiller. Then I gave the Sunfish a push and hopped on board. As we slid out into the deeper water, I began to raise the triangular sail, pulling on its halyard hand over hand while simultaneously trying to avoid the wildly swinging metal boom on the bottom of the sail. This probably took less than a minute, but again it felt like an age. I cleated off the halyard and slid the daggerboard halfway down.

I settled my butt awkwardly on the narrow strip of deck along the windward side of the boat. It was a challenge to accordion my long legs into the footwell. Somehow I hadn't thought about the fact that a Sunfish, which had fit my skinny ten-year-old self just fine, would be ridiculously small for a six-foot-something woman who hadn't been skinny since, let's see, she was ten.

I tugged the tiller toward me and pulled in the sail until it caught the wind. The *Swallow* jumped forward and we were off! For a moment I forgot that I was running away from a very bad man who might well want to hurt me. For a moment, I was just a girl on a boat, and I was happy.

I steered the *Swallow* between the moored Chris-Craft and Darth Vader's boat. While we were still close to shore, the wind was strong but nothing the *Swallow* couldn't handle. The boat heeled a little, and the side of the boat I was sitting on lifted a few inches out of the water. The leeward side, the side the sail was on, tipped down a bit. None of this alarmed me. Boats sail best on a slight heel. You just hike out, which is using the counterweight of your body leaning out of the boat to adjust the angle at which the boat is heeling. I did it as easily and unconsciously as most people adapt their bodies to upward and downward slopes when they walk.

I hiked out a bit, and the boat settled back a little. I was already at least thirty feet from shore and well into the channel that Jason and I had traveled only a few days earlier. To my left were the great boulders that ran along the Skaket shoreline on the Big Crystal side of the point. To my right, the big bay stretched as far as the eye could see. Ahead of me, across the bay, the view across to the long stretch of the Outer Beach was uninterrupted except for the bulk of Nickerson Island. I thought back to that day with Jason and our picnic in the marshes behind Nickerson. That had been a wonderful day, and now it was just a memory.

The wind picked up considerably as I made my way farther out from shore. Now I was grateful for my long legs. I slipped my feet back into my Vans, levered my toes under the opposite lip of the footwell, and leaned back out even farther over the water. When I was a kid, hiking out was my idea of wicked fun. But this time I wasn't hiking out for fun. This time, it was about sailing as fast and far as possible, which would mean getting as much wind into the sail as the *Swallow* could handle. Which would also mean that, as we got closer to the tip of Skaket Point and hit the worst of the wind, I would have to hike out even more to keep the boat upright.

My plan was to take the channel along the Skaket waterfront, then tack around the point and into Little Crystal, where I'd beach on a stretch of bayfront that had at least a dozen houses, some of them year-round. I could pull up the Sunfish on shore and find shelter with whoever was home. And if someone wasn't home, I knew where to find the spare key. This made me smile a little to myself. I'd probably been a little dramatic in my "escape" from Bits and Bites. And then I heard the motor. I turned to look behind me.

Darth Vader's boat was heading out from shore, coming straight for us.

THIRTY-FIVE

N O, NOT DARTH Vader's boat. Worse. Trey Gorman's boat.

"That fancy boat out there" Mr. Logan had called it. The *Mad Max*. The tinted windows that wrapped around the enclosed wheelhouse safely hid whoever was inside. But I knew it was Trey Gorman, Trey Gorman coming after me in the *Mad Max*.

Which was not actually my immediate concern.

In the few seconds it had taken to glance behind me, the *Swallow* had found the stronger winds that I'd been anticipating. As a formidable gust hit the sail, the boat tipped dangerously. I forgot the speedboat behind me. I leaned farther back, hiking way out to level the boat while at the same time letting the sail out a bit to spill some wind. The maneuver worked. The boat righted itself, and though we'd shipped some water into the footwell, it wasn't a lot. The boat's self-bailer valve would drain it quickly.

I pulled the sail back in, and glanced behind me again. The *Mad Max* was gaining on us. The fact that I couldn't see the man at the wheel made it somehow more menacing, as if the boat itself was after me. I scanned the bay. No one else was on the water. It was a Saturday, so no lobstermen were out and pleasure boaters would be waiting until the cold, gray, windy weather turned. I was alone with the *Mad Max*.

I told myself to breathe. What did I actually think was going to happen? Was Trey going to risk everything by running me down? Sure, we were alone out on the water. But he knew as well as I did that Mr. Logan was probably watching the course of true love from his vantage point on the shore. Nonetheless, I was scared, and I concentrated hard on getting as much speed out of the *Swallow* as I could.

I heard the *Mad Max* roaring up behind me. It would be on me in only a few seconds. I was determined not to look back. I wouldn't give him the satisfaction. He was just flexing his muscles, trying to put a scare into me.

The relief when I heard and then saw the huge craft zooming by my little boat—very close to it, to be sure, but *by* it, not *over* it—was enormous.

Probably Trey hadn't even known it was me on the Sunfish. To him I was just some sailor in a red hoodie out for a joyride. He was probably checking something along the Skaket shore, maybe looking for some more baby birds to stomp on. Nonetheless, I kept my face down and firmly away from him.

A heavy powerboat going at top speed creates a trail of wake behind it with waves that can reach two feet. That wake is no picnic if it hits a small sailboat broadside. And there's pretty much no sailboat smaller than a Sunfish. That's why powerboats are *supposed* to slow down when passing sailboats.

Trey's boat had not slowed down. I was so relieved that it hadn't actually hit us that it wasn't until the first enormous wave of its wake slapped the side of the *Swallow* that I woke up to what was going on.

Trey was trying to capsize me.

My fragile craft tipped violently to leeward and water began to pour into the footwell, much faster than the self-bailer could handle. In the space of a few seconds, we'd be over. Fortunately, my body and my instincts were working more quickly than my brain. I kept the sail tight to keep the wind and maintain our headway and threw myself back, hitching my butt right off the boat and hiking out until I was essentially straight, like some kind of human pontoon over the water. Three-quarters of my body—the heavy three quarters of my body—was outside the boat. I felt the *Swallow* begin to right itself.

This was both good and bad news. We were no longer shipping water. On the other hand, in the second or two that it would take for the wave to slide under the boat, the *Swallow* would rock back to its other side, the side I was on. When that happened, unless I moved very, very quickly, first my head and then my shoulders would slip under the cold waves. In all likelihood, I would be pulled off the boat.

I forced myself to keep leaning out to windward, waiting for my body to tell me the boat was righting itself. It was a risk, but I needed to be sure that, as I started moving my body weight back onto the boat, the water we'd shipped wouldn't pull the opposite side back down again. But if I waited too long and the boat tipped too far toward me, I was going to be taking a swim.

Finally, it came, the moment when the fulcrum had been reached, when my body knew we were safely upright. I jackknifed up. The Sunfish rocked dangerously, but stayed upright. Despite my best efforts, though, the sail lost its wind and flapped madly. We had no headway. We were literally dead in the water. But at least we weren't dead.

I knew I had almost no time before the second line of wake would hit the *Swallow* broadside and the whole nightmare began again. I needed to turn the little boat directly into the wave so its pointed prow could nose safely up and over the rough water. But to do that, I needed headway. I needed wind in my sail. I pulled the tiller toward me with one hand and yanked the sail in with the other.

"Come on, fill," I breathed (okay, I prayed). "Please fill."

The sail filled. If I'd had a hand free I would have done one of those fist pump things that athletes do.

The little boat jumped forward, and I used our momentum to turn its bow directly into the oncoming wake, which the *Swallow* obligingly sliced through as smoothly as a comb finding a center part. I could see the water in the footwell receding as the bailer did its work. We were out of danger.

The whole thing had taken no more than a few minutes, but Trey's boat by this time was well away, almost to the channel markers at the end of Skaket Point. It had not slackened its speed, nor come back to see the results of its little game.

So maybe I was wrong. Maybe Trey hadn't known it was me in the Sunfish. Maybe in his monumental self-absorption he hadn't even realized how close he'd come to capsizing it.

I watched, hardly daring to hope, as the *Mad Max* began to make the turn away from us and around the point into Little Crystal. And then I stared in disbelief as, instead of going through the markers, the sleek gray-black monster made a complete circle until it was pointed back at the *Swallow.*

This time there was no denying its intent. The *Mad Max* was coming back. At top speed.

There was nowhere to safely beach along the rocky shoreline to my left. The rocks would have made mincemeat of me and my little boat. To my other side, there was only the empty expanse of Big Crystal. Nickerson Island and the Outer Beach lay ahead, but too far ahead. I was alone on the bay with a crazy man. And I had nowhere to hide.

THIRTY-SIX

NOWHERE TO HIDE. The words seemed to echo in my skull. *Nowhere to hide.*

And then, in some kind of interior point/counterpoint, it came to me. *Jason's secret creek.* I could hide in the secret creek in the marshes behind Nickerson Island. If I could get to the island before Trey. Which was a pretty big if.

Both Trey and I were in the channel that circled the shallows created by the sandbars that stretched across to Nickerson. If I tacked around and stayed in the channel, following the route around the bars that Jason and I had taken the other day, there was no chance I'd get to the island before Trey got to me.

But I didn't have to stay in the channel. At this tide, the water over the bars would be about a foot deep. The *Swallow* drew only a couple of inches with the daggerboard out and the rudder tipped up. With the wind directly behind me, I wouldn't need the daggerboard and I could skim right over the shallows, making a straight shot to the island and then the river behind it in about five minutes. I had no doubt that Trey would try to follow me. But to get to the island, the *Mad Max* would have to stay in the looping detour of the channel around the shallows. It had taken Jason at least ten minutes in the Zodiac. The much heavier *Mad Max* would take longer, maybe even fifteen minutes.

I pulled the tiller toward me and let the sail out, turning the boat toward the bars and Nickerson Island. Looking over the side, I could see the deep darkness of the channel's weedy bottom change almost instantaneously into sandy bar only a foot or two below me. I pulled up the daggerboard. I was on my way.

Behind me, the *Mad Max* zoomed by harmlessly.

THE WIND STAYED with me all the way across the shallows, and soon I was dropping the daggerboard and tacking into the river behind Nickerson. I wasn't home free, though. The tide was going out fast, but I knew there was still enough water over the sandy mouth of the river for Trey's boat to get into the river. Before the island blocked my sight, I could see the *Mad Max* across the bay coming around the channel but still a good five minutes away.

I was glad when the island blocked my view of the channel. If I couldn't see Trey, he couldn't see me. I needed to find the spot that led into the secret creek, and I needed to find it fast. "Please, please, please," I prayed.

For the life of me, I couldn't see the entrance to the secret creek *at all*. There was a trick to finding it. *What was it?* I felt my brain fritzing as I moved into panic mode. What had Jason said?

"The opening is directly across from that high sand dune on Nickerson Island—you know, the one everyone used to run down when we were kids."

This, I knew, was not my memory working overtime. This was Jason's voice as clear as if he were right there with me in the boat. I didn't doubt it for a minute.

In about fifteen feet I would be exactly opposite the high dune to my left. To my right was, as far as I could tell, unbroken marsh. I knew that if I overshot the opening, I'd have to waste precious time pulling the *Swallow* off the solid peat of the marsh and trying to find the spot again.

I steered the boat along the marsh side of the river, so close that the grass on my right brushed the *Swallow* like a whispered warning. I was now exactly opposite Nickerson's high dune.

I yanked the tiller to turn the boat directly into the marsh grass and then quickly hauled up the daggerboard. In seconds I would know if I'd calculated correctly. In seconds, the boat would either slide over the small shelf of water and grass into the hidden creek or, more likely, drive itself onto a mud flat.

The *Swallow* glided over and through the grass and into the creek. Never had the words "safe harbor" been so real to me.

No time for celebrating. Time now for step two. I steered the *Swallow* across the creek and gently into the cordgrass on the other side until the marshy bottom took hold of the bow and held us fast. As quickly as I could, I uncleated the sail's halyard and let it down until it was just a heap of aluminum spars and nylon on the deck. I carefully crawled up to the bow, blessing the marsh grass for giving the very tippy boat some stability. Even more carefully, I stood and wrapped my hands around the light aluminum mast, then lifted it up and out of the shallow fiberglass cup in the deck that held it upright. I laid the mast down on top of the pile of sail and spars and heaved a huge sigh of relief. Now nothing of the boat could be seen from the river behind the island.

Nothing except you, you big dope.

I ducked down hastily and crawled back to the *Swallow*'s footwell, where I shoved aside enough of the sail that I could sit in it, knees up around my chin. To add insult to injury, a cold drizzle of rain, almost a mist, had begun, and I tried to wrap a bit of the sail around me to stay at least partially dry. I maneuvered my cell out of my jeans pocket, but still no bars. And I knew that even 911 wouldn't work if there were no cell towers in range. I considered the acres of treacherous, boggy marsh sheltering me but also effectively holding me hostage in my hiding place. There was nothing to do but wait . . . for what? My deliverance? Or my doom?

I HAD NOTHING TO do but think. Why would Trey go after me in clear sight of Mr. Logan? But he had. There was no doubt now that the man at the helm of that boat was after me.

The man at the helm of that boat . . .

Was it possible that the man at the helm of that boat *wasn't* Trey? What if Trey's "fancy boat," as Mr. Logan called it, was the *other* powerboat moored off Reedie's landing, the Chris-Craft, not the *Mad Max*? In that case, the *Mad Max* belonged to someone else. *Someone else like Krista's friend Curtis Henson?* Miles had said that Henson had an old family place on the hillside above Reedie's landing. That he had a boat moored off Reedie's where he and Krista met. Was the *Mad Max* Henson's boat, not Trey's? Was that Curtis Henson at the helm of that boat?

But, no. But Krista had told me that Curtis had been with her the night that Estelle was killed. Had Krista lied to me? Something in me protested the thought. Not Krista. Krista never lied. Plus, she didn't even like the guy. But still she'd given him an ironclad alibi. So, no, not Curtis Henson.

So it had to be Trey in the *Mad Max*. Had Mr. Logan told him I had Estelle's phone? I could just hear him, chatting away at Trey. "Do you know, I'm going to learn how to use one of those mobile cellular telephones. I have one that belonged to a friend of mine who passed away last week and Samantha Barnes is charging it up and she's going to teach me how to use it." And then, when Mr. Logan was sure I'd had time to make my escape, he probably took Trey into Bits and Bites to show him the phone. Which was gone. Because I'd taken it with me. And Trey knew it. *Oh, Mr. Logan, what have you done?*

Caught up in the dreadful dawning of what I was dealing with, it took me a second to register the soft chug of a powerboat coming slowly into the river behind Nickerson. The *Mad Max* had arrived.

I sat, huddled on my tiny craft, hardly daring to breathe. The motor got louder as it got closer to where I sat hidden and then, almost imperceptibly, the sound began to fade again. He was past me, checking the rest of the curving river. My hope was that once he came to the sandbar at the other end and knew I wasn't hiding behind one of the river's bends, he would assume he'd lost me, turn the boat, and leave the way he'd come.

I heard the sound of the craft coming back. And then, as if in a nightmare, the motor stopped, then cut out. It sounded very close to where I sat huddled in the marsh.

"Sam? Are you back in there somewhere? I think you must be. But it's okay. It's just me, Norman Logan."

THIRTY-SEVEN

M R. LOGAN. NOT Trey. Not Curtis Henson. Mr. Logan.

My first reaction was a wave of relief. *Of course.* He'd come out to tell me everything was okay, that Trey was gone. It didn't surprise me that Mr. Logan had no idea how powerful the wake of that borrowed boat could be. He'd only ever used it for fishing before.

But something stopped me from answering. Other memories, scraps of conversation were coming back.

"*. . . she was there alone. . . .*"

"*. . . she controlled the purse strings. . . .*"

"*. . . it might just upset her. . . .*"

"*. . . Mr. Logan was just here yesterday. . . .*"

"*. . . she told me that he had been there with her that night, that she had proof. . . .*"

"*. . . he says I got that confused. . . .*"

And the photo of an old, bald guy on a dock with the twinkling lights behind him. *The old, bald guy was Mr. Logan.* Mr. Logan prematurely aged by his illness, his thick hair temporarily wiped out by chemo. Almost unrecognizable. Almost but not quite.

Mr. Logan, whose last chance to beat cancer had been a hugely expensive treatment with no guarantee of success. Mr. Logan whose notoriously cheap wife had all the money and called all the shots. Had she refused to pay for that treatment?

In my mind's eye, I looked at the photo again. Yes, definitely Mr. Logan. But behind him not twinkling lights, as I had initially thought, but what as kids we used to call falling leaves—the last glowing embers from fireworks flickering as they fell to the ground. That photograph was of Mr. Logan watching Fourth of July fireworks, not from his own dock, which he didn't have, but from the dock at the Alden Pond boatyard in front of the Logan Inn.

Mr. Logan, who supposedly had been too ill to come to work for weeks. That's why, Jenny had told me, his wife had been closing up the restaurant by herself. *"She was there alone . . ."* when she'd come out to watch the fireworks and had had her stroke. *"She might have made it if they'd found her earlier."*

Mr. Logan not sick at home. Mr. Logan calmly watching fireworks while his wife's life had slipped away.

What had Suzanne said about Estelle? *"She told me that he had been there with her that night, that she had proof."* Suzanne hadn't been talking about an illicit romance as I'd assumed. She'd been talking about Mr. Logan and his wife.

No wonder he'd looked like he'd wished he hadn't mentioned Suzanne when we talked at Bits and Bites. No wonder he'd tried to discourage me from visiting her. *"It might just upset her,"* he'd said. No wonder he'd blown off his meeting with Miles and gone directly to the nursing home after our interview. *"Mr. Logan was just here yesterday,"* Jillian had said, *"We hadn't seen him for a while."* It wasn't only me Mr. Logan needed to convince of Suzanne's failing memory. He needed to convince Suzanne herself. *". . . he says I got that confused."*

Going one step further, had Estelle shown Mr. Logan

the photo? Had she been blackmailing him? Were his regular visits to the Bayview Grill to meet Estelle and pay her off? When had he had enough? When had he decided that Estelle and her demands were too much? That Estelle had to die?

One thing was for certain. The man at the helm of that boat was Mr. Logan.

And no matter what he said, that was definitely not okay.

THIRTY-EIGHT

~~~~~~~~~

FROM MY HIDING place in the high grass, I heard the unmistakable splash of an anchor being dropped.

Mr. Logan was settling in for the long haul, prepared to wait until cold or hunger or thirst drew me out. I bet the *Mad Max* was outfitted with an entire minibar. Maybe even a coffee maker. The vision of a mug of fresh coffee danced enticingly before my eyes. Right about now, I would kill for some coffee. *Nice choice of words, Sam.*

"Samantha, my dear? Can she hear me, I wonder?"

Mr. Logan. Talking to me. Or maybe to himself. Either way, it was creepy.

"I think you must be back in that marsh somewhere, so I'll just wait for you to come out. I know you saw that photograph of me on Estelle's mobile cellular telephone."

Honest to god, if you say "mobile cellular telephone" one more time, I am going to lose it.

"I could see the photograph over your shoulder. I'm sure you're wondering about it."

You got that right.

"So perhaps I can explain some things to you, help you to understand why I had to do what I did."

Good luck with that.

"You probably have never been given a sign, Samantha. But I have. Twice. The first, of course, was when Darlene had her stroke."

Darlene. Somehow I had never associated Mrs. Logan with anything as personal as a first name.

"It was the Fourth of July. I hadn't been out of my bed for weeks. But for some reason I had more energy than I'd felt for some time. I thought I could manage to drive over to the restaurant and watch the fireworks from the dock. I knew they wouldn't be very impressive from that far away, but I just wanted to see the fireworks, even from a distance, one last time before I died."

My heart almost went out to my captor. But whatever sympathy I might have felt for him was short-lived.

"Everybody was gone and I knew Darlene was busy closing up, so I just went out on the dock and waited for the fireworks to start. They'd just begun when Darlene came out onto the dock, too, I suppose for the same reason I did. She was surprised to find me there. She gave me this odd look, like she didn't know who I was. I asked her if she was okay. She'd been feeling rather unwell all day, making quite a fuss about it, which wasn't like her. She didn't believe in being sick. I don't think the woman ever really believed *I* was sick. I think she just thought I was trying to get attention."

Yes, that sounded like Mrs. Logan.

"Anyway, she took another step toward me, so close I could have touched her, and then one side of her face just sort of slipped down. And then she just *toppled* over at my feet. It was quite a surprise, let me tell you. She was lying on the dock, looking up at me but not really seeing me, if you know what I mean. She tried to say something, but it was all garbled. I knew she was having a stroke but I wasn't quite sure what to do."

Maybe call 911?

"And then it came to me. I had a choice. Darlene's life or mine. With Darlene gone, I could sell the restaurant, get the therapy that would save my life. All I had to do was *nothing*. Just as Darlene had done nothing to save my life. So that's what I did. Nothing. Except watch the fireworks. They were also a sign, of course."

Of course they were. The Fourth of July fireworks, watched by hundreds of other people that night, were a sign meant just for you.

"A sign of the beginning of my new life," Mr. Logan continued, blessedly unaware of my skepticism that the Universe was on his side. "When they were over, I could see that Darlene was still breathing, but only barely. I waited a while, maybe another hour or so, until she stopped breathing altogether."

And then he said it. I almost couldn't believe what I was hearing.

"So you see, Samantha, I didn't *kill* my wife. I simply let her die."

A distinction without a difference, I wanted to shout. I didn't of course. I just huddled and hugged my knees and wished I was anywhere but here, having a one-sided conversation in my head with a cuddly, cold-blooded killer.

"The next morning, I called the police and told them that I'd woken up to find that Darlene hadn't come home the night before. When they came to the house later to tell me that they'd found her body on the dock, I cried. My wife was dead. I cried from happiness."

Great. You were happy. But not for long, I bet.

As if he'd heard my thoughts, Mr. Logan said, "Of course, I didn't know about Estelle and the photograph then. I didn't know until she told me a few days later. Apparently, after everyone else had left the restaurant that night she'd stayed on, drinking up on the deck. Then she fell asleep and didn't wake up until she heard the booms from the fireworks. She decided to try to take a picture with her mobile cellular telephone, even from that distance. She didn't register me sitting out on the dock, she was too focused on capturing the fireworks. It wasn't until a few days later that she figured out what she had."

What she had was a motive for you to kill her.

"She came to me, showed me the photograph on her mobile cellular telephone. She'd just got my head in it and a little bit of the dock and the last of the fireworks, but it was clear where I was and when. And she said the camera keeps a record of the date and time when you take a photograph. She said nobody else knew, just her, but Suzanne told me when I was visiting her at Shawme Manor that Estelle said she'd seen her there. Suzanne said she never believed her, that Estelle was always talking trash, as she called it, about other people. And usually I could convince her she got it wrong, that she was confused. But it worried me."

I bet it worried you.

"Anyway," Mr. Logan continued, "at first Estelle wasn't all that demanding. I was sick and I really didn't have any money. I think she really just liked her power over me, her old boss. So every month, like clockwork, we met under the deck at the restaurant and I gave her a little money. But once I sold the restaurant and got my therapy and was given my life back, she got quite greedy. I'm not a big drinker, but I must say I really needed that Manhattan before I met her each month. I tried to explain to her that I needed all my money for the new restaurant, for my *new life*, but she wouldn't *listen*, she wouldn't *understand*."

This was not good.

"After Estelle had her accident, I thought the problem was solved. Nobody cared that she was dead. Nobody was looking for that mobile cellular telephone."

Something here was out of whack. But I was too exhausted to figure it out. And anyway, Mr. Logan wasn't done yet.

"I held on to the darn thing thinking it might be fun to

take photographs of Archibald if I could ever get it to work for me. When you offered to show me how, I thought that was so nice of you."

That'll teach you, Sam. No good deed, etc.

"And then I found you looking at that picture of me. So I knew I'd have to explain things to you. That was all I was trying to do out there on the bay, you know. Trying to get you to slow down enough so I could talk to you. Explain. Explain that I didn't kill my wife. I simply . . . let her die. I just needed you to *listen*. I just needed you to *understand*."

And what if I don't? Don't listen, don't understand? Do I end up dead like Estelle?

"So I'm sure you understand now what happened, why I need that mobile cellular telephone back, Samantha. Other people may not understand like you do. Why don't you just come out and we'll just throw that telephone in the bay and forget all about this?"

For a moment, I wanted to believe him. He might be crazy enough to do just what he said if I played along, if I convinced him I had *listened*, that I *understood*.

And then I remembered his words from our conversation at Bits and Bites. The words he'd said with such peculiar, unnerving intensity.

"Nothing is more important than your life. You have to fight for it. Illness will try to take it from you. Acts of God will try to take it from you. Other people will try to take it from you. You can't let them. It's yours, yours to live. You can't let anything or anyone get in the way of that."

No way am I getting in the way of that, chief.

The challenge was going to be how I was going to get *out* of the way of that.

THIRTY-NINE

W ELL, SAMANTHA," MR. Logan said, "I really do have to be going if I'm going to beat the tide out of the river."

He was right. The tide was going out fast. Soon the water over the sandy delta where the river met the bay would be too shallow for the *Mad Max* to cross back into the main channel.

"I'll wait for you out on the bay, shall I?"

The *Mad Max* rumbled back to life. I listened carefully as the soft chug gradually diminished, trying to determine if Mr. Logan really intended to go back into the bay. Which I did not for a moment believe.

What I believed he'd done, what it had sounded like to me, was taken the *Mad Max* in the other direction, back behind the first bend in the river. There he could drop the anchor at the very tip of the bend, then let out the anchor line until the *Mad Max* drifted back to where it would be hidden from me when I eventually ventured out into the river. And there Mr. Logan would wait for me.

Better then to sit tight? Eventually somebody might come looking for me. Maybe. But probably not. There was no reason for anyone to think I'd be out on the bay. What had started out as a gray day was now rapidly getting colder and wetter. Nobody in their right mind would be out on the water. Not to mention that, as far as anyone knew, I didn't have access to a boat. Jason might go looking for Trey, but Trey was somewhere on dry land. And he'd never be looking for Mr. Logan. No, nobody was coming to find me. And Mr. Logan in his nice dry boat could easily keep his vigil up for another twenty-four hours, maybe longer. And in this wet and this cold, exposed to the elements, perhaps overnight, how long could I last?

But what choice did I have? Try to make a run for it in the *Swallow*? Of course, I reasoned to myself, if I couldn't see Mr. Logan in the *Mad Max*, he couldn't see me either. That argument didn't hold water for long. I knew that all he had to do was every few minutes pull the boat noiselessly forward with the anchor line and peek around the bend. If I wasn't in view, he could drift noiselessly back again. If I was in view, he had me. Worst-case scenario, he'd start up the engine, run me down right there in the river. Best case, I'd make it out to the bay, where the whole cat and mouse game would resume until out of sheer exhaustion I lost control and my fragile craft would capsize. Death by hypothermia. Which wasn't much of a best case. And my old friend Mr. Logan would get away with murder. Again.

Unless . . .

I KNEW THAT EVERY minute I waited, exhaustion and cold and my cramping legs would make me that much less capable of what I had to do. But it couldn't be too soon. Maybe not for another fifteen minutes or so. For what I had planned, timing the tide was going to be crucial. With no cell service and thus no tide chart available, I was going to have to make my calculations based on the tides from two days earlier, which I'd noted because of my sail with Trey.

No sailor goes out on Crystal Bay without first checking the tide chart. So if the tides change by approximately an hour each day . . . I did the math in my head.

The minutes ticked by interminably. Finally I thought the time was right.

I crawled awkwardly up to the bow of the boat, stood up cautiously, and dropped the mast back into its step. Crouching back down I used the daggerboard to push the *Swallow* off the marsh bank and back into the creek. Still kneeling on the bow, I used the board to paddle the boat across to the other side of the creek and slide silently over the grassy hummock into the river. My heart was in my mouth.

There was no *Mad Max* in sight.

I crept back into the Sunfish's cockpit and dropped the daggerboard into its slot. As quietly as I could, I raised the sail. I was lucky that a couple of seagulls chose that moment to fight over a blue crab that one of them had snagged, and their angry squawks covered the creak of the sail's hoops sliding up the mast. I noted that the wind would be coming over the Sunfish's back quarter. This was good. We'd be on a close reach, always the fastest point of sail. The mouth of the river was only about a hundred yards away. We could make it in maybe two minutes.

I pulled in the sail, hoping the squeak of the pulleys wouldn't give me away, and the *Swallow* took off like the champ she was. Almost immediately I could see the water becoming progressively shallower as we flew toward the sandy delta where the river met the deeper channel of the bay. I tried to gauge how deep the water was going to be over that bar. It looked like about a foot. Fine for the *Swallow*. Not so fine for the *Mad Max*. The *Mad Max* would be trapped in the river. I crossed the fingers of the hand guiding the tiller. If I could have, I would have crossed myself. I told myself my luck was holding.

I spoke too soon.

Behind me, I heard the roar of a Yamaha 250 engine. I

didn't look back. He'd seen me. I'd always known this was a possibility. That's why I'd waited as long as I had. Mr. Logan had to know what would happen to the *Mad Max*, to himself, if he rammed his boat at top speed into the delta. Even if he rammed into me first, he wouldn't have enough time to stop. It would be a disaster when he hit the bar. He knew that. He'd have to reduce his speed. And, my reasoning was, if he reduced his speed, I'd have more time, I'd have a chance.

I could hear nothing but the roar of the motor in my ears. I could see nothing but the waters beneath the *Swallow* becoming rapidly shallower. And still the motor roared behind me. I could not believe what I was hearing.

He wasn't slowing down. He didn't care. He didn't care about anything but stopping me.

Still I didn't look back. What was the point? I'd either make it to the mouth of the river and over the shallows to safety or I'd be mowed down by two tons of fiberglass and steel.

"*Please, please, please,*" I whispered to the Universe.

And at that moment, a gust of wind caught the *Swallow*'s sail and literally blew us into the shallow water over the bar. Seconds later, I heard the monster behind us ground itself with a horrible screech of buckling fiberglass and metal.

I had no time to rejoice. The *Swallow* lurched and I realized that the daggerboard was digging into the soft sand of the delta. I yanked the board up and let out the sail to a full run, the wind directly behind me, the only point of sail I could steer without the board down. And glorioso! We were on our way once more, gliding over the bar on barely ten inches of water. Finally I looked back at the *Mad Max*. All was silence. Until the wailing began. Mr. Logan, climbing out of the wheelhouse, bloodied, shaking, and sobbing in a way that was almost as horrifying as his earlier, deluded monologue.

"You don't get to take my life away from me," he

screamed. "First, you won't sell the restaurant when you know it's the only way I can pay for that treatment. You want to let me die. Then you blackmail me, a little more each time, taunting me, watching my dream die. And now you pretend to be all sweet and nice and then you *steal* that mobile cellular phone from me, so you can steal my *life* away from me *again*. . . ."

He'd conflated us—Mrs. Logan, Estelle, myself—into one monstrous woman intent on denying him his life. It was chilling, but it was also somehow terribly sad.

I was grateful when the words trailed off behind me. I gave my full attention to getting over the delta. Any shallower and I'd be aground, forced to drag the *Swallow* across the next twenty feet to the channel. What I did not need at this point was to be trapped on the sand with my friend Mr. Logan.

Twelve inches of water. The bar continued to slide by below. Maybe eleven inches. Still eleven. And then, abruptly, the sand sloped away and the *Swallow* was in the deep dark of the channel.

I dropped the daggerboard, pulled in the sail, and almost fell off the boat.

Coming toward me was a twenty-foot Grady-White, the words "Harbor Patrol" emblazoned on its side.

FORTY

~~~~~~

I POINTED THE NOSE of the *Swallow* into the wind to slow my headway as the Grady-White reduced its speed to a crawl and pulled up next to me. Jason was at the wheel. I wanted to kiss him all over his face. Jenny, Helene, Krista, and Miles were leaning over the side of the boat, asking a million questions at a million miles a minute and sounding like nothing so much as a gaggle of geese quacking. A gaggle of geese that, at that moment, I also wanted to kiss all over their faces.

Miles tossed me a line, which I cleated onto the *Swallow*'s bow, and Jenny and Helene helped me up the stepped stern of the Grady-White. The gabbling continued, and again I couldn't really make any sense of it. It occurred to me I might be in shock. It also apparently occurred to Jason, who started bossing Krista around, telling her where she could find a blanket and brandy. It was very satisfying to watch someone boss Krista around.

Through all the commotion, though, Jason had never moved from the wheel. He'd said nothing to me, barely even looked at me. But one look at his set, drawn face told me why. This was a man keeping himself under iron control. His eyes were fixed on the *Mad Max* up ahead, lying awkwardly to one side, like a beached whale. Mr. Logan was nowhere to be seen, probably down below, for which I was profoundly grateful. Jason moved the throttle out of neutral and pushed it up slightly. We began moving very slowly up the channel, the *Swallow* trailing along behind like an obedient puppy.

Jason was steering with one hand. The other held the ship-to-shore radio as he barked out orders to invisible minions. I was seated only a few feet away in the relatively sheltered bow of the boat but the wind whipped his words away from me. My guess was he was telling someone he'd found me. Not that there was anyone left to tell. They were all on the boat.

Helene came forward with one of those silvery blanket things that you see in photos of people who have finished the marathon that never look very warm but, it turns out, actually are. Krista twisted the cap off the hip flask of brandy that Jason apparently kept at the ready in the boat's first aid kit and helped my trembling hands move it to my lips. Lately I seemed to be spending a lot of my time in blankets drinking brandy. This was not a good sign.

When he was done telling whatever to whoever, Jason clipped the ship-to-shore back into its holder. "We're just going to sit tight here and keep an eye on things until the crew brings the inflatable out and we can take him in," he said to his unorthodox crew.

Finally, he turned his attention to me. "Does he have a gun?"

I couldn't have been more surprised if he'd asked me if Santa Claus had a gun.

"Of course he doesn't have a gun," I said, almost reflexively adding something along the lines of *Mr. Logan would never have a gun,* but catching myself.

"Sorry," I said. "I mean, no, I don't think he has a gun.

If he'd had a gun, he would have used it." Not necessarily, I realized as I said it. Hard to aim a gun from a speeding motorboat at a girl on a bobbing sailboat. "Instead he tried to capsize me and when that didn't work, run me down."

Jason got very, very still at that, though the gabbling from the geese rose to a new high.

"Everybody needs to be quiet," Jason said in a voice that brooked no argument. The geese quieted themselves.

"Why?" Jason asked me. "Why did he try to run you down?"

"Because I have Estelle's cell phone, the one with the photo."

"The photo of him killing piping plovers?"

For a moment, I couldn't understand what he was asking. "No," I said, "the photo of him on the dock at Alden boatyard the night his wife died."

Jason shook his head slightly, as if he'd heard me wrong. But before he could say anything, Jenny, against orders, broke in.

"You mean *Mr. Logan*?" she asked. "Estelle had a photo of *Mr. Logan* at Alden that Fourth of July, that night his wife died from a stroke?"

"Not quite," I corrected her. "That night his wife had a stroke and he *let* her die."

Jason waved toward the *Mad Max*. "So you're telling me that's *Mr. Logan* on that boat?"

I nodded.

"Not Trey Gorman?"

"Not Trey Gorman."

"But Trey Gorman killed Estelle."

I shook my head. "Nope. That was Mr. Logan, too."

"Well," Jason said thoughtfully, "if Logan killed her for the phone, it would explain why Gorman didn't have it and wanted your mother's notebook so badly."

Something bothered me there, but I couldn't put my finger on it.

"It's good enough," Jason said almost to himself. "Even McCauley's got to admit it's good enough."

And for a moment, I felt the glow of vindication.

But not for long.

"And all this," Helene said incredulously, waving a beringed hand to encompass the *Mad Max* and my blanket-and-brandy thing going on. "This was your idea of being very, very careful?"

Helene was not pleased. Indeed, it would be fair to say that Helene was very, very displeased. I burrowed deeper into the blanket until only my eyes peeked out.

"That's where you went this morning?" she asked. "To confront this, this *murderer*?"

"I didn't go to confront Mr. Logan," I protested. "I had no idea Mr. Logan was a murderer. I thought Trey killed Estelle. I just wanted to check something out. I'd seen a cell phone on the kitchen counter at Bits and Bites. Mr. Logan doesn't own a cell, doesn't even know how to use one. I just wanted to see if it was still there and see if maybe it was Estelle's."

"We won't even go into why you didn't tell *me* where you were going," Jason said. "For now, just tell us what happened."

"Well, it was like this . . ." I began. I told him about finding the phone, seeing some compromising photos of people I didn't recognize (Krista made a little noise there, like she was going to interrupt but I glared at her and she shut up). "But Trey taking out plover nests and chicks was unmistakable," I said.

"But you didn't recognize Mr. Logan?" Jenny asked.

"No," I said. "Not at first. He looked so different, very old and haggard and bald from his chemo. Plus, I was too focused on Trey, and when he actually showed up at Bits and Bites, all I could think about was getting away from him."

I told them about taking the *Swallow*, what had happened out on the bay and then behind Nickerson Island.

"I hid in your secret creek," I said to Jason. I couldn't find the words to explain how his voice had come to me, how he had told me how to find the creek. "You saved my life."

For the first time Jason looked directly at me and allowed himself to show some emotion. "You saved your own life," he said, his voice rough. "I was looking for you on Trey's boat, but it would never have occurred to me to go behind Nickerson. No one takes a big boat like that back there. I figured he'd be heading out to the ocean."

"Whatever," I said. *I knew what I knew.*

I told them about figuring out too late that Mr. Logan had killed his wife, that Estelle had been blackmailing him for it. I did not mention my initial suspicions of Curtis Henson, of course. I really did not see any reason to bring that up now that we knew who'd actually killed Estelle. Krista would just have to lump it.

"But what I don't get," Jason said when I'd finally finished my piece, "is why you didn't tell me about seeing the cell phone in the first place."

"You were asleep," I said weakly.

Miles broke in. *"Wait? What?* He spent *the night* with you? What did I miss?"

I ignored him. Let him think what he wanted. It wasn't true and it would never be true.

"You could have woken me up," Jason said, his eyes back on the *Mad Max.* "Why didn't you wake me?" He wasn't being accusatory. He really wanted to know.

"You were so tired. I wasn't going to be long. I just needed to check on that cell. I'd be back before you even woke up, I thought."

"I don't believe that," Jason said quietly. We could have been the only two people on the boat at that moment. This was just between Jason and me. "Tell me the real reason."

I waited a beat. He wouldn't like the truth, but I was done avoiding our issues. "Because of what you always say," I said, almost in a whisper.

"What?" he asked gently. "What do I always say?"

"You always say, 'I'll take it from here.' That's what you say every time I try to work with you. Just like how Krista always says I'm off the story."

Krista looked up from where she'd been sitting on the equipment locker madly scribbling notes on a steno pad. Of course.

"I was just trying to keep you safe," she said.

"I was just trying to keep you safe," Jason said at the same time.

Suddenly I was sick and tired of being condescended to by Jason and bossed around by Krista. Well, okay, she *was* my boss, but still.

"I don't *want* to be kept safe," I said, sitting up and throwing off the blanket. "How come *I* have to be safe but you two get to stick your noses into all sorts of stuff?"

"It's my *job*," Jason said.

"It's my *job*," Krista said at the same time.

This Greek chorus thing was beginning to get to me.

"You *weren't* doing your job, Krista. You were trying to keep *me* from doing *mine*. You told me to cover Estelle's death and every time I tried to do that, you shut me down. You were completely in McCauley's pocket." *Which*, I didn't say, *is so much better than being the lover of a married man who I thought for a brief moment might be trying to kill me.*

"I shut you down, you big dope, because I suspected this was a murder."

"You *did*?"

"Of course I did. Granted, you raised the alarm. What with all your questions and all."

I looked at her in disbelief. "You told me I didn't have anything to go on!"

"Well, it was when you convinced me that Trey had deliberately stolen your mother's notebook. . . ." I'd *convinced* her? "So I took it to McCauley and he told me he was already working on it with Jason."

"McCauley?" I asked, incredulous. I looked back at Jason. "You were working with McCauley, too?"

"Of course I was," Jason said. "I told you it was his turf."

"He believed it was murder?" I asked.

Jason glanced over at me and had the good grace to look a little ashamed. "Not until I made the point, er, sorry, *your* point about the body being faceup."

I couldn't believe this.

"So both of you were working on leads *that I gave you,* but you still wanted me to let the case alone?" Suddenly I was angry again. "May I remind you that if I had left the case alone, you would *never* have known about Estelle's blackmail schemes, would *never* have known about Trey, who, even if he wasn't a murderer was a horrible person and completely corrupt, would *never* have known that Mr. Logan let his wife die and killed Estelle because he was being blackmailed by her. And may I remind you that *I* have the proof." I whipped Estelle's cell out of my hoodie pocket with a rather overly dramatic flourish.

"So," I said, "I have the same question that you had for me. *Why didn't you tell me?*"

"I couldn't," Jason said simply. "McCauley couldn't either. We couldn't risk it."

"Risk what?" I asked. "That I would keep finding out stuff and figure out who actually killed Estelle? Because I was ahead of you every step of the way."

"No," he said quietly. "We couldn't risk your life."

He had a point. I could see how they might want to keep this amateur detective off the case so that she wouldn't be, for instance, mowed down by a crazy man in a two-ton speedboat.

"Like that stopped her," Jenny said, and there was a certain amount of pride in her voice. Jenny always thought better of me than I deserved. But, still, I loved her for it.

Miles took up the banner. "Yeah, looks like she was going to risk her life no matter who told her she couldn't."

"Thanks, guys," I said. "But, honestly, I never intended to risk my life. That's why Jason was camping on my couch last night. I'm not a total idiot. And I did try to call him after I found Estelle's phone, but Harbor Patrol told me he was out on the bay with no cell service. And, believe me, if I could have called or texted for help once I was out on the bay myself, I would have."

They looked very disappointed at that, either because they had wanted to believe that I was the superhero they'd just invented or because I wasn't sleeping with Jason Captiva. Or both. Probably both.

This riveting discussion about my bravery or lack of same was interrupted by the sound of another engine. I stood and looked back over the stern to see the Harbor Patrol inflatable coming up behind us manned by two men and a woman in official patrol khakis and windbreakers. They were also all wearing holsters with guns in them. And what looked like bulletproof vests over their windbreakers.

I looked more closely at Jason. He, too, was wearing a gun. My heart began to thud. What if Mr. Logan *did* have a gun? *What were you* thinking, *Sam, putting yourself and others in danger?*

For a moment I wished I could rewind my life and go back to that first night at the Bayview Grill. That night when my only concern was explaining to Helene how to match an appetizer with an entrée. My future self would make sure that I'd never go wandering under that deck, never find Estelle, so that none of the rest would have happened. *And a murderer would still be living among us,* I reminded myself. *Right. There was that.*

The inflatable tied up behind the Grady-White. One of the guys with guns came up over our stern.

He greeted Jason with a brief, "Sir," handed Jason a vest, and took the wheel.

"Get these people away from here," Jason said to him as he shrugged on the vest, "and keep them away."

"Got it," the other man said.

Jason nodded at him and started back to the inflatable.

"Wait!" I cried out. *What if he does have a gun?* I wanted to say to him. *Just because he didn't try to shoot me doesn't mean he doesn't have a gun. Don't go. Don't risk yourself. You're the boss. Let the people who work for you handle it. Stay here. Stay safe.*

This, I realized suddenly, was how Jason had felt when I kept charging off to do what I did. What I *had* to do.

Jason had paused, was looking at me. I bit back my words.

"What happens now?" I asked him instead.

"Now," he said grimly, "I go get the bastard."

"Good," I said. "You do that."

FORTY-ONE

J ASON GOT INTO the inflatable and we in the Grady-White started back at full speed toward the municipal pier. Jenny, Helene, and Miles sat huddled together on the bench in front of the wheelhouse, silent for once. Somehow everything had gotten very, very serious. I sat apart from them at the bow of the boat, alone in my misery.

About ten minutes later, all of which I had spent whispering *please, please, please keep him safe*, the radio squawked. Our pilot picked it up, listened, said "Roger" (I swear, he actually said "roger"), and put the radio back on its clip.

"It's okay," he shouted up to us. "They got him. No resistance. He didn't even have a gun." He actually sounded disappointed. *What, would you have felt better if he'd started shooting?*

Back at the municipal pier, two of my not-so-favorite people were waiting for me—Chief McCauley and Jenny's husband, Roland. McCauley I could understand, but Roland?

"What's he doing here?" I hissed at Jenny.

"I texted him," she hissed back. "Once we got back into cell range, I texted him. You are going to need a lawyer."

I was going to need a lawyer?

Apparently so. Roland took me aside and patiently explained the situation to me. "You are going to have to make a statement to Chief McCauley," he said in his most lawyerly voice. "And he, I have already determined through our little chat before you arrived, does not like you. Not at all."

At this point he did something that changed my opinion of Roland Singleton forever. He smiled and said, "Which, in my estimation, speaks very well of you."

I choked back a laugh, and Roland turned back into a lawyer again. "He considers that you have obstructed the course of an investigation and withheld valuable information."

"Only because he wouldn't listen to me," I sputtered.

"Be that as it may, I believe you should retain me as your lawyer. In that way, I can advise you as you answer his questions and depose your statement."

I nodded. This sounded good to me. Roland, I realized, was someone you could depend on. Roland would have my back.

And then, still with his lawyer face on, Roland added, "After which, you and I will go out and get lit."

WHICH IS EXACTLY what we did. Well, not immediately. First Helene insisted on taking me home, but not before herself taking on Chief McCauley, who wanted me down at the station immediately to give my statement.

"This young woman has just helped to apprehend a suspect in a murder case," she said in her best I-am-the-town-librarian voice. "That suspect tried *twice* to kill her. If she is not in shock yet, she soon will be. I am taking her home to recover from her ordeal."

Truly, until that moment I had not thought of it as an

ordeal, but now it seemed like exactly the right description. Trust a librarian. They work with words.

McCauley still looked like he wanted to clap me into irons, but he let us go.

Helene shooed the rest of the gang away as we got into her car. "She needs a bath and a nap and her dog. Not you lot."

She was right. The bath was amazing. The nap was amazing. And Diogi was amazing. As Helene pushed the door to the ell open, he jumped off the bed (which he now clearly believed was his). I dropped to my knees to hug him. He rushed at me and then, sensing something, stopped short. He sat (Diogi sat!) in front of me, looked at my face, and very carefully and very deliberately raised one paw and gently put it to my cheek.

I gathered my dog into my arms and I cried.

When I was all cried out, Helene ran me a bath, and then ordered me into bed. Diogi settled himself at my feet and Helene settled herself on the couch with what looked like the new Scottoline mystery.

"Hey," I protested sleepily, "I thought I was supposed to get the new Scottoline." And then I conked out.

I slept for what seemed like days, though when I finally opened my eyes and looked at the bedside clock, it was only four in the afternoon. Damn. There was still time for that little talk with McCauley.

"Did I wake you?" Helene asked when she saw me stirring.

I'd been dimly aware as I'd come back to consciousness that Helene had been speaking softly into her cell.

"No," I said. "I'm not much of a napper." Which was true. I don't think I've napped since I was two years old. Apparently, it took an *ordeal* to get me to sleep during the day. "What's going on?"

"Miles wants to know how you are doing. Jenny wants to know how you are doing. Even Krista wants to know how you are doing."

I laughed at that.

"McCauley wants to know when you're coming in to make your statement."

I groaned.

"And the harbormaster wants you to call him and sends you his love."

I sat straight up in bed. "Wait. *What?*"

Helene smiled. "And I quote, 'Give her my love.'"

Whoa. Where did that come from?

To cover my confusion, I got up, began pulling clothes out of my minuscule closet and throwing them on my bed. There was no time, I told myself, to call Jason. I'll do it later, I told myself.

"What do you wear to a deposition?" I asked Helene.

"That one," Helene said, pointing to the dress I'd worn for my visit to the nursing home. "The one that makes you look like a nun."

Okay, that settles it. Tomorrow that dress goes to the Salvation Army.

R OLAND WAS AMAZING. He was like some kind of intellectual bodyguard. Every time McCauley tried to insinuate that I'd been impeding his investigation, Roland was in there, calmly pointing out that I had indeed reported my findings to law enforcement, that is, the Harbor Patrol, just not *his* branch of law enforcement.

In no time at all, McCauley had learned his lesson and simply shut up while I told my story. And to give him credit (some, not a lot), even his big red face got a little pale when I got to the part about almost being run down by the *Mad Max.*

Roland was true to his word (because a good lawyer is always true to his word) and squired me over to the best bar in Fair Harbor, the Windward. The Windward is notable for several things. First is its fine selection of scotches. The second is its decor—the walls are literally plastered with license plates from all fifty states and going back decades. The third is its fish and chips with homemade tartar sauce (the secret ingredient of which I am sure is Tabasco sauce. Lots of Tabasco sauce). The place was bustling when we got there, but we managed to snag a booth and Roland ordered us some fish and chips with the famous tartar sauce. He also ordered a Johnnie Walker Red for himself and, without asking, a brandy for me.

"You know," I said, "I don't actually like brandy."

"You've had a shock, Samantha," he said firmly. "Brandy it is."

I gave in. I kind of wanted to ask Mr. Bossy to order me a blanket, too, but refrained. He had his good points—most notably a remarkable ability to keep Chief McCauley in line—but Roland was Roland.

However, by our second round, Roland was no longer Roland. Roland was Rolly. It turns out, Rolly was a pretty fun guy. He told good stories about his early career as a public prosecutor back in the day when the most serious crime on the docket was shell fishermen misrepresenting Fair Harbor oysters as Wellfleets.

"Not that I am minimizing the offense, you understand," he said in a solemn parody of his usual demeanor. "It is equivalent to calling any sparkling wine true champagne." He considered this statement for a moment and then added, "Indeed, it is far worse."

When I snorted with laughter, he consented to smile, admitting in his own way to a sense of humor.

"You are full of surprises, Roland," I said.

"Rolly, please," he said with grave, and slightly tipsy, courtesy.

"Rolly," I said and added—since we were talking like something out of *Downton Abbey*—"and please do call me Sam."

"Sam it is."

We clinked glasses.

By the time Jenny found us, Rolly and I were firm friends. He'd solidified my warm feelings for him when he said, quite out of the blue, in the way one does when one is on their third Johnnie Walker Red, "She's an amazing woman, you know."

It took me a minute. "Jenny, you mean?"

"Of course, Jenny. What other amazing woman do I know?" He paused, aware of his gaffe. "My apologies. Other than present company, of course." The man could out-Grantham Lord Grantham.

"She's incredibly intelligent," he said. "Did you know that she does all the accounting for my law practice?"

"She works for you?" I was surprised. And then I felt guilty that I was surprised. When was the last time I had asked Jenny anything about her life?

"Well, she does it for free, of course," he said in his old Rolandy way. As if wives were expected to work for their husbands for free. I was on my way to not liking him very much again, when Rolly came back.

"And she also has that amazing—what do they call it?— emotional IQ," Rolly said. "This extraordinary ability to see below the surface, to understand why people do what they do. She knows, for instance, why you came back to the Cape."

"She does, does she?" *Because I would really like to know that.*

"Absolutely," Rolly said. "For one thing, she says you've never been able to fill what she calls the Cape-shaped hole in your heart."

I thought about that for a moment. It was true that everything had changed for me when my parents traded in their L.L.Bean boots for flip-flops. My visits to Florida were spent trying to keep up with their healthy lifestyle, which meant *hours* of yoga and swimming and jogging and tennis and eating nothing but tofu and what my mother insisted on calling "veggies." Steamed. With no butter. Also, it was very hot in Florida. The sun was always shining. That can get on your nerves after a while. My parents had friends, but nobody who really *knew* them. Or me. We had no history there, no connection to the land, the place itself. After a few trips, I had been amazed to find that I missed the Cape, maybe even missed mud season a little. I'd tried to talk my parents into moving back to the Cape until it occurred to me that maybe I wanted them to move back *so that I would have a home again*.

Of course, I could have come home all by myself. But no. Did I listen to my heart? I did not. What I did was read a bunch of self-help books that told me to look forward, to stop living in the past, to get a life in the big city, a real life, get on with my work, my career. And when work didn't fill the Cape-shaped hole in my heart, I now realized, I'd tried to do it by marrying a total creep.

And look how that turned out.

"Okay, Jenny may be right about that," I admitted. "What else does Jenny say?"

"She says you have unfinished business here. She wouldn't tell me what it is, but she's sure that's partly why you're back."

"Well, um, gee," I sputtered.

But Roland wasn't really interested in my unfinished business, thank goodness. He just wanted to keep talking about his amazing wife.

"And she always gives people the benefit of the doubt. She says that if someone disappoints her, she asks herself if that person is *doing the best they can*. And if she thinks they are, then she appreciates them for that effort, no matter how flawed or awkward they might be." He paused and I knew he was thinking of his own flawed, awkward self. "Which is why I love her," he added.

"And do you tell her that?" I asked.

"Well, it goes without saying," Roland replied with surprise.

"Actually, Rolly, I don't think it does," I said gently. "I think it needs saying a lot."

He looked thoughtful. "Perhaps you're right." He placed his glass carefully on the varnished tabletop. "I will take it under advisement." He gestured to our server for another round.

It was perhaps a good thing that Jenny showed up before the bartender, suddenly moving very slowly, was able to grant his request.

As his young wife pushed through the door, Roland's face lit up.

"Jenny!" he cried, standing up with just a little bit of a wobble. "What are you doing here?"

"Michael called me," she said, nodding over at the bartender. "He thought maybe you guys could use a ride home."

"How enormously considerate of the fellow," Rolly said, all Lord Granthamy again.

"Yes," Jenny agreed, adding dryly, "he thought it would look—unseemly I think was the word he used—for the town's most respected lawyer to have a DUI on his record."

"Quite right," M'lord agreed. "Good man, that Michael."

"And I wanted to talk to you, away from the house, away from the kids," Jenny added, suddenly serious. "So I asked Miles to watch the boys for a while."

Uh-oh.

"I'll go finish my drink at the bar," I said. I tried to get up from my seat, but Jenny pushed me back down unceremoniously.

"Sit."

I sat.

"Rolly, I . . ." Jenny paused, and I was filled with dread for Roland. *What? I'm leaving you? What?*

Roland, I noticed, was simply waiting for whatever his

beloved wife was going to tell him, smiling and sipping the last of his drink. I thought my heart would break.

"I'm renting some space in town, starting my own videography studio," Jenny said with a rush.

You could have knocked me over with a feather.

Roland, too, apparently.

"What's videography?" he asked blankly.

"Making videos," Jenny explained patiently. "You know, of weddings, bar and bas mitzvahs, sweet sixteens, quinceañeras, first Communions, class plays. You know, like the one I made of Evan's play?"

"You can make movies of class plays for recompense?" Roland asked, still trying to get his head around what he was hearing.

"The doting parents of the twenty-five kids in that class each paid me twenty-five bucks for that video," Jenny said. "I put exactly six hours, including the actual shooting, into it. You do the math. That's my hourly wage."

I tried to do the math in my head but I couldn't. Apparently Roland could.

He whistled. "What a wonderful idea!"

Jenny looked at him in disbelief. "You think so?"

"Of course I do," Rolly said. "I was just telling Sam here how talented you are at really *seeing* people."

Jenny looked at me doubtfully. "He was?"

"He was indeed."

"Oh, Rolly," Jenny breathed.

Roland reached for her, and I made a quick escape to the ladies' room.

When I returned, Jenny pulled away from her husband, who was looking rather flushed. "Okay, you two," she said, "time to get you home."

Taking each of us firmly by the arm, she escorted us out to her car like a Keystone Cop with two fumbling felons.

As she was pouring Roland into the front passenger seat,

he turned to her and said, "I do love you, you know. I may not say it with sufficient regularity."

She turned to me in astonishment. "Who is this man and what have you done with my husband?" she asked. But she was pink with pleasure.

Rolly gave me a big wink.

I T WAS STILL early but Jenny wouldn't leave until I'd changed into my jammies and climbed into bed. Diogi commandeered what had become his usual spot on my feet. I looked at him and realized that not only had I lost that battle, I'd lost the war. I *wuved* Diogi.

"Have you called your parents?" Jenny asked as she turned to leave.

"Um, no," I said guiltily. I looked at the bedside clock. "And it's past nine. Too late to call them." Which was not true.

"In the morning then," she said firmly.

"In the morning," I promised.

Once she'd left, I turned off the light, but I couldn't settle. It had been another very long day and that large snifter of brandy, rather than serving as a soporific, seemed to have put my brain into overdrive.

I kept hearing Helene's voice in my head, repeating Jason's message. *"Give her my love . . ."* What did that actually mean?

People say that all the time. I used to say it about Aunt Ida when I called my parents. "Give Aunt Ida my love." It didn't actually mean anything. I didn't actually love Aunt Ida. She was too starchy to love. I liked her, but I didn't love her. So Jason was probably just saying what people say, not really meaning it.

So why hadn't I returned his call? What was I afraid of?

Was I afraid that Jason could actually love me? Even if

I decided to stay in Fair Harbor to fill that Cape-shaped hole, was I ready for a relationship with Jason? Wouldn't I always wonder if I was just trying to make up for hurting him? And what if I hurt him again? How could I trust myself? How could *he* trust me, for that matter?

Or maybe I was afraid that Jason could never love me. Maybe he just liked me. I reminded myself that only a week ago, his friendship was all I was looking for. But now, if friendship was all he was offering, could I live in the same town with him? Just be his friend? Watch him find someone else, *maybe even Krista*?

I knew the answer to that. I reached for my phone.

"Hi, is this Plum and Pear? Could I speak to Caitlin Summerhill, please?"

FORTY-TWO

I GOT EVERY SINGLE player in this little drama wrong,"
I said to Helene, "and in one case disastrously, murderously wrong."

It was mid-morning the next day. Helene and I were walking along the long, golden sickle of Shawme Beach, leaning
hard against the wind, as Diogi played an endless game of
keep-away with the rollers breaking along the shore.

It was another chilly, gray, gusty day. We had the beach
to ourselves except for the sandpipers scuttling along the
wet sand at the water's edge and the gulls wheeling and
crying overhead. It was beautiful. It was paradise.

I was wearing my red hoodie and wishing I had something warmer. Helene was wearing her huge camel hair overcoat and Wellington boots. Turquoise Wellington boots. Of
course. We were taking turns sipping from a thermos of hot
tea. That's how you know when you're really friends. When
you don't mind swapping thermos germs.

I was explaining my theory about preconceptions.

"I got Roland Singleton all wrong. He doesn't take Jenny
for granted. He's doing the best he can. He's a warm, caring man."

"Well, he hides it well," Helene said dryly.

"And I got Jenny all wrong. She wasn't starting a new life. She was just starting a new business."

"Which you couldn't know until she saw fit to tell you," Helene pointed out.

"And I got Krista all wrong. She wasn't in McCauley's pocket. She was just doing her job, trying to keep me out of his—and harm's—way."

"And she was maybe just a little bit envious of your investigatory skills," Helene pointed out.

I didn't tell her the other thing I'd gotten wrong about Krista. I didn't tell her about my friend's affair with Curtis Henson. I didn't tell her about the incriminating photo. Because before I'd handed Estelle's cell over to the authorities, I'd made a few swift keystrokes and, *voilà*, no more picture on her phone. So sue me.

"And, boy, did I get Trey wrong. I thought he was just the weak-willed son of a bullying father. I remember once asking myself what kind of a man stomps on baby birds? And now I know the answer—a man who *enjoys* stomping on baby birds." I shivered, either with the cold or at the thought.

Helene stopped walking for a moment. "Don't blame yourself there," she said. "I should have seen how deep the damage was. A boy who had been emotionally, perhaps even physically, abused by his cold, distant father. A boy spoiled by a mother determined to make up for the father's failings, a mother who thought the sun rose and set on her son. That's a recipe for a callous narcissism."

I shivered again and took another sip of tea from the thermos. "But all this pales beside how completely and utterly wrong I was about Mr. Logan."

"It does appear that we might have read some of the players incorrectly," Helene said. It was nice of her to say "we," I thought. "I must admit I was surprised when you told us out on that patrol boat that it was Logan who'd killed Estelle."

"Why were you all out there on the bay in the patrol boat, anyway?" I asked. "Surely that's not the normal protocol."

"Well, when Jason woke up and saw your note, he waited for a while and then got a call from work and had to go out on the bay for a bit. He tried to call you when he got back to the Harbor Patrol offices. When you didn't answer, he came back to the house, found your truck but no you and naturally assumed you'd come over to see me. You can imagine his concern when I told him you hadn't. We thought maybe you'd gone for a walk, though it seemed odd that you hadn't taken Diogi with you. I called Jenny, Miles, Krista—anyone who might have come by, picked you up for some reason. Of course, none of them had. But within minutes, they were all at your house—"

"Aunt Ida's house," I corrected her automatically, but Helene continued as if I hadn't spoken.

"It was Miles who saw that the shed door was open, the bicycle missing. He'd seen it in there when he was looking for that snake thingy to fix the drainpipe. We figured the bike being gone was a good sign. At least you hadn't been abducted."

I snorted. "Abducted. That sounds a little dramatic."

Helene stopped short and looked at me reproachfully. "No more dramatic than what actually happened, surely?"

I was properly ashamed. "Point taken. Please go on."

"It was Miles who suggested we follow your bike's tire tracks. We all piled into the Harbor Patrol van. The tracks were clear in the sand. We followed you to Logan's new place. Your bike was there. But no you. No anybody. Krista started talking about how maybe you were following up something you'd found out about some politician, but then Jason noticed that the motorboat usually moored out front was gone. Somehow he knew it was Trey Gorman's."

"The harbormaster is in charge of mooring permits," I explained. "They keep a strict limit on how many new moorings are allowed. He would remember that one. Trey probably had to get a special permit for it."

Helene nodded. "At that point, Jason drove at, I must say, a *very* unsafe speed back to the municipal pier. He sent out some kind of all-points bulletin, then jumped into the patrol boat and so, of course, we all jumped in behind him. He tried to make us get off, but we weren't going anywhere and he decided not to waste time arguing with us."

She stopped and took the thermos of tea from me. "The rest you know."

"Thank you," I said, patting her arm. "Thank you for coming to save me."

"Well, we didn't actually save you," Helene pointed out. "Jason was right. You saved yourself."

I shrugged. That was true. "Still," I said, "I appreciate the effort."

"And just for the record, we all got it wrong, too. We were all sure by that point that we were looking for Trey Gorman."

"Believe me," I said, "nobody was more surprised than I was when I figured out it was Mr. Logan."

"Well, I wouldn't have pegged him as a murderer," Helene said, "but I never liked the man."

"Really?" I said, astonished. "Because I liked him a lot. I felt sorry for him, always under the thumb of his wife, always trying to be the good guy to make up for her bad guy. *Everybody* liked him."

Helene shook her head and her silver locks waved in the breeze. "I've seen that type before. Letting their wives do the dirty work, while they get to play the nice guy. It's a good gig."

We stopped talking for a moment, distracted by Diogi, who'd discovered a dead skate on the beach, probably discarded by a surf fisherman. I hate it when they do that. Why not throw it back if that's not what you're fishing for? Better yet, why not keep it and eat it? Skate wing sautéed in browned butter and capers is fantastic. Every French chef knows that.

I tried to call Diogi back to us before he did that thing that dogs do and rolled on the skate. He looked at me and rolled on it.

"Stupid dog," I muttered. "And stupid me. I just couldn't see how someone so nice could turn into someone so . . . bad." I meant Mr. Logan, of course, not Diogi. "Mr. Logan told me he'd had a sign. I thought he meant his successful therapy, but he meant the stroke that killed his wife. It was a sign, he said. And all he had to do was . . . nothing."

Helene took a swig of tea from the thermos. "I have to say, though, it's a big step from doing nothing while your wife has a stroke to actually drowning someone yourself with your bare hands. One is passive murder, the other active. It just seems so out of character for the man."

"But it wasn't out of character for him to try to mow me down out on the bay?"

"Not really. Even mild-mannered people become substantially more aggressive when driving cars. In a car—or a powerful motorboat in this case—people feel anonymous, and when we feel anonymous, we lose our moral compass and are more likely to behave badly. Psychologists call it deindividuation. It means a loss of self-awareness and along with it, individual accountability. And when you add anger into the mix, it can be deadly. Hence road rage."

I was speechless. "Okay," I said finally. "Spill. You weren't always a librarian were you?"

"No," Helene admitted. "I was a legal psychologist for the Manhattan DA's office for twenty-five years. And let me tell you, twenty-five years was enough."

"What does that even mean, legal psychologist?"

"It means I evaluated people facing criminal charges, talked with witnesses, consulted on murder investigations, that kind of thing."

I stared at her.

"So," Helene continued as if she hadn't just blown my mind, "while I think it makes some kind of sense that Logan could use the *Mad Max* to try to kill you, it's difficult for me to imagine him drowning Estelle with his bare hands."

I wasn't convinced, not by a long shot, but Diogi interrupted our discussion once again by dropping the dead skate at our feet. No wonder he had rolled in it. It stank to high heaven. Stinky dead things are doggy perfume.

"You do understand what you need to do next, right?" Helene asked me.

"Bury it?" I said, beginning to kick sand over the fish.

"Don't deliberately misunderstand me," Helene said in her I-will-brook-no-nonsense-from-you voice.

I gave in.

"Yes," I said. "I need to talk to Jason."

"How many times has he tried to call you?"

"Three," I said sulkily. It was true. Jason had been leaving a message on my cell every hour on the hour this morning. Each time it was the same: "Hi. It's Jason. Call me." Super romantic.

"And you let them all go to voice mail," Helene said accusingly.

"I'm not sure what to say to him . . ." My voice trailed off uncertainly.

"Well, you'd better figure it out soon, because, unless somebody else has adopted his distinctive *coiffure,* that's the man coming down the beach now."

Oh god, oh god, oh god.

FORTY-THREE

A S IT TURNS out, dogs are the perfect answer to so-cial anxiety. Not only do they break the ice in diffi-cult encounters, *they* can actually do what you wish *you* could do.

Diogi, for instance, once he'd realized that the man walking toward us was the Man with the Boat, ran up to Jason and showered him with kisses.

Jason in turn wasted a great deal of time giving Diogi a tummy rub. *So once again, Sam, you're jealous of a dog?*

Finally he turned his attention to me. "Where'd He-lene go?"

I looked around wildly. Helene had indeed done one of her disappearing acts. I was alone with Jason. And I highly suspected that she had engineered the whole thing.

Oh god, oh god, oh god.

"You're shivering," Jason said.

"Well, it's cold out here."

He took off his jacket and wrapped it around my shoul-ders. It was warm from his body and it smelled like him and I wanted to bury my face in it and never give it back.

"Thanks," I said inadequately and waited for him to ask why I hadn't returned his call.

He must have seen my apprehension.

"I've got some updates for you."

Thank you, Jason. Thank you for the reprieve.

"Did Mr. Logan confess?" I asked. "A real confession?"

"Well, it's complicated," Jason said.

I just looked at him.

"He's confessed to letting his wife die. He kind of had to do that, since you found the evidence that he was there that night. Plus, Estelle's photo has an electronic date stamp, of course. But in your case, he insists he wasn't trying to run you down, just wanted to talk to you, misjudged the distance."

"Yeah, he tried that one on me, too," I said. "For a minute I almost believed him."

"I'm glad it was only for a minute," Jason said. "If he had managed to . . ." His voice went wobbly and he stopped, cleared his throat, began again. "If you hadn't made it to the sandbar . . ." Another pause. "The bastard might have got away with it."

"Well, he didn't," I said, trying to give Jason some time to collect himself. "And he won't get away with killing Estelle, either."

"Ah, yeah," Jason said. He looked very uncomfortable. "There's that."

"What?" *I didn't like where this was going.*

"He categorically denies killing Estelle."

Of course he does.

"And here's the thing."

I waited.

"On this, I believe him."

I simply was not going to listen to any more "the crime doesn't fit the psychology of the man" nonsense. First Helene, then Jason.

"You *believe* him? How can you believe him? He had her *cell phone.*"

"Which he says he found under the deck when he went to meet her, to pay her. He says she didn't show."

"Well, he would say that, wouldn't he?" I knew my exasperation showed in my voice.

"Bear with me, Sam," Jason said. "What if Estelle made *two* appointments? If she was blackmailing more than one person, why not arrange to meet them both, one after the other? If she left fifteen minutes or so between them, she could save herself a trip."

I nodded reluctantly.

"You remember the reconstruction?" Jason continued. "How the killer is surprised by someone coming under the deck before he's had a chance to grab the phone? How he pushes the body down, sinks down himself up to his neck until that person goes away. And how, when the other person leaves, the killer goes to get the handbag with the phone in it and it's gone?"

"Of course I remember that," I muttered rebelliously. "It was *my* reconstruction."

"Well, I think you were right all along," Jason said. "It could have happened that way. Logan could have been the second appointment. He could have arrived at the meeting place and taken the bag with the phone in it when he didn't see Estelle."

"Because her killer was hidden by the darkness, holding her down in the water . . . ," I finished for him.

"Right."

And then I remembered something Mr. Logan had said in his rambling monologue on the river behind Nickerson Island: *"After Estelle had her accident, I thought the problem was solved."* I realized then that something about that was off, but fearing for my life at the time, I hadn't had the luxury of considering its implications. Now I did. *Mr. Logan still thought Estelle's death had been an accident.* And he hadn't known that the police were looking into it as a possible homicide, so he wasn't worried about keeping her phone. Until I'd found it and he'd seen me looking at that incriminating photo.

I told Jason what Mr. Logan had said, confirming his theory. Which brought us to the next and final question.

"So if it wasn't Mr. Logan who killed Estelle," I asked, "who was it?"

"It was Trey Gorman, of course. Gorman. Not Logan."

Trey, not Mr. Logan.

"There you go," I said to the Universe. "Got it wrong again."

"No," Jason said firmly. "If you remember, you were the one who got it right. You were the one who thought in the first place that Gorman had done it."

I felt somewhat better. "But you haven't got any solid evidence that ties him to her death," I pointed out.

"That's what McCauley says, too," Jason admitted.

Great, Sam. Now you're on the same wavelength as McCauley. Not a good sign.

"But I'll get it," Jason added grimly. "In the meantime, we need to get you a restraining order against Gorman."

I stared at him. Was this nightmare never going to end?

"What makes you say that?" I asked.

"Yesterday, after I talked to Logan, I staked out Gorman at his motel. Waited. Eventually some guy in a Lexus drives up, goes straight to Trey's room. Even from where I was in the parking lot, I could hear the yelling. So I go knock on the door, identify myself, tell them to open the door. They go quiet. Nothing."

"So what did you do?"

"I kicked the door open."

"Really?" I said, thrilled in spite of myself. "Just like in the movies?"

Jason grinned. "No, of course not. I had a passkey from the motel manager."

"Darn," I said. "It was such a good image. So what happened next?"

"I opened the door, and they stood there like deer caught in the headlights. Gorman and this other guy. Who turns out to be his father."

"His *father*?" I said. "What was he doing there?"

"The father says the son called him at his office, asked him to come out, said he'd tried to get some of his confidential work papers from you, but you sicced your dog on him."

I was incensed. "They were not his confidential work papers. They were my mother's confidential notes. And I did *not* sic my dog on him. My dog *barked* at him. And besides, Diogi's not even a dog. He's a *puppy*."

Then I had a thought. I paused in my defense of Diogi. "But why?" I asked. "Why would Mr. Gorman tell you that?"

"Because he needed to explain why he was standing there with a gun in his hand."

"A gun," I repeated blankly. *Uh-oh.*

"He said his son asked him to bring him the handgun he keeps in the office. Trey said he was going to go back and get the papers when you were out. So obviously, he's still worried about anything that connects him with Estelle. That right there is enough for McCauley to bring him in for questioning. I really doubt he's going to have an alibi for the night she was killed. And now that we know what we're looking for, we'll find someone who saw something. This was no perfect crime by any stretch."

I nodded. Trey really wasn't very bright. I had no doubt they'd find the evidence they needed. Even if it was McCauley doing the looking. But now something *else* was bothering me.

"But if he was going to steal the notebook while I was out, why did he need a gun?"

Jason looked uncomfortable. "He said he needed it to 'take care of the dog.'"

I felt the blood drain from my face. "*He was going to shoot my dog?*"

Jason took one look at me and gathered me into his arms. He said nothing, just held me close. I leaned into the reassuring bulk and warmth of his chest, resting my head on his shoulder. I felt as if I could stand there forever, wrapped in Jason's arms. Nothing bad could happen there. It was paradise.

FORTY-FOUR

〰〰〰

I EVENTUALLY MANAGED TO tear myself away from paradise, but only after Helene did one of her uncanny reappearances and convinced me that Jason had better things to do with his time than "canoodle" with me on the beach.

"Actually I can't think of anything better to do with my time than that," Jason said, laughing, "but you're right, Helene, there's other stuff I need to do first." *Yeah, like slap some handcuffs on that Trey creep.*

Jason turned back toward the parking lot, and Helene and I continued our walk. Diogi trailed behind us, proudly carrying his stinky fish. Helene made no attempt to draw me out, for which I was grateful. I needed some time to think, to process what had just happened and what I'd just heard.

Finally breaking the silence, I said, "Jason wants me to get a restraining order against Trey."

"Does he," Helene said mildly. "And why is that?"

"Well, he apparently said he was going to try to steal my mother's notebook again and shoot my dog in the process."

"Then a restraining order seems like a reasonable precaution to me," Helene said.

"And because he thinks Trey drowned Estelle," I said.

Helene didn't even break stride. "And why is that?"

"Because it wasn't Mr. Logan."

Helene nodded thoughtfully.

"You called it," I pointed out. "You knew it wasn't Mr. Logan. And even if you didn't expect it to lead to murder, you knew Trey had a twisted psyche."

Helene nodded. "It's beginning to look that way, I'm afraid."

It was. And it made me sad. And afraid.

"Let's go see Roland about that restraining order," Helene said.

I F YOU HAVE never had to take out a restraining order against someone, I sincerely hope you never have to do so. But if you must, then take a lawyer with you. Roland was, once again, superb, guiding me through the forms at the police station and ensuring that Trey would be served with the papers immediately.

"He'd be a fool to come anywhere near you now," he said as he dropped me off back at Aunt Ida's.

"Or near my dog?" I asked.

"Or your dog," Roland said.

So I wasn't afraid anymore. But I was still sad.

K RISTA ARRIVED AS I was frying up a nice comforting grilled cheese sandwich for lunch. (Tip: Swiss cheese, which in my opinion tastes like an old boot when it's cold, is *the best* all melty in a grilled cheese sandwich.) And by "Krista arrived," I mean just let herself in without knocking or anything. That's how I knew it was her without even turning around.

"Hi, Krista," I said, lifting a corner of the sandwich with my spatula to see if it was just the perfect shade of light toasty brown. It was. (Tip: Use mayonnaise on the bread when you fry it. You don't have to worry about softening butter to spread it and the sandwich crisps up better.) I turned to her. "You want half of my grilled cheese?"

"Sure," Krista said, throwing herself on the couch. "You make the best grilled cheese."

"I make the best everything," I corrected her.

"That, too," she acknowledged.

I cut the sandwich on the diagonal with the spatula (sandwiches always seem more special cut on the diagonal) and slipped half onto a plate. I held it out to her and she took it greedily. Then I grilled two more sandwiches, just to keep our strength up. When we'd finished gorging ourselves and had fed Diogi a few of the crusts, we wiped our greasy hands on paper towels and looked at each other. Suddenly things felt just a little awkward.

Krista finally jumped in.

"Any idea when the cops are going to come knocking on Curtis's door about that photo?"

"Like, never," I responded. "Because, duh, he's not a suspect." Then a thought hit me. "And how do you know they haven't come knocking on his door?"

Krista just grinned at me.

"You *told* him about the photo?" I couldn't believe it. "Why would you do that?"

"Because I wanted to pay him back," Krista said defiantly. "I wanted to scare the crap out of him."

Okay. I could see that.

"And did it?" I asked. "Scare the crap out of him, I mean."

"Oh yeah," Krista said with some satisfaction. "Not that he would admit to it. But he's one of those guys who if he's scared gets really pissed off. And he was majorly pissed off at me."

"At you? Why at you?"

"Because I told him that I told you not to delete the photo. I told him the cops would see it."

"Jeez, Krista. You really know how to turn down the temperature, don't you?"

"Not my strong suit," she admitted.

I relented. "Anyway, tell him not to worry. The cops never saw it."

"You *deleted* it?" Krista exclaimed. "I *told* you not to do that. You can't delete evidence!"

I grinned at her. "First of all, it's not evidence anymore. And second of all, what I actually said was that the cops never saw it. I deleted it from Estelle's phone, but just in case, I sent a copy to myself by text and then deleted the text from her phone."

Krista laughed with delight. "Oh, you clever girl, you."

"And you can tell that sleazeball that that photo now holds a special place in my phone's gallery and if he ever gives you grief again, I personally will make sure it finds its way into the public eye."

Krista looked at me with awe. "Badass," she said admiringly.

"Or just a good friend," I said.

"Same thing," she said, "but 'badass' sounds cooler."

FORTY-FIVE

WHEN I'D LEFT Jason on the beach earlier, all he'd said was he'd call me later. So I wasn't exactly expecting him that evening, but in my heart of hearts, I was really hoping he'd come by for some dinner and canoodling.

As Grumpy's fit of the sulks was apparently over, I drove to the fish market to pick up some scallops and stopped at Nelson's for a bottle of California chardonnay, just in case. I also took a nice hot bath and prepped my face in the tiny mirror over the sink. I had to stoop just a little to see the top of my head, but that was par for the course. The six-foot-something Julia Child had had her kitchen remodeled so that all the counters were six inches higher than the norm. When I decorate my dream house, every mirror will be hung high enough that I can see the top of my head. In the meantime, I would stoop. Some lip gloss, some blusher, a dramatic hair flip (more for how it made me feel than how it actually worked).

So I was a little disappointed when Jason texted me with "working tonight." Fortunately, he almost immediately followed that up with the only slightly more romantic "see you tomorrow?"

What the hell. I'd take it. I sent back what I hoped was a friendly "sounds good." No emoticon though. I didn't want to appear overeager.

I went over to Helene's to pick up the Scottoline mystery but declined her offer to stay for dinner. The scallops went into the minifridge and the bread and Swiss cheese came back out. *You like grilled cheese sandwiches,* I reminded myself. But it definitely felt like a letdown. So I dolled it up by adding some sliced sweet onion and chopped cherry tomatoes. *Yummy.* The chardonnay was the perfect accompaniment.

Maybe it was the second glass of wine or maybe it was residual exhaustion from my *ordeal* the day before, but even the Scottoline wasn't enough to keep me awake. I put it aside, snapped off the bedside lamp, and fell into a dark, dreamless well of sleep.

Exhausted new mothers will tell you that they can sleep through every kind of noise except their child's cry. The slightest sound from their child will snap them awake. Which might explain why, though I dimly registered some noise out in the driveway, I didn't actually wake up until Diogi's soft whine had me sitting bolt upright in bed like a spring toy. He was still in his usual place at the bottom of the bed, but his head was raised and cocked toward the door to the ell.

It seemed to me that I could hear movement on the other side of the door, but I needed to be sure. "Shut up," I whispered to Diogi, whose whining was getting louder. Diogi, bless his heart, shut up.

Yes, movement. A tiny rattling noise. My first thought was that a curious raccoon was sniffing around. Curious raccoons are the bane of existence for Cape homeowners. But raccoons tend to grunt softly as they explore, almost like they're talking to themselves, and my visitor was definitely not talking to himself. My visitor, I realized, was ever so quietly shaking the spare key out of the conch shell conveniently illuminated by the light over my front door.

Without taking my eyes off the door, I reached over to the bedside table and fumbled for my phone in the dark. Diogi seemed to sense my fear, for, though he stayed on the bed, he rose to his feet and began to growl low in his throat. This time I didn't shush him. Maybe the growl would hold the intruder—*no, come on, Sam, just say it*—hold *Trey* off long enough for me to dial 911.

But before I could even begin to punch the numbers in with my shaking fingers, the door opened. A man stood there, silhouetted by the light behind him. He was nothing more than a dark and menacing shadow. Diogi and I, on the other hand, were nicely illumined by the light behind the intruder. In my shock, all I could register was that there was something glinting in his hand. A gun. *But Jason had told me the authorities had impounded the gun.*

"Drop the phone and call off your dog." The voice was cold and uncompromising, the voice of a man who was used to giving commands, used to having them followed. And infinitely secure in the power of the gun in his hand.

This was not Trey. For one thing, the intruder was shorter than Trey. And this was not Trey's voice. This was the voice of a stranger. A stranger, it seemed clear to me, who would not think twice about hurting anybody, let alone a dog.

I put a hand on Diogi's collar. "Shush, boy," I said clearly. "Shut up now. Everything's fine."

Diogi quieted, but he did not for a moment think everything was fine. I could see the fur rising on the back of his neck, and I held the collar more firmly.

"What do you want?" I asked, trying to keep my voice steady.

The man gestured at my phone. "That," he said. I wished I could see his face. It was unnerving trying to deal with a shadow.

"My phone?" I said. I held it out toward him with the hand that wasn't holding Diogi's collar. "Sure. Take it."

The man laughed. It was not a nice laugh. It was a laugh like glass splintering. "I don't think so," he said. "The only fingerprints on that phone are going to be yours."

What did that mean? I tried not to go there. I said nothing. I honestly didn't know what I was expected to do.

Then the shadowy figure walked toward the bed. If I hadn't been more worried about Diogi getting shot than me, I would have fainted dead away right then. But as the hand without the gun moved toward me, I was swamped by terror. The relief when the intruder simply switched on the bedside lamp was almost as overwhelming as my fear had been.

In the light from the lamp, I could see him now. And what I saw, I didn't like. Improbably white teeth. A chin like the prow of a ship. Thinning brown hair carefully combed and gelled over the top of his head.

I saw Curtis Henson.

Why was Curtis Henson standing in front of me with a gun?

And suddenly I understood. *Krista had told him I still had that photo. Yes,* I reminded myself, *because you told her to tell him.*

"You want the photo," I said dully.

"Yes, I do," he said. "And you're going to give it to me. Or, more precisely, you're going to kill it." I didn't like the way he said *kill it.* I kept remembering that fingerprints remark.

"Okay," I said. I pulled up the photo gallery with shaking fingers and held the phone out so that he could see the photo.

He nodded. "Kill it," he said again, gesturing at me with the gun.

Diogi growled again, louder this time.

"Sure," I said. I hit delete, and when the phone asked me

again if I wanted to delete this photo, I hit delete again. The photo disappeared. "There," I said. "Gone. Nothing for you to worry about."

Curtis smiled at me. It wasn't a nice smile. What had Krista called it? His killer smile. "Well, it's a start anyway," he said.

A start?

"I've still got to delete you and my little friend with benefits," he said.

I stared at him. *Delete* me? *Delete* Krista?

"Come on," he said, "we're going for a ride. Bring the phone." He waved the gun at me and pointed to the door of the ell.

I could feel Diogi stiffening against my restraining hand as the growling increased.

"And get rid of that dog before I do."

My blood went cold. And though I doubted he'd actually shoot Diogi, I wasn't going to take the chance. I slid out of the bed and Diogi looked at me inquiringly.

"Come on, boy," I said. "Why don't you go find Helene?" At the sound of her name, Diogi's ears went up and he jumped off the bed, though never taking his eye off Curtis.

"Who's Helene?" Curtis asked, his voice deep with distrust.

"The dog across the street," I lied. "He loves her."

I walked Diogi across the room, shivering in my pajamas. When I pointed out the open door, he looked at me uncertainly. Did I really want him to leave me with this man? I tried to banish the fear from my voice. "Go on," I said. "Go find Helene."

And so Diogi went.

I had never felt so alone in my life.

FORTY-SIX

"COME ON," CURTIS said from behind me, nudging me out the door with his gun. "Let's go."

"I don't get it," I said as I walked toward his car where it was parked next to my truck. "The photo's gone. You've got nothing to worry about. And I'm not going to say anything. Krista's my friend. I'd never let anything hurt her. That's why I didn't show the photo to the authorities, why I pulled it off Estelle's phone in the first place."

"Yeah, well maybe you shouldn't have taken that bitch's handbag in the first place. Maybe you should have just left it on that old table."

Wait. What? I could understand Curtis thinking I'd taken Estelle's handbag because, after all, I had her phone. But how did he know that Estelle's handbag had been on the workbench? I didn't even know that. I had suspected it, but I didn't know it.

And then it all became clear. Curtis knew that the purse had been on the workbench because Curtis had *seen* it on the workbench. Because he'd been there himself. Drowning Estelle.

Not Trey drowning Estelle. Curtis drowning Estelle.

And then Curtis had heard someone coming, walking under the deck, though in the darkness under the overhang it would have been impossible to see who. And when that person had left, Curtis had turned Estelle over to see if she was well and truly dead and then climbed back up on the breakwater to get the handbag. Which wasn't there. Because Mr. Logan had taken it. Not me. But Curtis didn't know that.

Wait. Something didn't make sense here. Curtis had been with Krista the night Estelle was killed. She'd told me so. I thought back. What had she said, exactly? "That was the night after you got back, right? Sorry, but he was with me."

But Krista never knew what day it was. "I'm always behind," she'd said. And as usual, she'd gotten it wrong, and I'd missed it. She'd sent me to the Grill the *first* night I was back—a Wednesday night—not the night after, not Thursday. Not the Thursday night that I'd seen her getting ready for her mystery date.

Curtis Henson had been with Krista on Thursday night, not Wednesday night. *Not on the night Estelle had been killed.* I was willing to bet that Henson had no alibi for that night and had no intention of letting me alert the authorities to that fact.

In spite of the gun wedged between my shoulder blades, I stopped dead.

"You killed Estelle," I said dully, stating the obvious but somehow wanting, needing confirmation. And an explanation of sorts. "Why? Why not just pay her off?"

"She was getting greedy," he said. "She knew with the election she had me over a barrel and started demanding more and more money. I told her if the sums got any bigger, my wife was going to notice my withdrawals, but she just laughed and said in that case maybe she'd just sell the photo to the gutter press."

He said the words "gutter press" with great moral disdain. *That's rich*, I thought, *coming from a murderer.*

"Either way," he said, "I knew she had to go. And then you got involved, and I knew you had to go, too. And Krista, of course. It's like the three of you had it in for me from the start. I never asked for this. Once I've cleaned up your mess, I can move on." His self-pity was mind-boggling.

As we'd been talking, my eyes had adjusted to the dark and I could see the bulk of Curtis's enormous SUV next to Grumpy. It looked like a hearse. The gun jabbed me sharply between my shoulder blades.

"Come on. Let's get in your truck," Curtis said.

That surprised me. "Why the truck?" I asked. Curtis only grunted.

I opened the door so that the interior light illuminated the two of us, but didn't move to get in.

"Where are we going?" I asked. Not because I really wanted to know the details of his plan. I asked because I needed to stall for time. The woods at night are filled with many rustling noises, but what I had just heard behind us— and what Curtis hadn't yet registered—was not one of those usual noises.

"We're going to the beach," he said. "Sadly, you're very depressed. You lost your job. You've been humiliated publicly. Krista told me all about it. Finding that old biddy in the pond was the last straw. You've been through a lot of trauma. You want to end it all. So, you're going for a little swim. You're going to swim and swim until you can't swim anymore."

My legs went to rubber, and I had to hang on to the truck's open door to keep from sinking to the ground.

"Why would I do that?" I asked faintly.

"Well, it's going to be a choice between swimming out to sea or being shot. And my bet is you're going to keep swimming."

"And if I refuse? It's not going to look good if my body"— *Did I really say my body? Is this really happening?*—"is found with a bullet in it."

"Don't worry. If your body has a bullet in it, I'll just have to make sure it doesn't get found."

I thought about the miles of deserted dunes posted with Keep Off signs along the National Seashore, all the uninhabited islands on the bay. It wouldn't be difficult to bury a body out there.

"And Krista?" I asked. "You think nobody's going to think it's a little coincidental when Krista goes for a little swim, too?" I really didn't want to hear about his plans for Krista, but I had to play for time.

"Don't worry about that," he said. "You know that piece she did a couple of weeks ago on the opioid crisis? Well, it really pissed off some bad guys who owe me a favor. Plus, she made the mistake of telling me that the police think that loser Gorman killed the old lady, so they're not going to tie that to the mob offing some journalist."

Okay, I can't go on with this nightmare conversation. Let's get him to talk logistics. That will buy some more time.

"And how are you going to get back to your car from the beach?" I asked.

Curtis moved out from behind me and pointed to the bed of the truck, in which he'd placed a nice shiny tenspeed bike. Ah, the noise that hadn't actually penetrated my sleep. The guy really had it all planned out.

The only thing that was keeping me upright at this point was the rustling sound getting nearer. I searched desperately for something to say, something to keep Curtis occupied, maybe put him a little off balance.

"You know," I said wildly, "pasting your hair to your head doesn't really hide the fact that you're going bald."

For a second we stood staring at each other. Guys who are going bald really don't like being told they're going bald. Any more than really tall girls like being told they're really tall. It's a cold cruel world out there. Curtis looked at me in disbelief, which rapidly changed to hatred. *Good*

*move, Sam. Now instead of killing you in cold blood, he'll
kill you in a murderous rage.*

And then I heard the sweetest three words in the English
language. I heard Helene say, "Sic 'em Diogi."

And Diogi sicced him.

T HE REST SEEMED to happen in slow motion, though
it took only seconds. A huge, furry, barking cannon-
ball launched itself at Curtis. As Curtis fired wildly at the
beast attacking him, I, in some instinctive movement that I
wasn't even aware of, kicked the hand holding the gun. My
foot and his hand wouldn't have connected if I weren't so
tall, so there is some justice in the world. The shot went
wide, and the next thing I knew, Curtis was on the ground
with Diogi standing on his chest, his nose inches away from
the New Bad Man's face, snarling in a way that made it
clear that if Curtis wanted to keep that face he would do
well to *not move a muscle.* Curtis did not move a muscle.

Helene at this point stepped out of the shadows and
calmly picked up the gun from where it lay on the grass.
She pointed it at the man on the ground and said, "I'm going to call off the dog. But what you need to understand is,
I know how to use a gun. And I would be delighted to do so
in this case."

"Whatever," Curtis snarled. "Just get the dog off me."

"Diogi," Helene said, "come." *And Diogi came.* What
else—aside from sic 'em—had this amazing woman been
teaching my dog?

I walked shakily over to Diogi, still standing at attention
next to Helene, sank down on the ground next to him, and
clung to him while he licked me enthusiastically all over
my face. "Who's my good dog?" I whispered to him. "Who's
my very, very good dog?"

Finally, when I had stopped shaking all over, I stood up
and said to Helene, "So what happens next?"

At that moment, a white Ford Explorer with familiar blue lettering careened into the driveway.

"Jason happens next," Helene said.

I T SEEMS LIKE I'm always getting to the party after all the excitement's over," Jason said.

"Well, you had some excitement of your own," I said. It seemed that Jason's "work" that night had been raiding a boat suspected of being used as a stash house for heroin.

We were sitting on Helene's couch, where she'd parked us after Jason's partner, a strapping young woman who looked more than capable of handling the likes of Curtis Henson, took Henson off to what I hoped was jail for the rest of his life. I was once again wrapped in a blanket and drinking brandy (for which I was beginning to develop a taste). But, best of all, Jason's arm was warm around my shoulders. Helene had rewarded Diogi—whom Jason had dubbed Diogi the Wonder Dog—with a steak bone the size of Texas.

I was pleased that he didn't seem to mind that once again he had not been the white knight coming in to save the helpless girl. He seemed, in fact, to be proud of me. And of Helene. And of Diogi. Diogi had been *amazing*.

"When exactly did you teach my dog *sic 'em*?" I asked Helene.

"We were working on it all morning," Helene said modestly. "I just couldn't feel like you were safe until whoever killed Estelle was under lock and key. You should see that dummy I made when we got done."

I looked at my cuddly puppy and decided not to think about the dummy.

"So, let me make sure I fully understand this," Helene said. "Henson was the one who drowned Estelle and Logan was the one who took her cell phone?"

"That's about it in a nutshell," I said.

I turned to Jason. "I'm sorry I didn't tell you about Curtis Henson," I said. "First, I thought he had an ironclad alibi. And then all the evidence pointed to Trey Gorman."

"You thought the evidence pointed to Gorman because *I* wanted the evidence to point to Gorman," Jason admitted. "I was completely unprofessional."

"Actually," Helene said with her usual briskness, "you can both stop blaming yourselves. Yes, you were both worried about someone you care about and that colored your perceptions, but you were following the evidence as you knew it. And it's not like Trey Gorman doesn't have some serious offenses to pay for." She ticked them off on her beringed fingers with great pleasure. "Intimidation with physical violence, attempted theft of property, planning an armed robbery, deliberate killing of an endangered species . . ." She looked at Jason. "Did I miss anything?"

"Kicking a defenseless dog," I put in, holding Diogi close. "And planning to . . ." I couldn't say it.

"That, too," Jason said, tightening his arm around my shoulder. "Plus we're finding out a lot more. In exchange for immunity, Daddy Dearest is throwing his son completely under the bus for some other questionable practices in developments he's been managing. Easily enough to put the guy away for years. We're talking bribery of public officials, falsifying environmental impact reports, all sorts of good stuff."

He smiled at me with a distinctly unprofessional satisfaction. *Plus Trey put the make on me*, I thought, but didn't say. I just smiled back at him.

Helene brought us back to reality. "The bigger issue is that you no longer have that photo you need to prove Henson's motive for murder."

I looked at her in amazement. "Of course I have that photo. After I forwarded it to myself, I downloaded it to my phone's picture gallery. So I told Krista it held a special place in my gallery and that's what she told Henson. That's what I showed him and that's what he saw me delete. He didn't think any further than that. He's not the kind of guy who deals much with technology, I think. He has people for that. But the original's still in my texts, of course."

Now it was Helene's turn to look embarrassed. "You kids and your technology," she muttered. And then she stood up and disappeared into the kitchen, leaving me alone with Jason.

Oh god, oh god, oh god.

Jason's arm tightened around me. It was late. We were alone. For a moment, I lost my nerve, but then the moment was past. Just like that, I didn't care.

Because Jason Captiva was kissing me.

FORTY-SEVEN

I WAS LYING IN bed, a quiet thrum of happiness running through me, remembering that kiss, luxuriating in that half world when you are moving from sleep into wakefulness and the day lies ahead of you with all its possibilities, when my phone shocked me out of my reverie. I picked it up and looked at the caller ID. The 'rents. Oh well, I had to get it over with at some point.

"Hi, Mom. Hi, Dad."

To which my mother responded as she always did. "Hi, Sam, it's your parents."

"Right," I said and waited for them to figure out the speakerphone on my mother's cell. Usually this resulted in them hanging up on me once or twice, but this time they got lucky on the first try.

"Hi, Sam," my father shouted.

"Hi, Dad," I said. "No need to shout, I can hear you fine."

"Good, good," he shouted. "Now tell us about what's been going on up there. Some neighbor of yours called us this morning, got our number from Krista she said. Told us Mr. Logan tried to run you down with a motorboat? And then that the DA held you at gunpoint?"

"And why didn't you call us?" my mother added. "We had to hear this from a stranger?"

"Helene's not exactly a stranger," I protested. "But you're right, I should have called. It's just that after the thing with Mr. Logan I was really busy, what with making my statement to the police—"

"Not that moron McCauley?" Not one to mince words, my mom.

"Yeah, to McCauley. And then Roland Singleton took me out to the Windward and we ended up having a couple of drinks. . . ."

"Roland Singleton took you drinking at the Windward?!" my father shouted. "Good lord, what's gotten into the man?"

"And then I thought it was too late to call you. And then I put it off yesterday because I didn't want to worry you and then after last night with the Henson thing, I was really busy again dealing with the authorities. . . ." *That's what you call it, Sam?*

My father took pity on me. "No need to apologize, pumpkin. You've been through a lot. Just tell us what happened."

And so I told them, as briefly as I possibly could. I admit, I left out a lot.

When I was finished, my father said something that absolutely floored me. "So this harbormaster you keep talking about. Is that Jason Captiva?"

"Well, um, yes," I said, and waited for the explosion.

"I heard he'd been promoted, come back to Fair Harbor," my father said. "Must have been just after we left."

"I guess," I said, still waiting.

"Well, I'm glad he was looking out for you," my father said. "Jason Captiva is a good man. Always thought so."

WHEN HELENE HAD banished Jason the night before so that she could run me *another* nice hot bath and send me to my nice soft bed, the two of us had agreed to meet at Nellie's Kitchen for breakfast. Sure, that was where I'd made my first big mistake with Trey, but far be it from me to hold poor Nellie responsible. And was I going to give up those buttermilk pancakes just because of a few unpleasant memories? Not likely.

"Do you mind telling me why my father thinks you're a good man?" I asked as I began perusing the Nellie's menu, which never changed. Nor did my order. But I love perusing menus.

"I didn't know he did," Jason said easily. "But that's nice. I think he's a good man, too."

"I don't get it," I whined. "I thought he hated you, ran you out of town."

"Why on earth would you think that?"

"It was in one of his notebooks. He said you met with him, agreed not to see me again."

"Well, not for *forever*," Jason said. "Just until you were older. Remember, you were just a kid. Still under age. I was already ashamed of myself for taking advantage of you, of kissing you that night. It wouldn't have gone any farther, even without the Estelle thing. But your father was right to talk to me about it."

"Good lord," I said. "How positively *medieval*. Did he ask you what your *intentions* were?"

"More or less," Jason admitted.

"And what did you tell him?"

"I told him my intentions were just to be your friend."

My face must have registered my disappointment, because he reached over and took my hand, smiling gently.

"Just to be your friend," he repeated, "until you were older and really knew, from your *own* experience, what you wanted out of life." *Oh dear, and here I was still trying to figure that out.*

"And until I had more to offer you," he added.

I stared at him. "*Offer* me? Like what?"

"Like a man who was worthy of your respect. And your father's respect."

"Well, apparently you've got his. He seems to think you're very impressive."

"That's good to hear. How about you? Do *you* think I'm impressive?"

"Well," I said, mock doubtfully, "I'm sort of impressed with your job, what with you being harbormaster and all."

"Aw shucks, ma'am."

"And you have a truly impressive head of hair," I said as Jason tried and failed to look modest.

"But the clincher," I concluded, "was last night. Your kiss. That was *very* impressive. 'Sam,' I said to myself, 'that's a man with a lot to offer a girl.'"

A S I DOWNED my last bite of bacon, I considered the face of the man sitting opposite me. It was a noble face. Not handsome. Not golden. It was the face of a man who had weathered tragedy. It was the face of a man who knew how terrible the world could be—and how beautiful. It was the face of a good man.

And one who desperately needed a haircut.

"Jason?"

"Sam?"

"Why didn't you tell me at the time about that talk with my father?"

"I didn't want to influence you," he said. "You had a life to live, and I didn't want you to make any decisions based on what you thought our future might be. I wanted you to build your own future. The future you'd dreamed about, told me about."

I remembered doing that. I remembered my surprise at the time when Jason, having poured out his heart to me, had then asked me about *my* hopes and dreams. Never before had a boy asked me that. (And never since had a man asked me that.) I talked, and he listened. I'd told him about my passion for cooking, my conviction that the wider world held as yet undreamed of experiences and knowledge. I'd told him I wanted to become a chef, wanted to live in a big city, wanted to own my own restaurant. That I didn't have the courage yet to tell my parents that I didn't want to go to college, that I was afraid of their disappointment. And apparently, he'd never forgotten any of it.

"You weren't angry at me for what I did that night when Estelle found us under the deck?" I asked him. *Why are you trying to ruin things, Sam?*

"I don't know what you're talking about."

"You were upset," I said. "And I didn't ask you why."

"And I didn't want you to," Jason said. "I just wanted all the bad stuff to go away. I just wanted to kiss you."

Oh that sweet, sweet boy.

"And I didn't stand up for you," I added. *Still can't leave well enough alone, Sam?*

"Seriously?" Jason asked, incredulous. "A truly awful woman essentially calls *you* a spoiled, rich slut and you think you have to defend *me*? Quite frankly, I was amazed by your self-control, your dignity."

Self-control? Dignity? Well, okay, I would take it.

"Another question, then," I said.

"Shoot."

"Why didn't you keep in touch?"

"I told you. I wanted you to make your own future. And it was pretty clear that you were making it in New York City. What was I going to do, call you up and say, 'Hi, it's Jason. You remember you had a crush on me when you were a kid? I was wondering if you wanted to give up your life and your career in the big city and come back to this hick town and be my girl?'"

Part of me wanted to say, *I wish you had*. There was so much of the past ten years that I wished I hadn't had to go through. Then I remembered what Helene had said. *"You did not waste the last ten years of your life. You honed your craft and built a career. You learned about life and you learned about love. You are a better, wiser, more compassionate person for the challenges you've faced."* So, Jason was right about letting me live my dreams. But not about everything.

"Fair Harbor is not a hick town," I corrected him.

"Well, it's not New York," he pointed out.

No, it's not New York.

I thought about my call to Plum and Pear. I really needed to tell Jason about that.

"I had a job offer," I said abruptly. "A really good job offer. Back in the city."

Jason sat very, very still. He said nothing.

"I turned it down," I said. "I'm staying here."

Still nothing. I waited.

"Not because of me," he said finally. "Please tell me you didn't turn it down because of me."

What? Was he going for sainthood?

"No," I said, in all honesty.

"So why?" he asked softly.

I heard Helene in my head again.

"Because suddenly I knew that here—the Cape, Fair Harbor, Aunt Ida's house—was exactly *where* I was supposed to be *when* I was supposed to be."

EPILOGUE

~~~~~~~~

W E PILED INTO Miles's truck, with Helene up front and me in the back. Miles was blasting the *Hamilton* soundtrack from a Bluetooth speaker he kept permanently on the dashboard. It was nice. Driving in Miles's truck was nice. Even on Snow's Way, the ride was pretty smooth.

"When did trucks turn into cars?" I asked Miles.

"About ten years ago, when I bought this baby," Miles said. "You should see what they've got now though. Some of them have sound systems and coolers *built into the bed.*"

I could see Miles imagining himself at his beloved Patriots games wowing all his tailgating buddies, of which he had quite a few, all straight. Which I'd always thought was wonderful.

We pulled into Jenny's driveway, and she hopped in back with me, waving to Roland and the three Things standing in the doorway. The boys waved back madly. Roland did not.

"Be good for Daddy!" she shouted out the window. "I'll miss you!"

Then she leaned forward and said to Miles, "Drive, drive, drive!"

Miles drove.

It had been all of three days since my little run-in with Curtis Henson, but Krista had decided that three days off was enough. I'd promised her I'd review the Crying Tiger and, by god, it was time I did. I didn't have high hopes for the restaurant, but even pale imitation Thai food was better than no Thai food at all. So I was pleasantly surprised by what was on offer. In true Thai style, we ordered a half dozen dishes for the table, ranging from a green papaya salad to the house specialty, the Crying Tiger itself: supremely tender flank steak, marinated, grilled, and sliced thin, then draped over a cone of steamed rice. I was delighted with the spicy hot pad Thai and the rice noodles with chicken and garlicky greens. A stir-fry of crunchy hearts of palm with shrimp came adorned with two giant prawns, heads still attached, and I thought Jenny was going to pass out.

"I don't eat food with eyes," she said, waving the dish away with her chopsticks.

"Don't be ridiculous," Helene said as she calmly snapped a shrimp's head off and began peeling it with her fingers. "You eat lobsters, for Pete's sake."

"That's different," Jenny said with finality, as if she'd made a point whose logic could not be denied.

Helene just rolled her eyes and reached for the other shrimp.

We washed down the feast with cold Thai beers (except for designated driver Miles, who pouted) and pronounced the meal a success.

As we were finishing up, a trim Thai woman wearing a floor-length silk skirt and long-sleeved collarless blouse came over and introduced herself as Madam Phi, the restaurant's owner. She insisted on knowing all our names, though when she came to me, she said, "Of course, you need no introduction. I have seen you on the computer."

My heart sank. *Was my infamy going to follow me forever?*

"You are so amusing."

Really? Because that was a reaction I hadn't come across before.

"I did not know the story of the spaghetti tree."

"The spaghetti tree?" I repeated inanely. *Not YouTube?* And then, with a sinking heart, I remembered the video of me and Mr. Logan at Bits and Bites. The video in which I said to a man who every *Clarion* reader now knew had tried to run me down with a speedboat, "I've really enjoyed our time together." How long had that clip been online? A week? Krista needed to pull that thing down!

"It is surprising, what people do not know about the food they eat," Madame Phi continued. "I once had a patron who said there was no chili in his pad Thai. I pointed to the dried red chilies in his meal, but he was confused." She laughed. It sounded like a bell ringing. "He wanted American chili, you know, with ground beef and red beans!"

Jenny turned to me and said, "'The Cape Cod Foodie, Episode Two: Where's the Chili?'"

ACKNOWLEDGMENTS

An author could have no more trustworthy guide and champion than my tremendously supportive agent, Sandy Harding, whose smarts and professionalism are surpassed only by her warm and caring heart. Plus, she totally gets my sense of humor.

To my editor, Michelle Vega, at Berkley Prime Crime, a thousand thanks. Michelle's sheer enthusiasm (this is a woman who has never met an exclamation point she didn't like!) and spot-on editorial judgment have made working with her an absolute joy. And many additional thanks to fellow foodie Jenn Snyder for all her help in guiding *A Side of Murder* into print. Plus, they both totally get my sense of humor.

I would be remiss in not mentioning that all three of these remarkable women have been models of grace under pressure, working with unflagging dedication and optimism in "a world turned upside down." I am in awe of their strength and resiliency, and I thank them for their example.

And, of course, all love and gratitude to my wonderful husband, Bill Schwartz, whose devious mind started the whole ball rolling!

RECIPES

A Casual Dinner with Friends

This is a lovely, informal meal to share with good friends. I like to serve it "European style," as four small courses (appetizer, soup, salad, and dessert). This lets you and your guests really appreciate each course—and keeps you around the table, laughing and talking, much longer!

BEACH SHACK ONION RINGS

These delicate rings are dipped in a light flour and water batter and cook up into lovely "nests" of fried onion goodness. As an appetizer, bring out a platter piled high with the golden nests and put it in the middle of the table, encouraging your guests to pull it apart and eat the nests with their fingers. It's so much fun!

(SERVES 4)

2 large onions, thinly sliced (no more than ¼ inch)
2 cups water
2 cups all-purpose flour
1½ quarts neutral frying oil such as canola (or more as
    needed)
Salt

Warm oven by preheating to 150-200 degrees, then turn it off.

Slice the onions as thinly as possible, no more than ¼ inch. (A mandoline, if you have one, makes short work of this, but a nice sharp chef's knife will absolutely do the trick.) Separate the onion slices into rings.

Put 2 cups of water in a shallow bowl and gradually whisk in the flour, until the batter is smooth. It should have the consistency of sour cream—you can add more flour or water if necessary.

Fold the sliced onions into the batter with a spatula.

Pour the oil into a large, heavy pot until it comes 2-3 inches up the sides and place over high heat. When the oil is very hot but not smoking, test it with one batter-dipped ring—the oil should be hot enough to sizzle on contact.

One large forkful at a time, slip about ⅓ of the onions into the hot oil. Use tongs or a long fork to stir them around a bit and to make sure they are not sticking to the bottom of the pot, but do not try to separate the individual "nests."

Cook until a fine golden crust forms, about 2 to 3 minutes, turning the "nests" occasionally. Using the fork or tongs, transfer the onions to platter lined with paper towels and sprinkle with salt. Place in the warmed oven.

Repeat the procedure two more times, until you have fried all the onions (this should only take about 10 minutes total).

Serve immediately.

AUNT IDA'S
CAPE COD CLAM CHOWDER

~~~~~~~~

A real Cape Cod clam chowder is a thing of modest beauty. It is not thickened or overly creamy. It is nothing more than tender clams, little crispy cubes of salt pork (or bacon), some minced onion and celery, and a couple of diced potatoes—all swimming in a rich, milky, buttery broth redolent of the sea.

Aunt Ida would go out and dig her own quahogs, but any reputable fishmonger should have fresh hard-shell clams on hand. If these aren't available to you, frozen or canned clams are a perfectly respectable substitute.

Also—and this is important—do not add your clams to the chowder until just before serving. They will only need a few minutes to cook (for canned clams even less). Anything more than that and they turn to rubber.

(10-12 SERVINGS)

2½ pounds hard-shell clams such as littlenecks, cherrystones, or quahogs (in order of increasing size) *or* 1 pound frozen clams (unshelled) *or* 2 cups of chopped or minced canned clams, drained (six 6.5 ounce cans)

¼ pound salt pork (or thick cut bacon), cut into ¼-inch cubes

2 tablespoons butter

1 medium onion, finely chopped

2 stalks celery, finely chopped

4 cups bottled clam broth (if using canned or frozen clams)

1 quart whole milk

2 bay leaves

    1½ pounds (about 3 cups) russet (baking) potatoes,
        peeled and cut into cubes no larger than ½ inch
    Salt and freshly ground black pepper
    Optional: 1 cup heavy cream (Aunt Ida never would,
        but it does make it extra yummy)

If using fresh clams, rinse them under running water to clean the shells and set aside. If using frozen clams, thaw them in the refrigerator overnight and chop them roughly, if necessary. Canned clams are fine right out of the can.

Put the cubed salt pork (or bacon) into a heavy-bottomed stock pot or Dutch oven over medium heat. Cook until it begins to get brown and crispy.

Add the butter, minced onion, and celery and cook for about 5 minutes or until onions are softened but not browned.

If using fresh clams:
Add the clams and 1 cup of water to the pot and turn the heat to high. Cover and cook, opening the lid every once in a while to stir the clams, until they begin to open (about 3 minutes). As the clams open, remove them with tongs into a large bowl, keeping as many juices in the pot as possible and keeping the lid shut as much as possible. After 8 minutes, discard any clams that have not yet begun to open.

Roughly chop the clam meat and put it into a separate bowl with any juices.

Add the milk, bay leaves, and cubed potatoes to the pot. Bring to a boil, then reduce the heat and simmer for about 20 minutes or until the potatoes are very tender and starting to break down. Add salt and pepper to taste.

Add the clams to the pot. Add the cream if you are using it, bring to a simmer and cook for two or three minutes. Serve immediately. (I like it with a pat of butter melting on the top, but that's just me.)

If using canned or thawed clams:

Add the bottled clam juice, milk, bay leaves, and cubed potatoes to the pot. Bring to a boil, then reduce the heat and simmer for about 20 minutes or until the potatoes are very tender and starting to break down. Add salt and pepper to taste.

Add the clams to the pot. Add the cream if you are using it, bring to a simmer and cook for two or three minutes (one minute for canned clams). Serve immediately. (I like it with a pat of butter melting on the top, but that's just me.)

NOTE: If you are making the chowder in advance, do not add the clams and the cream until you reheat it for serving.

ARUGULA, MANGO, AND GOAT CHEESE SALAD WITH HONEY DRESSING

The trick here is to arrange the ingredients in layers on a pretty platter and drizzle the dressing as you go rather than tossing the whole shebang in a salad bowl. This keeps the salad light and the flavors wonderfully distinct. Plus, it makes a beautiful presentation!

(4 SERVINGS)

3 tablespoons honey
4 tablespoons olive oil
Kosher or sea salt and fresh black pepper
5 ounces baby arugula
½ cup small basil leaves or larger ones torn into
    pieces (plus a handful of whole leaves for garnish)

    2 ripe mangoes, peeled and cut into ½-inch cubes
    8 ounces goat cheese, in small pieces (not crumbled)

Whisk together the honey and olive oil and season with salt and pepper to taste.

Arrange the arugula, basil, mango, and goat cheese in layers on a platter, drizzling the dressing over each layer as you build it, finishing with a final drizzle of dressing on the top. Garnish with whole basil leaves.

Guests should serve themselves from the platter onto individual salad plates.

SAM'S THIN AND CHEWY CHOCOLATE CHIP COOKIES

The trick here is to use high-fat butter, which usually means a French or Irish brand. Many supermarkets carry Irish Kerrygold butter, which works beautifully. Make sure the butter is really room temperature, which means so soft you can poke your finger through it. Also, if you use salted butter, you may want to skip adding any more salt to the batter.

(MAKES ABOUT 4 DOZEN COOKIES)

10 ounces high-fat French or Irish butter, softened to
    room temperature
1¼ cups dark brown sugar
¾ cup white sugar
1 tablespoon vanilla extract
2 teaspoons kosher salt (or 1 teaspoon table salt like
    Morton's)

2 large eggs
1¾ cups all-purpose flour (plus another 2 tablespoons
    of flour set aside to coat the chocolate chips)
1 teaspoon baking soda
8 ounces semi-sweet chocolate chips

Preheat oven to 350.

Combine butter, brown sugar, granulated sugar, vanilla, and salt in a bowl and cream on medium-high speed until light, about 3 minutes. Add the eggs and mix on medium speed until blended, about 2 minutes.

Whisk the flour and baking soda together in a separate bowl, then mix into the dough at medium speed for 2 minutes.

In another bowl, combine the chocolate chips with the set-aside 2 tablespoons of flour. Use a spatula to stir the flour-coated chips into the dough by hand.

Drop the dough by slightly rounded tablespoons onto cookie pans, preferably lined with parchment paper. To allow for spreading, 12 cookies per sheet works well.

Bake until golden brown, 8-10 minutes. Let the cookies cool for 5 minutes before transferring them to a wire rack to cool completely.

Ready to find
your next great read?

Let us help.

Visit prh.com/nextread